~ ALSO BY CAROL BUCHANAN ~

GOD'S THUNDERBOLT:
THE VIGILANTES OF MONTANA
2009 Spur Award winner for best debut novel

"This accomplished Western examines one of our nation's formative episodes of vigilantism from an inside perspective and finds substantial moral ambiguity. Set in a southwestern Montana that's experiencing explosive growth centered on gold mining while the Civil War rages back east, citizens take action to curb a wave of robberies and murders. ... It's an excellent western with an intense moral gravity." – Publishers Weekly

"This book will appeal to the western rancher as well as the New York literary circle." – Sam Morton, author of *Where the Rivers Run North*

"I've waited three decades for someone to write a great novel about Montana's Vigilante era, and here it is. *God's Thunderbolt: The Vigilantes of Montana* brims with courage and tragedy, with brooding menace and tenderness." – Richard S. Wheeler, five-time Spur Award winner

Available in select bookstores and through your favorite online retailer

GOLD
UNDER ICE

A novel

Carol Buchanan

MISSOURI BREAKS PRESS

Gold Under Ice

© 2010 Carol Buchanan

ISBN-10: 0982782217

ISBN-13: 9780982782217

Printed in the United States of America

Missouri Breaks Press

2915 2nd Ave. South No. 102

Billings, MT 59101

missouribreakspress@gmail.com

In Memoriam, William B. French, who first inspired my love of Montana history and told great stories. Thanks, Dad!

PART I:
ALDER GULCH

~ 1 ~

AS IF ALL THE CANNONS OF NORTH AND SOUTH fired a ragged volley, as if all the black powder in Alder Gulch blew, the ice over Alder Creek broke, boomed, split into clashing chunks; echoes rebounded on echoes, pulsing in Dan Stark's ears, and blanching the faces of two men who had been skating just a minute before. The fat man walking on the ice disappeared.

"Get a rope!" yelled Dan over the rolling thunder. "Run!"

Martha McDowell hoisted her skirts to run stumbling through soft snow up Wallace Street, where men already hurried toward her with ropes in their hands.

Dan could not wait for them. "Your scarf!" One of the skaters wore a muffler several feet long. Dan bolted toward an outcropping into the stream, cursing the snow that mired his ankles and pillowed the banks, obscuring their outlines. As he ran, a sense of relief rolled below the uppermost thought – save him, save him—

From the time the ice riming the shores had joined in the middle and thickened, all of Alder Gulch had waited for it to break and melt away, so they could return to work their gold claims. Now, in mid-April, the ice was breaking.

The skater made a ball of his muffler, and pitched it to Dan, who caught its fringe, made a hasty loop, and ran as in a nightmare, seeming to get no closer. The black water foamed white, flung up slabs of ice, damming itself, then tore the dam apart, rampaging against its banks, scouring away snow, rocks, contraptions, claim markers, and hope. A few yards upstream, the fat man, arms flailing, broke the surface, gasped and coughed. How long could a man survive such cold?

Dan threw the loop toward him as hard and as far as he could. Fell short. The man fought the water. Dan reeled the loop in, pushed through the snow as close as he dared to the tip of the outcrop. The sodden loop threw better when Dan flung it out and slightly downstream. The fat man plunged for it, and the creek hurled arm and shoulder into the loop. A slab of ice hit his head, and he sank. Dan braced himself, wrapping the scarf, stretched to a rope, around his hands. Squatting against the water's jealous pull, he dug his heels into the snow. Yelled for help.

Up the man came again, unconscious, his body given to the water and the cold, his arms limp. The roiling water tossed him, played with him, sent him past Dan. Though thinking he was dead – then why fight the flood? – Dan braced himself, hauled on the rope. His boots could not find purchase; the creek dragged him toward its brink. He would drown, too, if he did not let go, but he could not bring himself to unwrap the cord biting into his hands, though the bank, leaning outward, settled under his feet.

Christ, he thought, don't let us both be carried away. The man rose higher in the water – or did the ground sink? Dan clenched his jaws and dug in his heels, almost sat in the snow: Goddammit he would win this battle with the creek, even if for a corpse.

"Hold on!" A new man grabbed him around the waist from behind, stopped his slide toward the water. They fought the creek together, bringing the drowned man a couple feet closer to the bank.

A third man seized the cord ahead of Dan, and then more men arrived to battle the current for the stranger's life. The soaked ground sank a little more as slowly, too slowly, the man's grey face came up above the edge, and then his torso, and two more men risked the sinking bank to pull on his arms and coat, and haul him up. The bank cracked near the dead man's knees. "Pull!" They all pulled as one and scrambled back, dragging the body.

A one-armed man in a Confederate greatcoat wrapped the rope around his upper arm, and they all yanked Dan back from the bank as it broke off into the water. He lay and gulped for air, as if he'd been the one drowning rather than the fat man lying inert in the wet snow.

"My God," said the one-armed man's Southern voice. "I think he's alive."

"Roll him over!" Dan unwound an inch or two of rope from his hands, gasped at the pain. Peeling the cord out of bloody cuts, he held his lower lip in his teeth, damming an outcry behind them. Men rolled the stranger over onto his stomach, head downhill toward the creek, and turned his face to the side. A man straddled him and leaned on his back. Water ran out of his mouth and nose.

Someone said, "Careful with him! Don't break a rib."

They pressed, and again. And again.

The fat man sputtered, gasped, coughed, and vomited.

"If he don't die of pneumonia," said the skater who owned the scarf, "he might live."

"We better get him up to the recovery," said another man. "Someone go for a doc."

They made a stretcher of the stranger's greatcoat. "One, two, three, now!" Together they raised him up. Someone said, "Too bad this ain't you, Jake, you wouldn't be half the weight."

Jacob Himmelfarb laughed. "The ice I do not walk on."

"Let's go," said one. "We can't be standing here with him all day." Grumbling at his weight, they set off up the slope toward the recovery, where men with no place else to go recuperated from accident or illness.

The muffler, stretched thin, three times its length, and soaking, lay on the snow. The skater who owned it stooped to pick it up. "My wife knit that for me last year, before I come out here."

Dan said, "I'm sorry about ruining it."

"Don't be. I'll tell her it saved a man's life, and we'll both treasure it."

"Who do you suppose he is?" The skater asked.

"He come in on the stage about an hour ago," said the man who had come first to help. Timothy. In the battle to save the fat man, Dan had not realized it was his own stepson. He'd mistaken Timothy McDowell for a man. Or had he? Timothy was only sixteen.

The boy was saying, "Everyone looked mighty glad to make it. They had theirselves a time in the passes, the driver said. Nigh killed the horses."

Dan scrabbled to pull his feet under him. "Maybe something in his valise will tell who he is." He tried to stand, fell back. Strength had drained from his legs. Timothy bent to him, and Jacob, too; the fringes of Jacob's prayer shawl escaped his overcoat and brushed Dan's face.

Together they raised him up, slung his arms across their own shoulders. "Let me go," said Dan. "I'll be all right."

"Puny, ain't you?" The one-armed man picked up Dan's hat. His Confederate greatcoat was faded almost to the color of squash. Butternut, they called it

"Go to hell, Fitch." Dan smiled as he said it.

Laughing, the Confederate handed him the hat and walked away.

"Let me go." His friends stood aside, and Dan set the hat on his head. "I'm grateful to you both, but I can walk." He tottered, not at all sure where his numb feet were. "Whoever he is, he'd be dead without you. Me, too, maybe." Me, too. Understanding shivered up Dan's spine. "My God, that was close." Another step, and he wobbled, stumbled, would have fallen had not Timothy and Jacob taken hold of him again.

Timothy said, "You don't know how close. There for a bit I thought you was a goner."

Applause and cheers made Dan look up. Most of Virginia City seemed to be gathered at the foot of Wallace Street.

Dan tried to free his arms. "I had better walk home under my own steam." He smiled. "Don't tell your mother."

"Too late." Laughing, Tim held onto him.

Martha emerged from the crowd, relief and pride glowing on her face, and she touched his cheek as if to reassure herself that he stood here in the flesh.

Some in the crowd called out, "Good work!" "You saved him!" "Hurray for Dan Stark! Hurrah for —"

A shrill boy's voice shrieked, "Damn Vigilante!" People stepped aside from a as if avoiding a dog's mess. "You should'a drowned, you goddam murderer —" The sheriff strode toward him. "—you and your whore!" The boy pointed at Martha, screamed, "Whore!"

Dan jerked his arm from Timothy's grasp and rushed for the boy, but Timothy outstripped him, cuffed the younger boy into the mud. Fending Timothy off with an elbow, the sheriff hauled him to his feet. Dan caught sight of Martha's face, her dark eyes shocked in the bleached mask of her face. He drew her to him, wrapped his arms around her, and held her, trembling like a small and fragile brown sparrow. "You are my wife," he whispered, "nothing less."

Seeing a few secret smiles on some faces, Dan shouted at the boy, "Jacky Stevens, you should be horsewhipped for slandering my wife!" It would not prevent people from thinking as they liked, but at least it made his intentions clear.

~2~

MARTHA TOOK COMFORT from Dan'l's arm holding her close enough to grow together as they made their way up the rising ground toward home. Timmy walked alongside Dan'l, and Dotty ran ahead and held their yellow dog, that barked and wriggled and wanted to play.

While Dan'l changed to dry clothes, Timmy stirred up the fire in the iron cook stove and Dotty put hot water on. Martha hung her cloak on a peg to the left of the front door (the rifles laid across pegs to the right), and put her outside shoes on the mat next to the others. They didn't hardly need it, and the wood pile was getting low, but she built a fire in the round stove standing next to her rocker. She didn't think the house could be too warm. Huddled in the rocker, her arms around herself, she tried to take comfort from this clean big room, better than any house she'd ever lived it. It had a window with real glass in three outside walls. The cook stove stood kitty-corner from her. In front of it, an eating table big enough for the four of them and a few guests did double duty as a work table. In the right-hand corner, between the two bedroom doors, stood the trunks where she stored their off-season clothes and extra bedding.

Even though the fires needed building up, the room warmed her, because here they took their meals together, argued some, got to know Dan'l. They were forging a family, and already she'd begun to think of her and Dan'l and the two young'uns that way, though she and Dan'l had come together just over two months ago. After McDowell left them, like they was – were – so much extra baggage, a stick of furniture or a dry cow. What they'd have done without Dan'l she didn't know, made out somehow, maybe, though she might have had to work as a hurdy-gurdy dancer, but dear Lord never worse. Never. There'd have been no schooling for Dotty, and no comfortable cabin with separate bedrooms, so the child didn't have to be aware of what grown folks did in bed. There, as everywhere, Dan'l treated her like she had feelings and wasn't just something for him to, well, do what men did with a woman. They were getting to be a family like they hadn't been with McDowell, though he was their real Pap. And her lawful husband.

That's why the thought of him coming back scared her so. He could take her away and beat her for going with another man, and no one would stop him. He had the legal right.

At Dan'l's touch on her shoulder, Martha started. She hadn't heard him come out of the bedroom. Turning her head to smile at him, she caught sight of his hands. "Lordy," she gasped.

His smile twisted. "I'd forgotten my gloves."

Martha fetched the bandages and medicaments she kept handy, her being a healing sort of woman. Sitting at the eating table, the young'uns across from them, she laid his hand out under the ceiling lamp.

She felt Timmy's anger beating its wings to be free. He'd be wanting to give Jacky Stevens a good whipping, and that scared her. It was something his Pap would do. Dotty, only twelve, liking pretties and how things looked, slumped in her chair and showed herself plumb mortified. The meaner ones at school would say plenty if they hadn't already.

She set to work, tried to put her whole mind to this task. The muffler had been knit from a hairy sort of wool, and being strong like most wool when wet, it had stretched thin enough to cut. Tweezing wool hairs out, she felt him flinch, heard an occasional hiss, but she worked steady, just like her stomach wasn't about to give up its doubts. When she'd bandaged his left hand, she couldn't keep them to herself. She could be some temporary arrangement for Dan'l. He'd had a fiancée back in New York. Martha had seen her picture once – blonde, beautiful, and stylish – and her just a little brown mouse.

"Only I'm not your wife. Not all legal-like." Tears started, and Dan'l reached out and wiped them away with his thumb.

"You are my wife." He took her chin between his thumb and two fingers and turned her face up to him. "We are legally married, under common law, till death do us part. When we can, we'll do it right."

"A wedding?" Dotty sat up straight. "A real wedding?"

"Whatever your mother wants." Dan'l kept her chin prisoner and looked into her eyes, his own a changeable blue like a lake she could drown in.

Blinking fast, Martha pulled her chin out of his grip and bent to work on his right hand, but her feelings spun too fast to take hold of, and she couldn't see proper.

"How can you get married, with Pap still alive somewheres?" Dotty, playing with a blonde curl, twined it about her index finger. In build and coloring, both young'uns took after their Pap.

"Your mother can divorce him on grounds of desertion." He spoke to the child, but Martha understood he was talking to her more'n the young'uns, letting her know how things stood, not just between them two, but between them and everyone else that thought it their business to have an opinion.

"That takes a court, don't it?" Timmy's deep man's voice, that she still was not used to. "Can the People's Court do it? Or, or the, the —"

He stumbled on Vigilante Tribunal, knowing Dan'l to be one of its prosecutors, but Dan'l said, "Neither court can grant a divorce. The People's Court handles disagreements about property under fifty dollars. We" – meaning the Tribunal – "hear suits for more than fifty dollars." Almost like an afterthought he added, "And capital crimes."

They were all silent, thinking, Martha guessed, about the winter's events, the twenty-four men hanged. Or was it twenty-two?

"Two and a half months aren't enough to say he's deserted us?" Martha gave the words an uphill tilt that made them a question.

"The only courts that have jurisdiction over divorces are the Territorial courts – Ah!" as Martha pulled out a long thread "– in Lewiston. If we traveled there and petitioned them to hear your mother's case, they might refer it to the Legislature. Then we would have to wait until the next session."

Martha thought about the journey to Lewiston, 500 miles over the Bitterroots, the snows twenty feet deep in the passes. Spring hadn't begun even here, more'n a mile up, while another three or four thousand feet higher, it wouldn't be thought of till maybe June. They could travel sooner, down to Salt Lake, then up the west side of the Bitterroots, a round trip she'd bet on being almost as far as from here to New York City, and taking longer. Besides the expense.

She sighed. "Nothing for it, then, but to wait on Mr. Edgerton."

"Pooh!" Dotty tossed her curls. "What did that ugly old man want to see his pal Abe Lincoln for, anyway? Dratted Yankees."

"None of that!" Martha scolded, Dan'l being himself a 'dratted Yankee,' but he answered Dotty like she'd asked a regular question, except for an extra edge in his voice to correct her.

"Chief Justice Edgerton went to petition Congress to split our side of the mountains away from Idaho, into a separate territory, called Montana, so we don't have to make that long journey across the Bitterroots. We won't know whether we're in Idaho or Montana until he returns." A secret joke lit in his eyes. "We might arrive in Lewiston only to find that we had made a useless trip and could have stayed home."

Timmy reared back in his chair and slapped both palms on the table. "That damned Jacky Stevens! If he crosses my path, I'll kill him."

Dan'l's head snaked around, quick as a biting horse. He aimed his finger at Timmy. "You will not. Do you hear me? If the Tribunal tried you for murder, I would not be able to save you. You will leave that boy alone. Do you understand?"

This was another Dan'l, the hard man, the Vigilante, who had, so folks said, put the noose around a few necks himself during the winter. For certain, his nightmares tormented his sleep, so that a time or two she'd cradled his head between her breasts to comfort him.

And while they all sat there dumbfounded, Dan'l said again: "Do you?"

Timmy slumped back in his chair, mouth open, eyes staring at Dan'l, and Dotty half rose, like to run.

When he found his voice, Timmy said, "Yes, sir."

Martha breathed again, realized that she clung onto Dan'l's wrist, and loosed her grip.

"Good. Now apologize to your mother and sister for your language. And for scaring them."

The boy mumbled out something, and Dan'l told him to speak up and be plain. Martha wanted to say it was enough, but seeing in Dan'l's profile still the man who could do what he had done, no matter what it cost him, she held her peace, because Dan'l was in charge, and knew what he was about. It was only when Timmy had spoke plain and they'd forgiven him that Dan'l's face relaxed into the man they knew.

Later, listening to his breathing in the dark, Martha understood that he'd bent Timmy to his will without offering his fist. Unlike Timmy's Pap.

~ 3 ~

MUD EVERYWHERE. Heavy clay mud, what folks called gumbo, that clogged wagon wheels and hooves ankle deep so that horses or oxen, straining as they might, hauled a load a mile in an hour. Martha felt like she spent most days on her knees, scrubbing the floor, though Dan'l and the young'uns was – were -- good about leaving their muddy shoes on the mat, and most storekeepers had laid down boards for walking on.

After lunch, when Dan'l suggested they go for a walk, it being such a beautiful spring day, she had her reasons for saying no.

Like always, his yes overcame her. "Men don't hide their wives," he said.

"I'll just put on my outside shoes." She wanted to put on McDowell's old boots, but Dan'l wouldn't want to go walking with her wearing those old things, so she wore her own shoes, though they weren't much, except they fit better. Fingers trembling, she changed into her good dark blue walking skirt, too, which she'd hemmed three inches shorter than fashion, to keep it out of the mud, with a hem protector for good measure. She struggled a mite to button the waistband (living with Dan'l making her put on weight). Pausing a moment, she made a prayer on account the idea of this walk scared her, being paraded around.

They walked just about twenty feet from their door when she changed her mind. A man walking up their street, Jackson street, greeted Dan'l and touched his hat to her. Dan'l introduced her as Mrs. Stark, and the man bowed a little and said as he was happy to meet her. That was new to Martha. Men hadn't bowed or touched their hats to her when she was connected to McDowell. She loosened her grip on Dan'l's arm.

After the winter quiet, the town was noisy. Horses neighed and oxen bellowed, a dry axle screeched. Carpenters hammered and sawed, the blacksmiths' anvils rang, and music escaped the saloons and hurdy-gurdies through open doors and windows.

On the corner of Wallace and Jackson, three men stood talking in a vacant lot, mud to their ankles. They talked loud, not arguing but just to be heard over the Creek running high and the reawakening sounds of commerce, Wallace Street being the center of business in Virginia City. One man came forward, pulling his feet out of the sucking gumbo.

Dan'l introduced her as Mrs. Stark, and added, "Solomon Content, my dear."

Mr. Content took off his hat. His dark eyes smiled, full of humor, and made a little bow. "If men are bringing their wives into this wild country, it will be civilized in no time. Ladies have a civilizing effect on a man."

Martha wasn't sure about that, considering she'd had no civilizing effect on McDowell, a-tall. Judging it safest, she smiled at him and said nothing while the glow spread through her. No one had ever called her a lady before.

"What are you building?" Dan'l asked.

The man seemed fairly to expand, like a grouse or some such, he was so proud. "I intend to put up a two-story brick building."

Imagine that! Martha couldn't hardly credit it. Two two-story buildings in one town. "Like Kiskadden's?"

Mr. Content smiled. "Not exactly. It'll be built of brick, with Romanesque windows on the upper floor. Rounded tops, you know. It'll be a fine building. A good addition for our fair city." A man with a ruler in his hand called to Mr. Content, who touched his hat brim to her. "Will you be in your office later, Stark? I have a proposition I'd like to discuss."

Dan'l nodded. "I'll be at there in an hour."

At that, Mr. Content said, "I'll come see you then. I have a proposition."

When they had crossed Jackson, watching for horse droppings and puddles, Martha asked, "What did he mean by that?"

"I'm not sure, but I think it's the Masons. They want me to join."

Before she could ask anything more, they crossed Jackson, and he held open the door to John Creighton's store for her to walk in. Martha lingered in front of the display cabinet to admire the ladies' watches, one on a velvet ribbon and two on gold chains. At the back of the store, men sat around a square stove. On seeing Dan'l, Mr. Creighton himself stood up to greet them, and Dan'l put his hand at the small of her back and ushered her forward, instead of leaving her to noodle among the new items for sale. The other men stood up, and Dan'l introduced them. They all smiled and nodded or bowed and mumbled polite greetings.

Sheriff Fox reached for her hand and bowed low over it. "Your virtues and your courage are well known, Mrs. Stark." Almost she wondered if that were an insult, when a thin man, whose gaunt face and deep shadows under his eyes showed that he'd come through a great trial, said, "You helped my brother and me in the typhus. You truly have the healing gift."

"Oh, we – we all helped," Martha stammered. "All the women helped." She blushed like a schoolgirl, and plumb forgot about the things she'd thought she wanted to look at.

When they continued their walk, she couldn't ask Dan'l why they'd stopped in there because he was too busy greeting and exchanging pleasantries with other men, and introducing them to her. The few ladies out doing their day's shopping smiled at them, and Mrs. Wilbur Sanders stopped with her two little boys to comment on the balmy spring day. "We must enjoy this while we can. I'm told winter is never far away in this country."

As they walked on, there was to Martha's mind an odd sound to the day, and she listened hard to all the parts, something like splitting a band into its separate instruments. Over the Creek's thunder, men hammered and sawed, like they kept time with the tin pianos and fiddles that played in the saloons and hurdy-gurdies, and the blacksmiths' hammers clanged metal on metal, sharp and clear in a tum-te-tum rhythm she could almost have danced to herself. Men shouted to their friends across street, horses whinnied, and oxen lowed. All that was ordinary, the town getting ready for gold season.

A snarling dogfight rolled under a yoke of oxen, and only the mud slowing the oxen's hooves saved the dogs from being trampled. A teamster yelled words she didn't allow in her house, cracked a whip, and the dogfight broke up, dogs kiyi-ing and yipping as they ran away.

The yell and the whip crack told Martha what puzzled her: the silence under the noise.

Being in their cups and taking a dislike to the way another's mustache drooped, men used to holler angry insults and end their irritations with bullets, but now all was calm amidst the other noises. She used to listen for those shouts, and judge how close she was to Kiskadden's so's she could duck into one of the stores behind stone walls if the shooting started. You could never tell where bullets might fly.

Not now. Now she could walk about with Dan'l and visit with folks on street, there being no need to worry about stray bullets. They'd done that, Dan'l and the other Vigilantes. They'd made the town safe, except if someone went on another rampage.

They turned up hill on Van Buren Street, and Martha began at an angle to what she wanted to know. "With all this building, it won't be long until everyone lives under a roof." During the whole of Virginia City's first year, men had lived in tents and wickiups like Fitch and Berry Woman, or the wagons that brought them west. Some even dug into caves like the man who'd spoken to her in Creighton's store.

"True enough," said Dan'l. "I marvel that they survived the winter."

"Virginia City will be a real town before long."

On Idaho Street, that ran parallel to Wallace, they stopped, and Dan'l pointed to where a crew hammered stakes for a new street crossing farther on. "See where they're laying out logs? There'll be a new street up there. And another one after that."

"I see." Martha didn't particularly notice the street being marked. She'd seen someone else, much closer. Berry Woman stood alongside Major Fitch, who directed some men laying out logs. Berry Woman, wearing a deerskin dress, tall moccasins, and a red shawl that Martha had knit for her, shook her head at something Fitch said. He waved his hand again, and the men holding one of the logs moved a few inches outward, all the time keeping their eyes on Fitch who gestured this way and that at them. Martha wondered what they thought of moving that heavy log a trifle here and a trifle there.

In picking one foot and then another out of the mud, Berry Woman turned enough to see Martha and Daniel. She smiled and waved, and Martha sketched a little wave in return. Her friend was due before summer's end, and when she clasped her hands under her protruding belly, Martha knew her back hurt.

Fitch looked to see what had caught Berry Woman's eye, and gestured at them to come on.

Dan'l said, "We'd better go see."

"They're laying out their new house," said Martha. "Berry Woman told me, it's on account of the young'un." Berry Woman was a full-blooded Crow, to Martha's one-quarter Eastern Cherokee. "It must be the young'un. The Major always wants to keep what's his." Yet why he was keeping her didn't so much matter as him doing it, on account so many white men who took Indian women for convenience, sent them back to their tribes – along with the young'uns – when they could marry a white woman. Mr. Dempsey, who owned the stage station at Ramshorn Creek, wasn't like that, though. His Indian wife had give him a passel of young'uns, and they all lived happy enough, as far as Martha had ever heard.

Knowing that Fitch wasn't fixing to throw Berry Woman away, why, that made her think better of him. Not much, but some. She recollected him with McDowell, their heads together in the lamplight, across the table, clicking their beers together and laughing about how rich they'd be. And all the time she knew what McDowell was doing with the dust he collected from Major Fitch, from her, from Timmy's labors in Alder Creek's frigid water. It all went to the cards and the rotgut whiskey, and to the women at Fancy Annie's Saloon. Which was why she hadn't let him touch her since they come here. Thank the Lord he'd been too drunk to force her.

While the men trucked around, they talked about outside walls and which side would catch the best sun and which would have the best view, almost like they was friends, Martha talked in sign language with Berry Woman. Having carried two to term and lost one between Tim and Dotty, Martha could help her be more knowing about her condition. Aside from Lydia Hudson, the Quaker who befriended everyone in the name of Jesus, and herself, Berry Woman had few friends here, being Crow Indian. She felt sorry for the Crow woman. The Shoshone had stole her as a child from her own people, then traded her two years ago to Fitch for four ponies.

The workmen laid the logs down and dusted their hands. Fitch said, "That'll have to do, I suppose." He gave an order to the crew about a load of lumber.

The men rejoined them, and then the back of Martha's neck prickled because in answer to Dan'l saying it would be a fine house, Fitch got a prideful tone in his voice and said, "This is only the start. You'll see. Someday I'll have the finest house in the Territory, and Berry Woman will queen it over all them that won't give her the time of day now." He put his good arm around her shoulders, and Berry Woman blushed.

"Louise," she said.

"That'll be her white name," said Fitch.

"Louise." Berry Woman cocked her head at Martha, as if to ask what she thought.

"'Louise.'" Martha tasted the word, said it again. "'Louise.' That's real pretty."

Berry Woman smiled.

~4~

OPENING THE RECOVERY DOOR, Dan regretted his impulse to visit the fat man. The odor of used chamber pots in the steamy air assaulted him almost to gagging, and he had to stand while his eyes adjusted to the gloom. There were no windows, and one lamp on a table by a cot showed him where to go. He rounded his shoulders to pass under the low rafters. Short men must have built this cabin, he thought, if this was the highest they could lift the wall's top logs. Why had they not used a block and tackle?

The fat man, too weak to sit up, lay on the cot by the table, while Tabby Rose, the Negro woman who helped as needed in the recovery, spooned up soup for him from a bowl. The dark-stubbled skin of his cheeks folded in on itself, testifying to some weight loss overnight. As Dan stood beside her, the woman rose from her stool.

"Hello, Mrs. Rose." Dan greeted her.

She nodded an unsmiling response, but he was accustomed to Tabby Rose's disdain for white people, even those – like him – of the abolitionist mind. Her sleeves were rolled to the elbows, revealing muscular forearms a man might be proud of. Water bubbled in two buckets on the stove, and a pair of wash tubs squatted on a long table. A scrubbing board stood in one, and a stout stick lay by the second.

25

On the floor a pile of dirty cloths waited for washing. She handed him the bowl and went back to her washing.

Pulling up a stool beside the cot, Dan offered the soup. When the fat man shook his head, Dan set the bowl on the floor and hung his hat on one forefinger.

"Who are you?"

"I pulled you out of the water." He looked, Dan thought, to be in his forties. Old to travel this far in winter.

He offered a soft, plump hand. "You must think me a fool, but I'm grateful."

Dan took the hand. The fat man's grip was strong, seeming oblivious to the healing rope cuts, and he winced. "You could not know the ice would break just then. Two other men were skating there." He pulled his hand back, hid the pain behind his hat.

"My name is Joel Van Fleet." He smiled, but his eyes assessed Dan, as if wondering about him. "May I know yours?"

"Daniel Stark."

The fat man's belly pumped. He was laughing. "Do you appreciate irony?"

"Somewhat," said Dan.

"I owe you my life and you're the reason I'm here." Van Fleet's voice was hardly above a whisper, yet Dan recognized a New York accent that put him on his guard. "I was sent out to find you and bring you back."

The hat dropped to the floor. "To find me? Has something happened to my family?" Only a dire need could force anyone, especially one as apparently accustomed to his comforts as this man, to travel nearly three thousand miles now.

The scrub board bumped and rasped as Tabby rubbed cloths down and up over its rounded wooden rungs. Dan bent closer to hear Van Fleet.

"Have no fear on that score. Everyone was well when I left. Your mother had a slight rheum, I believe, but nothing more. They send greetings. I have letter from your mother and grandfather. No, I'm here on business. I represent the Bank of New York."

"The Bank of New York?" He had seen the list of everyone to whom Father had owed money, but the bank was not on it. He retrieved his hat from the floor, felt like a schoolboy at the teacher's deck, anticipating the ruler across his knuckles.

"Yes. The Bank has bought the debt instruments."

"I see." The Bank of New York had bought the papers Dan had signed agreeing to reimburse the debtors in full at 10 per cent interest. Why? Banks never did anything unless they saw a profit in it. Meaning, Dan thought, that the bank considered it a sound investment to pay off the three outstanding debts so it could collect the gold from Dan. Again, why?

"That's the irony, you see. Thinking I was tracking down a debtor, I find myself indebted to you. For my life."

Dan said nothing. Tabby rumbled the washing over the scrub board, and then lifted a bucket of hot water off the stove, poured it into the rinse tub, and dropped in the clean wash. Taking up a flat stick, she stirred the cloths around.

"So you see," Van Fleet said, "our duties are plain. Mine, to collect the debt and bring you back to New York. Yours is to accompany me forthwith."

Like a damn criminal? Heat flared along Dan's veins. He turned the hat round and round, studied the bandages on his hands. "I have never intended to default."

"I am happy to hear you say that. It gives me hope that my long and arduous journey will be soon rewarded." He regarded his broken fingernails, and his upper lip curled. "You have tarried here so long, your grandfather doubts your intentions. As does the bank."

Clamping his jaws shut on his thoughts, Dan swore to himself. Grandfather had sold the papers to the bank. Had he set their dog on him? This dog in particular? The old son of a bitch.

Van Fleet said, "I expect we might leave for New York as soon as I have strength to travel."

What had the poet – Donne? – said? Something about lovers bound by strands of gold beat to airy thinness? Obligation and duty could bind more than love, could draw him back to New York, and choke him. Dan leaned both elbows on his knees and willed his mind to clear of the anger pounding at his temples.

"What have you heard from your grandfather?"

"Nothing since October."

"The mails are so slow, then?"

"They can be. This is remote country."

"You will be happy to have your Grandfather's letter in my portmanteau, then, wherever that may be now."

"It will be where you left it." A letter from Grandfather. There could be no good news there. "I can fetch it to you, if you wish, but it is safe where it is."

"At Oliver's Stage office?"

Dan nodded. A bug crawled up between the floorboards near his foot, and he shifted his toe to crush it. "I can't leave yet." He concentrated on scraping the bug mess through the same crack. He would not return before time. He had not collected enough gold. Above all, he must safeguard Martha against McDowell's return.

"Surely you can pack quickly. I was able to travel here; you can travel out." Even whispering, pausing between breaths, Van Fleet spoke as one sure of his ground, convinced he held the moral initiative, that Dan would do his bidding. "Your grandfather expects it."

Dan almost laughed out loud. Did they expect Grandfather's domination to have extended over such distance and time that at his mere command Dan would not delay? "No, I cannot. I have not acquired enough gold to accomplish my purposes." Dan looked him in the eye. "You may depart whenever you like. I shall return when I am ready."

"I had expected, if you were truly dedicated to repaying your family's obligations, you would be prepared to return with me immediately."

Dan's temper might have broken then and led him to say something regrettable, but as his mouth opened, his right hand folded into a fist and his middle finger gouged a rope cut in the palm. Blood reddened the bandage. Dan smiled inwardly at the twisted black irony. Blood on his hands. His hands had held a rope to hang a man and suffered no injuries, but that was an irony he doubted Van Fleet could appreciate. He kept silent, though his amusement must have showed in his eyes, to judge from Van Fleet's baffled expression.

"I shall return when I have enough gold," Dan said. "You may suit yourself."

Watching Van Fleet's changing ideas scud across his face as the banker reassessed him, Dan spoke to him in silence: I am not the man you expected to find; I am no longer the grieving son who signed those papers. I am not the bewildered greenhorn I was.

~5~

SOON'S SHE PUT this venison pie in the oven, Martha promised herself, she'd curl up in her rocker, wrap herself in Grandmam's quilt, and read the Good Book while she drank a hot cup of tea. She'd be having a reading lesson with Lydia Hudson soon, and she wanted to keep up with Dotty so's the child wouldn't be ashamed of having an ignorant Mam. Folding the top crust around the flat pastry stick, she laid it across the pie, then, lower lip between her teeth, she turned the stick to begin unfolding it.

Barking and growling, Canary, the yellow hound, set up a fearful row outside.

Martha jerked, the crust tore. She let out a word in Cherokee, her Grandmam's tongue, and snatched up the butcher knife. Why hadn't she barred the door? It was on the latch, the string out. McDowell could walk on in if he got past the dog.

"Mrs. McDowell, will you call off the dog? Please?"

Not Sam McDowell. Praise the Lord, not him coming back, but someone reminding the world that she wasn't married to Dan'l, which was the next worst thing.

Martha stepped over her threshold, under the overhanging front eaves that gave some shelter from wind and snow-mixed rain.

29

Straining at his rope, Canary faced Tobias Fitch, late Major in the Confederate States Army, who kept just outside the dog's reach, his hat streaming water onto the cape of his greatcoat.

Putting the knife in her belt, Martha reeled Canary in until she could close his jaws, but the snarl wrinkled his lip under her fingers and the growl rumbled in his throat. "Mr. Stark isn't to home." She might be friends with Major Fitch's Crow wife, Berry Woman, but she couldn't welcome him. He brought back bad memories of life with McDowell. She could not like him.

"Yes, I know. I came to see you."

Drat the man, picking himself a time when he knew Dan'l would be at work. "You best come back when Mr. Stark's here." Her reputation had already suffered, maybe beyond repair, living with Dan'l when she had a live husband someplace. Entertaining a man not related to her in Dan'l's absence would finish it off.

"He's not involved in this. It's business McDowell left unfinished, about the contracts. This is between you and me."

The contracts. Before McDowell ran from the Vigilantes, he and Fitch had been partners. In exchange for his expenses and a half share in each claim he found, what the miners called grubstaking him, McDowell had prospected all over the area and located eight claims, and the two of them, Fitch and McDowell, had writ it all out on paper. Two papers Dan'l had won from him at poker, but she kept the others hid in the chifferobe, under her nether garments.

"I won't leave until I speak my piece." The wind, as if telling her it wasn't Christian to keep him out here, veered around and slapped wet snow in his beard. He used his short left arm to brush at it.

Holding Canary's rope, Martha stepped aside to give him room to walk past them before she let go and followed him in. Fitch waited on the mat, his hat off and his eyes glancing around the room. The man irked her no end. Near as tall as Dan'l, he had a way of looking down his nose, like he wouldn't bend his neck to the likes of her. To meet him eye to eye, she would have to invite him to sit. At least, if they sat at the table, she could keep it between them.

He hung up his hat and coat on pegs driven between the logs while she went about repairing the pie crust. His muddy boots tracked across her clean floor.

"You can set yourself there." She pointed her chin to a chair. "What have you got to say?" Laying the knife to one side, she attended to piecing and patching the crust.

She felt him watch her, and kept her hands steady.

"I had rather you gave me your full attention."

"I can listen and work, together. This pie is our dinner, and Mr. Stark and the young'uns will come home hungry." Her fingers worked just like common, like she wasn't facing off a man used to commanding soldiers in battle, now trying to command her. She'd knowed worse. He couldn't raise his hand to her like McDowell done. Like Dan'l never even thought of. Yet, hissed a tiny doubt in the back of her mind.

His irritation hummed in the silence, like a plucked string after the pick left it. Martha let it draw out while she finished patching the crust, put it in the oven, and seated herself.

"All right, then," she said. "What do you want to talk about?"

"I want to buy the contracts Sam McDowell and I made."

She cocked an eyebrow at him. "I can't sell. They ain't – aren't – mine." If she knew that, he had to know it, on account he was an educated man, his family had owned slaves in Virginia before the Union Army burned their plantation, and she was an ignorant hill woman just now learning to read. "They belong to McDowell." Martha picked some crumbs of pie dough one by one into a little ball.

"Begging your pardon, he is probably dead."

"Only we don't know for certain." Her worst nightmare, that was, not knowing if McDowell lived or not, that he might come back and catch her alone. "Till we know if he's alive, the contracts belong to him, and I have to give them to him if he comes back."

"This would protect you. You'd only have to send him to me to get them."

Before he had finished, she was shaking her head. That would only infuriate McDowell, his temper being too quick at any time. He'd only to think a thing for it to be true in his mind. Her fingers rolled the dough ball a bit faster.

"I'll give you three ounces of dust for those pieces of paper."

Dust. He meant gold dust, the fine grains and flakes that miners washed out of the dirt, occasionally with a nugget. Gold dust traded for $18.00 an ounce in Virginia City. More, other places. She had enough ciphering to figure that he offered nine dollars each for those bits of paper. Timmy earned a dollar a day clerking in Dance and Stuart. Fifty-four dollars was two months' wages.

Her bump of suspicion swelled. Why did Fitch want those papers so bad? As she tried to figure that out, he added, "Each."

31

One hundred and eight dollars? Some claims brought thousands, but not generally before an assay. "That's generous," she said, "but they still aren't mine. I can't sell them."

"Suppose we call it the right to store them. I'll pay you for having stored them for me."

A bribe. He was offering to make it so her conscience would give him his way. However she looked at it, though, it was a bribe. He was asking her to whore herself, only in a different way than Jacky Stevens meant. That bump of suspicion burst into full-blown anger. "How dare you? Offering me a bribe. I'm keeping those papers safe for McDowell, for when he comes back."

"Wait a minute. I have no intention of offering a bribe. None whatever. You've misinterpreted my attempt to be of help." He placed his right hand over his heart, and his eyes were full of hurt that she would think him capable of such a base act.

Not believing a word of it, Martha was forced to apologize, hating herself for every syllable. She had caught him out, and they both knew it, yet he had won.

Fitch pulled a piece of paper from an inner pocket and smoothed it out on the table. From another pocket he took a pencil and tapped a place at the bottom of the page. "This paper is called an option. It says you'll let me buy the claims someday. If he's, uh, no longer living."

"He could be alive and well in California."

"True." Fitch tapped the pencil point on the paper. "If you wouldn't mind signing here."

"I don't understand," Martha lied. She knew full well what this meant. She didn't own the shares unless McDowell was dead, and this paper bound her to sell to him whenever they discovered his death.

"I'd need to read it first." Martha rolled the dough ball between her fingers. "You leave it here, and I'll let you know what I make of it."

"You mean you'll have Dan Stark read it for you." The contempt of the educated for the uneducated – and a woman – thickened his voice.

Her temper threatened to flame, but she piled ashes on it. Losing it would let him win again. She smiled as sweet as she could. "I'd be a fool not to, wouldn't I? A good lawyer like him." Maybe if Fitch wasn't trying to bully her into giving up the claims, she wouldn't take pleasure so in the way his jaw muscles bunched.

"I didn't have to offer you anything. I could just jump his part of those claims. You'd do well to accept my offer, because it will be withdrawn when I walk out that door."

Stifling the urge to throw the dough ball at him, she said, "You can't jump them yet. The Creek is at high water."

By the way he worked his lower lip, she knew she had rattled him. Did he think she was a witless ninny? Dan'l called it the winter dispensation. During the summer a claim was considered abandoned if the owner didn't work it for three straight days. Other times, when no one could work account of ice or high water, that rule was suspended.

His voice struck a higher pitch. "Pah! This offer expires when I walk out that door. I wanted you to have something from this, but if I jump them, you'll have nothing. Besides which, you will have enough to do just to keep the one claim that's registered to McDowell. That son of yours wants to clerk in a store rather than work hard, and don't tell me Dan Stark would pay to have that claim worked either, because he's saving all his dust to take home to New York, and he won't come back."

Maybe because she was scared of just that, she answered him sharp. "I said I'd let Mr. Stark look at it. And I'll think on it. That's my answer." She stood up, closed her fists around handfuls of her apron. He could do nothing but stand, too, and not for the first time she wished she was big so's men like him and McDowell couldn't loom over her or think they could bully her.

"Dan Stark won't find anything irregular about my offer." Raising the stump of his left arm, he rubbed his jawbone. He'd left his hand at Antietam, Martha had heard. A defeat for the South, and him not one to take defeat easy. Especially from a female.

She held Canary close to her skirts until Fitch had walked away. Shivering, she went inside, but she couldn't settle herself to read the Good Book. Her thoughts, like scared rabbits, jumped here and there. What if McDowell came back? Why did Fitch want to buy the claims? If McDowell showed up while Dan'l was in New York, could she send him to Fitch? Fitch had that look in his eye: like he knew something she didn't.

Sly. That's what he was. Sly. A knowing lurked behind his eyelids, a secret. Fitch was up to something, but what? Or was it just that he thought he knew what sort of woman she was?

The easy kind. The kind he could bribe.

Drat the man. She rubbed her hands together to warm them. The dough ball smeared all over her hands, and she'd squished it into the fabric of her apron. "Oh, drat!" Muttering to herself in Cherokee, she took up two buckets. Fitch's visit wouldn't disappear from her mind, but she could scrub his muddy tracks off her floor.

Oblivious to fat, wet snowflakes plummeting onto her head and shoulders, she pumped the buckets as full of water as she could carry and toted them into the house. She boosted one onto the stove to heat, and set to shaving soap into the other from the soap block. The knife slipped, and blood sprouted from her thumb. Wheeling, she flung the block across the room.

~6~

"YOU HAVE A CHOICE." Dan spoke to two men sitting on boxes in front of his makeshift desk, warped planks laid across a couple of boxes that served as pedestals. One crate was taller, so the planks sloped a degree downhill to his left. At his right, Dan's client stood squeezed into a corner formed by a pile of boxes and the board-and-batten wall separating this storage room from McClurg's Dry Goods store. Arms folded, he glared at the other two men.

"You can make full restitution, or I'll report your theft to the Tribunal."

Someone tapped at the door. "Later," Dan called, then lowered his voice.

One of the men in front of him wore a beard and hair untouched by scissors since his arrival. His eyes shifted from Dan's left shoulder to his right and back again. The other man, who smelled of bad whiskey, turned to him. "I'd advise you to own up and do as Mr. Stark says."

"What sort of lawyer are you? You're supposed to be on my side." The thief's eyes flicked toward Dan's client and away. "Anyhow, I don't got the money. I spent it."

"Then we'll confiscate your tools and your horse," said Dan, "and you can get the hell out of the Gulch."

Something crawled out of the thief's hair and back in again, but he did not seem to notice. "I'll be broke. You can't do that to me, Charlie." His bloodshot eyes filled with tears.

"Go to hell, Ben. You didn't give a shit about me being broke when you stole my dust."

"All right, I'll give you my tools, but not Babe. That horse is like family. Besides, the tools is worth more'n what I took."

"Not no more. They're all bunged up. You never could learn to keep your tools, and Babe will be better off with me. I'll feed her good. It's that or the Vigilantes."

"Take the offer." The lawyer groped into a coat pocket, and came out with a flask.

"God damn it, you're all agin' me. All right! I'll do it." He turned on his lawyer. "As for you, give me back the fee I paid you. You done nothing for me."

The lawyer said, "I did so. I gave you good advice."

Dan said, "I'll draw up the formal agreement and we can meet in front of Judge Duncan in a couple of hours to have it registered."

The thief's lawyer said, "We don't need the judge for a simple agreement, do we? This is all between friends."

"Friends!" Dan's client burst out. "Friends don't thieve from each other. Damn you, Ben—"

"We need the judge to ratify an order of banishment." Dan pulled a piece of paper toward him. "In the meantime, you can sign this." He uncapped the ink bottle, dipped his pen, and scribbled so fast that the nib caught. A drop of ink splattered onto the plank and rolled downhill, but he did not pause to blot it. He wanted the men gone; their odors were choking him.

When the thief and his lawyer had left, Charlie said, "Thanks, Mr. Stark. I thought Ben would make more of a fuss." He took a deerskin pouch from his pants pocket.

"That's why you hire a lawyer, Charlie." Dan hitched his chair back and stood up. He needed fresh air.

"I didn't just hire a good lawyer. I hired you, on account of you're a Vigilanter. Ben knew he couldn't weasel out of nothing with you." He sidled around the desk.

Dan snuffed the candle between forefinger and thumb, and followed him into the store. Jacob Himmelfarb and McClurg stood, heads bent as though in prayer, studying two rectangular boxes lying on the floor. The clerk leaned over a display case to stare at them, too. "What have we here?" asked Dan.

"We've been waiting for you," said McClurg.

Jacob smiled. "It is to you they belong. They have your name."

"All the way from New York." The clerk drummed on the counter top.

Dan's rope cuts tingled. "Open them up."

McClurg held out the crowbar he had held behind his back. "Here, Pat. Don't waste any time." The clerk came around the counter and grasped the crowbar. "Hurry up. But be careful."

Rolling his eyes at that, Pat set the crowbar's teeth under the lid. Wood screeched as he pried up the top to expose a large rectangular bundle wrapped in oiled cotton and bound many times with string.

The men looked toward Dan. "Lift it out."

Pat placed the bundle on the counter and set the crowbar at the second box.

The cuts on both hands tingled now. Newspapers. By its shape, the bundle had to contain newspapers. Something new to read after the long winter. He had read Kenilworth almost to shreds, nearly memorized *Henry IV*, and worn out his Emerson. Penknife in hand, Dan put it to the string, but McClurg stopped him. "Don't cut it, save it." Dan shifted the knife point to the knot and pried it loose, stood aside while McClurg and Jacob unwrapped the bundle. They had the wrapping off, McClurg folding the cloth.

"Newspapers!" someone breathed.

What if the War were over? But wouldn't Van Fleet have said?

Pat lifted up the second bundle. Newspapers again.

"God damn." Pat sounded like he'd found the Mother Lode, or the Holy Grail. "I'll give you a week's salary for one of these." And when Dan did not reply, he said, "Hell, Mr. Stark, I'll give you a week's salary for one page. God damn. The *New York Times*."

Behind him Charlie asked, "Who's winning the damn war? That's what I want to know."

Jacob lay his hand on one of the piles of newspapers. "Dan Stark's newspapers they are, and to say they are rented is for him." A German-Yiddish speaker, for Jacob the English 'th' slid between his front teeth like a soft z.

"I'll look through them," Dan said. "Day after tomorrow —"

Charlie craned his neck around Dan's shoulder. "November 27, 1863," he read. "Hell that's only four, five months old."

Dan said, "Come back Monday, Charlie, and you can rent something then." He folded the blade back into the knife. "In the meantime, you can pay my fee."

McClurg moved to his balancing scales. "How much?"

"Half an ounce." The tingling in the cuts was almost more than he could stand, yet Dan dared not scratch. Nine dollars, a sum Pat would earn in nine days.

"And worth every flake." Charlie gave his poke to McClurg, who placed the thin metal wafers on one pan of the scales, and poured gold dust into the other until they balanced.

Dan watched both men. He trusted McClurg, who was not one to put his thumb on the weight pan, and Charlie was satisfied to have his former partner's tools and horse, but no one was completely above temptation. It was a philosophy McClurg believed in; he allowed no one but Pat or his business partner to handle the scales.

When Dan had poured the dust into his own poke, he and Jacob carried the newspapers into his office. He slid a plank aside and dropped the poke into the pedestal box, replaced the plank, and pulled the kerosene lamp close. He seldom lighted it, but if newspapers were getting through the passes, supply wagons would come soon, and he could buy more kerosene before he ran out.

Jacob laid the bundles on the desk top. Dan lifted up the lamp chimney and set it aside. With a small scissors he trimmed the burnt strip off the wick. Taking his tinder box from his jacket pocket, he struck flint and steel together until a spark caught the scrap of cloth and shavings. He lighted a splinter from the tiny blaze and touched it to the wick until it caught, then replaced the glass chimney (in need of a good wash). Turning the wheel to adjust the wick higher for greater light, "There. Now we can see what we have." He closed the small metal box and set it aside to cool before putting it back in his pocket.

As he lifted the top newspaper to see the next one, a letter slid out. It was addressed in Mother's hand. Had she collected these papers for him? Risked Grandfather's displeasure? The old tyrant did not permit women to read newspapers; he considered they ruined a woman's natural delicacy and unsexed her. Mother. A rush of homesickness stung Dan's eyes. How had the family borne this winter of their disgrace?

Jacob picked up a *Times*. "Wunderbar! Aber, es ist nicht alles." His long fingers sought inside his overcoat, past the fringed prayer shawl he wore over his jacket, and from an inner pocket brought out a packet of letters. "All this mail, they came on the stage yesterday."

"First the ice breaks a week ago, and now the stage brings mail. Winter must be over."

"Ja, aber —" Jacob stopped, and shut his eyes while he changed to English.

Letters. Dear Lord, letters. News of home. After all this time. Someone, where they lay waiting to be collected for the last leg of the trip, had tied the letters into one package, with a knotted double bow.

Dan set the letters aside and hunted through the newspapers for the latest, but among the *New York Times*, the *Herald*, the *Tribune*, none was later than December. Old news. Battles had been fought, armies had marched and retreated. All over months ago. Perhaps the War was won, but by which side? He still would not know.

Jacob said, "Ja, the stage has this brought." Jacob smiled. Dan smiled with him while he organized another sentence, but Dan remembered the joke about the German language: Throw Mama from the cart a kiss. English word order defied Jacob as much as the th's. "The stage, it is not far behind the mule train." Another pause. "Perhaps two weeks behind."

Then Van Fleet had come out with these letters and the newspapers without knowing it. "Excellent, Jacob." Dan shook Jacob's hand. "Your English improves day by day."

"Everyone teaches me. Timothy, too, in our cabin." Jacob winked. "The Morris brothers and Solomon Content, they tell me perhaps his English is not kosher."

Dan laughed. "I agree. Definitely." He gestured at the newspapers. "How shall we divide these?"

"Dates." Jacob laid one paper aside, took the next. "They are, I think, arranged already."

"So they are." Mother had sorted them and packed them in order. He separated them into two piles. "You take one pile. When I've finished the others, I'll give them to you."

"Nein." Jacob put his hands behind his back. "Nothing has been to read in months. I read, sell the pages, give you half the dust."

"You keep —"

"Nein. I pay. Half." Jacob shook his head, his long beard touching each shoulder in turn.

"Nonsense, Jacob. You should save every flake against the day you want to find a wife."

His friend said, "What I owe you, who gave me job, brought me where I can someday be rich —" He swallowed, his adam's apple bounced in his throat . "Someday I go back, ja? And I find a wife, but now is too soon. I have not enough to offer. Her father laughs at me." He tapped a finger on the desk. "She must keep a kosher house."

"Perhaps a wife will come here."

"Ja, I hope, though maybe wish, more like." As he pulled the door open, he asked, "How mends —?" His English failed him, and he made a helpless gesture.

Dan did not wonder how Jacob knew he had been to visit Van Fleet. People had nothing much to do but notice their neighbors. "He will live. He does not have pneumonia." Glancing at his hands, Dan added, "His name is Joel Van Fleet and he was sent by the Bank of New York to find me and bring me back with him." As if I were a common criminal, he added to himself, they have sent a bailiff, a bounty hunter.

"Do you go home?"

"Not yet. Later, when travel is easier, if I have enough gold."

"Ja. Then you pay back your father's debt." Jacob took a deep breath. "Do you come again to Virginia City?"

"Of course. Martha is here. My life is here now."

When Dan had closed the door behind Jacob, he lighted the candle, blew out the lamp, and sat down. Pulling the candle closer, he flipped through the letters Jacob had brought. All were addressed in Grandfather's hand, and he set them aside. Without reading them, he knew what they contained: Complaints and grumbling, first about him, secondarily about the economy, and the War. Lincoln's War, his Copperhead Grandfather called it. They could wait, damn it. He had no wish to encounter the old man either on paper or in person, but all too soon, as he had told Jacob, he would have to take his gold home. A long trip and very little good at the end.

He slit open the letter from Mother, held it to the candlelight. "My dearest son," he read, "you are sorely missed," and then had to wait because the damn candle light shook so, and her writing swam on the paper.

~7~

LOVING MARTHA ALWAYS BEGAN with a tightness in Dan's throat, a warmth that spread outward from his loins along his veins, and the awareness of joy waiting for him. The anticipation at once made him impatient and calmed him. He could wait as long as necessary, even for days if it was her time. In their weeks together, he had learned he could not live without her, that he dreaded the trip to New York, loathed the thought of leaving her here for the three or four months the journey would keep him away. As if already missing her, he held her in his hands, buried his face in her neck, and plunged into the age-old dance of man and woman that finished in an exploding crescendo of joy.

Lying back, her head on his shoulder, their mingled sweat cooling on his chest, he let his left hand explore her body while he floated on the peace of the moment.

Martha said, "Tabby Rose tells me the man you pulled out of the Creek is doing right well. He should be up and about in another couple of days."

Dan's spirits plummeted. How much had the Negro woman heard? Had she said anything to Martha about their conversation? He would have to tell her now, damn it.

He said, "I went to see him this morning. He's weak, and not so fat, but he'll live." After a pause to kiss her temple, he added, "His name is Joel Van Fleet and he came all the way from New York City to find me."

"To find you?" Martha raised herself on one elbow and tucked the quilts in around him. Chuckling, she slid down again. "What a way to find someone he's looking for."

"Yes." How much of it must he tell her? About Father's gambling? His suicide? It was safest to say as little as possible. "My Grandfather sent him. They want me back soonest."

"I always knew you come out here to get gold for your family. Now you won't have to carry it back there. He can take it back for you."

Van Fleet take the gold back? What assurance did he have that the banker would deal honestly with the family? No, he could not allow that, but now was not the time to tell her about Van Fleet's connection with the Bank of New York. If he ever told her. It was best to say nothing and not worry her. "The stage brought mail, too."

"Mail? What kind of mail?" He tickled her neck with the end of the braid she wore to bed.

"Newspapers. Letters from home. From my Grandfather."

"How are your folks doing?"

"Very well." Mother had written of their good health and had made light of the adjustments to living in her son-in-law's house, but in what she had not written Dan had felt the pain of her comedown from social queen to pariah. He changed the subject. "When I go back to New York, come with me."

"No," she said.

"Why on earth not?"

"On account your family will hate me."

He kissed her breast. "No one could hate you."

"They'll say I'm no better'n I should be, and I'm out to catch me a rich husband."

He laughed. "If that were the case, you made a very poor choice. My father left such a mess of everything before he died that my family is deeply in debt. I'm about your worst choice."

"I don't think so. They won't think so, either. I don't talk right, I can't read much yet, and I ain't got – don't have – manners." Her fist beat on the mattress. "I don't have grammar either. They'd talk about me, and you."

"I wouldn't let them." But he knew she was right. Mother, having lost money, jewels, carriage, horses, and house, would cling to whatever shreds of her social position remained.

"You couldn't stop them. If we married proper-like, they might swallow everything else, but we can't."

God damn Sam McDowell, thought Dan. It wasn't enough that he beat this little sparrow, ran away and left her for dead. He hadn't the decency to let her know where he was, so she could divorce him.

In her uncanny way, she seemed to read him. "It was the drink and the War made him act mean. He weren't – wasn't – like that in the beginning."

"You were thirteen and he was fifteen when you married him. Nobody's like that at that age." He knew he lied. Old school friends had grown up to be more like themselves, not less.

"Phht." She blew out a sharp puff of air. "If'n I wanted a rich man, I made the right choice. You ain't the sort to live poor. You won't stop till you're comfortable. You come out here to get gold, and you'll get it."

Thinking of his obligations to the family in New York and the family he'd acquired with Martha, he said, "I hope you're right, because I'll need a lot of it. For all of us." He nuzzled into her neck, and she turned to him, and for a time he had no thought but the soaring joy while sinking flames in the pot-bellied stove cast flickering lights toward the rafters.

As the bedroom chilled, he thought to bank the fire before they fell asleep, but just now he could not bring himself to shift her head from his bicep, or to stop exploring her body.

She said, "Fitch was here today."

His hand jerked.

"Ouch! You pinched."

"I'm sorry. Fitch? What did he want?"

"The contracts. He wants to buy McDowell's shares in them – those claims."

Damn Fitch. How dare he come visit Martha uninvited and try to buy the shares? And why make an offer? Fitch should know they were not hers to sell. As long as McDowell was presumed to be alive, they belonged to him and no one else.

Martha said, "I told him to come back when you were to home. He wouldn't hear but he'd speak his piece right there and then. I didn't know what else to do."

He kissed her hair. "You did the best you could. Fitch is hard to resist."

She turned over and curled against him, her back turned. He felt her shaking, and moisture trickled onto his bare bicep. She was crying.

Not knowing what to say, he held her and let her weep, cursing Fitch soundly to himself.

When she spoke, halting between sniffs and pauses to wipe her eyes, her voice was full of old, remembered hurt. "You don't know what it's like, being poor white trash in the South. Folks like Fitch don't ever treat us like proper humans. Not as bad as they treat the darkies, but near enough. My family was lucky, living in the hills. We owned our own farm, and never had nothing to do with sharecropping. I 'member Fitch telling McDowell how he grew up on a big plantation in Tennessee, with lots of slaves, and he talked to McDowell like he was dirt under his shoe. That's how he was today." She sat up and reached for her flannel nightgown hanging on the bedpost by her pillow. "You come from money. Nobody ever figured you could be bought on account you're poor. He said he'd keep the papers for McDowell, and it was a storage fee."

Damn Fitch to hell. That he should find Martha alone, and try to bully her into doing something so wrong, so against her own moral fiber — it beggared thought. The son of a bitch claimed to be a gentleman, did he? Yet he would bully a woman in her own home.

Dan slid out of bed, tiptoed to the stove so as not to put his feet flat on the cold floor. Despicable. That was the word for Fitch. The bastard. Wrapping a towel around his hand, Dan swung the stove door open. Firelight leaped across his face, and he grasped the small fire shovel, scooped ashes from the ash box, and shook them over the embers to keep the fire alive but damped down for the night. Fitch thought he could get away with it, did he? Like hell he would. He hadn't reckoned on Dan Stark.

As Dan bent to replace the shovel, a drop from the ceiling splashed down on his bare buttock. Damn! The snow on the roof was melting. Shivering, he dashed across the floor, pulled his nightshirt over his head, and slipped under the blankets.

"How much did he offer?"

"Three ounces of dust. Each." Her voice quavered.

"$108? For six contracts? That's either far too much or too little. What did you say?"

"I told him I'd talk to you. That was right, wasn't it?"

"Yes. Very much so. I'll look at the contracts in the morning, and from now on, I'll deal with Fitch. I'll tell him that as your husband now, as well as your man of business, I represent you. I'll tell him to conduct whatever business he has with you only in my presence."

"What if —" Martha's voice squeaked; she cleared her throat. "What if McDowell comes back? What do I do then?"

Damn McDowell. "You let me handle McDowell. As for Fitch, I'll talk to him tomorrow."

"Good." She snuggled down under the quilts, burrowed in against the cold beginning to creep over the house.

Long after her breathing steadied into its sleeping rhythm, Dan lay awake while questions glimmered among the rafters.

~8~

THE NEXT MORNING at breakfast, Martha handed him the cigar box, battered at the corners, its fancy gilt lettering mostly worn off the lid. "What does it say?" she asked.

Dan read aloud, "Best Havana Cigars. For the Discriminating Connoisseur."

She pronounced the words after him, a crease forming between her eyebrows. "What is that when it's to home?"

"It means someone of refined tastes who can appreciate the finer things of life."

She laughed. "That had to be Fitch. McDowell wouldn't be any sort of connoisseur of anything." She added. "It's a funny-sounding word."

"It's French," said Dan.

"No wonder," Dotty said. "Professor Dimsdale says French is a slippery sort of language."

Laughing, Dan heard Martha whispering the word to herself as she turned over the bread frying on the flat stove top.

Dotty poured milk onto her mush. "I like how the words sound, though. Discriminating connoisseur. "

"You can take them to the Professor," Dan told her. "He'll be pleased you're learning new words. Even a French word." Taking the papers from the box, he slid it over to his stepdaughter. As she chewed her mush, she traced each letter with the handle of her spoon, whispered its name to herself. Something about her earnest concentration, or perhaps the way the lamp shone on the planes of her face, caught Dan's attention.

Good God, Dotty was maturing, becoming a young woman. Both she and her brother favored their father in looks. They had McDowell's light brown hair and big bones. Someday, people might refer to Dotty as "statuesque." Men would notice and seek after her, bees to honey.

Her mother would guide her steps to womanhood, but he was her stepfather. He was responsible for her protection. He had not thought, when he knew he loved the mother, had not considered that loving her made him responsible for this child as she blossomed into a handsome young woman.

"More tea?" Martha stood beside him with the teapot.

He held up the mug, surprised to find it steady under the pouring stream of pale green tea. "Thank you." He was responsible. He smiled up at Martha, who squeezed his shoulder.

As he looked into the mug, he saw the liquid surface shimmer, though his hand was steady. Exactly, he thought. Like me. He blew on the tea, and brought his mind back to the contracts.

There were six of them, written on papers torn from a school exercise book. On one side, Fitch's full name – Tobias Wayne Fitch – headed the sheet in a childish printing, followed by line after line of cursive letters in a Spencerian script: thin strokes upward, thick strokes downward, but with a tendency to return the downstrokes of the small t's and l's on the same line rather than in a loop. Closed, rather than open, Dan thought. Secretive. Fitch had written out the contracts on the unused reverse of each sheet. The mature penmanship was practiced and skilled, the loops tight.

Each read the same. "We the undersigned agree to share fifty percent (50%) each in the risks and profits of the claim at the following location. One and one-fifth miles upstream from its confluence with Daylight Creek and Lee's Creek, on the north bank, the corners marked by a cairn of pale stones." Someone, presumably Fitch, had printed his name and McDowell's below his signature and McDowell's mark.

Which of any number of little feeder streams had been named after Robert E. Lee?

Dotty carried her bowl to the dishpan. Standing at the stove with her mother, she whispered the letters, and Martha repeated them. The two of them giggled at something, and at the happy female sound homesickness gripped Dan in a hard, sharp spasm. Mother and his older sister, Florentine, had sometimes laughed that way. Could they laugh now?

He flipped through the papers. All were similar to the first, except for the locations and the names. The names. Dan studied the papers. Either Fitch's name or McDowell's appeared on all, but on only the first one did they both appear, though Fitch had both written and signed all the agreements. Each signature bore the significant tight loops.

Martha brought him his breakfast, and he set the papers aside for her to put down the plate. Venison strips and fried bread. Again. God hurry the freighters, and let them bring canned peaches, beans, spinach. Always the same breakfast – venison or beef and fried bread – since deep snow had made the passes too difficult for freight wagons. He and Timothy hunted deer themselves, or they had bought beef from Con Kohrs's butcher shop when he could get it. Strips for breakfast, stew for dinner. He smiled at her, knowing his luck. She was a good cook, who could use herbs to flavor the food. They had enough flour to make the bread. "Should Tim and I go hunting again?"

"Not yet," she said. "Con Kohrs said he'd have fresh beef in his butcher shop today."

Dotty, examining her face in the mirror, said, "Maybe there'll be pork. I'd love a chop."

"There will be soon." Ignoring Martha's exasperated sigh for his cooling food, Dan went into the bedroom. In a small top drawer of the dresser, that Martha called a chiffonier, he kept extra buttons, a couple of nuggets, two spare handkerchiefs. His notecase. After winning the half shares in two claims from McDowell at poker, he had put the papers in his notecase and forgotten about them in the press of other business. Vigilante business. Courting Martha.

"Is everything all right?" Martha called.

"I don't know. There's something odd about those agreements." Three different names appeared on them, all written in Fitch's hand. He spread his own two out on top of the dresser.

Martha came to stand at his elbow and said something that Dan, reading, did not hear.

He said, "One of these agreements is signed by Fitch, with

McDowell's mark, but the other has McDowell's name and that of one Thomas Whipple on it."

"Who might Thomas Whipple be?"

"I don't know. I've never heard of him." Dan folded the papers and put them back in his notecase, slid the notecase into the inside pocket of his suit coat on the back of a chair. "Of course, with thousands of men in the Gulch it would not be difficult to miss one or two." He smiled despite the questions bumping against his suspicions. If this Thomas Whipple had entered into an agreement with McDowell or Fitch, why had he not signed his own name?

"Finish your breakfast," Martha said. "These things will still be here when you're done."

"Yes, Ma'am." He forked up a mouthful and chewed while he thumbed through the papers. Fitch and McDowell had agreed to a fifty-fifty split on two claims. For the rest, either McDowell's name or Fitch's appeared along with another, Thomas Whipple. Two more were signed by Edgar Isaacson, and two by William Yancey.

While he ate and washed the food down with cooling tea (let the freighters bring coffee), and teased Dotty about nonexistent spots, his mind worried at the questions popping up like mushrooms. He had thought that studying the agreements would banish the questions of the night, but instead they had multiplied. Thinking hard, he barely knew when Dotty left for school.

Fitch had grubstaked McDowell on all of the claims, so why did their names appear together as partners on only two claims? Who were Thomas Whipple, Edgar Isaacson, and William Yancey? All the names and signatures were in Fitch's hand. Had McDowell put down his own mark? Dan looked again. The shaky slashed check was typical of an illiterate man.

He held the paper out to Martha. "Was this McDowell's mark?"

"Seems to be."

"You can't be sure?"

She shook her head. "I never saw him make his mark. Only time he did afore we come here, he sold the farm without I knew a thing about it." She took her lower lip in her teeth and was silent. "I never saw the bill of sale."

"What happened to the money?" Dan asked.

"There wasn't none that I knew of. He come back with the wagon and the outfit and said he was moving West." Her eyes brimmed with tears. "He wasn't best pleased when I told him me and the young'uns would come, too." The tears spilled over, and Don stretched his hand across the table to her.

"I would never have met you if he had not done that," he said, inwardly cursing McDowell, who had not recognized the real treasure in his life. The son of a bitch had been involved in possibly shady mining ventures with Fitch, and again Martha had known nothing.

So now. He and Fitch had entered into these agreements, with three other men whom his own wife did not know. By and large, that in itself was suspicious. Men did business all the time that their wives knew nothing of, but this was different. Where were the claims? Did they even exist? McDowell had been gone for days at times, and generally had plenty of money. Had he after all been a road agent, a highwayman? Fitch had suspected him; had Fitch been right?

"I'll talk to Fitch today if I can," he said to Martha. "He has some questions to answer."

"But — " Martha began, then stopped. Her pupils were dilated, so that instead of brown, her eyes appeared black. What was she afraid of? Dan wondered.

"Go on."

"We can't handle all them — those claims. And we, the young'uns and me, we've already got the Alder Creek claim."

"Yes?"

"I'm thinking we give Fitch back all them papers that don't have McDowell's mark on them." Her hands lay clasped on the edge of the table, and her fingertips dug into the backs.

Dan smiled at her. "You're right." Her hands fell into her lap, her shoulders relaxed, and she closed her eyes as if relieved of a great fear. Damn McDowell to hell. "That still leaves four, including the two I won from him." He could not say McDowell's name aloud, but only in his mind, with curses. "I'll meet with Fitch and see what we can work out."

~9~

DAN AWAITED FITCH in the company of the dead.

Between this knoll, where rocks and mounded rotting snow covered five unmarked graves, and the farther slopes rising towards distant mountains hidden in a low overcast, Virginia City bustled into a pale gray day. It was fast becoming a town, its increasing population stretching boundaries that bulged like a self-indulgent waistline.

At the foot of the knoll, Dan saw Fitch cross Daylight Creek. The Southerner waved to him, and Dan lifted a hand in return. Fitch had insisted on meeting here. When Dan asked him, Why? he had replied, 'Because you and I, we share history with them.' Did the memories whisper in Fitch's mind, too? It didn't have to be this way. Then you should have chosen a different life, he said to the whisper and to the silent corpses in their graves.

Was Fitch, now climbing the knoll, ever troubled by nightmares? A breeze brought laughter and tin music clashing in drunken hilarity from exuberant saloons and hurdy-gurdies. People celebrated spring runoff as if they could work the claims already.

Dan waited as Fitch joined him, panted around the tobacco chaw in his mouth. "That's a climb, that is."

"We could have saved ourselves the climb, and the mud, by meeting somewhere else."

Jerking his thumb over his shoulder toward the graves, Fitch said, "I didn't want to be overheard. They're safely in hell, where they belong. Most of them, anyway."

"We got them all," said Dan. He would not think otherwise, would not think it had all been for nothing.

"Maybe. Take McDowell, for instance. His pals are up here. He should be with them."

Dan shook his head. "McDowell wasn't much, but he was no murderer, no armed robber."

Fitch went on as if Dan had not spoken. "All the times he said he was prospecting? God knows what he was really doing." He spat a yellowish brown stream of tobacco juice.

As in stud, watching the tells, the small unconscious signs that revealed a man's true intentions, Dan said, "Then if you think he cheated you, why do you want to buy those agreements my wife has? You don't pay good dust for nothing."

"I don't want Mrs. McDowell to be out anything because her husband was a son of a bitch." Fitch stretched his lips in a smile that did not hide his calculating gleam.

Mrs. McDowell. Not Mrs. Stark. McDowell her husband, not himself. A porcupine jab at Dan, a quill under the skin.

Very well. Let Fitch think he had led him astray. In a lawyer's most stilted phrasing, Dan said, "It is an untenable situation that is beyond our power to correct just now, but when she can, she will sue him for divorce on grounds of desertion." He took a deep breath, "In the meantime, please refer to her as Mrs. Stark."

Fitch turned his head away to spit, but

Dan caught a tic at the corner of his mouth, perhaps the beginnings of a secret smile.

"As for visiting her yesterday, we would prefer you dealt with me, as her husband and man of business." He could not prevent his own tells, the tone of voice hardening with the effort of not throwing Fitch down the bluff. "She will continue to hold McDowell's shares until we know he is dead. Until then he is the legal owner." And Fitch damn well knows it, he thought. "In the meantime, I have no choice but to safeguard his interests, supposing he reappears alive."

"Safeguard McDowell's interests? That son of a bitch? Are you mad?"

"It's the best way to protect her."

"His name's not even on all of them."

"I noticed that. Who are Thomas Whipple, William Yancey, and Edgar Isaacson?"

"Investors. In Atlanta."

Fitch had been expecting that. His answer had come too pat, too neat. "Atlanta. I see." Where, because of the war, verifying their existence and their interest in potential Western gold mines would be difficult, if not impossible. "Given that McDowell's mark is not on them, why were those agreements in his possession to begin with?"

Instead of answering, Fitch grubbed at a snow-covered rock with the toe of his boot. "You're going back to New York soon, right?"

"Not soon, no. What has that to do with the issue at hand?"

"Not much, but that's what the fella you pulled out of the creek says. He was looking for a room, said he wouldn't need it more'n a few days while you tidied up your affairs and traveled back with him."

The clouds veiling the distant mountains darkened. Dan's hands doubled into fists. "That bastard." I should have let him drown. The bastard. Damn Van Fleet.

Dan swept off his hat, wiped sweat from his sideburns. He waited for his breathing to slow, for the clouds to return to pale gray before he spoke to Fitch's triumphant face. "I am not returning to New York any time soon, and when I do go it will be a short trip, to take care of some business and return as soon as possible." He paused. "If Van Fleet says anything else, he is mistaken." He settled the hat on his head, tugged the brim low. He would deal with Van Fleet as soon as he could. Damn him.

"I wondered, considering you're so determined to protect Mrs. Stark's interests."

And damn you, Fitch. "I have asked her to come East with me."

Fitch's jaws worked harder on the chaw, the muscles bulging and flattening.

Dan wanted to laugh. Let Fitch think that if Martha came with him, the shares would either be hidden or she might take them with her. He changed the subject. "Did McDowell bring back ore samples? Have you had an assay done?"

"No." Fitch coughed, spat a gob, and cleared his throat. "I intended to, but what with one thing and another." He let the sentence trail off, cocked his head toward the graves. "My boy was killed about then."

"Where are the samples?"

"I don't know. I thought he left them with the contracts."

Dan forgot tells, forgot strategy to stare into Fitch's eyes, as blank as his own mind. "Do you mean to say that McDowell brought back locations but no ground samples?" The first thing a prospector always did was to dig up some dirt from a potential claim, then mark the four corners so the dirt came from the middle of the claim.

"He said they were at home, and he showed me a couple." Fitch took the plug of tobacco from his pocket and bit off another chaw. "But Nick was late coming back, and I was getting worried. After that, well, you know. Then McDowell ran off and there was no more to be done about gold claims till the ice broke."

Dan nodded. For a moment he was united in memory with Fitch. Finding Nick's body had been the first step that led them here. The living and the dead alike.

"Until spring runoff is down enough to let the claims be worked," Dan said, "not much can be done. But we have to find those claims and get them assayed."

"Shit," said Fitch. "He stole them. We'll have to do it all over again. Damn it, Stark, I told you he wasn't on the up and up."

Through a hole in the clouds, a shaft of sunlight shone on a farther slope, where dark conical junipers pierced the snow.

"This is a tangle," Dan said. "If McDowell lives, he owns his shares until three days after the first day the claims can be worked. Then someone can jump them. If he is dead, and he left no will, his widow and her children inherit his shares equally, one-third each. If he left a will, everything depends on who inherits. If McDowell lives and can be found, you can, in fact you will have to, communicate with him directly. He did not appoint her his agent, and she has no authority to act for him. She cannot sell or promise to sell."

"God damn that son of a bitch." Fitch yanked his hat from his head and thrust it under his short arm, scratched among his long hair. "We're all in limbo with this, aren't we?" Finding something, he studied it, cracked it between his fingernails, and flicked it out over the edge.

"Yes."

"Except for my shares. The ones I have with the Atlanta investors."

"Granted," Dan said. "Those rightfully belong to you, and we're willing to give them to you." He took his notecase out of his inside coat pocket and removed Fitch's shares. "Here they are." Fitch reached for them. "Don't you have your own copies?"

"No. There are just these." Fitch glanced through the papers. "They're not all here."

"That's right. We're keeping all those with McDowell's name on them. Except for two."

"Two? What two? Where are they? I don't get it."

"They're the ones I won from him." Dan faced the Southerner. "Remember? I won two contracts McDowell had with you and one Thomas Whipple."

"I'll buy you out of them, too. Name your price."

Dan shook his head. "It may be premature to sell them now. I want to see how they prove up. It would be a pity to sell for a few flakes of dust when they might be worth millions."

"God damn it, I said I'd give you a fair price."

"But there's no assay to determine what would be fair. It wouldn't be good business."

"I have to think of the shareholders."

"Who may have bought a pig in a poke. We won't know until there's an assay."

Fitch's mouth opened, and his beard moved as if his throat worked. Thinking he choked on a bit of tobacco, Dan swung his arm to pound Fitch's back, but the short arm rose and blocked his hand. A shock ran down Dan's arm to his shoulder as though he had struck a log, and jarred his thoughts into a realization:

Fitch wanted all the shares. All the claims.

"Shareholders be damned. You want them all, don't you?"

"Yes, God damn it! Why the hell not?" Fitch shouted, his short arm stabbed toward Dan. "I paid for them. I grubstaked McDowell." He paused, looked toward the moving sunbeam sliding across the far hill. "I aim to be the richest man in the Territory someday. Then in the whole damn country. I'll build the biggest mansion on Manhattan Island. I'll dress Louise in silks and hats with ostrich plumes, and society women will call on her." His words rushed on, a spring run-off of plans and dreams. "I'll buy me a Senator, maybe a couple of Congressmen, and put right what happens in this damn War, if the South loses."

"You're committing fraud to get around the two claim rule. What you plan is illegal as hell."

Fitch's cheeks swelled, the hairs of his beard seemed to bristle, "Who in God's name are you to tell me what's legal? You fucking mudsills invaded my homeland. Your man Lincoln sent troops into

Virginia. You're fighting a God-damn illegal war dressed up as a righteous cause to free the niggers."

Mudsill, the Confederate's ultimate insult to Unionists. People scraped the mud from their shoes on a mudsill when they entered a house. Dan clasped his hands behind his back, so as not to slug Fitch. He would not give the son of a bitch the satisfaction. Through tight lips he said, "Then you'll be one greyback to have a mudsill partner." Greyback, a Yankee insult to Southerners, a double allusion to the Confederate uniform, and lice. Duels were fought over these insults.

Fitch stomped two steps away, stopped, wheeled about. "The hell I will."

The two men glared at each other.

Fitch broke first. "Ah, shit, Blue. You and I, we've been through too much. I can't forget you helped bring my boy's murderers to justice." Fitch liked to call him Blue, because he favored the Union.

"Then let's trade the shares out. I'll give you the one I hold with your name on it, and you trade me your other share with McDowell."

"No, damn it. Fuck this." He wheeled about to walk away.

"Why the hell not?" Dan called after him. "It's a reasonable offer."

Fitch turned, stared at Dan. The straight lower lids rose to narrow his eyes, and his chewing changed its rhythm. "Because the Mother Lode might be on one of those claims." And when Dan had to swallow his laughter, Fitch spat the tobacco juice and the remains of the chaw at Dan's feet. "You don't believe in it, do you? The more fool, you, because someday I'll own it, and all the God damn gold in this Territory."

The Mother Lode. A belief persisted that in the beginning molten gold, like lava, flowed from one source to the places where men now found it. That one source believers called the Mother Lode. "I'm the fool? Damn it, Tobias, the Mother Lode is a myth. It does not exist."

"Like hell it doesn't. Look at the lode they found up in Highland in January."

Dan said, "That's just a big pocket of gold. There are lots of them in gold country."

"I know. Bigger lodes, and the Mother Lode. I've grubstaked prospectors up at Summit City, but they've been stopped by the cliffs. We'll find it, though. I know we will." He gazed toward the opposite slopes, and his voice vibrated low in his throat. "I will own the apex of all apexes."

He's mad, thought Dan. Possessed by gold fever,of all diseases the worst. He thinks he can use the apex rule to corner all the gold in the Territory. Whoever owned the apex, the highest point of a gold source, owned all the gold that proceeded from that point. Men were always filing claims higher than a successful mine in hopes that they could find the apex of the ore being mined. Mining companies paid lawyers hefty retainers to guard them against such lawsuits.

"What will you do if McDowell comes back, then? You'll have to pay him half of whatever the claims are worth, plus half of whatever you've made from them. Until it is known that he is dead, his shares belong in an escrow account to be held for him until he does surface."

"I own those claims, and I won't pay that bastard one red cent."

"You'll have to," Dan told him. "You signed agreements with him. You'll have to abide by them. If you don't, I'll take you to court, and force you to keep your word."

"My word? My word?" Fitch's voice rose. "Go to hell, Stark." For a second or two, Dan thought the Southerner would attack him, and he shifted his feet to defend himself, but as if pricked with a pin, Fitch deflated. "Hell, I don't want this. I'll always be grateful that you put yourself in the line of fire for my boy." He raised his good arm and scratched his cheek. "But gratitude stops when you come between me and what's mine."

~10~

"THEE HAD BEST come quick, dearie," said Lydia Hudson. "There's a new shipment of ladies' boots at Dance & Stuart. Timmy said to tell you."

"New boots? Praises be!" Her friend stood on the mat while Martha flung her shawl around her shoulders, and the two women set off down Jackson, leaving Canary to bark his protest at being left behind. "New boots at last. I'll buy a pair, even if they don't fit just right." With a few hundred women in the Gulch, against thousands of men, the storekeepers had a habit of forgetting to buy for them, and this old cracked pair of McDowell's didn't keep out the cold or the wet, no matter how many rags she padded her feet with. "Thank you for telling me."

"Thee are welcome," panted Lydia.

"Glory be, here I'm plumb running your legs off you." Martha slowed her steps for Lydia to keep up. Sometimes she forgot the difference between them, her being built thin and spare and quick, and Lydia short and round and slower moving, though a body would never know it from the deal of work she did at her Eatery.

When they crossed Wallace and fetched up in front of the Eatery, Lydia stopped.

"Come in and get thy dust." In the spring breeze all the ruffles and furbelows on her black dress quivered.

Inside, two tables spanned nearly the entire width of the room, with an aisle on either side, and benches to sit on. Martha smelled beef browning in the pan, while Tabby Rose's knife drummed a rapid beat on the chopping block.

While Tabby sorted out Martha's poke from all the others in Lydia's warming oven, Lydia said, "Thee are blessed in Daniel Stark, my dear. Thee does not have to hide thy money from him."

Unbidden, McDowell's shadow loomed between them. The dust Martha had earned from boarding Dan'l and another man, and from baking pies for the Eatery – not all of it had gone down McDowell's gullet in bad whiskey. She hefted the poke in her hand and thanked Tabby.

"I'm willing to bake more pies for you when you have the fruit," Martha said. "I have a proper stove now."

"And he would be willing?"

Martha was brought up short. She had no idea if Dan'l would be willing or not. "I don't think it's good, a woman depending only on a man. Something might happen to him."

"Indeed it might, dearie. There were Dr. Hudson and I, and Tabby and her Albert all ready to leave. The farm was sold, the wagon packed, the horses hitched, and the doctor went to check if he'd forgotten anything. He slipped and fell down the cellar stairs and broke his neck." She sighed. "I don't know what he thought he was looking for down there."

Against the tear trickling down Lydia's cheek, Martha could think of nothing to say, and anyway, sometimes nothing a body could say would help at all. She hugged her friend. Lydia clung to her as a drowning woman might seize a rope. Drawing back, she said, "Dearie, thee are a port in a storm. In this country a woman needs her friends, and the good Lord sent you."

Over her friend's shoulder she caught on Tabby Rose's cheek a glint that might have come from candlelight on a tear or a stray bit of gold, before the black woman turned back to the chopping block and picked up the knife.

~11~

LEAVING THE EATERY to walk down to Dance & Stuart, Martha heard Dan'l call her name. He smiled at her, but by the way he tapped his gloves against his leg, she could tell he wasn't best pleased about something. Before she could get up a proper worry about that, he caught up to her and laid her hand in the crook of his elbow.

"Where are you going?" he asked.

"Dance & Stuart. Lydia Hudson says they have a shipment of women's boots."

"Have you enough money?"

"I had some dust at the Eatery." She showed him the poke, something she would never have done with McDowell, who would have took it and drank it up.

His smile seemed tight to her. "You don't have to use your dust for boots, you know. I do well enough for that." People passing by said How-do and stopped for a few friendly words about how the weather was moderating. At last he was able to tell her, "Fitch wouldn't trade like we hoped."

"He wouldn't? I don't understand."

"He wants them all."

They walked along Kiskadden's Stone Block, next door to the

Eatery, where the three little shops offered groceries, dry goods, and stationery. Mr. Baume, in the middle store, was stocking his shop window with mining supplies like quartz picks and bottles to hold acids, and beckoned them in. "I sent you a client," he told Dan. "Seems this fella's a miner who bought a cat to catch the rats in his cabin. It proved to be so good a rat catcher that he rented it out, but the cat took to one renter in particular and keeps going back to him. The man refuses to pay because it's the cat's free choice. So the cat's owner was asking about a lawyer." Mr. Baume stopped. His serious face didn't match his mirthful eyes.

After a second or two, Dan'l sighed. "I'll bite. Why does he want a lawyer?"

"To sue the renter for alienating the cat's affections."

Dan'l's laughter rumbled up from his belly and boomed out, mingled with her own delight and Mr. Baume's satisfaction in his joke.

"Tom," Dan said between spurts of laughter, "you are a caution."

Outside, when their laughter had faded, Dan'l said, "Fitch thinks the Mother Lode could be on one of the claims."

"The Mother Lode? Oh, Lordy. McDowell believed in that, too. He was so sure we'd be richer'n that old king, what's his name?"

"Midas. Everything he touched turned to gold, including his daughter." Under his breath she heard him mutter, "Damn fools."

Martha sniffed the good smells coming from the City Bakery. They walked on past LeBeau's Jewelry, where miners brought their gold for assay and to be made into jewelry. Maybe when she and Dan'l could marry, LeBeau might make her ring. Inside Goldberg's Pioneer Clothing Store, Jacob Himmelfarb talked to Mr. Goldberg. Martha wondered why Mr. Goldberg didn't wear the beanie like Jake did. He didn't wear a shawl, either.

The Virginia City Hotel occupied the second floor over Goldberg's and the Millinery Shop, and its door was set between them. The door flung open, and the man Dan'l had pulled out of the Creek nearly collided with Martha. With hardly a glance at her, and no greeting for Dan'l, he said, "I'm on my way to purchase tickets to Salt Lake."

"Have a good journey," said Dan'l.

If Martha had been the man, Van Fleet his name was, she'd have paid attention to the tight way Dan'l said that, but no, not him. "I shall purchase two tickets. One for you and one for me."

"Then you will waste a ticket. I have told you I shall return when I am ready and not a moment before."

"Your obligation is to return with me."

"So I understand you have been telling people, but you are mistaken. My immediate obligation is to my family here," Dan'l said. "My dear, may I present Joel Van Fleet of the Bank of New York?"

Van Fleet gaped as if he'd never seen a woman before, and Martha wished she had taken time to change her skirt when Lydia came for her.

Dan'l, cool as if butter wouldn't melt in his mouth, said, "My wife, Mrs. Stark."

Van Fleet's mouth opened and closed, and Martha thought he'd forgot to take off his hat, like a gentleman should when presented to a lady, until he recollected himself, dashed off the black city hat, and made a bow just short of rude. "Madam."

"I shall return to New York when I have enough gold, in addition to making suitable provision for Mrs. Stark and the youngsters." Dan'l sounded like he squeezed the words between his lips. "Until then, I'll thank you to refrain from announcing my business to everyone in earshot." He guided Martha around Van Fleet and continued toward Dance & Stuart, but Van Fleet hailed them.

"Wait, Stark, wait."

They stopped. When Van Fleet had caught up to them, he held out a letter. "This is from your Grandfather Stark."

Dan'l thrust it into his side pocket.

"It has instructions in it for your immediate return."

"I'm not surprised," Dan'l said. "Grandfather loves to give orders. It's his chief pleasure in life. He must be greatly chagrined to have had to let the servants go." He smiled, and Martha did not like the look of that smile. "Then again, he has you, does he not?"

~12~

MOTHER AND FLORENTINE had enjoyed shopping. Too often, to Dan's mind, he had accompanied them and hidden his boredom while they tried on new shoes, chose the modish styles that tortured their feet while ensuring that if ever a man should glimpse their ankles, he would have a favorable impression. He had stifled yawns while they exclaimed over their choices, and carried their purchases while wishing himself elsewhere.

None of that, though, prepared him either for the pandemonium in Dance & Stuart or for Martha's excitement. Six or seven women were already in the store. They crowded the single center aisle, grabbed a shoe box as fast as Timothy could unpack it from the shipping crate it had come in, passed boxes back and forth, called to each other: "Here try this one." "Is there a blue anywhere? Did they get blue?" "I need black, size five." "Dear me. A man must have selected these. Has anyone seen something with style?" Martha dove into the melee.

Dan stood back. "My God."

"It's something, ain't it?" Timothy stood with him. "I never seen nothing like it before."

"Neither have I." Dan rubbed his chin. "I forgot to tell your mother to buy two pairs." When Timothy protested, "That's too dear," he replied,

"It's less expensive in the long run to have a pair set aside for good. Then, when the everyday pair wears out, the good ones become —"

"I get it," Timothy said.

One of the women asked for a chair to sit on while she tried on shoes. Walter Dance invited them into the area at the rear where a white picket fence cordoned off Oliver's Stage office and some chairs by the round black stove. "Help yourselves, ladies."

Tim called, "If you have any questions, just ask."

Pulling a poke out of his pocket, Dan said, "Give your mother this when she's ready to leave. I'll be at my office."

"Mam won't believe it." Tim hefted the poke on his palm. "She ain't used to being pampered. Two pairs? She's hardly ever bought one pair."

"If the Alder Creek claim pans out well, she could buy as many shoes as she wants." Dan thought, now. "As it is, we'll have trouble keeping it unless you work it."

"No. Damned if I will. I hate mining. Everything hurting all the time, in muck to your knees. I'd have had to sink a shaft this spring. With no one to help, who'd know if it would cave in and bury me. You can find someone else. Maybe work it on shares."

"It could be your claim."

Tim looked startled, then shook his head. "No. I quit mining. I'll work here till my speculations get me enough for a horse farm and then I'll do that. But I ain't going back to mining and you can't make me. Don't even try."

A woman called to Tim for help, and the boy stepped around Dan to go to her. "You ain't my Pap."

~13~

DAN POKED A LETTER-OPENER at the pile of envelopes he had arranged in date order, oldest on top. He eyed the tight, judicial writing, the reflection of Grandfather's tight, judicial mind, each character narrow and upright, the ascenders on the small *d*'s and *b*'s and *k*'s a single line.

Memory, that random trickster, took him back:

Sunshine lay a carpet of light, crisscrossed into smaller panes a foot square, over the low table where he sat on his heels across from Father. On the table, stacks of poker chips stood in their colors – blue, white, red, yellow. He scratched his bare knee, wished he were old enough to wear trousers. He dealt the first card to Father and himself, face down. The next four face up, the hand for five-card stud. Turn up your hole card, said Father, and turned his up, too. I win, said the boy, amid a singing in his ears. Father's relentless smile stopped him. Why? Father asked. My hole card is an ace of spades. Your hole card is only a three of clubs.

He wriggled from one heel to the other, hardly able to contain his joy, for winning at five-card stud. He said, A pair beats high card, even an ace. Father leaned across and ruffled his hair. Good boy. You'll be a player when you grow up.

Heavy, imperious steps tolled toward them down the hallway.

The parlor door swung open, revealed Grandfather leaning on his cane: Here you are. Corrupting your son. You should be ashamed, do you hear me? Ashamed.

Father rocked back on his heels, stood up without using his hands, adjusted his waistcoat. Smiled and winked at the child. "I have some business downtown." Back straight, shoulders squared, he brushed past Grandfather. The front door shut; the latch lifted and fell. Father had run away. Again.

"Leave the cards and come here, Daniel. Do as I tell you. Now!"

He rose and walked toward Grandfather, prayed not to pee his pants.

Grand Central Station, at trackside, voice raised over the train's chuffing, Grandfather said: "You're just like him. You'll throw everything away on the turn of a card or a horse's nose." The old man jabbed his forefinger at his grandson's breastbone, though Dan topped him by a full five inches and outweighed him by fifty pounds. No matter. All his life, the Judge had succeeded in dominating larger men, starting with those in his family. "How can we trust you to carry out this mission? I'll expect you home in three months. A month to travel there, a month to collect enough gold, a month to travel back. See that you complete our business with dispatch."

He had boarded the train, found a seat. When he saw the new trees of Central Park, he allowed himself to breathe.

July seventeenth of last year. Getting on for a year, today being April 14, 1864. Even after so long, he doubted that he had enough gold to pay the debt. With the interest, it must be somewhere around $30,000, depending on the ever-fluid price of gold. In Virginia City, the price was $18.00 an ounce. Elsewhere, $20.00 or $22.00. At $20.00, he needed 117 pounds. He did not have it. He could not go home until he did.

Even then, how could he leave Martha?

Dan wiped his palms on his trouser legs, slit the first envelope with his pen knife.

Dated October 15, 1863, it began:

"Grandson: I desire that you complete your business and return directly. You have had sufficient time to gather enough gold to meet our requirements." The paper fluttered as if a breeze stirred it. Dan let it drop onto the desk. How did the Judge think gold was acquired? By finding it under bushes like Easter eggs?

He clenched his fists, cracked his knuckles. "I would not have survived the return trip," he muttered, thinking of travelers robbed and murdered before he and the other Vigilantes acted. The roads were safe now, but he had not enough gold.

To calm his mind, he picked up a *New York Times* and leafed through it. He hungered for news; even six months old, it would be new to him. He skimmed accounts of battles long won and lost, an alderman arrested, political scandals stale in Albany these many months.

A small headline on an inner page stopped him. He read:

"Financial Report for November 2, 1863. The price of gold was down to 145 1/8 – 1/4 this forenoon, but recovered 1 cent later in the dealings."

Down the columns, another paragraph continued, "The general course of the market for Gold and Stocks through the course of the week is thus noted," jumped over another line, to read: "American Gold Coin … 145 1/2 @ 148 1/2 ."

What did that mean? What did he know of gold trading? Damn all. He hadn't been much interested when Peter Yates, who worked on Wall Street, talked about it.

Setting his elbows on the desktop, his jaw on his doubled fists, he screwed his eyes shut. Think, man, think. The Lincoln Administration printed money – greenbacks – to finance the War. Peter had talked about how gold related to the greenback. Why the hell had he not paid attention? The two monies floated on the Gold Exchange. No, that wasn't quite right. How did they float? Like any other commodity, cotton, for example, or potatoes. All right, but so what? He remembered Peter's hands brushing up and down against each other. Ah! The values of gold and the greenback floated against each other, like currencies of separate nations. When one went up, the other went down, because the greenback was not pegged to gold.

Gold was not, did not have to be, pegged to anything. Gold was the standard.

He recalled Peter's hands raised shoulder-high, palms up: "God help us, the greenback is pegged to faith in the Union. As the Union goes, so goes the greenback." God help us, indeed. If people lost faith in the nation, in the Federal government, in its paper money, the Union would not win the War.

Said the *Times*, in November gold fluctuated on the Exchange between $145.50 and $148.50. If he remembered Peter's lesson correctly, that meant in New York his gold could be worth almost half again its current value. Was that right? But what was the value of gold now? Was it rising? Or – God forbid – falling? Perhaps Grandfather had mentioned it. He grabbed up the letter. Nothing. He slit the envelope on next letter, dated after Thanksgiving.

"I demand that you return forthwith." Dan snorted at it: Hmph. He skimmed the rest of the page, clenching his jaw. Grandfather had no real news, merely complaints about him, about the War; the Copperhead in the old man hissed, fulminated against Lincoln (that madman in the White House), his ruinous economic policies (printing money ... criminal.) In the envelope was a letter from Mother that Dan set aside to read after this, a reward for plowing through Grandfather's diatribes. He picked up the old man's next, written on New Year's Eve. More grumbling: Dan had not come home before Christmas.

On January 8, Grandfather ordered, "Return immediately, by the next train." Dan laughed aloud. The old fool understood nothing of the distance, the difficulties of travel. For him the edge of the world was the Hudson River. "Everyone continues in low spirits," he wrote, as if accusing his absent grandson of causing their situation, then turned to the state of the nation. As usual, he took a dim view. "...Nothing less than a national scandal that men go on trading gold even after the Stocks Market ordered the Gold Exchange to move. They trade in the the street, if necessary, and think nothing of blocking traffic. With the onset of cold weather, I understand they occupy a nasty dim basement, called the Coal Hole, which should be named the Snake Pit because they are perfidious vipers all. They drive up the price of greenbacks with every Union victory, while honest gold sinks in value. Men lose fortunes, as well they should. It is nothing more than a gambling den."

At what price did gold trade? Dan's jaw ached. He heard a small grating sound; he was grinding his teeth.

He flipped over the page and swore aloud: "God damn it!" Grandfather had written more, but it had got damp, and smeared. Pulling the candle closer, he bent close, but the figures there could not be right, however much he wished for it. Blood pounded in his ears, and sweat ran on his temples. He rubbed his eyes, read it again.

His desire had not deceived him.

"The only good," wrote Grandfather, "is to drive down the value of that madman's perfidious paper. Against $100 in gold, $100 in greenbacks this week fluctuated in value between $65.75 and $65.37½."

Good God. What did this mean? Dan stood up. He needed to

walk, to pace as always when he had a problem to work out, but there was nowhere to go. Stretching his arms behind him, jigging his shoulders to work out the stiffness, he wracked his brain: What had Peter told him? His friend's jibe sounded in his ears: Why are lawyers so thick at finance?

All right. Start with par.

Greenbacks and gold at par meant, $100 in greenbacks could be exchanged in a bank for $100 in gold. He seemed to hear Peter's voice, speaking as if to a child. But in January they had not been at par. If you took $100 in greenbacks to the bank, the teller would give you only $64 in gold. If you wanted $100 in gold, you had to pay about $156 in greenbacks.

At the bank.

The white tail of an idea flashed through the undergrowth of his confusion. Dan picked up the letter. "In the opinion of some," he read in an unbelieving whisper, "the price of gold has not yet reached its maximum, but my sense of it is that it will soon drop and ruin all the gamblers who batten on it."

He sat down, laid the paper aside, snatched up the last letter, written on January 16. "The greenback has fallen to under $64 against $100 in gold. It serves that madman and his gang of Federal sycophants right, trying to foist paper money off onto citizens to pay for this unconscionable war, while the purveyors of this swindle refuse to accept anything but gold in payment of customs and, of course, taxes."

His hand opened, the paper floated to the desk. And yet, when it came to buying something in a store, a gold Double Eagle, face value twenty dollars, would purchase the same quantity of goods – milk or property – as $20 in greenbacks, because the Legal Tender Acts made the greenback the same as gold. The greenback was legal tender. Legal for everything, except – as Grandfather had said – for taxes to the Federal Government, and customs duties. Legal for repayment of debts —

Legal tender for repayment of debts already incurred.

The idea had antlers now, a full rack.

His brain stuttered to a stop. He drove his fist into his palm. No wonder Van Fleet wanted to return so quickly. The bank wanted the gold because it was more valuable by the hour. Take in gold, pay out greenbacks.

God almighty. What the bank would do, he could do. Pay the debt in greenbacks.

If he did not have $30,000 in gold, he might have it in greenbacks. If he only knew what the exchange rate was now.

Repay Father's debt in greenbacks. Not in gold.

He thumped his fist down on the planks. The candle tipped, and he grabbed for it to steady it, flinched from hot wax dropping on his hand. He saw the tail, the rack of the idea, but not the entire animal. He had too many questions, all needing answers. He picked at the wax cooling on his hand. What was the exchange rate now between the two monies? How much gold did he have? How pure was it? Men had paid his fees in gold dust from claims all up and down the Gulch, and purity varied as much as two percent.

Even if he knew all that, he could not exchange it for greenbacks on the Gold Exchange, because the Exchange did not trade in raw gold. They kept no scales to weigh out dust. "Thank you, Peter," he breathed to his absent friend. Raw gold had to be converted into coin or bullion at the Assay Office in New York. Then he could exchange it.

Hilarious laughter leaked through broken chinking from Fancy Annie's saloon next door. Repay the debt in greenbacks. Not gold. He laughed out loud.

As he raised his hand to lick the small burn, he remembered the letter Van Fleet had given him. He tore it open, noticed the judicial letterhead, the formal salutation to Daniel Bradford Stark, Idaho Territory, and read the date, February 27, 1864, over a few scrawled lines: "You are to return forthwith in the company of Joel Van Fleet, emissary from the Bank of New York and from me. Your presence is required here soonest with whatever gold you have acquired. The remainder you will finish repaying here. By order of – " Grandfather's official scribble – "Judge Jason Quincy Stark, Esq."

Grandfather had sent him a summons from the bench.

Damn the old bastard. Thought his grandson would drop everything because he had received a formal notice to return, did he? Maybe he would have, before.

He held a corner of the paper to the candle flame.

~14~

THE LATE AFTERNOON SUN slanted Dan's long shadow uphill, into the ice-rutted street. Watching his footing, Dan crossed to Kiskadden's Stone Block, the biggest and only two-story building in Virginia City. The second story had a peaked roof hidden by a long false front that served as a sign board; the upper room served as a meeting hall for the Union League, the Confederate Club, the Masons. The Vigilantes. Below, three commercial spaces fronted Wallace street. D. W. Tilton's Stationery store occupied one end, its display window so far empty of paper and books, which had been used up months previously. In the middle window Tom Baume flicked a feather duster among the display of mining tools. Smiling, Baume beckoned Dan to step inside, but when Dan tried to indicate urgent business up the street, Baume came to his doorway. "You have to hear this, Stark. It's even better than my cat joke."

"That was a joke?" Dan said. "Why, the miner came to visit me this morning, and tried to hire me to represent his suit for alienation of affections."

Baume goggled, realized that Dan was teasing him, and threw back his head to laugh. "Good one, Stark, good one." Then, "What did you tell him?"

"I had to refuse. It's a tom cat."

Baume's laughter in his ears, Dan went on his way. Not even when a bullet had creased Baume's scalp did his humor fail: "If you want me to change the part in my hair, there are better ways of telling me." He had made even grim Vigilante business a little more bearable.

Next door to Baume's dry goods store, Morris Brothers' Grocery occupied the third space. Joseph Morris waved at Dan from his window, where he stood enjoying the sun. His window displayed a pyramid of potatoes only slightly wrinkled. Dan smiled, waved back and walked on.

Dwarfed by Kiskadden's, the log cabin that housed Ma's Eatery stood at the corner of Wallace and Jackson. Albert Rose, the former slave who had come here with Lydia Hudson, tossed a bucket of dirty water into the street. "You coming in here, Mistah Stark?"

"Yes, Mr. Rose, I am." Dan smiled at Albert's answering frown. The Emancipation Proclamation had been in effect since January 1863, but Albert seemed to reject its implications of equality.

"You don't want to be a-calling me 'Mister,' suh."

"And you need not call me sir. It's a new day."

"Not so's I been noticin', suh." Albert held the door wide for Dan, who knew defeat when he met it, and yet Albert had a point. The Fugitive Slave Act was still in force, and what if Albert were a slave on the run instead of a free black? Among the Confederate majority in the Gulch, some would be only too happy to own Albert. A big, strong man, he could talk and weigh gold dust at the same time, and not miss a flake on the customer's side or his employer's. He could read and cipher, too. Dan asked him how he had learned, but Albert walled off his past, and Dan understood. He could guess that someone had taught Albert, despite it being a crime in most of the South to teach a Negro his letters. The less known about Albert and his wife, Tabby, the better. Some people would view them as valuable properties. Dan made a silent promise to Albert: God help anyone who tried to take them back, and damn all slavers.

Pausing on the threshold to let his eyes adjust to the dim interior, Dan reflected that among them Lydia Hudson, the Eatery's owner, and the Roses presented a mystery he would like to solve. Just to know. Feeling Albert's presence close behind him, he stepped forward before his eyes had quite adjusted. He wished Mrs. Hudson did not conserve kerosene quite so vigorously. She had not lighted the wall lamps, nor the lamps on the two long tables. At the back of the room, she and Tabby prepared dinner in islands of dancing candlelight. They sang a freedom song to make the work go faster, Mrs. Hudson's high soprano fluted over the Tabby's cello tones. Savory aromas of beef frying in a skillet floated to him from the stove, along with something else, something he had not – Coffee.

Coffee. At long last. Coffee. After months of sage tea and beer. Coffee.

The singing stopped. "Who is that?" Mrs. Hudson called.

"Dan Stark." Behind him, Albert closed the door.

"What can I help thee with this time of day, Mr. Stark?" Mrs. Hudson called. "I have coffee. Would thee like some?"

"Would I! As much as you can spare, Mrs. Hudson. I'll pay well, too." A dollar a cup. Twenty times the usual price would not be not too much to pay to quench his coffee thirst. His mouth filled with saliva. He swallowed.

By not looking at the candles, Dan's night vision returned. He walked down the aisle to the bench at the back table, and seated himself facing the stove. He took off his hat and combed his fingers through his hair, in need of washing and cutting. "I came to count up, Mrs. Hudson."

While she poured his coffee, Albert opened the warming oven over the stove and held a candle up to read the tags.

"Good afternoon, Mrs. Rose," Dan said. Tabby Rose ducked her head the merest fraction, a tiny acknowledgement. She did not speak, and Dan wondered – not for the first time – if she hated all white men, or only him. He wanted to tell her he had never owned a slave, never would, despised slavery and all slave owners, but he kept quiet. No matter what he said, she would hold to her ideas until she was ready to change her mind.

Dan's four pokes were heavy, perhaps a pound or more each, but Albert held them all in one hand as he set them in front of Dan. Mrs. Hudson gave him a lighted candle on a stand. "Do thee want the scales?" she asked.

"Yes, thank you. And would Albert have time to help me?" Each time he had added some dust to one of the pokes, he had weighed it in haste, but now he had need of accuracy. With Albert weighing his gold, he would have an accurate accounting.

Albert brought the scales and the thin metal wafers that served as weights, and stood waiting for instructions.

"Sit down, Albert, please."

"Yes, Albert, please help Mr. Stark," said Mrs. Hudson.

"Yes, Ma'am. Suh." Seating himself across from Dan, Albert poured the first gold onto the scale pan. As he laid a third weight on the other pan, Mrs. Hudson set a speckled blue tin mug in front of Dan.

The dark hot liquid smelled like heaven. Dan tasted it. "This is the best coffee I have ever tasted. Let Albert weigh out a dollar for it."

"My goodness, no. I couldn't charge thee. Sip it, though. I only have half a pound left until more freight comes in."

"They stretch it with chickory in New Orleans." Tabby pronounced it Nawlins.

While the women compared notes on various ways of stretching coffee without destroying its taste, and Albert weighed his gold, Dan sipped the coffee and jotted the weights in his pocket notebook as Albert gave them to him. As each poke was refilled, he knotted the drawstring, jotted the weight and date on its tag, and finished off with his signature knot, a bowline topped with two square knots. A slow, tedious process, but if the idea taking shape in his mind were to yield the results he wanted, he had to know how much gold he had and how much he needed. He could not go home with too little, or he would have done everything in vain.

The thought stopped him. No. He would not even think that. He could not have done it all for nothing. He could not. He would stay until he had enough gold to pay the debt and secure the family's future. Both families. He put the mug to his lips and inhaled the good aroma. He wanted to drink the coffee all in one gulp, and then drink more, but he sipped it instead.

"How are banks run?" Mrs. Hudson seated herself beside Albert.

Dan took his time swallowing the coffee. "About like you do now," he said, thinking of Van Fleet, "except on a much larger scale. You keep our pokes for us and charge us a small fee for the service. You could make loans and charge a larger amount, per day or week or month, to cover your risk." He sipped again, aware that he had to make it last. "If someone wanted to take their gold out, you'd have to make it good, so you would need to keep a reserve equal to the amount on deposit. Are you thinking of starting a bank?"

"I might be. We could use one here, couldn't we?"

"We certainly could."

Albert told him another amount, and Dan set the cup down to make a note. He would not know until he returned to the office, but the amounts seemed more than he had thought.

"I'll need good financial and legal advice. How do lawyers charge?"

"By retainer or by the hour. Do you need a lawyer?"

"I will before I'm done. Do thee want the job?"

"You realize a woman isn't thought to have a mind for business. It might be difficult to persuade miners to trust you." Writing, he heard her intake of breath and looked up to see her lips pinched together, her eyes narrowed. "Then again, all of Alder Gulch has trusted you not to poison us. Holding our gold is a minor matter."

She giggled, and the giggle became laughter. She leaned backwards, so far that Dan thought she might topple off the bench. When she could speak, she said, "Is there anything about life that's easy?"

"Not that I know of. There's someone in town, though, who could tell you more than I can about banking. Are you acquainted with Joel Van Fleet?"

"He's the man thee pulled out of the creek, that wants thee to go back with him?"

"Yes, but if he wants us to travel together, he'll have to wait until I'm ready." Dan looked at her over the rim of the cup. "He may have quite a wait."

Albert gave Dan the last weight and poured the gold into its poke. He pulled the drawstring tight, made a note on the tag, and tied his signature knot. "I have to go back to the office. I want to pay you for the coffee?"

"No, thank thee all the same." The candlelight exaggerated her dimples. "It's by way of being thy fee for the legal advice."

"As to that—" he raised a cautionary finger "—mind you, a warming oven might not always be considered adequate storage for quantities of gold."

Her laughter pealed out again as Dan swung one leg and then the other over the bench and rose to his feet.

The opening door let in a fresh draft that fluttered the ruffles on her black widow's dress. Dan reflected that she either wore the same dress day in and day out, or she had them made to the same pattern. He waited for two men who walked down the aisle. One carried a pick on his shoulder, with a gunny sack dangling from it, and the other carried fishing poles and a pail. As Dan stood aside for them, they nodded to him, and touched their hat brims to Mrs. Hudson.

Dan asked, "Catch anything?"

"Enough for a few dinners." The man carrying the pick swung it off his shoulder for Mrs. Hudson to take the sack.

The man with the fishing poles said, "Even the fish are hungry these days."

Dan escaped into the clean bright air, his mind occupied with the numbers he had written in his pocket book. He would have to weigh the gold he kept at the office, and then do the sums, but even at best it would be a rough guess how much gold he had. Until the mint in New York finished, he would not know for certain how much gold he truly had.

~15~

HARDLY BELIEVING THAT DAN'L had paid for two pairs, Martha wore her new shoes in the house to break them in. And learn how to walk in them, where no one could see her wobble on the heels. Never in her life had she worn shoes with heels, or such impossibly pointed toes, that looked so pretty. Not that both pairs looked like that. She had bought this pair for show and the other for everyday, and she watched her toes as she walked back and forth.

So when Timmy's knock came at the door, she was right there to open it.

Every time Martha saw her son these days, it appeared like he'd growed more. No, Martha reminded herself, he'd grown more. If she didn't practice talking proper even in her thoughts, all her studying from Dotty's readers would be for nothing. She might even embarrass Dan'l. Bless the man, he didn't say nothing – anything – about how she talked, but she talked some different from him, and she didn't ever want folks to wonder what he saw in her. Bad enough she wondered that for herself.

Timothy changed into the house shoes she kept for him. His back and shoulders were that broad, she found it hard sometimes to imagine the baby she'd borne and suckled. He'd be as big as his Pap, and Sam McDowell had been a very big man, taller and stronger than Dan'l, who was no mouse himself.

She had a dried apple pie still warm from the oven, and she set it in the middle of the table, poured a mug of her wild berry tea that she'd brewed up special for him on account she knew he liked it. It was a singular pleasure to make something extra for her son and see him relish it so.

He tucked into the pie and tea with a will, and not until his fourth or fifth bite did he stop to look around at the muslin-covered walls. "Mam, you've done up this house real pretty."

"It was both of us. Dan'l did a deal of it himself. He strung the muslin." Bought it, too, when she'd said she could appreciate white walls instead of logs. "I cut it and he helped put it up." She thought the effect was real pretty, too, though sometimes she caught a wry twist at the corner of Dan'l's mouth when he didn't think she noticed. "It lightens the room, don't you think?" She even liked the way the muslin bloused where they'd driven nails through it into the logs for hanging up pictures.

To her way of thinking, the only thing lacking in the house was music, but she had hopes even that would be remedied in time.

"It's good of Mr. Dance to let you off work early," she said. "It's been a long time since you and I had ourselves a talk without nobody else around." There, she told herself, she'd opened the talking, what Dan'l might call the negotiation.

"Mr. Dance is a good man," said Timothy around a mouthful of pie. He washed the bite down with a gulp of tea. "You have something on your mind, Mam?" His blue eyes seemed to darken, the way they'd done ever since he was a baby when she'd pulled her breast away from him before he was ready.

"You know your Pap left behind the contracts he had with Major Fitch." She felt it hard to get a full breath now because she was going to have to persuade him of something he hated to think of. She breathed like she was running as she explained to him how Dan'l had given back the papers that didn't have McDowell's name on them, and tried to trade the others even with Fitch, and Fitch wouldn't have none of any trade on account he wanted it all.

A drop plopped from the ceiling into a bucket standing on one end of the table and distracted her, but she recovered and went on to tell him that because McDowell had run off somewheres, people could say he'd abandoned the Alder Creek claims and jump it as soon —

"You want me to work Pap's claim again."

He said it flat, and with such sadness in his face, she almost took it all back, but she firmed up her resolve, though it hurt her to speak. "Yes. We can't see no other way."

"No, Mam. No." He shook his head like a horse trying to rid itself of a halter. "I can't do that no more."

She stretched across the table and took hold of his hand, callused from all the hard work on the claim. The skin had cracked in the cold, cold water of December, just on the point of freezing, when his Pap had made him keep on. "You'll be working for yourself now, because Dan'l will register the claim in our names, your, mine, and Dotty's and we'll share in thirds. He don't want none of the gold from it, not one flake."

Across the room, his coat hung on a peg, and his boots stood side by side under it. She had reinforced the back seam now that he was growing so, but the sleeves could not be let down no more, and it wouldn't hardly button. The boots were old and split, and too small for his lengthening toes, and he'd thrown away the ragged gloves some weeks ago. His Pap wouldn't pay for new clothes, said the boy should work harder and earn them himself, but how could he when McDowell had took all the dust for his own pleasures? But since he'd run off, why was the boy still wearing the old clothes?

"Why haven't you bought yourself warm things?"

"I don't know. Didn't seem much need, now that I ain't slaving in the Creek no more." He moved a bit of pie around on the plate, studied the fork like it was the most important thing in the world to him. "I been saving my wages, as much as I could, to buy land for a horse farm. I want to breed good horses, Mam. Not the plugs you find out here so much. I want to raise the best horses in the Territory."

"You can save faster by working the claim."

"Maybe. Maybe not." He put the last bite of pie in his mouth, but this time he swallowed it before he asked, "Do you think it's worth the risk? Mining's awful chancy. What if it's all played out by summer?"

"Nobody can answer that without reading the future, but do you know of a better way? And if the pay dirt's shallow, you've still got that speculation that Dan'l helped you to."

"Yeah, but that shipment of boots hasn't come in yet." He smiled. "Wouldn't you know the women's boots come in before the men's?"

He picked up his mug and held it to his lips, but forgot to drink, only stared past her toward Dotty's bedroom door. She had a hunch he wasn't seeing it, or her, or anything, but a possible future, the content of which was mysterious to her but not to him. Her son was turning into a man right before her.

He set the mug down with a thud. "All right. I'll work the claim so's we don't lose it. But only till I've enough saved to start my farm." His cheeks sank under his cheekbones, and his face became that of the man he so nearly was. "I purely got to liking farming, back home. You don't know how I hate mining."

~16~

DAN WADDED UP Grandfather's letter and flung it at the crates in front of his desk, and laid his face in his hands. He had not nearly enough to repay the debt in gold. Not quite seventy-five pounds, total. The desktop wobbled, and he smelled salted fish from the barrel supporting it at one end, the other support a wooden crate labeled Canned Beans. His desk in New York had been oak: two pedestal columns of drawers, a center drawer, and a fine-grained top. He would swivel his chair to look out the window, and dream of hunting deer upstate, in the Adirondacks, among red and gold trees.

Father's blood spread wide over his gleaming mahogany desktop, gray brain matter splattered the law books' leather spines behind him. Where was that desk now? Had someone cleaned it of blood, or did they only see the stains when they opened a drawer and wonder then what had happened? A dead man's desk.

Damn.

Damn Grandfather, too, for ordering him back to New York. "Return forthwith," he had written.

And double damn Van Fleet, who daily ambled about town with the self-satisfied air of one who had run his quarry to earth.

Getting up, he retrieved the balled-up paper and smoothed it out on his blotter, drew the candle closer. Preemptory, commanding, domineering, Grandfather from the bench, Judge Stark, issuing an order as he might a bench warrant.

"Like hell I will!" His own voice startled him. By God, he had obligations here. The sooner he let Grandfather know that, the better.

The ashes floated in the unquiet air. When one sank to the floor, he ground it under his boot. Seating himself, he drew clean paper and pen and ink toward him. "Dear Grandfather?" Too affectionate. "Dear sir?" "Honored sir." Or just "Sir." He stared at a barrel labeled "Flour." The old man was expert in commanding other people to their duties. He had ordered Father to the law, the family firm. Father had broken early and came in right out of school.

He'd viewed the law, joining the firm as a life sentence, wanting to work out of doors, had become a surveyor. He loved tramping through the forest, laying down the chain, reading the land through the transit, imposing the clear order of mathematics – trigonometry – on Nature's chaos.

As water wears stone, Grandfather had worn him down. A Stark did not dress in jean overalls or other rough clothes, hike about in forests like a savage, forgo the benefits of advanced education, grow calluses on his hands. All that was for the lower orders.

A Stark was not free to follow his own inclination. He had a duty to the family, to uphold that which his great-grandfather, his grandfather had built: Stark and Sons, Attorneys at Law, in gold lettering on three tall windows.

When he had gold enough, he would make the trip.

How much more gold did he need? He laid down the pen and corked the ink bottle.

He must think. Clearly, from what Grandfather had said in his letters, and from the newspapers, and from Van Fleet's urgency, gold was rising. Or it had been, as late as a month ago. Dan reached for his slate and a piece of chalk. He held the chalk poised over the clean black surface of the slate, a fresh start. Like coming West for some men, the chance to start over. The song went, Oh, what was your name in the States? He shook his head, and thought of gold, its weight, its values, and his mind swung into a hunt, familiar yet strange, among numbers and probabilities. His hand dove for the slate; the chalk squeaked, a white dust rose. (Voices rumbled from the store, on the other side of the wall.)

Would they not be quiet in there? Someday, he'd build himself a true office with thick walls, not just a cleared space in a merchant's storeroom. Dissatisfied with the calculations, he wiped them all away. Began anew. (Quite an argument the store's clerk was having.)

Surely supplies would be replenished any day. At this rate he would run out of chalk. If he weren't careful, he'd be writing drafts, doing calculations, in the dust on the floor, ink being far too scarce for a draft. (A shout: "I gotta have it," the words as clear through the wall as if he stood beside Dan.)

He reined in his wandering thoughts, let the chalk scratch across the slate until it seemed fairly covered in small numbers and tiny notes. (The clerk bellowed, "You'll get nothing from me. Not without Mr. McClurg says so.") Damn it! Would they stop? He had lost his train of thought. He wiped the slate on his sleeve, leaned back and closed his eyes.

At $18.00 an ounce, the amount raw gold exchanged for in Alder Gulch, he had $16,200. Just over half of the debt. Grandfather himself had told him that in January, gold had traded at 156, because it took $156 in greenbacks to buy $100 in gold. At that rate, he might have — Chalk dust rose, and Dan sneezed. The chalk squeaked, broke. He gripped the short piece and stared at the total. He might have more than $25,000 in greenbacks.

But what was the price of gold now? How pure was his gold? How much bullion would he get out of it?

All that figuring and he still did not see how to do it. Trade in the Gold Room? Damn, he wished he'd paid more attention to Peter.

(The stranger's voice: "You know I'm good for it!" And the clerk: "No, you owes the store too much!")

He had not solved his problem, the ammunition to write to Grandfather. He laid a piece of paper on the blotter, pulled the stopper from the ink bottle, and dipped his pen. Without even stopping to sharpen the nib, he dashed off a note to Grandfather: "Sir: Circumstances of business detain me here; specifically, I have not yet enough gold to satisfy the Bank. Regards to the family. Your respectful grandson, Daniel Bradford Stark." Succinct, and as formal and pompous as he could write it. He was folding the note for mailing when shouting burst through the wall.

("Take your hands off me!" The clerk's frightened voice, and the other shouted, "You got no right to refuse me credit. I always pays my bills.")

Dan leaped to his feet and yanked open the door into the store.

A man wearing baggy trousers that might have been corduroy, might have been any color between tan and black, topped by a torn black suit coat smudged with dirt, held the clerk's lapels in his fists across the counter. He gaped at Dan, who banged the door shut behind him and took two steps into the space between the counters. The corduroy man opened his hands, and the clerk sagged back, coughing, against a nearly empty shelf of canned goods. Unspeaking, Dan waited. Sweat shone on the clerk's face. The corduroy man looked above Dan's left shoulder, then his right shoulder, as if he studied the various sizes of coiled chain dangling from the rafters.

The clerk's greasy dark hair had fallen into his face, and his waistcoat was awry. He tugged at the points, cleared his throat. "I have to ask McClurg to extend credit." His voice was ragged, harsh.

"I'll pay in full when I can work the claim again. You know I will."

Using both hands, the clerk smoothed his hair back. "It won't be long till you can work the claim, now the ice has broke."

"Damn it! See if you get any more of my custom!" The man's glance raked across Dan as he pivoted to the front door, jerked it open. "You and your God-damned Vigilante!" The door slammed behind him.

Across the agitated interior bell, the clerk said, "Glad you were here. He was getting tough until you showed yourself." His hands trembled, and he clasped them together, leaned his elbows on the display case. "He knows better than to tangle with one of you."

Meaning the Vigilantes. Dan could think of nothing to say, but nodded to show he understood. He understood all too well, that the sight of hanged men had seared people's memories, so when people looked at him, they knew he was capable of using a rope.

The clerk wiped his face on the counter rag. "Thank you."

"You're welcome." Dan returned to his office, sat down, stood up, put on his greatcoat. He would mail the letter at Dance & Stuart to go out on the next stage, then look for different office space, where empty crates and barrels did not close in on him, and no invisible sign on his door read: Vigilante on Premises.

~17~

IT WAS NEARING SUPPER TIME when Dan walked down Idaho Street. He had not been successful in his hunt for office space; the town was filling up fast, and space was at a premium. Tomorrow he would talk to Solomon Content about renting a room when his building was finished. God willing, he would have returned from New York by the time it was built. Ahead of him, Dotty walked uphill toward Jackson, perhaps a long block away, near the livery. He raised his hand to wave to her. She appeared to wave back, and then he knew her arm flailed to keep her footing against something that snatched her into the livery barn. Her schoolbooks dropped into the mud.

Dan leaped into a run, cursed the infernal clay mud that choked his feet, damned a team of great bay horses pulling a beer wagon up Jackson that threw up their heads to avoid bumping him as he plowed under their noses, half-stumbled on the new boardwalk, and thanked his stars for his boots' faster drumming. He swung into the barn through the big door where Dotty had disappeared.

Jacky Stevens had backed her against a wall, and one hand covered her mouth while the other pawed her where no male's hands should ever be until her marriage. Her fists pummeled his shoulders, and she kicked at his shins, but though small for his age, he was bigger and stronger, and determined to have his way. Dan's punch knocked him sprawling into a pile of steaming dung, and the horse squealed, jumped forward, and kicked, barely missing his head.

Putting himself between Dotty and the snarling boy, Dan said, "You ever come near my family again, and I'll haul you before the Tribunal." He snatched Jacky up by his coat collar and flung him toward the door. "Now get out."

Watching Jacky scoot out of the barn, he reached behind him for Dotty, gathered her to him. Sobbing and trembling, she put her arms around him and clung to him. He enfolded her in his greatcoat, and held her, murmured, "He'll never bother you again. You're safe now. You'll be all right." At the same time he wondered if anything could ever be right for this child, whose innocence Jacky had shattered.

The hostler came through the big door. "Here, what's this?" He picked up a pitchfork.

"Where were you?" Dan demanded. "Jacky Stevens attacked my stepdaughter."

The man lowered the pitchfork. "A man's gotta take care of business once in awhile."

From the smell of his breath, Dan knew his business had included a drink.

The man said, "I saw Jacky hightailing it down the path to Fancy Annie's as I was coming up, and I guessed something had happened on account of the horse sh— " a glance toward Dotty "—uh, manure in his hair." The man talked as he picked up Dotty's books, used his handkerchief to wipe them. "That little – he's a wrong'un, for sure, and his Ma's no better."

Dan set the child outside his coat, but she would not let him go, so he put one arm around her shoulders. The hostler tucked the books under the other arm, and with Dotty's arms clasped tightly around his waist, Dan took her home.

Canary greeted them, but as if the dog sensed something was wrong, his tail wagged slowly, and he sniffed at Dotty's skirts and whined. The house smelled of savory stew, and hot apple cider. Martha, knitting in her rocker, dropped everything to take Dotty from him, and the two vanished into Dotty's room. Dan hung up his coat, changed his boots for house shoes. Their voices came to him through the single-board walls. Martha soothed her daughter, "My baby, my baby, there, there, you're all right, you're safe now," and by the time he had hung up his suit coat and poured himself a generous shot of decent whiskey, Dotty sounded calmer.

When Tim came in, Dan said, "Come here. I want to talk to you." As he spoke, Tim's anger grew until the boy half rose from his seat.

"I'll kill him. I'll damn well kill him." By his low tones, Dan knew Tim meant what he said.

"You will not, or you'll have the Tribunal to deal with, and they won't listen to justifiable homicide. They will just hear homicide. Murder." When Tim settled back onto his chair, Dan continued, "You let us deal with Jacky. He's a menace, and neither he nor his mother belong among decent people."

"You'll hang 'im?"

"Probably not." He might have said more, perhaps mentioned banishment, but Martha came out of Dotty's room, slumped onto a chair next to Dan.

Laying her hand on his open palm, she said, "The child will be out soon. She's all right, but mighty shook up."

"Of course. It's an awful thing." Dan lifted the drink to his mouth, and the glass clanked against his lower teeth. He set it down. His hand shook, and his teeth chattered as if he were cold, but he was warm enough. A haze settled on the room, and he saw as in the notch of the Spencer's forward sight Jacky Stevens pressed against Dotty, his hand on the small, immature breast. His index finger curled as around the trigger, and he thumbed back the hammer. Squeezed.

"Dan'l?"

Dotty stood at his elbow, between him and her mother.

Dan tore himself away from his vision. It could never be, much as his rage would have it so. "Yes?" He hoped his smile reassured her.

"I'm sorry."

"You're sorry?" Dotty's brother broke in, and Martha raised a quelling hand.

"For – for – you know. What happened."

Dan met Martha's look over her daughter's shoulder, and thought he read a warning. "My dear child, you have nothing to apologize for." He breathed deep, and sent up a kind of prayer: God help me to say this right. "There are some bad people in the world, and that nasty boy is one of them." Martha smiled at him now. "He didn't need a reason to act badly. He is bad. You are innocent. You did nothing wrong." Perhaps in their minds, as in his, was the knowledge that Martha had saved Jacky

Stevens during the typhus epidemic. And this was how he repaid her for saving his life? I wish that horse hadn't missed, he thought, but he kept his face from showing his anger, lest Dotty think it was meant for her.

She sank back against her mother, and a weak smile curved her lips. "Mam? I'm hungry."

~18~

THE MORNING WAS WARM ENOUGH not to need a greatcoat. Men who had been in the Territory for a decade or so said winter could blow out of the mountains again, but right now it receded in his wake, a country he would not return to, and sunshine lay in folds over the greening hills.

Dan walked up Idaho to Van Buren, then down to Wallace in hopes that prolonging the walk to his office might stir his brain. He had lain awake much of the night thinking how best to protect Dotty, what to do about Jacky Stevens, but no good answer had come to him. Walking along Wallace, he found the door to John Creighton's Dry Goods standing open. On impulse he went in. It was always good to talk to John.

In the back, though, Creighton sat with four other men in a companionable group around the square box stove. When Dan walked in, they called to him, and scraped their chairs to open a space between Creighton and the sheriff, Jeremiah Fox. Fitch sat on the sheriff's left, facing Judge Alex Duncan, on Creighton's right.

Removing his hat, Dan sat down, laid one ankle over the opposite knee. At a nod from Creighton, Duncan poured him a cup of coffee strong enough to walk on and topped it up with a "drop or two" of passable whiskey, not Valley Tan, that Mormon mixture of water, white lightning, and tobacco for flavor. The drink warmed his gullet going down, and a knot in his shoulder began to relax.

Fitch, seated on the other side of Sheriff Fox, blew on his coffee. "We're mighty sorry to hear your little girl was frightened yesterday."

They all murmured regrets, their smiles fading, their faces mimicking the return of winter. Dan, sipping his coffee, glanced around. "The damn hostler."

"It was bound to get out. You can't keep secrets in a place like this," said Creighton. A lock of his thick dark hair fell over his brow, and he combed it back with his fingers. When he's older, Dan said to himself, people will describe him as "leonine."

Fox tapped the ash of his cigar into the bucket between himself and Fitch. His long fingers could have belonged to an aristocrat, instead of the rough and ready sheriff of a booming settlement. "Is she all right?"

"Yes. Just badly frightened." Thank God the stableman had not seen what happened.

"That won't happen again." Fitch spat into the bucket.

"Damn right," Fox said. In the muttered agreement from the others, Dan heard an echo of his own outrage and anger.

"But what can we do about it?" That question had kept him awake without an answer. Dan heard his frustration vibrate in his voice.

"Hang the little bastard," said Fitch. "Nothing else will stop him being a menace."

Creighton, disliking foul language even in a stag group, clicked his tongue at Fitch.

Dan and Judge Duncan spoke together: "We can't do that," said Dan. "He's done nothing to warrant being hanged."

"No!" The Judge pounded his fist on his thigh. "That's what you always say: 'Hang him!'"

"That kid's not right, and you know it. He's a baby rattler, and the only thing you can do with one of them is not let it get bigger."

"No," Creighton said. "People can change. Our Lord can work miracles if we let Him. Look at St. Paul."

Fitch leaned forward. "You feel that way about them?" He tilted his head back, in the direction of the graves on the knoll.

Before Creighton could answer, Fox tipped his chin up to blow smoke into the blue cloud drifting above their heads. "There's whipping.

We could give him ten, twenty lashes."

"And he'd take revenge on my stepdaughter." That was the point of rocks on which Dan's every idea had wrecked in the night. Any punishment they gave Jacky would rebound on the child. It would not keep her safe.

Fitch said, "That's the point. That little bastard – sorry, John, but that's what he is – he's not like the rest of humanity. Whatever part of us carries a conscience, that was left out of him."

"Besides," said Duncan, "when you-all revised the miners court, you kept criminal cases to yourselves. Right now, the People's Court doesn't have jurisdiction for this."

"You got any more of that coffee, John?" asked Fox.

"Help yourself." Creighton looked toward his doorway. "I've got a customer." He went to tend to the customer, and Dan heard him ask, "Is there something you're looking for, sir?"

Was Creighton ever troubled by the doubts and second thoughts that plagued himself, Dan wondered. Or did being Catholic give him an extra certainty? If he had ridden with us, could he confess, pay some sort of penance, and still be sure of his place in Heaven? Except there were no clergy of any kind in Alder Gulch, let alone priests, or a church. Just an occasional visit from one of the fathers from the mission at St. Ignatius, 200 hundred miles north.

Fitch and Duncan had begun to argue about the court. "The Court must have more scope." Duncan's Southern accent deepened as his feelings grew stronger. "It can't be limited to boundary disputes, petty theft, and claim jumping. It must have jurisdiction over criminal cases."

"All right, tell us what you'd do to stop Jacky from bothering little girls." Fitch's unlovely grin, that could have been almost a snarl, came at Duncan over the rim of his cup. "You tell us and we'll enforce it. Without enforcement any court's a sham. A damn sham." His lower lids crinkled with fun.

A poor thing, but mine own, Dan said to himself about the rhyme.

"I'll enforce it." Fox regarded Fitch with no humor in his eyes. He was reminding them all that he was the Sheriff, and in this tangle of jurisdictions between Judge Duncan's People's Court and the Vigilantes, he was Virginia City's chief law enforcement officer.

Its only law enforcement officer, Dan reminded himself. Did Fox ever consider that his position as both the town sheriff and a member of the Vigilantes' Executive Committee held inherent contradictions?

Whether he did or not, whether the position did or not, until a proper system of justice could be installed, we have to do the best we can.

Duncan stared at the floor until Fitch spat a stream of tobacco juice into the bucket. "I thought as much."

"If we had a jail —" Duncan began.

"But we don't, damn it." Dan stomped his resting foot down on the floor. "How do we keep my little girl safe in the meantime?"

Returned, Creighton dumped his cold coffee into the slop bucket between Fox and Fitch, and poured himself some fresh. Sitting down, he said, "A jail wouldn't guarantee her safety," Creighton said. "We couldn't jail someone indefinitely for scaring a child. And when we released him, what are the odds jail would have shown him the error of his ways?" He sighed. "Someone like Jacky – any sinner, actually – needs the conviction of sin in order to mend his ways. Repentance must be sincere."

If Fitch's snort of laughter held any humor, it was night-black. "We had a lot of repentance when the noose settled around their necks, didn't we, Stark?"

"Good God," Duncan whispered.

"You have no hold over criminals," the Sheriff told Duncan. "Nothing that will make them straighten up."

"And you do?" Duncan's right hand was wrapped around his cup. He lifted his middle finger and pointed it at Fox.

Fitch broke in. "Damn right we do. The rope."

"No, Fitch —"

Dan broke in, "All right then, Alex, once again, how would you control Jacky?"

"I don't know that anyone could control that boy," said Creighton.

Duncan turned his free hand palm up. "I don't know. If jail wouldn't work, if corporal punishment would not work, I don't see what would."

"That's what I thought," said Dan. "That's what kept me awake most of the night. The law has nothing to prevent a crime from happening. It can only act once a crime is committed."

"I'm afraid that's true," Duncan agreed. "I'm sorry, God knows I am."

Sheriff Fox said, "There is one thing we can do. The patrols. They can watch him. And his wretched mother. They can arrange to patrol the route between your house and the Professor's school in the morning and in the afternoon."

"I'd appreciate that," said Dan, "but I walked her to school this morning, and her brother will collect her this afternoon."

"Good," said Fox. "You do that much, and the rest of us will keep an eye on Jacky. He'll soon learn he can't pan dirt on our claim."

"I still say we should take care of that particular problem permanently." Fitch picked his teeth with a fingernail, examined the result. "Baby rattlers are as poisonous as when they've got ten rattles on them."

Behind them, someone gasped, and Dan knew the customer, whoever he was, listened. He cast back: Had anyone mentioned the Vigilantes? This conversation was no place for strangers.

"Capital punishment doesn't work," Duncan said. "People still murder people."

Fitch showed his teeth in a tobacco-stained smile. "Tell that to them up on the hill. They won't be murdering anyone else. Ever."

"True enough," said Fox.

"You know what I mean," said Duncan. "You might have hanged them, but it won't stop others. And that's what I mean. Capital punishment is no preventative to crime."

Creighton reached for the coffee pot, gestured with the pot to ask if anyone wanted more. Shaking his head, Dan put his hand over his cup.

Duncan said, "I hate capital punishment."

Fitch struck a match on his thumbnail. "If you ask me, we didn't hang enough of them."

Under cover of Fitch's remark, Dan muttered toward the floor, "Not as much as we do." He swirled the coffee in his mug, and the liquid seemed to reflect his memory: Sad, hate-filled eyes glared as he snugged the hangman's knot behind the left ear, and a voice whispered: It didn't have to be this way. Cracked boots swung across snow. How else could it have been, given the choices they had made? He would drink up and be gone.

Duncan had heard him. "How can you say that, Stark? If you hated it, you would not have put the noose around anyone's neck."

"That's why, damn it," Dan said. "I hope I never have to do that again."

Behind him, a man's voice: "My God!"

Duncan leaned forward, jabbed his index finger toward Dan, his voice rising. "You hope? You hope? You mean you would do it again? More than a score of men weren't enough? Tell me, who's your next target? Me, perhaps, because I defended them?"

Fitch said, "Hell, Alex, if we'd wanted to hang you, you wouldn't be sitting here."

"Good God." Duncan slumped back in his chair as if Fitch had punched him. "You mean that, don't you?"

"Damn right." Fitch spat into the bucket.

"Nonsense," said Dan. "You were never in any danger of that. We want to work with you."

Fox said, "Stark's right. We banished Thurmond and Smith, after all."

"Yes." Duncan slapped at an early fly buzzing around his face. "Though I've often wondered, why banish them and not me?"

Behind Dan someone breathed as though he'd been running hard. Who listened? Damn, the talk had gotten out of hand. "James Thurmond threatened to kill Sanders, and H. P. A. Smith connived with him at suborning perjury. Absent a true court system and a jail, that was the only other recourse open to us. You were against us at every turn, but you're a principled man. We never thought you were in league with the roughs. We had good reason to believe they were."

"Then why do you think I oppose you? Tell me, Stark, I want to know. Do you think I was afraid not to back the roughs?"

Dan glanced at Fox, his fellow member of the Executive Committee, who said nothing, a silent signal to go ahead. "No one could think you a coward."

"Then, why? Why did you leave me here, set up the People's Court, and appoint me judge?"

"The law decrees that everyone deserves the best defense possible. Even murderers and cannibals. You were true to the law when you chose to defend those bastards."

"C – cannibals?" said the voice behind Dan.

"Where does that leave you, then?" Duncan asked. "Or Sanders? Why did you prosecute? Because you have no principles?"

Dan clamped his teeth down on what he wanted to say, stared into the cup as if reading the dregs that were cold and thick as mud. "I can't speak for Sanders. I chose to prosecute, because just as the law demands a defender, it demands a prosecutor, and my sympathies lie with the victim. As they always will."

Duncan's face reddened, seemed to swell. "You crossed the line. You weren't only prosecutor, you were judge, jury, and executioner. All of you. And you still are."

Dan jabbed the cup at Duncan. "What in God's name would you have had us do? The miners court was a failure, those charged with enforcing the law were corrupt, and we had no law to enforce in the first place. Not even the Constitution." Other memories crowded in on him: foul-smelling threats from the dark: You're a dead man, Stark. "Would you have had us pretend men were not being robbed and killed? Should we have played dead? Because if we had done nothing, we would have been dead men."

Behind him, Dan heard the new voice begin to ask something, but Fitch jumped up, and his chair fell back onto the floor. "God damn it, Alex, if it was up to you, my boy's killer would still be walking around free as a bird and you know it." He jammed his hat on his head; the brim, surmounted by the tarnished crossed rifles symbol, sagged so that he tilted his head upward to glare down his long nose at Duncan. "It's a crying shame that nigger lovers like Stark and Sanders did the needful." He pivoted on his heel. "'Scuse me, John. I need air." His heels resounded down the aisle between the display cases.

Duncan, his ears pulled back like a horse about to bite, called after Fitch, "If y'all hang a man or a boy before he commits a crime, it's murder."

The door slammed, and the bell's shrill clanging made Dan want to cover his ears.

Creighton said, "Fitch can be mighty hard on doors."

"And on chairs." Sheriff Fox leaned over and righted the chair. As calm as if they debated the outside temperature, he said, "You're right, Your Honor."

Dan wondered if he detected a tinge of sarcasm in the sheriff's voice.

Fox went on, "Only, nobody has yet thought of a decent solution to preventing crime. Like Stark says, even if we had us a jail, it wouldn't guarantee what John calls a sinner come to repentance. Throwing a drunk in jail don't mean he'll quit drinking when he gets out."

"I'd better go to work," Dan said, rising to his feet. "In the meantime, until someone unties this Gordian knot, we maintain vigilance." He set the cup on the table next to the stove.

Fox, standing up with him, clapped him on the shoulder. "Damn right. We've done it all winter, and we have no call to stop now."

Turning to leave, Dan came face to face with Joel Van Fleet, who straightened now from leaned his elbows on the display case. Oh, shit,

Dan said to himself. How much had he heard? Had anyone used the word, Vigilante?

Duncan said, "I still maintain that you committed murder. You violated due process."

Van Fleet gaped at Dan. "What did you do?"

Dan had had enough. Swinging around to Duncan, Dan snubbed his anger down and spoke in a low voice that nevertheless had Duncan getting up to put his chair between Dan and himself. "Tell me how we violated due process of law when there was no law. Tell me how saving men's lives, destroying a gang of robbers and murders, violates due process. We did nothing unconstitutional because the Constitution still does not apply here."

"You can never reconcile me to what you did." Duncan glared at Dan and Fox in turn.

"We don't expect to," Dan said. "But you have our backing for your court anyway."

Duncan barked a short, humorless, laugh. "Now there's a devil's pact if I ever heard of one."

~19~

IN PROBABLY WHAT was a vain hope, Dan decided to check for new books at Tilton's Stationers. Waiting for a mule train to haul itself past, he glimpsed Martha in front of the Eatery and raised his hand to wave to her. Something caught his sleeve, and he swung around to face Joel Van Fleet. "You want me?"

Van Fleet snatched his hand away. "Yes," he stammered. "Yes, I do."

"Well? Here I am." Not waiting for him, Dan crossed Wallace behind the last mule, his jaws tense, head down to watch for fresh droppings, and avoid his fear. In front of Con Kohrs's butcher shop, he tugged his hatbrim down to shade his eyes from the sun, and from Van Fleet. How much had the fool overheard? Worse, what would he make of it? What would he tell Grandfather when he returned? Damn, but Dan could do nothing to stop him.

"I thought perhaps you might allow me to buy you a drink." Van Fleet shifted from one foot to the other, as if his feet would not bear his weight for long, though he had shed pounds, and the skin of his jowls pouched loose from his cheekbones.

His eyes showed innocent, and the invitation sounded sincere, but why would a banker, in effect a bill collector, a bailiff, travel twenty-five hundred miles in winter time to drag him back to New York and after he failed, offer to buy him a drink? Pulling him out of the creek was not an invitation to friendship, and the sooner Van Fleet understood that the better.

"I don't think so." Martha waited for him across Jackson. "I have to meet my wife."

"I'm sorry. You saved my life and I would like to show my gratitude." He licked his lips, his tongue moist and pink.

"That is not necessary."

"My life is not so negligible an item."

"Then you can show your gratitude by returning to New York. I have a letter for my grandfather for you to take back."

"You know I cannot return without you. I explained why." He had a slight lisp, and an S-sound hissed out at Dan.

"So you said. Your duty and mine do not coincide." Pausing to steady himself, to remind himself that Van Fleet was a smaller, softer man, Dan linked his hands together behind his back. "If you'll excuse me, I have business to attend to." He crossed Jackson, but Van Fleet kept close behind him.

"Hanging business?"

In the shadow of the Eatery, Dan spun around. "What the hell do you mean by that?"

"That talk in there. That was about hanging men. I've heard talk about them, what happened during the winter. Were you part of all that?"

Damn, that he had let himself be goaded in that conversation. He should have stopped the talk when he knew someone was listening, but the opponents, Duncan or others, always made him angry. It would have been so easy to have let the others go after Nick's killers, let other men clean up Alder Gulch; after all, he had not intended to stay here. Then. Before he loved Martha. "Part of what?"

"Were you one of those men who hanged people? Were you part of that lynch mob?"

By what right did this soft man, with his soft conscience, demand to know what he had done? By what right did he presume to judge them, when he was never here? And God damn it, he would tell Grandfather, and everyone he could think of in New York, and Dan's reputation would be shattered, because how could he ever explain it to those who knew only a regular police, a working judicial system? Yet, he would have to try.

"Have you ever lived in a place without law? Where ruffians rule and murder is common?"

"New York City had the draft riots last summer —" began Van Fleet, but Dan cut him off.

"Draft Week? Five or six days of mayhem? The law crushed it. The police, and the Army. The City has law. The City has police, and can call in the Army. The City has jails, and courts, and judges. The Constitution. Here we have had none of that. When men were murdered for their gold, no Army could come to our rescue. You think I should have left it to other men?

"Digging gold takes work. Hard, back-straining labor, and only a few have a small chance, because every inch of the creek, bed and banks, is taken. Fourteen miles, men packed together like ten to a bed, everyone armed – guns, knives, axes, picks. God knows what else.

"Then add to that, there is no police. No laws except those made for each mining district, by the miners themselves. No courts except the miners court, a separate one for each mining district, whose primary function is to settle rival claims to property.

"No law, not even the Constitution, because we don't know what territory we're in. Is this Idaho or Montana? Who knows? Who knows if there will be a Montana Territory?

"Stir all that with whiskey and easy consciences, and you have thefts and murders by the score. Then tell me we should have let someone else take care of the problem. And I'll ask you, Who else?" He paused to catch his breath, panted as if he'd been running. "Who else should have made this place safe for honest men and women?" He had backed Van Fleet against the windowless wall, and jabbed his forefinger at the man's breastbone. "Who else was there to put the law in place? If not us – if not me – who?"

Dan came to himself, aware that Van Fleet's face had turned a grayish hue, that he had collected a small crowd, that Martha was tugging at his arm.

"You can stop demanding my return to New York. I will go when I am ready. Do you understand? In the meantime, I suggest that you go back where you came from. Sooner rather than later."

With that he stepped back, let the fool busybody go, and allowed Martha to lead him home.

~20~

Martha purely didn't understand Dan'l's anger. No swearing, no lashing out with a fist, like McDowell. Instead, it flowed silent like Alder Creek under the ice. When it broke, would it sweep everything before it, like the Creek?

He hung up his coat on its peg to one side of the door. Took off his boots and put on his house shoes. On the other side, the Spencer rifle and the English shotgun lay across their pegs. He was so proud of that rifle, it being a rare thing, a repeating rifle. He'd took it with him always before he wrote the rule against carrying firearms in town, and he had a habit of patting the stock when he came in the door. Today, though, he took no notice of it, but went to the window over the wash stand and stood looking out. She didn't think he saw whatever he was looking at.

When she had set the meat – a beef roast – in the bowl so's it wouldn't leak on things, she heard him whisper, "Stupid. Stupid. Stupid."

She thought he was talking to her. "What did you say?"

He talked toward the window. "I've been incredibly stupid. I let them goad me. First Alex Duncan and then Van Fleet. I should have controlled my temper."

"Mr. Van Fleet would have found out soon anyway. Everyone

knows you're a Vigilante. Y'all did everything in broad daylight, out in the open for everyone to see."

Dan'l made a disgusted noise in his throat. "People climbed the walls for a sight of it. Men being killed." He spat into the slop bucket.

In silence she corrected him: to watch you-all kill them. And they told me whose neck you put the noose around. "Some of the Vigilantes make no bones about what they did."

"I know they do. I don't. It had to be done, but it's nothing to brag about."

"It's nothing to be ashamed of, either. Like you told Mr. Van Fleet, if you-all didn't do something about the crime here, who would have?"

"Cold in here," he said, though to Martha it was warm enough. He lifted the burner lids from the stove and thrust a quarter-round in, but it stuck, and he jammed it over and over, fought the stove, the fire, the mostly burnt wood, while Martha held her peace in her teeth along with her lower lip. Brushing his forelock into place, he said, "You don't understand. He'll tell everyone in New York. He'll tell Grandfather."

His cheekbones jutted out like rock under the skin. "It don't matter none what that old man thinks. He's not here. And you ain't – aren't – in New York."

"I have to go back. I have to take the gold home."

"Why? Why can't Mr. Van Fleet carry it for you? Why do you have to go?"

"Because I don't trust him. And because the gold is not the whole issue. " He swept his coat tails behind his elbows, slid his hands in his trouser pockets.

Questions fluttered in her head, flew to her tongue and up again, until one magpie question crowded out the others: "What do you mean, the gold is not the whole issue?"

Although he stayed as he was, a distance came into his eyes, and she felt like he didn't see her for the things he looked at inside his own memory. She waited until he came back from wherever he'd been. "I don't know that I can explain it."

Her own temper surged. "You're planning to take your gold back to New York, which is not needful on account Mr. Van Fleet can take it, and you won't tell me why?"

He strode about the room, beat one fist into the other palm. "It is a matter of family honor. My father – died owing a great deal of money, and I obligated myself to repay his debt in person. I have to keep my word. It's not just repaying the debt. It's – I have to restore my family's honor. My Grandfather is a judge, and without honor he won't be reelected, and my mother, my sisters, have lost all their friends and their prospects, and my brothers won't get an education. I told them I would repay it." He rubbed his face, let his hands drop to his sides. "I must go back. My father's son must be seen to repay his debts, money and honor, both. I have to do it."

A sunlit rectangle on the table faded, reappeared further over, and faded again. The shelf clock ticked, and a gust surprised the windows in their frames. Her questions perched on a line: Why wasn't paying back the money enough, no matter who carried the gold to New York? Why didn't he trust Mr. Van Fleet?

She asked. "Why don't you trust Mr. Van Fleet?"

"He works for the bank that bought up all my family's debts, and he will act for the bank's benefit and not the family's good." The shelf clock whirred, pulling back its striker.

"Which family? Me and the young'uns or your New York family?"

He pulled on one of his outside boots, and stomped his foot to settle it on him. "Both." One boot on, one foot still in its thick sock (thin at the toe, she noticed), he said, "Don't you see? If I would not do the honorable thing there I would not do it here, and you would be more endangered by my staying here than my going. I'll come back. You know I will."

She could not wrap her brain around that. All she knew was the here and now, that if he went back there, he'd be tempted to stay. He wasn't used to the hard life like she was, he'd growed up on linen sheets ironed by servants, and matched teams of carriage horses to carry him around. He'd had someone else to empty his slops every day and clean the bucket, if rich folks used buckets. It was why he didn't let her empty the night jars now, though she was used to it. "How do I know you won't stay in New York?" The clock struck, and she raised her voice over its deep bong.

Lifting his hands at his sides, he let them fall so they slapped against his legs. "Because I promise I'll come back. You're here. Without you, I have no reason to remain in New York." He put the other boot on, stomped his foot into it while she watched him, her fear roiling inside her, churning up debris from her life with McDowell, an angry gesture, a raised fist, the smell of bad liquor and rotting teeth in the night.

He took his greatcoat off its peg. "What more can I say to convince you?"

"Don't go." Her voice creaked out as stiff as her lips.

"I must, in order to salvage something from this situation." He settled the coat on his shoulders and took up his hat. "You'll have to trust me."

Her throat felt stiff, and she could not force words past it, but inside she screamed at him, How can I trust you? I don't know you. I knew McDowell all my life and look how he turned out, and now I've took up with you, a man I don't hardly know, and how should I have chosen right this time? How should you be better? Fear flowed strong, unsteadied her, so at first she only dimly heard Dan'l speak as from a long way away off.

"I'm invested here in all the ways a man could be. I've given you my heart, and my soul to the Gulch and its people. I bought the house to live in with you. What more can I say?"

"Don't go back to New York."

He took in two or three breaths. "I've told you. I must, but not right away."

Something in his voice warned her away from it, and she knew she'd lose him for sure if she clamped on too tight, like a baby bird she'd wanted to keep once, for a pet. Mam had said, If'n you keep it, it'll die. Did that go for men, too?

He looked so sad she wanted to cry, tell him lies and keep her fears secret, but her throat crimped and she could not bring up the words. He said, "You don't trust me, do you?"

"I'll try," she whispered. It was all the comfort she had to give him, or herself.

He swung around, yanked up the latch. "Then you will have to learn trust by what I do. When I come back, you will know." For a moment he stood at the open door, his back to her. Outside, clouds blew overhead. As if to the clouds, he said, "I'm going to Dance and Stuart to find Tim and arrange to look for the claims."

After he closed the door behind him, she stood for a time, looking at a blank where the future should be. Learn to trust him by what he did? Trust he'd come back?

Heels beating across the wood floor, she went into their bedroom. Her search led her to the closet shelf, and in an inner side pocket of Dan'l's portmanteau she found the framed daguerreotype, and brought it to the window to see better. It showed a blonde woman's head and shoulders dressed in a low-cut evening gown. She had a long straight nose, full lips, big eyes, and a cleavage that Martha, thin and small-breasted as she was, could never attain. The woman looked toward something above and beyond, like an angel seeing God.

Martha had seen this picture once before, when she tended Dan'l's bullet wound. He'd been engaged to her in New York, and now he would go back, and even though he'd promised to return, she didn't believe him. Little Sparrow, Dan'l called her. Why would he choose a common brown sparrow over a shining angel?

~21~

RAIN BATTERED on Tim's wide-brimmed hat like fifty drums, each beating out its own rhythm. Ahead rode Dan'l, shoulders hunched, water rolling down his oilskin slicker, and behind plodded Jake on his saddle mule, ponying the pack mule loaded with surveying equipment. Tim estimated they'd ridden some five miles upstream along Daylight Creek, and now they followed Dan'l through a feeder stream, but the ground on the other side was so wet Tim thought the animals wouldn't hardly notice the difference. Creek or ground, all the same to them.

Spring. Who the hell could love spring but poets? Melting snow rushed into dry gullies and thawed the frozen ground into a slime of mud over frozen layers. Who the hell would be out in this but idiots?

Dan'l stopped to let them catch up. Tim's mount brought him alongside, and the horses moved to put their tails to the shifting rain. "Men are damn fools for gold," Dan'l said.

Tim could only nod, but Jacob said, "Ja. Is maybe all gold fool's gold."

"You mean all gold is fool's gold," Tim said. Jake had told him to correct his mistakes in English, but it still felt odd to be schooling a grown man. Jake nodded, and his lips moved as he repeated it, but Tim lost the words in the rain.

Dan'l dug under his slicker for a compass and sheltered it against his chest. Tim pictured the rough map they had made from Pap's locations. Lucky he could make a mental picture of it, on account the storm would destroy it in seconds if he brought it out. Dan'l's horse stamped a protesting hoof. The pack mule brayed a complaint.

Without looking up, Dan'l said, "We could leave this to a better day."

"No." Shaking his head, Tim scattered water over his shoulders. "No. Come good weather, the claim jumpers will be all over this country."

"Jake?"

"We're out. I think we stay," Jacob said.

"All right." Dan'l studied the compass, looked toward the horizon.

Pap would've gone back or pushed on, without any say-so from Tim. But Dan'l, now, Dan'l was as different from Pap as white from black. Dan'l asked what he thought, and listened like what Tim said mattered.

"I read it that we go along this side gully." Dan'l pointed across Tim's horse. "That's north."

"What is Lee's Creek?" asked Jake.

Dan'l smiled. "Damned if I know."

Tim opened his mouth to ask then why did Dan'l think this was the way, but Dan'l lifted the reins and clucked to the horse, who had his own opinion about walking farther from its home barn. Dan'l kicked him with his spurless heels, and the critter walked on. Tim fell in behind.

Jacob caught up to him. "Daniel, it is that he has – how you say – a knowing sometimes, though not knowing." He beat his fist on the saddle horn. "I must more English have."

Tim understood. Jake was saying that Dan'l sometimes knew a thing though he couldn't say how. He lifted up his hand to adjust his collar, and rain slithered down his arm. It was like they tracked a ghost, because winter had wiped out any sign that live men ever walked here. Maybe they were on the wrong trail. Pap's locations were screwy, somehow.

What if Pap lied on them papers to get money from Major Fitch? Maybe Pap was a road agent. The thought ambushed him so he couldn't get his breath, and he tasted something bitter on his tongue. His stomach heaved, and he leaned over the off side of the horse and vomited. The rain washed the foul stuff away, down his slicker, his boot and stirrup. He wanted to lie in the mud and let the rain drown him.

Jacob rode up on the near side and shouted to Dan'l, who turned his horse back. Tim couldn't look at him, he was that embarrassed.

"What's wrong?" Dan'l called over the wind.

Tim shook his head. He couldn't say it.

"You ate something bad?"

"No!" Tim could say no more.

Dan'l took hold of a rein. "We'll go back. If you're sick, we can't do this."

"Ja," Jake said. "We go back."

"I ain't sick," Tim yelled against the rain blowing in his face, and Dan'l took his hand off the rein. Now that he was in this, Tim had to get rid of it. "Maybe Pap was a road agent. Maybe you should a hung him, along with them others. He spent a lot of money in the saloons. Mam never gave him any more'n she could help. Me neither."

Dan'l swung down off his horse. "Get down." When Tim stood on the ground, Dan'l pulled him close, and held him in the circle of the horses' bodies, one hand snubbing the reins to keep their horses there while Jake managed his own and the pack mule. "Say it," he hollered.

"There ain't no record of any payment Fitch made to Pap, is there? How'd he come by the money he spent in the saloons? Major Fitch said he'd been a road agent."

"Don't believe Fitch. He wants the claims for himself."

"What if there ain't no claims?"

"We'll find them. Your father was no thief. He was a mean son of a bitch with a bad temper, but he was honest."

"How do you know? How the hell do you know?" Tim felt like he was six again, and wanted to cry, instead of almost seventeen and near a man grown.

Dan'l stood so close the brim of his hat brushed Tim's. "Sam McDowell was a rotten poker player, but he didn't cheat. He lost those two agreements to me fair and square. He did not cheat at cards. The claims exist. We'll find them. Mount up."

"Now?"

"Hell yes." Dan'l put his left foot in the stirrup and hopped on his right foot as the horse sidestepped away, then bounded upward and into the saddle. "This is no time to quit."

Jake edged his horse to block him so Tim could mount up, his right arm stretched backwards to hold the pack mule. When Tim was secure in the saddle, Jake said, "You will see. Daniel, he is right."

They rode on, zigzagging around small rivers rushing through gullies, until Tim wished to hell they'd quit. At last, Dan'l pulled up. "We should see something pretty soon," he said. The wind had dropped so he just talked loud, instead of shouting. "What do you think?"

Rain poured off Tim's hatbrim, and nothing came to mind except that his butt was wet. The skirt of his slicker covered the saddle, but a seam leaked, and water trickled down the cantle.

"Come on, dammit, Tim, think."

Forcing himself, Tim fitted his mental map to the terrain. "I think it could be that way." He pointed toward a rise about a quarter mile off.

"As good a guess as any." Dan'l nudged the horse into a walk, the wind at their backs again. "You have any ideas, Jacob?"

Jake shook his head without speaking.

At the top, the low rise turned out to be a broad ridge above a narrow, snow-filled valley. Beyond the valley a range of mountains disappeared into the clouds.

"Damn." Dan'l wiped his face with a handkerchief. "I thought we'd find it down there, but that could be ten feet of snow."

So Dan'l had been wrong. They wouldn't find a claim, and Pap was a road agent. The bitter taste was in Tim's throat when Jake pointed along their back trail. "There something is. See? "

Dan'l nudged his horse toward the downslope, shielded his face from the rain. His hatbrim bobbed, and he prodded his horse downward.

Tim squinted beyond the horse's nose. With a whoop he kicked the horse toward an object the rain uncovered, a white cone in front of a larger dark one. The horses slipped and tossed their heads, not liking to move so fast on unseen ground beneath the melting snow, their riders keeping them to the job. Below the ridge, they were sheltered from the worst of the storm. The object was a cone of light-colored rocks in front of a tall cone-shaped juniper. Dan'l lifted his right leg over the saddle horn, cleared the scabbard, freed his left boot, and jumped. Tim laughed at the surprise on his face as he sank into snow up to his knees.

They grabbed stakes off the pack mule and drove them into the ground for tethering the animals. That done, they took shovels and cleared snow around the rock cone, dug down to the ground. It was what Tim had not dared to hope for – a pyramid of rocks, a marker to show one corner of a gold claim. They leaned on their shovels and stared at each other. Tim's thoughts rioted in his mind: Pap had been prospecting, like he'd he said. He hadn't lied. A mean son of a bitch. A wife beater. An honest man. At least he had that. Whatever else Pap was, he was honest. Tim straightened his spine. He could hold his head up, because Pap was not a thief. Not a road agent, like some said. Like Fitch said.

Dan'l consulted the compass and pointed. "There. Fifty paces. And the other corner, maybe there." The three of them paced to the supposed corners and dug like they were gold-crazed. Nothing. They shifted a few degrees, dug some more. Nothing. They moved uphill and dug. Once more, nothing. Then downhill. Despite the chill in the air, sweat ran down Tim's sides. Fifty feet away, Dan'l stopped digging to wipe his face and neck. Jacob leaned on his shovel and breathed hard.

Tim struck rock. He scraped away snow and more snow, felt for the stones, and scooped snow away in his hands until he found a fallen pile of stones, and he straightened, turned his face up toward the rain, and laughed. Right then, Dan'l's shovel clanged on rock, and Jake plowed through the heavy snow to help. Three corner markers soon stood free.

Tim had an idea. His boots sucked at the ground as he hurried to the two men. "You know, Pap was bone lazy."

Dan'l made a note in his pocketbook and stowed it in his breast pocket. "Oh?"

It took Tim a bit to round up his thoughts, so's he could make them, Dan'l 'specially, understand how Pap would have gone about this. They waited. "He was always hard to live with. Ma worked damn hard. Even when he showed me how to do things, hunt and fish and plow, it wasn't like he wanted company, just for me to learn how to do things so's he wouldn't have to."

He had to force the rest of it past his throat's tightness, the words rasping against his vocal cords. "Pap wouldn't take no more steps about prospecting than about anything else." He coughed, and cleared his throat, spat downwind.

"So you think he wouldn't have ridden very far from one claim to locate the others."

Dan'l's matter-of-fact tone, like they were speculating on which way the wind would blow, let Tim save himself from blubbering. "Yeah, that's what I think."

"So the others wouldn't be far away from this one."

"Right. Pap wouldn't exactly hunt real hard even for gold. It'd have to be more or less sticking up and shouting come and get it."

Dan'l fished in an inside pocket for a handkerchief, wiped his face. "Lazy, huh?" He stowed the handkerchief and studied the surrounding terrain. "What do you think, Jacob?"

Jake must have been thinking ahead of them both, because he didn't stop to make a sentence. "We can perhaps this idea keep, ja?"

Dan smiled in a way that reminded Tim of a fox drawing in one of Dotty's readers. Crafty. "You're right. Fitch knows McDowell as well as anyone. Timothy has helped us draw a conclusion about him, and it's one Fitch could draw as well." He clapped Tim on the shoulder. "Let's find the fourth marker and go home."

They trudged to where the fourth buried corner should have been and found no marker, no pyramid of white stones. Tim heard himself speak his horrid thought: "You don't suppose Pap marked someone else's claim, do you?"

"No. Like I said, McDowell was honest. We'll dig around more. Let's spread out, but not very far. I think we're close."

The rain stopped, but the wind blew until Tim gave up holding onto his slicker and tied it behind his saddle. Between the rushing clouds, the sun played peek-a-boo, shone here and there. Tim dug and scraped at the snow until he felt sweat sting his eyes. They had uncovered nearly every square inch of ground for twenty feet around where the fourth marker should have been. Nothing marked the fourth corner, except a scatter of stones, like they'd been dropped.

Dan'l spoke. "Look here. Does this look odd to either of you?"

Amid the white rocks it looked like someone had dug a box-shaped hole, the sides largely fallen in from the weight of snow melting, but man-made, clear enough, and a film of thin ice lay over the water in the bottom.

Jacob said, "Someone has samples taken, perhaps?"

Tim scratched at the hole with his shovel, and through mud and shards of ice, a gleam caught his eye. Figuring if it was pretty, he'd clean it and give it to Dotty who liked pretties, even stones, Tim picked it up. Its weight surprised him, and hardly daring to think what it might be (spitting on it and rubbing it some) though a chill along his forearms warned him that the lump of rock on his palm might carry he didn't dare think what (rinsing it in a puddle to clean it better and scouring it on his trouser leg), and hearing Dan'l breathe like running and Jake's muffled "Mein Gott," and it was, God almighty, gold. A nugget the size of his thumb.

He felt the two men waiting, holding their breath as he scored it with his thumbnail and left a dent – not a scratch – in the soft gleam. "Gold," he whispered.

Jake, his English all gone, muttered in German; his hands flailed about.

Tim held the nugget out to Dan'l, but he wouldn't take it. "It belongs to you. You found it." Tim wrapped the nugget in his handkerchief and pocketed it. Straddling the hole, Dan'l sighted to the first and third markers. "Jacob, we'll have to survey it."

"Ja, ja. Aber, es ist — " Jacob could not yet manage English, but Dan'l was already moving toward the pack mule, to unload the surveying equipment. The business of the survey steadied Jacob like a kind voice to a fractious colt. Tim stood aside and let them get to it.

Even if Tim had knowed what to do, he could not have helped, on account his mind was savoring the nugget, like it was something to taste. Only he'd never had nothing to eat that tasted as good as the nugget had felt in his hand, and now in his right front pants pocket; the heft of it, the crinkly-smooth feel of it under his fingers, the gleam.

Riding home in the thickening dusk, Tim let his horse pick its own way, following Dan'l's lead, because the critters knew they was headed for home and would get them there. He was wet and cold and tired beyond what he'd ever thought he could be, but he no longer cared that his ass had settled into a puddle. The nugget poked into his groin and bulged against his pants, and all his ideas of how he wanted to spend his life – keeping a store, raising horses – what he'd thought was solid ground making up what he knew and felt and believed, had shifted and melted away like the ice in a spring runoff.

He watched Dan'l's shoulders moving with the horse and imagined Dan'l and Mam alone together. This must be what it's like, he thought, feeling the solid lump of the nugget. Falling in love and finding gold. There couldn't be nothing better in the world.

~22~

SHOUTING OVER THE PELTING RAIN, Tim announced their find almost before he opened the front door. "Mam, Dotty, we found it." A few feet behind him, Dan and Jacob exchanged smiles. Jacob waved goodbye and strode down Jackson toward his kosher meal with the Morris brothers. Inside, Canary stood up from his mat to greet them, his tail whipping his sides.

Dan hung up his slicker, pried his wet feet out of his boots, and made for the bedroom to change into dry clothes. As he toweled his hair, Martha came in, shut the door on the youngsters' excited voices, and took the towel from him.

"Did you ever see anything like that nugget?" She rubbed his back from his neck to his buttocks, and the scratchy toweling warmed his skin.

"No. I don't think any of us did." Turning, he took the towel from her to finish drying himself. "It was on the claim McDowell marked. Tim will come with me, and we'll register it and the Alder Creek claim in the morning." Answering a question she did not ask, he said, "We brought back samples besides the nugget for assaying, and I'll take them to LeBeau's." A sudden memory compared the Assay Office on Wall Street with the double duty Frank LeBeau performed in his jewelry shop, and he laughed to himself: ironic that the temple of gold should be so far from the point of origin.

He arched his back and stretched, and saw her face turned up to him reflected in the rain-streaked window. He had forgotten to draw the curtains, he noted before the blood rose at his temples, and he reached out for her. The storm rattled the window panes.

He held her to him as if he would merge them together. Her mouth opened, and as his tongue found hers, and their dance began, he sought under the bib of her apron, worked a button free in her shirtwaist as her hands stroked downward to his hip bones –

"Mam?" Dotty's voice came through the closed door. "Mam? Do you want I should dish up the stew?"

Dan's tongue retreated into his own mouth. He rested his chin on the top of her head, and laughed silently. Giggling, Martha pulled away from him, turned to the mirror to adjust her bodice, check her hair, and froze. One hand at her mouth, she pointed with the other. "Oh, Lord, no!" she whispered. "The window."

"It's so dark no one could see anything."

Martha yanked the curtains closed.

"Mam?" Dotty called again, and the latch scraped against wood.

"Don't open the door!" Martha held it closed while Dan skipped behind it as Dotty's voice complained to her brother, "What do you suppose is keeping them in there?"

Tim's voice sounded choked. "They're probably talking like grown people talk. Better give the stew an extra stir."

Dan tried to say, "Be out soon," but laughter, squeezing through his lips, splattered the words against the door as Martha went to join the youngsters.

When Dan emerged, carrying his wet clothes in a bundle, Dotty squealed, "You found it! You found the claim!" She would have thrown her arms around him, but Dan held up the bundle, and she backed away.

He tossed the wet clothes into the laundry basket. His hands and face needed a good washing. From a bucket standing on the stove, he dipped hot water into the wash basin, and hung the dipper on its hook. Behind him, Martha's mellow voice interlaced with Dotty's high squeaks and Tim's new bass in a three-part round of questions and answers. A pot lid scraped, and the savory aroma of venison stew set Dan's mouth watering, yet he longed for a different meal. He had shot that deer himself, dressed it out and brought it in. It was one of many, and he was tired of venison. Tomorrow he'd give Martha some dust to buy beef at Conrad Kohrs's butcher shop.

He dried his face and poured the soapy water into the slop pail. As he straightened, he caught Martha looking at him. A big wooden spoon in one hand, the lid to the stew pot in the other, she smiled at him with such glowing happiness that his breath caught in his throat. Later, alone in their bedroom, they would talk while he lay in bed and watched as she let her hair, thick and nearly black, fall down over her shoulders, and brushed it a full hundred strokes. And then he would raise the covers for her to come to him. He smiled. By the flush spreading over her face he knew she read him, his wanting her, and her smile became private, full of shared secrets. Little brown sparrow.

"So Pap didn't lie about finding the claims, then," said Dotty.

"Nope." Tim stretched out a long arm and snared a piece of bread. "It was right about where he said it was. Though I'd never have found it without Dan'l and his compass."

"Pap didn't lie," said Dotty. "Pap's not a liar."

Finished combing his hair, Dan put the comb in his pocket and dipped drinking water from the clean water bucket. While he drank, he watched rain flow down the night-black panes.

"Nope, he ain't," Tim said. "And Dan'l said he didn't cheat at cards, neither. Our Pap's no card cheat."

Dotty wrapped her arms around herself. "He ain't a road agent." She burst into tears, her emotions drowning all her hard-won grammar. "He ain't. He ain't." Martha put down spoon and lid, gathered her daughter to her, smoothed her hair, patted her back. Tim's cheek bulged on a chunk of bread he could not chew. They all had the same tearful happiness that McDowell had told the truth.

Night and the storm turned the window panes into running mirrors: his own face swam in one pane, Martha wavered partly in another and partly in a third, grouped with the youngsters in a watered distance. His family – but not his family. His wife – but not his wife. They rejoiced because McDowell, bully and brute, was also honest, something he could not say of his own father, who had yet been a kind man, a good father. Grandfather had driven him to his gambling, to his thefts. To his death.

"We'll be rich." Breaking out of her mother's embrace, Dotty twirled so her skirts flared out around her, a grass-green flower, like the dancers' skirts the night Dan had won the claim from her father.

Sitting on the table, the nugget's planes and edges caught the lamplight in various colors of gold, as if gold had power to change other colors into itself. Yet under the ice it had been nothing much, a lump of mud from which a single gleam had escaped to catch Tim's eye. This nugget was his inheritance from Sam McDowell, along with Sam's abandoned obligations to his family as Father had left him his place, his obligations, and to fulfill both, he would have to return to New York, because the real value of gold lay there. In the Gold Exchange.

~23~

LeBEAU'S JEWELRY STORE lay between the City Bakery and Goldberg's Pioneer Clothing, toward the foot of Wallace Street. Knowing gold as he did, working with it daily to fashion the "pretties" Dotty admired so much, Frank LeBeau did a smart side business as an assayer. Though he insisted his fire and chemical assays were not rigorous enough to satisfy the Mints in Philadelphia, New York, or San Francisco, Alder Gulch miners swore by them, and now with spring runoff showing signs of peaking, two men stood in his shop and talked with LeBeau's clerk about the strikes they would make this year. Except that LeBeau served no beer, Dan might have heard the same talk in any Virginia City saloon. Having no expectation that the nugget would remain a secret longer more than one minute after he and Timothy left the jewelry store, he laid it on LeBeau's table.

LeBeau put the jeweler's lens to his eye, and his eyelids clamped down on it as he picked up the nugget and scored it with his thumb nail and nodded to himself. Taking up a touchstone, a piece of black quartz, smooth and shiny with a tooth sharp as a knife point, he scored the nugget deeper and stared at it for a long moment that stopped the talk of strikes and lodes and stiffened the atmosphere with concentrated listening.

Dan resisted the urge to wipe his palms on his coat. The jeweler held the nugget out to Dan, who gave it to Tim.

Removing the lens from his eye, LeBeau asked. "Where did you find this?"

"I won it at poker last winter." Which was true, in a way. At least he had won the claim then. Dan produced the bag of ore they had dug out of the hole and set it on the table. "Here's a larger sample." He turned his palm up, and LeBeau dropped the nugget onto it.

"It's high grade," LeBeau said. "Very high. I'd say better than 98% pure." He dropped his voice to the level of a sigh. "Maybe 99%. You'd need a Government assay to know for sure."

"Christ almighty," breathed Tim.

Absolute pure gold was one thousand. Even in a region known for its high grade gold, where purity of .97 or .98 was not uncommon, this was extraordinary. Aware of the excited murmur behind him, Dan managed a natural-sounding laugh. "It could have been salted."

Behind them, he heard an excited murmur, and sounds of the door opening and closing.

The jeweler scratched his chin. "This sure got them going. They'll be on your back trail forever, now." He blew a speck off his lens, and replaced it in a velvet bag. "Till the next rumor hits. If'n I was you, I'd hightail over to the recorder and register it pronto."

The door crashed open, bounced off the wooden frame of a display case, and shattered the glass. Fitch strode in, out of breath, shouted between gasps, "You found a lode, did you? It's mine, damn you, that claim is mine."

"God damn it, Fitch!" shouted the jeweler. "You owe me for that glass!" He leaped up from his table, dashed around it to Fitch, and pulled at his short arm. "Get the hell out of here."

Dan said, "It's not yours. I won it from Sam McDowell." Someone pushed at his back, as the jeweler pulled at Fitch, and then they were outside on the street. Fitch bellowed that the claim was his, goddammit, his and no one else's. Dan yelled, "Your name is not on the contract."

That stopped Fitch. His mouth gaped open, and his short arm, that had been thrusting at Dan's face as if it still wielded a fist, dropped to his side. "That can't be."

"It is," Dan said. "We can settle this any time. I'll meet you in court whenever you say."

"Now, damn it," said Fitch. "Alex is holding court at the Nugget now."

"Let's go, then." He set off up Wallace toward the Nugget Saloon. He knew Tim walked with him, and was aware of others falling in, but his mind busied itself while he caught up with one idea: Fitch contended the claim was his, but his name was not on the agreement.

"No," Judge Duncan said.

As always on court days, men and their combined odors of long unwashing, cigar smoke, and spittoons crowded the Nugget Saloon. Many of them would linger after court, celebrate wins and drown their losses, and the odors would intensify until the owner aired the place out.

The Judge liked to sit at a table in front of the window. It gave him a good look at the faces before him, while hiding his own thoughts in the day's backlighting. Today, Dan could see nothing of his expression, read nothing of his real thoughts, for the bright sunlight that won against the window's grime, threw his shadow across books and papers, and shaded his face.

No mistaking Alex's voice, though. His irritation was plain, and he flipped through a pocket calendar to settle on a date. "I want you two to try to work this out. I'll give you until Monday the sixteenth."

Outside, Fitch wheeled about to face Dan. "What's this about my name not being on that paper you won from McDowell?"

"See for yourself." Dan took the agreement from his notecase and held it for Fitch to read. Damned if he'd let Fitch hold it, or touch it. "It's plain as day." And almost laughed at his unintended pun, the sunlight on the paper showing the rough places where a pen's nib, in need of sharpening, had scratched the sheet. "McDowell and this Thomas Whipple you say is in Atlanta."

"He is in Atlanta. I'm his representative. His surrogate." His voice rose, his booted feet ground their way deeper into the mud of the street as if seeking a firmer base from which to attack. "They asked me to be on the lookout for opportunities in case the War went bad."

It might be true, Dan thought, but fighting for what was rightfully his – having won that claim fair and square – he could not back down. Even if what Fitch said was true, Fitch's name was not on the agreement. Dan said, "I won this claim in an honest game. I made no such agreement with any Thomas Whipple. If he should appear, I'll pay him what the claim is worth today." Dan folded the paper into his notecase and tucked it into his breast pocket. "Now, if you'll excuse me, I have a claim to register."

As he walked away, he heard Fitch's shout, "I'll see you in court, Stark. God damn it, you won't get away with this."

~24~

DAN PUSHED OPEN THE DOOR of the Nugget Saloon for Tim to walk in before him. Blinded by the dim interior after the sunshine glinting off puddles and window panes, he heard feet shuffling and low coughing, and smelled the saloon odors of winter underwear long unwashed, and beer. Stale cigar smoke thickened the atmosphere, and the cuspidors had needed emptying for days.

The two threaded their way among the crowd of men attending court. Despite the Glee Club, the Choral Society, and the Drama Club, court was still the best show in town, a way of passing the slow while waiting for high water to drop enough for miners to work their claims. Add to that the possibility of serving on the jury, of being a player in someone's real-life drama, and few men could resist attending.

No seats remained at any of the poker tables, and people stood three deep against the walls. At the front, the proprietor had kept three tables free. Duncan and the recorder of the mining district sat at the Judge's usual table. Plaintiff and defendant sat with their lawyers at two tables facing Duncan. Shotgun resting muzzle down in the crook of his elbow, Sheriff Fox leaned against the bar. Decorum would reign throughout the proceedings.

When Dan and Tim reached a place where the crowd thinned

somewhat, they stopped. Just like a New York omnibus, Dan thought, the crowd was thickest near the door.

Duncan's voice rose: "The jury of the whole will now consider a verdict in the matter of Sullivan versus Jones. Did Mr. Jones take Mr. Sullivan's kit, including his poll pick and his four-pound hammer?"

As the discussion buzzed around them, Dan smiled to himself. Ten months ago, he had no idea what a poll pick was, but now he knew it was a one-sided pick, the other side blunt and squared off to serve as a hammer. A prospector could use the pick to pry promising ore out of its bed, turn the tool around and crush the ore with the hammer to extract the gold. A versatile tool. He whispered to Timothy, "What happened to your father's tools?"

"I've got 'em," the boy muttered. "Most of 'em, anyway. I mixed some in with mine and sold the others."

"You have a pretty good kit, now?" He asked because he had not thought before that perhaps Tim might need tools, but Tim's arm, pressed against Dan's own, stiffened. "Yup."

Dan glanced at him. "A man has to have good tools." When Tim relaxed, he wondered why the boy had been alarmed, maybe even afraid, because he had sold his father's tools. No business of mine, Dan said to himself, but Tim had been immediately on guard. Sam McDowell had a great deal to answer for if he ever returned.

Judge Duncan banged the gavel on his table. Around them, conversations stopped. "Will the foreman poll the jury for a verdict?"

A small thin man made his way through the crowd, pencil and paper in hand, questioning those present. "We say he done it." A miner gestured with an empty beer mug. "Stands to reason, or why'd Jones have a good poll pick when two days before, he didn't have none?"

"I don't think so," another man said. "I believe Jones. He said he bought it."

"Then why the hell did the damn thing have Sullivan's mark on it? That double S?"

"I still believe Jones. He might have bought it from him or stole it, not knowing."

The miner stared into the mug. "It could have gone that way, I guess."

Around him other men listening, mumbled their agreement. The small man made a note and went on. When he had finished his circuit of the room, he marched to the Judge's table and handed the recorder the piece of paper. The recorder glanced at the paper and gave it to the Judge, who read it and beckoned the small man closer. "You sure about this?"

"Yessir."

"I'll have to poll the jury."

The small man nodded. "Figured you would."

The room was silent. No foot shuffled, no one coughed. It seemed to Dan that the room held its collective breath and waited for Duncan, who blew his nose and scrubbed the handkerchief over it three or four times before putting it in his coat pocket. Alex could have been an actor. He certainly knew how to milk a room.

The Judge spoke. "I'm calling for a show of hands because the foreman's report is not conclusive. All who think Jones did not steal Sullivan's poll pick and hammer raise your hand."

A forest of hands went up. Dan kept his hands down, and a man poked him in the back. "Why ain't you voting?"

"I didn't hear all the evidence."

"Don't matter. You got to vote. Jones is a good man, and we ain't about to let him get stung by that Irisher."

"Right," put in another man. "Jones bought them tools fair and square, not knowing they was stole."

"Who sold them to him?"

"He don't know," said the first man. "Fella said he needed a grubstake to leave town 'cause he couldn't find a job."

It could have happened that way, and it looked like one man's word against another man's, with no real evidence on either side. But he had not heard Sullivan's side of it. Tim's hand rose into the air, as Dan shook his head. "I can't vote. I don't know what Sullivan said."

The second man said, "He says he didn't see the thief, only the tools was gone one day and then he spotted them when Jones was a-sharpening the pick."

The first man nodded. "That's right. You can put your hand up now."

Judge Duncan gaveled for order. "All of you that think Jones did steal the tools, raise your hand." A few hands went up amid a low growl from the men who had voted not guilty, and several of the more timid lowered their hands.

Judge Duncan gaveled again. "Not guilty."

Cheering, applauding men turned toward the bar, but Sheriff Fox stood in their way. "Court ain't over yet. The bar's not open."

"Then we'll go on over to Trottman's," someone shouted, and the crowd began to disperse, taking the defendant with them.

As if beached by the current of men pouring out of the saloon, Joel Van Fleet, who had stood unnoticed against an opposite wall, joined them. Dan acknowledged him with half a nod. "Is this what passes for court in this country?"

"It's democracy in action," Dan said. "It works well enough for small cases."

"What if Jones did steal Sullivan's – uh, whatchamacallit?"

"Miners' tools," Tim laughed. "Jones is in real trouble now."

"How so?" asked Van Fleet.

"They'll expect him to stand them a round, seeing as how they voted him not guilty."

"Dear Lord. Can they do that?"

Tim's smile vanished. "They can. And he'll stand the round, too, even if he has to sell the rest of his tools to do it. They voted to free him on account he's a popular fellow, but they're not sure but what he might have 'found' the tools, if you see what I mean."

"What about Sullivan?" Van Fleet asked.

Dan watched the judge's table. Duncan leaned forward and shook his finger at Sullivan, who seemed to be arguing with him, but Dan could not hear over laughter and noise of the departing crowd. "He lost, so he'll have to pay court costs. Besides, Alex will probably fine him for wasting the court's time and bringing a frivolous suit. He'll have to sell his outfit and move on."

Duncan brought the gavel down and waved Sullivan away. The man shuffled out, hat jammed into a pocket, his face like murder. It wasn't fair, Dan thought, if Jones truly had stolen his tools, but his lawyer ought not to have allowed him to bring a suit he could not prove. Now he would have to pay the court costs, a fine, and his attorney's fee.

Judge Duncan banged his gavel on the table. "Next case."

Sheriff Fox said in a voice just below a shout, "All who have business with the court rise and identify yourselves."

"Here you go," Tim said. "Good luck, Dan'l."

When Dan and Fitch stood in front of him, Judge Duncan demanded, "What are you two doing here? I told you to settle your affairs between yourselves."

"We tried, Your Honor," Dan said. "We could not do it."

"Oh, all right. Tell me in one sentence what is at issue. We don't have all day."

Wishing Alex had taken a break between cases to ease himself of whatever bothered him, Dan summarized his side of the dispute. "Your Honor, I won Sam McDowell's half share in a claim. The other shareholder is one Thomas Whipple, but now Major Fitch says he owns the entire claim."

"Is that so?" Duncan asked Fitch.

"I do own it, Your Honor. Dan Stark is trying to steal a valuable property from me."

Nearly, he fell into the trap, the denial loud on his lips before he bit it back with an acrobatic twist of his brain in time to say the politic thing, "That will be for Your Honor to decide. I won the contract from Mr. McDowell, and Major Fitch's name does not appear on it." He reached into his inside coat pocket and drew out his note case. Unfolding the agreement, he laid it before the Judge, smoothed it out. "Here. See for yourself." He stepped back, wishing he could read the Judge's expression, but the afternoon light behind him, though the day was dull, shadowed his face. Clever of Alex, to choose that position, but damned difficult for anyone with business before him.

Beside him, Fitch rocked back and forth, heel-toe, heel-toe. "That's my claim, Your Honor. I grubstaked McDowell to find it and —"

Without raising his eyes, the Judge held up a hand. "You will have your turn, Major Fitch."

They waited. From somewhere, Dan heard hammering and sawing. Thinking to sharpen a pencil, he reached into his trousers pocket for his penknife, but thought better of it. Fidgets could be interpreted as the sign of guilt. He willed himself to be quiet, to appear calm, though a muscle fluttered in his right calf.

"Major Fitch," said the judge. "Can you prove that you are the lawful owner of this claim?"

"I, uh, I give you my word, Your Honor. I grubstaked Sam McDowell to find claims for me, and this is one of them."

"Is that true, Mr. Stark?"

"I believe so, Your Honor, although I have no personal knowledge of any business arrangements Major Fitch made with Mr. McDowell. I did not act for either of them."

"I see." The Judge tapped his chin while he thought about what they had said.

Dan breathed, counted to six each time he inhaled and exhaled.

Judge Duncan asked, "Mr. Stark, do you have any other contracts?"

"Yes, sir, I won a second contract in that poker game." Dan removed the second contract from his note case and handed it to the Judge, who read it, compared it with the first, and laid the two of them on the table.

"Major Fitch, the second contract clearly names you and Mr. McDowell as sharing equally in the claim listed thereon. The first contract, however, names Mr. McDowell and a Thomas Whipple. Who is Thomas Whipple?"

Fitch cleared his throat, licked his lips. "He is a shareholder currently residing in Atlanta."

Duncan stared at Fitch, his hand spread out on the papers. "Are there more of these?"

"Yes, your Honor," Fitch answered him. "There are six more. I hold three, because McDowell's name does not appear on them, and Mrs. – uh – Stark holds four, because McDowell's name does appear. And his mark."

"Do they name other shareholders besides yourself and Mr. McDowell?"

"Yes, sir. The other shareholders besides Thomas Whipple are —"

"Never mind their names. How many are there?"

"Three altogether, including Mr. Whipple." Fitch rubbed the stump of his left arm with his right hand.

"Mr. McDowell has left the country, I believe?"

"We believe so." Dan had a sense of matters passing by him and Fitch both, being taken out of their hands because Judge Duncan was becoming interested. It showed in his straighter posture, in the square set of his shoulders. After all the cases of petty theft, and public nuisance, and drunk and disorderly, here was something for a legal mind to grapple with, a problem worthy of his education. Never mind that he did not yet know the case, had not begun to follow it in all its labyrinthine ways along the twists of jurisdiction. Never mind that he would have to rule at some point under some body of law, Idaho Territory or Montana Territory, as yet unknown. Edgerton had left in January and it was now the middle of May, and no one yet knew which territory this region belonged to. If they remained in Idaho, they would have to use the Idaho statutes; if they were in Montana, well, there were no laws for Montana Territory.

Duncan tapped his chin.

"I suggest that you gentlemen take counsel. It appears that we have an interesting problem of ownership to sort out."

Overriding Fitch's explosive protest, Dan said, "Your Honor, I should like to request that you rule on this case. Ownership of this claim is separate from the rest because that is one of two claims between Sam McDowell and Mr. Whipple, and McDowell passed his ownership to me at poker. Mr. Whipple not being present in the Gulch, in my opinion, he forfeits his rights in this claim. You can establish clear title on this one claim."

"Does this claim exist?"

Ah. Alex, no fool, had grasped an essential point without seeing the other contracts. "It does, Your Honor. Timothy McDowell and I surveyed it and I registered it with Mr. Fergus." He nodded toward the recorder, sitting at Duncan's left, who returned half a nod. James Fergus, who hailed from Minnesota, was a staunch enemy of the Vigilantes.

"That's correct." Fergus opened his claim register, a ledger book the size of a small table top and thick as a family Bible. He slid his finger down a page to find the entry.

Fergus said, "This claim is registered to Timothy McDowell and unnamed persons with whom he wishes to share ownership." A gasp from Tim, audible even over the sounds of construction, a low-voiced conversation in the back of the room. Over his shoulder, as a hint to Tim, Dan added, "Perhaps his mother and sister."

Duncan waved Dan aside to have a clear view of the boy. "Young man, do you agree with this disposition?"

Dan beckoned him forward, and Tim stepped up to stand between Dan and Fitch. "Beg pardon?"

"Would you like to own this claim?"

"I can't."

Dan muttered at him, "Your Honor."

Tim started over. "I can't, Your Honor. Dan'l – uh, Mr. Stark, he won it fair and square from Pap, and Pap left his Alder Creek claim, and I'd rather own that'un."

A pause while Duncan considered. Dan, who could not catch his breath, willed him to give ownership to McDowell's family. "A man can own two claims, you know. Did your father stake any claims other than these two in Fairweather District?"

Tim shook his head. "Not that we know of, Judge. Uh, Your Honor. The others, they ain't been surveyed or recorded." He looked at Fergus. "Have they, Mr. Fergus?"

The recorder shook his head. "No. The only claim registered in Sam McDowell's name is the one you've been working."

"I see." Duncan lifted his gavel above the table, scratched his head with his other hand. Dan inhaled to the bottom of his lungs, let out his breath slowly. The gavel banged down on the table and the room fell silent. The Judge said, "Please register both of these claims in the name of Timothy McDowell – son, are you of age yet?"

"I'm almost seventeen, Your Honor."

"Then we shall have to have an adult co-owner. Who would you name?"

Only a moment's hesitation before Tim said, "My Mam, sir. Martha McDowell."

"Your mother?" Judge Duncan's voice reflected the raised eyebrows Dan could not see. "A woman owning a gold claim? Women are incapable of understanding business, let alone doing the heavy work of mining."

Dan forced his hands to remain loose at his sides. He saw Martha poring over the Bible her children had given her for Christmas. She had memorized whole Psalms, and the first ten or so verses of the Gospel of John, this woman who had never read a word six months ago. She had been quick to understand the snarl McDowell had left with the shares, and the legal morass of their own situation. And now Duncan questioned that a woman could have the business acumen to own a claim? So Dan might have thought had he stayed in New York, where the women of his circle led frivolous lives devoted to fashion and balls, and the acceptable charities, but a man who held that opinion here was a fool. He overlooked Lydia Hudson, who kept a restaurant and a quasi bank, and Helen Troy, who owned Fancy Annie's. Saloon and brothel it might be, but it was also a thriving business.

"Your Honor," began Fitch, "that's the very reason —"

"My Mam's as smart as they come, sir," said Tim. "She ain't been to school, but she has a head on her shoulders, and she can sort out sense from foolishness."

The Judge held still, except that he twiddled a dry pen between two fingers. At last, he nodded as if he had come to the end of some internal debate. "Very well. I shall do as you wish, with one proviso."

"Sir?" asked Tim.

"Condition, young man. One condition. An inexperienced woman and a boy cannot be left alone to manage properties potentially worth considerable. I will only do this if you name a responsible man of business."

"Dan'l Stark," the boy said. "My stepfather."

"Daniel Stark, do you agree?" Judge Duncan was at his most judicial, all seriousness and propriety to impress Timothy with the gravity of his choice.

Dan suppressed an urge to laugh. "I agree."

"Then I hereby appoint you attorney of record for the McDowell family until Timothy McDowell's twenty-first birthday."

So it was done and going in the record. Dan watched James Fergus's pen scratch across the paper. When he finished recording the claims, the Alder Gulch claim and the nugget claim, and the agreement appointing him attorney of record, it was done. He was officially the McDowell family's man of business until Timothy's twenty-first birthday. The two claims belonged to them for all the world to know. Anyone having business with the McDowells regarding the two claims would have to go through him. No one could bully Martha or her children ever again. They were safe from Fitch.

All that remained was to settle the business of his partnership with Fitch. Because he'd be damned if he'd be partners with a Secesh.

~25~

OUTSIDE THE SALOON, Fitch stomped back and forth, a few steps at a time, mud squelching outward from his boots, and men dodged out of his way.

Dan would not dodge, but stopped on the walkway, in effect dared Fitch to hit him.

"You goddam mudsill," Fitch said, "you stole my claim." His mouth was full of tobacco juice, and he spat and wiped his mouth on the sewed end of his short sleeve, a smear of tobacco juice staining dark against the butternut.

Mudsill again. "I won McDowell's shares fair and square, and you damn well know it. If it was your God damn claim, why the hell wasn't your name on it?"

"Whipple is a shareholder, I told you! I put his name on it because —"

A drum beat in Dan's ears, and he saw Fitch as through a pale mist. "Shareholders? I told you before, damn it, prove it! Do they even exist? Or are they dummies —" Dan stopped, this public accusation a plank he had made and walked out to the end of his own accord, charging Fitch with attempted theft by demanding ownership of the nugget claim, and more, of swindling the McDowells by putting on the contracts the names of other shareholders who might or might not be real, instead of McDowell's name. If the other men did not understand all the implications, Fitch did, but he was caught, unable to say anything, even in his own defense.

A low growl among Fitch's friends, muttered, "mudsill," "Nigger lover," and "debaucher," accusing him of soiled intentions toward Martha, of seducing her. He shot a quick glance toward the speaker, and noted the lank beard, the eyes close set on either side of a wide nose. He would know the man again. He could not fight him, not now, but he would. He would.

As soon as he had won this battle with Fitch, who could sue him and win with a jury made up mostly of Confederates, though he did not have to prove the shareholders were faked. Fitch, mouth gaping, the chaw bulging out one cheek, his countenance as open an admission of guilt as Dan might ever hope for, took in a breath to roar his outraged innocence to the world. Before he could, Dan raised his voice, "I'll give you a chance, though. You can win the other claim back, the same way I got it. Meet me in a poker game at Con Orem's."

Came a voice from somewhere in the crowd, "Just like your father." It was Van Fleet, he knew, though he could not stop to fight that side battle, either. The banker shouted, "You can't do this. You'll lose."

Van Fleet caught Fitch unprepared, too. The Southerner gaped around at his cronies, while Dan held his lips shut, until one of Fitch's pals called out, "Go on, then, Major! It ain't only on the battlefield we'll lick those goddam Yanks."

"Like hell you will." Dan planted his feet wide apart, changed his stance foursquare to Fitch.

"I –," Fitch gulped, "I'm not a poker player. I don't gamble."

No, Dan told him silently, you want a sure thing, so you'd make up shareholders and try to cheat my family. "Find a surrogate, then, dammit. I'll play anyone in an honest game, as long as it's at Con's Melodeon Hall." Because Con Orem kept honest cards, and had the strength, as a pugilist, to back his rules.

"No," shouted Tim. "Dan'l, you can't. You might lose —"

"What do you say, Fitch?" A man wearing an evil-smelling buffalo coat much too warm for the day came out of the growing crowd. The coat's stench went before him, and other men made way like the Red Sea parting for Moses. The man twined his fingers in his coat's rough fur as if he petted a dog. As he stepped out to face Dan, Dan's eyes watered. "I'd jump at the chance, if I was you, Fitch. You might win. Hell, I'll play, too." He smiled and winked at Dan. "I've wanted another chance since New Year's Eve."

Jim Sloan. He'd been in the game when Dan won the claims from McDowell. The ice had been thick on the windows, shutting in the almost visible stink from Sloan's coat. Where had he been all these months? Still Fitch said nothing, but his pals watched him with sobered faces while Dan waited, thought of the price of gold in New York and the gold waiting to be dug out of Alder Creek, and telegraphed a thought: It takes balls to get in this game.

Sloan said, "I'll deal the game, gentlemen. How about it? I've been wanting to win a claim, but so far no one has been fool enough to risk one when I'm playing. I'll play both of you."

Fitch could leave everything alone and still have half the claim, and Dan wished the gambler would shut up, but Sloan went on talking. "You-all want to know why Fitch is afraid to sit in a game with Stark? I'll tell you. I've played cards with him. That was the damnedest game. I didn't do too bad out of it, but Stark, looking like mother's milk is still drying on his lips, he turns out to be a goddam card shark. Hey! That rhymes — Stark the shark. He was the big winner that night." Pausing for a moment to let his words sink in, he finished, "But honest. Here's a man don't cheat at cards. Or anything else."

Blood rose in Fitch's face, the vein across his forehead swelled under his skin.

Dan said, "Anybody else want in? Fitch and me and Sloan, but we need at least two or three more. Who else wants to be partners with the Major?"

Fitch's backers muttered among themselves. Some stepped away, walked on down the slope.

"Stark, don't do it," shouted Van Fleet. "Think of why you're here. Think of your father." And he began to talk, to tell everyone that Dan's father had gambled away his life.

"Shut the hell up, Van Fleet," said Dan without looking away from Fitch.

"No, you can't," Tim said. "Dan'l, don't do this. God damn it, don't."

Fitch burst out, "All right. You're on. Both of you. Stark and you, Buffalo Coat. But I won't have a partner. It'll be winner take all." He wet his lips, and his shoulders moved under his coat. "You'll eat your words, Stark. I don't care who's my partner in this claim so long as he ain't a goddam mudsill."

Dan showed his teeth. "I don't much fancy a greyback, either."

Someone grabbed his arm from behind, and Dan swung around, elbow cocked, fist ready to strike, but it was only Tim. Dan dropped his hands to his sides, and did not see the roundhouse blow from his left side that staggered him into the path of a fast-trotting horse. The horse shied, its rider came out of the saddle and landed in the mud, got up cursing.

"You son of a bitch, you drunk or something?"

Dan turned his face to bring his nose and mouth out of the mud. A horse's hoof, too long in the toe, shifted in front of his eye. Warm breath, smelling of hay, on his ear. No, he tried to say, not drunk, just —

~26~

DAN'L LAY QUIET with blood seeping out of his left ear. Tim sank to his knees beside him, shouted at him to get up. He'd just wanted to stop Dan'l from gambling away the claim. He hadn't meant to hurt him. The rider backed the horse away from Dan'l and stood over him.

Dan'l wasn't getting up.

"Good God," the rider said, "I thought he was drunk. I thought he was drunk. My God. Did I kill him?"

Oh, God, Dan'l wasn't getting up. He lay still. Like death.

"No, I did." Tim raised Dan'l's head and shoulders out of the mud. Blood from Dan'l's ear trickled onto his coat. "Oh, God, oh God, I've killed him."

One of the town doctors come running, and felt of Dan'l's neck, leaned over to listen to him breathe. "He's alive, thank God. Here, you men," he said, "help me. Let's get him home." Home. So Dan'l was alive; he hadn't killed him. Thank you, Lord.

They took Dan'l out of his grasp, lifted him up. Using Dan'l's coat for a stretcher, they started up the street, Tim slogging ahead as fast as his long stride could carry him.

Mam had set the washtub on the sawhorse, and was scrubbing clothes up and down the washboard while Dotty read to her from the

Good Book when Tim pulled up the latch and walked in.

"There's been an accident," he said. She turned white as paper, and he thought she would faint when she saw they carried in Dan'l, still out cold, but breathing. Dotty screamed. That brought Mam around, and she ran toward their bedroom, stripped down the quilts, and told them to put him there. Then the men crowded her and Tim out of the room, while they stripped Dan'l and put him to bed with the kind of experience that comes when people have to do such things for each other. They brought out his muddy clothes and gave them to her, and spoke some reassuring words to Mam as they left, all except for the doctor, who stayed behind.

"He caught a massive blow to the head, Mrs. Stark," with a glare at Tim, "and all we can do is let him rest and come out of it himself." Then he was gone, too.

Tim followed Mam into the bedroom where someone had lighted a lamp.

"Bring me some warm water and the tincture of woundwort," she said without a glance at Tim. Dotty obeyed, while all the time Tim stood at the foot of the bed and wishing the last minutes away, out of his life, wishing himself on the moon or dead, because he'd acted just like Pap, and now Dan'l, who'd rescued him from Pap, rescued them all from Pap, lay in his bed pale like death, and Mam looked more struck than when Pap hit her. And it was all his fault. He'd done it.

"I done it," he told Sheriff Fox sometime later. The Sheriff sat at the eating table, where he could rest his writing arm and a notebook, but somehow Tim couldn't sit with him. This wasn't a social visit. It was a questioning, and he stood before the Sheriff like he was already on trial, which he was even if he was judge and jury convicting himself. "We got to arguing, and I lost my temper and I hit him." It was a relief to tell it, and he almost broke down like a baby when he added, "I'm sorry as I can be." He couldn't stop one or two tears that squeezed out.

Behind him, at the bedroom door, Mam gasped at his telling. He knew she'd never have believed that he could pay back Dan'l's kindness this way. He didn't believe it himself.

Sheriff Fox rose to his feet. He wasn't as tall as Dan'l, and Tim looked at him straight across, but that didn't matter none because the man's authority towered over him. Sheriff Fox, lawman. Vigilante. "I guess I don't need to tell you what'll happen now. You'll have to appear before the Tribunal. We'll meet to decide what to charge you with, and then notify you to appear. You'd better pray Daniel Stark doesn't die."

"I didn't mean to, Mr. Fox, I swear I didn't. I was afraid he'd gamble the claim and lose it and go back to New York and never come back, and he'd leave Mam, leave us —" He didn't have to explain what Dan'l's going would mean for Mam, what with some folks already saying she was a hussy, and after what someone had called Dan'l. Debaucher. "I just swung on him."

Stepping over the threshold into the twilight, the Sheriff paused. "Hold yourself ready for when I come for you, young man. It won't do you any good to run." There was a deal of meaning in his face when he said that; in January the Vigilantes had tracked guilty men more than a hundred-fifty miles, through better'n two feet of snow, twice across the Divide to Hell Gate and hanged them there.

"No, sir. I'll be here." He didn't say that if Dan'l died he wouldn't be able to live with himself anyway, so they could do as they pleased.

When he shut the door behind Sheriff Fox, Dotty was there to wrap her arms around him and he come as near to being undone as made no difference. Neither of them could think of aught to say, then or on into the evening. Mam tended Dan'l, though there was not much to do, once the bleeding stopped, except wait. Dotty put together some soup, but they ate precious little of it. He tried not to look at them because he couldn't stand the disappointment in their eyes, and the terror that they might lose both their menfolk.

Jacob Himmelfarb came by and sat with them. "He will not die," said Jacob.

"I wish I knew that," Tim said.

Lydia Hudson came to sit with them, too, and when Tim opened the door to her, he saw, at the end of the path on Jackson street, two men waiting. One called out, "Any change?"

Tim called back, "No change." He didn't invite them in and they didn't come any closer, and he knew, with a lift of the hairs on his arms, who they were: Vigilantes. On guard to be sure he didn't escape.

Mrs. Hudson went into the bedroom to sit with Mam. After awhile she came back into the big room where she made coffee, and cut some of the bread she had brought with a jar of preserves. She and Jacob made a strange pair at the table, him in that prayer shawl he wore with the knotted fringes and wide stripes. Her in the black shawl she draped across her back and somehow held with her elbows as she poured coffee and cut the bread.

The Quaker lady and the Jew. Tim had never knowed any such back home, but here he'd learned the world was made of a heap of different folks.

Another tap at the door that they almost did not hear, but Dotty opened it, and Berry Woman came in. She carried a laden basket, and smelled of wild things – sage and wood smoke and faintly, bear. Lydia Hudson took the basket and called out to Mam that she'd come. Mam came out to greet her with a watery smile. They signed to each other, their fingers making flying shapes and gestures, and the only one he understood came at the end of their conversation, when Berry Woman hugged Mam.

After the women went into the bedroom, Dotty whispered to Tim that Fitch was outside with the group at the end of the path. Tim did not go look.

Van Fleet came to ask if there was anything he could do, and to wish them well. He took himself off again, for which Tim was glad on account he recollected the man shouting something about Dan'l's father, and losing the claim, and he'd scared Tim. Which wasn't no excuse, there being no excuse for what he'd done.

Other people came to ask about Dan'l, and went away again. No one asked him what happened, why he'd slugged Dan'l, or what made him do such a thing. But there was in their silence a slight drawing aside of skirts, as if they were reconsidering what they knew of him and finding it not to their liking.

Or maybe he thought that because it was what he was doing, reconsidering what he knew of himself. And telling himself it must never happen again. Of course, if Dan'l died, the Vigilantes would see to that, but if he lived, Tim would have the rest of his life to know this about himself, what he was capable of, and he didn't rightly know how he'd live with it.

The grandmother clock bonged out the hours, and not long after it had counted ten, Berry Woman brought Mam out for coffee and made her eat some bread. It pained Tim that his mother couldn't look at him, like he'd turned into Pap.

Oh, God, was that what he'd gone and done? Was he more like Pap than he'd ever thought? He couldn't be – he just could not –

"Martha." A weak voice from the bedroom. Everyone at the table sat up straight. Mam set down her cup and bread, and ran to the bedside. Tim stopped in the doorway to see how she bent over Dan'l who tried to sit up.

Mam laid her hand on his shoulders. "Just rest," she said. "You'll be fine, but for now, go back to sleep."

Dan'l slid down, his expression puzzled. "What did you say?"

~27~

THEY TALKED AS LOW as might be, the bedroom door closed so as not to disturb Dan'l, sleeping. After staying home from school to help her for a couple of days, Martha had insisted Dotty go back-$150 a term couldn't go to waste- but Timmy sat at home with her to help with Dan'l and, so Martha thought, because he couldn't face the town yet.

He'd hardly spoke since they'd brought Dan'l home. Head down, staring at his big hands knotted together on the eating table, he broke his silence. "Mam, what's to become of me?"

"I don't know." She wished she had some comfort to give him, come to that, some reassurance for her, too, but it all depended on Dan'l's recovery, and the Vigilantes. "It's in the Lord's hands, and all we can do is pray." Which she'd been doing without stopping, like the Bible said: Pray without ceasing. Keeping her head down and her eyes on her needle, she stitched at a seam on a dress of Dotty's she had decided to let out before the fabric faded so the seams showed too much. The child was growing a woman's shape, and it wouldn't be long before she'd have to put darts in her bodices —

She lay the sewing in her lap, unable to hide behind other thoughts any more. She'd held the question in, hoping Timmy would tell her of his own, and because she was afraid of what he'd say. Now she had to know. "Why did you do it?"

He must have been thinking on it some, because he spoke right up. "I got scared, and then I was that crazy angered with him."

"Why?" In that simple word she put all the meaning possible: that Dan'l had rescued them, that he was as decent a man as you'd ever hope to find, that he shared what he had with them all, though his obligations to his mother and brothers and sisters in New York scared her.

A good man, like all folks not perfect.

She loved him.

"Judge Duncan fixed the nugget claim, so's we own it all, and —"

He went on for a few words, but Martha was caught: "We own it? We who?"

"The Alder Creek claim, too. You and me. We own both of them. Dan'l didn't register the nugget claim to hisself. He registered it to me, and the Judge, he wouldn't let me be the only one on account I ain't twenty-one yet. So I named you co-owner, and when Judge Duncan didn't like that any better, you being a female, I named Dan'l as, what-do-you-call-it, our attorney of record? Man of business, anyway. So that satisfied ever—"

He stopped, and stared off past Martha's right shoulder, his eyes blue pebbles in snow, and she reckoned he was putting what he'd just told her alongside him hitting Dan'l, and convicting himself of the worst ingratitude. He'd always had a punishing conscience, even as a little'un.

She knew better than to take him in her arms the way she would've done then, because he was near to man-grown, and had to face his wrongdoing. But she prodded him to tell it all, because she wanted to know, and it would be the best comfort to him. The Papists knew a thing or two about confession being good for the soul. Right along with penance and atonement.

Obedient, Timmy went on, though he looked like he saw something rotten, but when he came to the part where Dan'l had challenged Fitch to a poker game, Martha couldn't stand it.

"A poker game?" Her voice, pitched higher than normal, rasped in her throat. "He accused Fitch of —? Of fraud?"

"Yeah. That's what it sounded like. And Dan'l, he sounded confident, like he knew. Fitch couldn't say nothing against it, either. And it just come over me, sudden-like, how Dan'l couldn't be let to gamble it away."

Martha could not think. It was like her mind stopped between one thought and the next, and there was only a blank where thought should be until, like pulling her foot out of the gumbo, her mind lurched into motion again. She stabbed her needle into the fabric, laid it on the table. She had to move about. Opening the bedroom door a crack, she looked at Dan'l. The bed, a full double, was barely long enough for a six-foot man stretched out, but he lay curled on his right side, one arm laid out toward her side of the bed. As she watched, he slid his hand under her pillow and drew it to him without waking up. He let out a long sigh, snuggled his face into it.

She wanted to weep. He loved her, and he'd told her so just then, in his sleep, but her thoughts were too jumbled in her mind. Loving her, he would gamble their future away? Worse, even, what if he lost and then went to New York and didn't come back, there being nothing to hold him here but love? Love was never a thing to bet a life on. Sam had loved her once, for a time. And there was that woman, that shining angel in New York. If he stayed there, she didn't see how she could stand it.

How could she live without him? As quiet as could be, she closed the door.

Sitting down again, she took up the dress where she had set it aside, pretending to Timmy, and maybe to herself, that everything was normal. She was just fixing a dress and talking to her son, while her man slept in the other room. "You said Judge Duncan awarded us the two claims? The nugget claim and the Alder Creek claim?"

"Yep. Dan'l got that for us." He drew in a long breath and stared at his hands spread out flat on the table. "And then I hit him." A few tears flowed down his cheeks, into the three days' growth of light brown stubble that had started because he hadn't been home to the cabin he shared with Jacob, and he wouldn't use Dan'l's razor without his say-so.

He had such a lost look in his eyes that she forgot her resolution about him being almost a man. She set her sewing aside again, rose and gathered him into her arms just like when he was a little boy and done something he was ashamed of.

A shudder ran through his body. "Mam, I won't be like Pap. I won't. I swear it. Good God, I'll die 'fore I'll be like him. If I'm growing up like Pap, I'd rather the Tribunal hung me."

It was a cry from the heart that must surely carry all the way to Heaven. Martha could only pray that the good Lord heard, and watched over this boy of hers, because he was sore in need of help.

After he wiped his eyes and blew his nose, he wouldn't look at her, for being ashamed that he'd played the baby to her, and him with a beard on his cheeks.

Martha dipped water out of the drinking bucket and set it on the burner for tea. Pretending like they talked of might-be rain, she thrust another fat stick into the firebox, and said, "You don't have to be like him. You can be better'n that. You can be like —"

A heavy knocking at the door must surely be a man about important business. Martha stared at her son while the knock sounded again. There was no help for it, but she must answer the door, and her fears leaped into her throat as she stood aside for Sheriff Fox and X Beidler. Another time, maybe, she might laugh at the contrast, the Sheriff being so much taller than X, as people called him, whose rightful first name, she thought, was John. It wasn't that the Sheriff was so tall, but that X was the shortest man she'd ever thought to see, barely topping the shotgun he carried on his arm. A little man, but tougher than saddle leather. She closed the door behind them, and went to stand with Timothy, who stood up square to face them.

They removed their hats like gentlemen, and greeted her, but it was plain the business they come on, and Martha, recollecting the day the Vigilantes had come for McDowell, thought she might faint. She sat down on a chair before her knees gave way.

"How's Mr. Stark?" asked Sheriff Fox.

"He's mending." Martha spoke as if through a mouthful of cotton, and her words had a thick, mushy sound in her ears. "He's sleeping now, and I'll thank you not to wake him."

"Glad to hear it. For all your sakes." Taking a paper out of his inside pocket, Sheriff Fox said, "I have a warrant for the arrest of Timothy McDowell on the charge of assault with attempt to murder Daniel Bradford Stark." At his side, X held the shotgun ready to swing up and cover Timothy.

"Except that I'm not preferring charges, Jeremiah." Dan'l leaned on the door-jamb. He was dressed in a flannel shirt and trousers, his feet in thick socks against the drafts rising through the floor. "The boy didn't mean to lash out like that."

"He could have killed you, though, and we have to put a stop to people striking out from pure meanness. An apple doesn't fall far from the tree."

"You'll have to speak up a little more." Dan'l lifted himself away from the doorjamb and shuffled across the floor, an old man's way of walking. Martha wanted to leap up and give him her shoulder to lean on, but she knew he wouldn't thank her for that, him needing to make his way on his own, so on account she had to be doing something, she got up to see to the tea, the water now boiling ready for it. "I seem to have trouble hearing." Martha swung around. Dan'l ignored Timothy, who breathed in sharp, like he'd jabbed himself on something.

Raising his voice, Sheriff Fox repeated what he'd said.

Dan'l dropped onto a chair and held out his hand for the paper. He read it and gave it back to Sheriff Fox. "All right. It's properly drawn and properly executed, but you can't take him now."

Martha bit her knuckles, too late to stifle the short scream that burst out. Dan'l turned his head, like he wasn't sure where the sound came from, reached a hand toward her. She seized it and hung on like she'd drown without it.

"Why can't we?" Beidler shifted his weight from one foot to the other, and the shotgun's close-set stare looked at Timothy's knees.

"X, didn't you ever learn it's not good manners to come into a man's house with a loaded shotgun? And point it at people?" Dan'l waited until X lowered the weapon. "Because we don't have a jail to keep him in and I'm not ready. It'll be a few days yet before I can appear."

"Why do we need you?" The shotgun looked up a few inches.

Sheriff Fox put out his hand, palm down, toward Beidler, and the weapon stared at the floor. "You aim to defend him?"

"Yes."

Martha sucked in her breath, and with a squeeze Dan'l let go of her hand. From a canister, she took out a couple of pinches of sage leaves and dropped them in the old brown pot, poured in the water, and put on the top, wincing at the small clatter it made on account her hands shook.

"You're the Vigilante prosecutor, not a defense attorney."

"I can change places in a good cause. I can't prosecute a case that has no merit."

"The boy hit you, knocked you cold, and by his own admission, he thought he killed you."

"He didn't, though. And even if he had, it would have been an accident. He lashed out, but there was no intent to murder, and I'll say so at the tribunal."

The Sheriff looked Timothy up and down. "We can't have people lashing out. We can't have men settling their quarrels by fighting each other, with fists or with guns. We've had enough of that around here, and there has to be an end to it."

Dan'l said, "I know that and—"

"Especially a man as powerful as he'll be. As he is right now, without his full growth."

"— so does he." Dan'l turned his head and regarded Timothy for the first time, his expression graver than Martha had ever seen on his countenance.

"Yes. God as my witness, yes. I never meant —" Timothy choked, like his tears were handy to coming. He swallowed two or three times and couldn't speak.

"If we delay this," Beidler said, "how do we know he'll appear when we call him?"

"He was here today, wasn't he? He knew you'd come for him sometime, and he stayed. That's not the action of a guilty man."

The Sheriff put away the paper. "Will you guarantee his appearance at the tribunal?"

"Yes."

"Very well, then. We'll postpone it for maybe two, three days. Will that suit you?"

"Two days. I won't be out of commission longer than need be."

Martha went to the door to shut it after them and hurry their leaving, but Sheriff Fox paused in the doorway and turned toward Timothy. "You should be damn grateful to Dan Stark. He's sticking up for you, when a lot of men would gladly see you hang just to prevent the next time. If I were you, I'd give a lot of thought to the man you want to be, and be very sure that man was a credit to your stepfather." He put on his hat and gave a tug to the front of the brim. "Begging your pardon, Mrs. Stark." Because he'd cussed in the presence of a lady.

~28~

DAN DRANK HALF his mug of tea before he trusted himself to speak, or even to know what he wanted to say. His head ached, and nausea lapped at the edges of his stomach. He was not certain how long he could stay upright. His voice sounded odd inside his head; he had never heard it that way before. Martha stood behind his left shoulder, her hands kneading the muscles along his upper spine; he smelled her anxiety mixed into her usual scent, as of juniper and sage smoke together. The boy's fear beat at him, and as he sat there, the steam rising from the tea, not knowing just what to say, the feeling grew in him that it was not only the summons from Fox, the threat of the Tribunal that frightened them. They were terrified of what he might do or say. They had lived their lives afraid of the man of the house; they did not know how else a man acted in times like this.

If I had my full strength, Dan said to himself, I'd be tempted to go a round with him and whip his ass. But that's what he expects, it's what his father always did. The son of a bitch never taught Timothy there was another way to be a man.

"You're out of chances." He made it a simple flat statement, like telling someone his fee for a survey. Tim said nothing, only stared at him out of eyes that peered out from under his frontal bones like creatures from their caves. "If you strike out that way at anyone again, ever, I'm done with you." He swallowed some tea, felt its heat all the way down to his stomach, clamped his jaws together on the threatening reaction. When Tim did not speak, Dan said, "Do you understand?" He lowered his voice, because he did not know how loud he had spoken. "I want an answer."

"Yes, sir."

Dan waited while it dawned on Tim that he had to say something more.

"Yes, sir. I'm sorry." Big though he was, man though he almost was, he looked ready to cry, a child half his age. "Oh, God, I'm sorry, Dan'l. I never wanted to act like Pap. I don't want to be like Pap."

Steeling himself against his own rising pity for the boy's agony of fear and guilt, Dan said, "You did, though. Do you know what you've done?"

"I – I hit you."

"Yes, but beyond that." His voice sounded different to him now, and he tried to hear it through a ringing in his right ear. "Do you know what you've done?"

"I knocked you out."

"Yes. But do you know you've done?"

Tim was silent. His shoulders slumped, and his head turned from side to side.

Neither of them could speak. Dan raised his hand, palm up, to Martha, who hesitated before she laid her own on it, and he closed his fingers around hers, the little bones like a small trembling bird in his grasp. Little brown sparrow. That the boy should have brought this upon her made him even angrier, hardened him toward Tim's misery.

"Do you?" he demanded once more.

Tim said, "Not—" The rest Dan lost amid the ringing of his right ear.

"What did you say?" His voice thundered inside his head.

Martha's hand jerked in his own, and Tim flinched, ducked his head as if Dan had slapped him. Dan tried to speak more calmly, but his anger vibrated full out in the words, and maybe the more harshly because he kept his voice low. "You've deafened me. I can only hear a ringing in my right ear." Tim's head came up, his eyes dark pools of grief. "I'll learn to cope with that. What's important is how you've hurt your mother."

"Mam, I never meant to—" His voice broke.

Sensing that Martha might speak, or go to her son, or do something else to ease the burden on him, Dan tightened his grip on her hand, and felt an answering pressure followed by a stillness, as a sort of permission, that she trusted him to do this right. He tightened his lips against an uprush of gratitude as he would against the rebellion of his stomach. He had to concentrate. Whatever he said now could help make a man of Tim or break him. Too much leniency, and the boy might think he could get away with it, like McDowell, never knowing the right way to use his size and his strength. Too harsh, and it might end up the same.

"How's the water?" Dan asked.

"The water?"

"Can the Alder Creek claim be worked yet?"

"I don't know. I haven't been to see."

"Then go and see, because I won't have you throw it away for pitying yourself. As soon as you can, get to work on that claim. And don't let anyone jump it." He took a sip of tea. "We're lucky that Judge Duncan awarded you and your mother both claims, but you can't work two claims at once, so you'll have to find someone honest to work the nugget claim. On shares to start with, or sell it. We'll talk that over later."

Just above whispering, Tim said, "You're trusting me to do all that? Mr. Stuart wouldn't. He fired me. Said he – he wouldn't have someone working for him that could hit that way."

"You're not acting for me. It's for your mother and your sister. You have to take a man's part now. Can you do it?" He fixed the boy under his gaze, held him impaled on the question as a fly on a pin.

Tim took a deep shuddering breath and nodded. "I can. I have to, don't I?"

"Yes. You do." He held Tim a moment longer, then dropped him. "All right, then."

Martha tugged her hand away from Dan's grip, and he let her go. She pulled out a chair beside him and sat on the edge of it, her knee pressed to his thigh. In this, she was saying, they were together.

He was not so sure she would be with him for the rest of it, the hardest part, for which he needed a clear head, and his body insisted. "I have to go outside." He would not use the chamber pot; if he could not go outside, one of them would have to empty it. Pushing back from the table, he stood up, steadied himself with a hand on the back of Martha's chair. He fixed his eyes on the rifle lying across its pegs, snake-like in its suppleness, and when he reached the wall and tried to pull on his boot, he fell forward and caught himself with a hand on the peg holding the rifle. A scramble of feet. Tim's strong arms steadied him and put him on a chair, and Tim pulled Dan's boots on his feet while Dan cursed his weakness. An old man not yet twenty-nine.

All the way out to the privy, he leaned on Tim. The dog followed them, a doubtful wag in his tail, as if he sensed something awry. "I don't need help unbuttoning my pants," Dan grumbled, and slammed the door behind him. Hiding himself in the sunlight-striped darkness, he felt his face flame at his echo of Grandfather.

Going back, he kept himself upright as much as might be without Tim's arm, though it was there when he needed it.

"What have you told your mother about this?"

"She asked why I'd hit you and I had to tell her."

As if it were a matter of mild curiosity, Dan asked, "Why did you? To stop me from playing poker with Fitch?"

"Yeah. That's what I said."

Canary crowded against his knee. Keeping one hand on the wall of the house, Dan reached down to scratch behind an ear and wait for the earth to settle. With care he brought himself erect, wondered if this were how a baby felt, when it took its first steps. He leaned against the house. "What did you keep back?"

"I heard what someone called you. Debaucher. He meant you'd —" Tim's mouth twisted, his fist came up and his shoulder went back.

Canary snarled. The fur ruched up along his backbone, and his muzzle curled over bare teeth. Dan grabbed the loose skin at the back of his neck.

"Christ." The boy dropped his arm, opened his hands. "Thinking that – that – you —"

A house on fire holds in its flames and heat until someone opens a door, and it bursts out, to char anything, anyone, standing too close. Dan clamped his jaws together, closed his eyes, leaned his head against the unpeeled logs. Through the incendiary words he dammed inside himself, he heard a young girl cry out, "Dan'l! You're up! You're up!"

Dotty, home from school. Her face rapturous, delight brimming over, joyful tears splashing onto her coat. Running as best she might through the thick slippery mud, she would have clasped him around the waist except that Timothy caught her and held her from running into him full tilt. Even that was enough to unbalance him. Dan braced himself against the house, eyes closed to shut out their spinning faces.

He heard the tears in her voice.

"I'm sorry, Dan'l, I didn't think. I didn't mean, oh, Dan'l."

Forcing his eyes open, he smiled, though her face slipped in his sight. "Of course you didn't." He steadied a bit, knew he could not stand away from the logs just yet. "You go on in. Your brother and I will finish our talk. Tell your mother we'll be along in a moment."

Closing his eyes, Dan listened to her steps going away. He sensed that Tim stood close, ready to save him from falling. Dotty had jarred more than his precarious balance, and he found the words that would not come before. "If you are ever lucky enough to love a woman as I love your mother, that will be the greatest blessing in your life."

"So you'll stay here? You won't go back to New York?"

"I have to go back. I have to keep my promises there, but I will come back here when my business there is finished."

"How do we know that?"

"God damn it, I don't know." Dan opened his eyes to find the boy's face only inches from his own. "Maybe when you see me here again." He stood away from the wall. "That scared you? That I might go away and never come back? Why?"

"On account, I don't know why you have to go. Van Fleet can take your gold back. You could pay him here and stay with us."

"I see. All right, let's go in." Taking Tim's arm, he let Martha's son support him into the house. He would have to tell them all of it, all the secrets he had kept to himself, because they had to understand why he would return to New York, and that he would come back to them.

Martha met them at the door and scolded him across the room. "You'll catch your death, going out without a coat that way, and you not yet in the clear." When he sat on his chair at the table, she said, "No. You go back to bed. You're plumb tuckered out."

He shook his head. "I have things to say. All of you, sit down." When Dotty hesitated, he told her, "With everything you've been through, you are not too young to hear me. It's all right."

While they settled themselves, he looked at his hands resting on his thighs, hoping his strength would last long enough for this. "In court, Judge Duncan awarded you the nugget claim and the Alder Creek claim. That leaves the third claim, the second I won from McDowell." He said, "As things stand now, Fitch and I have equal shares in that one. Fifty-fifty."

Dotty let out a little squeal, wrapped her feet around the legs of her chair. Timothy shook his head, his lips tight, tension raising his shoulders almost to a shrug. Martha covered her mouth with her fingers.

"I can't be partners with Fitch, nor he with me. He demands full ownership, and I won't give it to him. So I've challenged him to a poker game. The winner will own that claim."

Martha gnawed on a knuckle. "You could lose."

"Of course I could lose. There is always some loss at poker. The trick is to never lose more than you can afford. I won't risk your claims. I'm gambling the half-share I won from McDowell." He wished he were not so weak, that what little strength he had did not drain from him word by word, so that he doubted he had enough to go on with the rest of it. But he had to say it, all of it.

He said, "I will not jeopardize your future. I am not my father, to do that." Against their mystified voices, his raised his own to be heard, spoke more sharply to make them listen because he was fighting his waning strength: "Hear me. It's a rather long story, but you have to know it. My father never wanted to be a lawyer, but that was what Grandfather wanted, for him to carry on the family name, in the law firm that Great-Grandfather founded, Stark and Sons, so he forced my father into it. Father hated the law, and he took up gambling as, I suppose, a kind of revenge. He taught me to play poker. I think my mother and my grandfather knew he gambled, but they did not know how much. He gambled everything away. His own money, the family's money. Then he embezzled our clients' money. Everything. And when it was all gone, he shot himself." My legacy, he thought, my father. Gambler. Thief. Suicide. Coward. "I'm his eldest son. I'm responsible for paying the debt, ensuring the family's future."

As they stared at him, perhaps not fully comprehending what he was telling them, he hurried to tell it all before he lost his courage and hid all the rest.

"Grandfather forced me to the law, too. I was a surveyor, but together, they both – Grandfather and Father – wore me down. I hated it, too, the law. Nothing but contracts and business, and so dry I thought I would die of thirst. Then I came here, and to stop the murdering, I became a prosecutor, and to establish the law I joined the Vigilantes and became their prosecutor." In that, he told them no more than they knew. "To Grandfather all vigilantes are rebels against the rule of law. When Grandfather learns what I've done, he will never forgive me. He will never understand."

He breathed hard, his knuckles bulged pale on his fists, and the rope scars stood out across the backs of his hands. "An odd thing happened." He laughed short, with a humor in it he doubted they would understand, but he treasured the irony of this part of the truth. "Prosecuting criminals here, I began to love the law. Murder taught me to love the law."

He took Martha's hand and held it in both of his, spoke to the youngsters because this was probably just as necessary for them to hear as any of the rest. "More importantly, though, I met your mother. Outside, I told Tim that if he ever loved a woman as I love her, it will be the greatest blessing of his life."

Martha brought her free hand over his, and her fingers traced the scars, soothed them. No one spoke, only waited for him to go on.

"My father and I are different. True, he taught me to gamble, but I don't plunge. This appointment with Fitch, it's for one claim and one claim only. I will go no further. If Father had thought of the family, he would never have plunged, he would have known when to quit. But no. He must have thought each time that he could win on the next card, the next horse."

"Oh, Dan'l." Martha's voice sounded full of pity for him, and he rejected that, would have nothing to do with it.

"No, Martha, don't. Understand me. My family is disgraced. It is said that the Starks are thieves and their word cannot be trusted. I have to show everyone that a Stark keeps his word and pays his debts. Do you understand now why I have to go back? No one else can do what I can. No one else can pay the debt. If I don't do it, my mother and sisters and brothers will never be free of dishonor."

In the silence, they fidgeted. He thought the youngsters waited for their mother to speak, but Tim said, "That means you promising to come back here when you've finished your business there is worth something."

"Yes."

Dotty dabbed at her cheeks with the dish towel. "I wish you didn't have to go, Dan'l. I'll miss you so."

"I'll miss all of you, too. Your mother most of all." His energy was draining fast away, and he wished Martha would say something that showed she understood.

After another moment, as she fidgeted with a loose button on his shirt cuff, speaking as if still thinking things through, she said, "I understand why you think you have to go." Then, maybe thinking – rightfully, to his mind – that was less than she might have said, she kissed his cheek. "I'll pray every day for your safe return."

It was not enough. Not nearly the faith in him that he had hoped his confession would bring from her. Levering himself up with his hands on the table, Dan stood and walked toward the bedroom, in those few steps, drained of strength, an old man weighed down by the care of years. Through the floorboards he felt quick feet behind him, then Martha's shoulder slid under his armpit, and she draped his arm over her shoulders. And steadied him.

~29~

Dressed in a pair of old trousers and a plaid flannel shirt, Dan sat reading in his favorite chair, that shared the corner with Martha's rocker, a round stove, and a lamp table on which stood a kerosene lamp and Martha's Bible.

Yesterday, Oliver's stage coach had brought another package, from Mother, who had sent it "in hope that it might alleviate the tedium of travel home." She had written, along with some scant news, that they managed by the grace of God, and that Flo expected a child in October, and everyone was in good health.

The package contained a bound volume of the *Atlantic Monthly*, July through December 1863. Dan handled the fat black book with care. It had cost the family perhaps a dollar, and the shipping another two dollars. Three dollars, three days' wages for a working man. One day's wage for an underground miner who bet his life that the timbers he himself erected would hold up tons of rock and soil overhead.

After awhile he laid the book on his lap. He loved the *Atlantic*, with its scientific articles by Louis Agassis on the formation of glaciers, stories by Louisa May Alcott and Bret Harte, poems by Longfellow, and John Greenleaf Whittier, and essays by Thoreau and Nathaniel Hawthorne. Secretary of War Charles Sumner wrote about how the

Rebels should be treated after the War. Victory for the Union was, he said, "inevitable." The volume was a treasure for minds deprived of intellectual stimulation, and he was sure that the next meeting of the Philosophical Club would pounce on it.

Just now, though, the effort of keeping his mind on Sumner's essay tired him. The dog snored on his mat. Martha had gone shopping. She hoped to find canned citrus fruit, because everyone was weary of the sage tea that warded off scurvy. In her absence he had one duty: to turn the beef roast on the half hour, a duty he took seriously because it was their first beef in weeks. He wished it were his most serious duty, that he did not have to think of Tim's fate.

He stood up, waited for the small unsteadiness to settle. He did not even have to grab for support. "Progress," he told himself, and noted with pride that he could stoop to turn the roast without toppling over.

As he crossed the room back to his own chair, Canary lifted his head, ears up. What did the dog hear over the street sounds? Dan tried to listen. Wheels creaked on axles. Men shouted at their beasts. The hairs rose along the dog's spine. A few seconds later a knock sounded at the door. Canary stood up and barked.

When Dan pulled open the door, Sheriff Fox stood with his hand poised to knock again. His bony face split in a wide smile. "You're looking better today."

Canary walked between them and sniffed at Fox's boots. Tail slowly wagging, he returned to his mat and curled onto it.

"Thanks. I'm doing much better." Dan stood aside to let the Sheriff in and while Fox was taking off his coat, he brought up a chair for him. "I can put coffee on."

"Wonderful," said Fox. "I haven't had coffee in months. How'd you come by it?"

"Mrs. Hudson brought some by."

When they were settled with their coffee, Fox licked a drop off his mustache. "That's good." He leaned forward, the cup cradled in both hands, and rested his elbows on his knees. "I come to tell you Judge Duncan is kicking up rough over this business with Timothy."

Dan waited.

"He wants the trial in his court. Says it don't belong with the Tribunal at all."

"That's crazy. It's a criminal case. He knows that all the criminal cases belong with us."

"He's afraid we'll hang the boy." Fox swirled the coffee around in his cup, drank a little. "We might, too. Depends a lot on you."

A chill raised goose bumps on Dan's arms. "There will be no hanging. Not this time."

"I don't want to hang him any more'n you do." Fox stared into his cup. "You have to know there's some feeling for making an example." Shifting the cup to his left hand, he nibbled at the nail of the other index finger.

A pulse throbbed behind Dan's eyes. He rested his head against the back of the chair. Christ, that it should even be possible they might hang Timothy. The boy had so much good in him that he'd had to find for himself. True, he had Martha's guidance, but a boy needed his father to teach him how men behaved themselves. "It's a matter of trust, isn't it?"

"What do you mean?"

"Which venue—"

Canary's bark interrupted Dan. A heavy knock sounded at the door.

Dan opened it to find Joel Van Fleet standing there, holding a bottle, and as he tried to think of an excuse not to let the man in, Alex Duncan strode up Jackson and turned onto the path. His words of welcome were lies, but Dan stood aside for both men. Fox, with only a tightening of the corners of his mouth, brought two more chairs and helped settle everyone with the last of the coffee.

It was good whiskey, and had cost Van Fleet something. Dan guessed it was both a peace offering and a sick room gift. "I'll save this for the celebration."

"Celebration?" Van Fleet's glance moved from Duncan to Fox.

The Judge sat between Van Fleet and Fox, but sideways to Fox, one leg crossed over the other. He would have to look askance at Fox, and Dan thought that was probably intentional. Fox studied his fingernails. As Sheriff, Fox worked for the court, but being a Vigilante meant he had another allegiance, and Duncan knew it. Why, Dan asked himself, could Duncan not see they all worked for the same end? Duncan would probably never acknowledge the Vigilantes had done right to hang the criminals, but if the miners court had been left to deal with crime, the Gulch would still be ruled by murderers.

"Celebrate Timothy's acquittal," Dan said.

Fox's eyes narrowed, and his head came forward. Duncan stared at Dan, and his thumb, which had been drumming on his knee, stopped. It was a brutal opening, a challenge to both Fox and Duncan, but Dan was bone weary of tact, of pussy-footing as Martha would say. Both men must have expected that Dan would say nothing in Van Fleet's presence. Maybe he should have kept silent until Van Fleet left, but damn it, Dan thought, the man knew nearly everything, and no oath of secrecy bound Duncan, who was fond of talking, especially against the Vigilantes. As soon as the Judge left, he'd spread his version of this meeting all over the Gulch; at least, Van Fleet would have a different view, if he talked.

Duncan plucked at the pants leg stretched over his knee. "His trial should be in my court, and you-all know it."

Van Fleet seemed to shrink back at that, to withdraw as if he found himself on stage by mistake when the curtain went up.

"Why?" Dan dropped the simple syllable among them, an invitation to argue the venue. There was no doubt in his mind who would handle the trial. Or should. The Vigilantes should take it, no matter what they said here, no matter what case Duncan tried to make for having it in his court, and if Dan had any influence, being both Tim's defense attorney and the victim, as well as a member of the Vigilante Executive Committee, it would go to the Tribunal.

Van Fleet drained his coffee and set the cup on his belly, which was not so ample as when he went into the creek.

"Yes," Fox said. "Tell us why the People's Court should try a potentially capital case."

Careful, Dan told himself. That was a side issue he would argue with Fox and the other Vigilantes later. Under no circumstances would he allow Tim to face the death penalty.

"Because justice should be administered by a court that is independent of law enforcement, and judgment should be impartial." Duncan turned his head to address Van Fleet. "The Vigilantes have been much too prone to administer the death sentence."

Van Fleet's lips parted, and his free hand plucked at his top waistcoat button.

"Only when a man earned his fate." The backs of Dan's hands tingled. He rubbed them to stop the irritation while he explained to Van Fleet, "The People's Court handles the smaller civil cases, those involving property worth no more than fifty dollars."

Fox smiled. "Sure has cut down on time-wasters. Men aren't so eager to go to trial if they think the Tribunal will handle their cases."

"It's ridiculous," said Duncan. "Y'all say it's the People's Court.

Well, let me tell you, the people can judge big cases as well as small ones, and when it comes to men's lives, they'll take far more care than a mob bent on hanging."

Sheriff Fox sat upright. "Whoa, there, Judge."

Dan's hands gripped each other for fear of what he might do if he let himself go. The dog stood, the hairs standing along his spine, his upper lip quivering in the beginnings of a snarl. Dan lowered his voice. "We are not a mob. The mob was the so-called jury of the whole that let John Dillingham's killers go last summer."

Barely hearing his own words, Dan said, "Put another way, whom would you trust more, a group of businessmen intent on ensuring a peaceful environment in which to encourage prosperity, or a collection of men who have no stake in the future of this Territory? Men who judge other men by the color of their coats?"

"Doesn't everyone, in these times?" Duncan returned.

Dan's head throbbed. He raised his chin. "I want this trial in the Tribunal, not in front of your so-called jury of the whole." Because, he added but did not say, a mob jury was likely to be a greyback jury, damn them, so much for your God-damn democratic experiment, because the greybacks were the majority here.

"You want it in the Tribunal?"

"Damn right. The boy will have a fair hearing there."

The clouds parted and sunlight laid a parallelogram of light across the rug and everyone's toes, across Dan's scuffed leather slippers, the Sheriff's black slip-on boots with one or two loose stitches, Duncan's worn but highly polished brown shoes, and Van Fleet's new work boots.

Duncan had said something. Dan said, "Beg pardon? My hearing's a bit off."

"And you're content with that?" Duncan said.

"Very much so." Dan added, "So is Tim." Fox leaned forward once again, rested his elbows on his thighs, examined his fingernails for snags. So that was what the Sheriff had come for, Dan thought: Reassurance.

"It doesn't matter to you that you are both victim and judge in this case?" Duncan asked.

Dan laughed through the heavy throbbing in his head. "It's worse than that. I'm victim and defender. I'm representing Tim."

Duncan leaped to his feet. "I should have expected no less of a mudsill. You're blurring the roles of judge, defense, and jury, and justice cannot be served unless they are separate. That's the only way they can balance each other. Damn it, then, I quit. You can find another judge."

He slammed the door so hard it bounced open again. Fox closed it and dropped the latch. The dog sniffed at the air, stretched front and back, and turned around a couple of times on his rug before he lay down, chin on his paws, watching the men.

Sheriff Fox slapped his hands on his knees. "My, my. 'Pears we have to find us another judge for the People's Court."

"The Vigilantes." Van Fleet spoke with the air of a man feeling his way into a dark room, or walking across thin ice. Thinking of that metaphor brought an internal smile to Dan's mind. "I don't think I have ever heard the entire story of what happened."

Dan said, "You won't hear it now, either, but the only way to ensure that anyone – man or woman – traveled safely with his gold was to break the back of a criminal conspiracy."

Fox folded his arms across his chest and appeared to grow taller, though sitting down.

A glance at the Sheriff and Van Fleet asked, "When will you be ready to leave with me? I can't stay here indefinitely."

The Sheriff's raised eyebrows told Dan that he had not heard of any such journey. He said, "Another month. Perhaps more. This has set me back. I have to attend to Timothy's defense, and there's a little matter of a poker game."

~30~

TIM COULD NOT STOP SWALLOWING. His Adam's apple rubbed up and down against the buttoned collar of last year's best wool shirt, but he could not stop himself. Sheriff Fox leading, him behind with a Vigilante on either side and one behind, and Dan'l following, they made a sort of parade from the bachelor cabin he shared with Jacob, down Jackson, across Wallace, and then into Kiskadden's Stone Block. Next door, in the Eatery, Mam said she'd wait with Lydia Hudson. People huddled into themselves as they walked by, and no one smiled, no one waved. Did they think he'd meant to kill Dan'l?

Mr. Baume barricaded himself behind a counter as they walked through his store to a stairway that wasn't much more than a ladder rising to the upper floor. Everyone knew Kiskadden's Upper Room. That's where the Union League met, and some other civic men's groups. And the Vigilantes. The Sheriff didn't hesitate, but led the way up. Tim stubbed his toe on one of the stairs and nearly pitched into the Sheriff, but caught himself, and then a step or two later, his head emerged into the big room. There was one window, and daylight slanted through it onto a raised platform with four chairs ranged behind a long table.

Would this be the last time he'd see daylight shining through a window?

He had to piss more than he'd ever had to in his life.

Sheriff Fox took hold of his upper arm and stood him at the far side of the platform away from the stove. The room struck cold, like winter hadn't all leaked out of it yet. The stove was lighted, but its heat didn't reach this far. He shivered and couldn't stop.

Dan'l took one of the chairs and laid a paper on the table in front of him. Men stopped to talk to him. Tim heard them ask him how he felt, heard Dan'l say he was much better thank you, but had trouble hearing out of his right ear. Dan'l lied. He couldn't hear anything out of that ear. And it was all his, Tim's, fault. He'd done that to Dan'l. Almost, he thought the Vigilantes should hang him; then he wouldn't have to be on guard the rest of his life against being like Pap.

The mayor of Virginia City, a thin, round-shouldered man with a funny name, Paris Pfouts, sat in the center chair, on account he was also the Vigilante president. Wilbur Sanders sat on the other side of Mr. Pfouts, leaned behind him to talk to Dan'l. Pretty soon, the two of them – Dan'l and Mr. Sanders – got up and went over by the stove to talk. Tim couldn't hear anything they said. He thought Mr. Sanders and Mr. Pfouts made a strange pair to be leaders of the Vigilantes. Them and Dan'l. Mr. Pfouts was loud for Secession, and Mr. Sanders was a veteran of the Union Army. He'd been next thing to a general. Dan'l wasn't a veteran, but a Unionist who held against slavery as hard as Mr. Sanders did.

Men come in quiet-like and sat on benches or stood, everyone solemn, some with their arms folded across their chests. Mr. Sanders and Dan'l sat down, and Mr. Pfouts rapped a gavel for order. "This tribunal is now in session."

So these were the Vigilantes. Tim recognized James Williams, who owned a stock ranch on the Stinking Water river and a livery in Lower Town, as they sometimes called Nevada City. It was Mr. Williams who'd led the Vigilantes all the way up to Hell's Gate in January, after some road agents. They'd caught them all and hung them as they caught them.

Would he be next? Dan'l would do his best, but would that be enough? Would this shirt be his shroud?

Mr. Pfouts gave him a Bible, and told him to put his left hand on it and raise his right hand. "Do you swear to tell the truth, the whole truth, and nothing but the truth?"

"Yes, sir."

"Very well."

He had to piss. It was all he could do to hold on, and he didn't quite hear what else Mr. Pfouts said, but Mr. Sanders stood up and spoke, in a kind of thunder that after a second or two became words telling what happened. He ended up, "Mr. Stark has recuperated enough to be present here today, although I am informed he cannot hear out of his left ear."

Mr. Pfouts asked Dan'l, "Is that an accurate statement?"

"It is," said Dan'l.

Now Mr. Pfouts was looking at him for an answer, and Tim could do no more than nod, but when Mr. Pfouts said, "Speak up," he managed to croak: "Yeah. I mean, yes sir. That's right."

"The facts are not in dispute." Mr. Sanders held his hawk's profile toward Tim, not looking at him, but Tim thought that his dark eyes were like a hawk's, too, that they could see over a wide range without moving much, and would catch the mouse moving through tall grass. Not a man to try to fool. "What we are to decide is what penalty this assault should carry, it being of an extreme nature and might well have ended in the victim's death."

"May it please the gentlemen of the committee," said a voice. Tim looked for the speaker as Major Fitch rose. He was not a member of the Executive Committee, but Dan'l had explained that any Vigilante could attend the Tribunal and have his say, though only the Executive Committee could vote.

Mr. Pfouts said, "The chair recognizes Major Tobias Wayne Fitch."

All real proper, thought Tim, like some damn minuet, not that he'd ever seen one.

"Considering the severity of the blow the victim suffered, and that damage to his hearing might be permanent, I would venture to suggest to the honorable committee that the charge be attempted murder rather than assault." Surprised by how like a gentleman he sounded, like Dan'l, only with the Southern accent and as much at home with big words as Dan'l, who never thought to put on a low-class voice just to be like someone he wasn't, Tim caught up with the sense of what he had said only when Dan'l leaped up and had to catch himself and lean on the table. Attempted murder? Tim opened his mouth to shout that he'd never thought of killing Dan'l, only Dan'l himself was glaring at him, warning him plain to close his mouth tight. So he did, and heard his teeth snap together.

Meanwhile, Major Fitch was going on, "Painful as it would be, I'm convinced we must set an example that violence towards one's fellow man will not be tolerated. Further, in striking out against Mr. Stark, the defendant demonstrated ingratitude in the extreme. I question whether he is amenable to change." With that, he sat down again, and one of the men sitting with him leaned over and whispered something that brought a smile to the Major's face.

Several men nodded and whispered among themselves.

"Have you anything to add?" Mr. Pfouts asked Dan'l.

Dan'l was so smooth that if Tim hadn't knowed him so well, he'd never have seen how Dan'l would've liked to kill Fitch right then. Dan'l spoke like he had to force the words out between his lips, and one of his hands shook so he thrust it into his pocket and leaned on the knuckles of his other fist. "I believe the lad hit out in a moment of extreme emotion, and that he has learned from his own jeopardy and mine what the consequences might have been. He has expressed to me his deep desire to have no repetition of that incident. I have no fear of such a recurrence either against myself or any other person. Therefore, I consider the charge of assault to be entirely adequate, from both a legal perspective and a personal one."

With that, he sat down again, and began talking behind his hands with Mr. Pfouts and Mr. Sanders, and some other men who joined them at the table. Sweat rolled down Tim's ribs. He knew what it meant, charging him with attempted murder instead of assault. Attempted murder carried hanging along with it. Not for sure, the way Dan'l had explained it, but possible. Assault did not. He wished his collar wasn't so damn tight.

After too long, the other men went back to their seats, Mr. Pfouts called for order, and Mr. Sanders stood up. "It is the prosecution's opinion that attempted murder is the failure to carry out an intent to murder and that whether or not the victim lives is due not to the will of the assailant but to the will of God." He paused, "There being no intent to murder on the part of the defendant, the prosecution considers the charge of assault to be adequate to the incident."

Some of the Vigilantes stamped on the floor, but two or three called out, "Hang him." Tim watched the Major, but Fitch sat quiet-like with other men wearing scraps of their Confederate uniforms, like he'd had his say and was done.

Using the back of his chair to steady himself, Dan'l stood up. Tim's throat tightened. Dan'l being still sometimes dizzy, was his doing.

"The defense agrees with the prosecution. The defense maintains that the charge of attempted murder should not be brought. There was no intent to murder on the part of the defendant. My stepson simply lashed out because of fear." Dan'l looked at Tim for the first time. "Is that not so?"

"Yes, sir." In Tim's own ears, his voice sounded stronger than he expected.

Mr. Sanders stood up. "May we know what that fear was?"

In silence Tim asked Dan'l, did he have to say, and Dan'l replied with a nod so small as to be near invisible. "I was afeared that Dan'l, uh, Mr. Stark, would go to New York and not come back here."

"Do you still have that fear?" asked Mr. Sanders.

Tim could not answer, because all he could think was the noose tighter around his neck than his collar.

Dan'l said, "You have sworn to tell the truth, remember."

Swallowing, he said, "No, sir. I don't."

"Why not?"

They had rehearsed this part. At the time Tim had argued, but Dan'l had said men sometimes forgot what to say in the Tribunal, even things that would save their lives. Now he understood. "On account you're standing up for me now. I hurt you, but you're defending me." The way the skin crinkled at the corners of Dan'l's eyes, and his lips lifted into almost a smile, brought Tim close to tears again, where he'd been so often these last few days. Almost, he couldn't get the words out, that they had not rehearsed, but he managed without choking. "You ain't Pap. I was scared you'd turn out like him, and run off and leave us, but I ain't scared of that no more."

At that, Dan'l said, "The defense rests," and Mr. Sanders echoed him for the prosecution, and they settled down to consider what to do with him. After a bit, Tim understood they were finished asking him questions, and he could sit, too. So he did.

Jim Williams rose to his feet. "I agree that the boy had no thought of murder, but he lashed out in a sucker punch, and he's got to learn not to do that. Never again. So I'm recommending two years' probation in the custody of Dan Stark, with this rule: If he ever again raises his hand in anger against Dan Stark or any other man except in self-defense, we may seek a more severe penalty."

Mr. Pfouts asked, "Is that a motion?"

"Yes, Mr. Chairman, it is."

Someone seconded it, and Mr. Pfouts called for discussion. Most men shook their heads, one man said that Jim Williams had spoken for him, too. At that there was a general chorus of agreement, even from Major Fitch.

They wrote out an agreement and Dan'l signed it. Tim could read enough that they'd turned him over to Dan'l. They could go. He was free. They would not hang him. For a few minutes, Tim could not comprehend that the danger was over. A quaking in his belly gave him a new fear, that he'd disgrace himself, so he said to Dan'l, "Let's go."

But Mr. Pfouts said to Dan'l, "Wait a moment, Stark. We have something to talk about." The way he said it so serious-like, nearly undid Tim, and maybe Dan'l understood, on account he said, "You go ahead and give your mother the good news," like he was talking about the weather, and Tim escaped, come close to falling down them stairs, his knees being so weak, and hurried out the back door to find an outhouse. It was close, but he sat there in the sun-streaked darkness and let himself go, sobbing into his hands like a baby as his bowels emptied. When he was done, he had to rest a spell, dry his face on his sleeve. He cleaned himself with a handful of damp sage leaves, but had to stay there awhile longer before he trusted his legs to carry him, what with all the feelings that rampaged through him, but at last he could step out into the spring sunshine and breathe the air. Even carrying somewhat the smell of the outhouse, and old bad whiskey from the nearby saloons, it smelled good.

He was free.

~31~

BELLS RANG IN MARTHA'S SOUL, the like of which she'd never heard for real, peal after peal of bells in a foretaste of Heaven, a joy that couldn't be kept inside the limits of her own body but overflowed in tears, so that she sobbed and laughed all at the same time. She didn't care about the tears running down her cheeks, only that Timmy was safe.

Not until someone come to the Eatery and told them had she broken out, drenched Lydia's shoulder, and held onto Dotty, happy beyond speaking because she still had two children. Albert smiled wider than she'd ever seen, said over and over, "Lord be praised, Lord be praised. He's delivered your boy." But Tabby surprised Martha most, laughing and crying all at once, like Timmy was her own, until she plumped down on a bench and threw her apron over her head. Martha wondered amid her own uncontainable joy why Tabby wept so for another woman's child. She hadn't thought Tabby cared much about her and her young'uns.

When Dan'l came in, folks trailed after him clapping their hands. Albert barred their way, there being no room for so many. "Well done!" they called after him, as he walked down the aisle to her and Dotty. He gathered them both to him, and she let go and wept on his waistcoat. She could have clung to him the rest of her life, her cheek pressed to his breastbone, like he was a pillar in the sea and if she let go, she'd drown. He held her like nothing could ever take her away from him, until Timothy came in to even louder cheers and clapping, and Dan'l handed her over to her son.

She wept so she couldn't see him proper, only smelled on him what he'd been through. Touching his face, the shape of his nose, the scratchy cheeks, she had a thousand pictures in her mind of him as child, baby, young man, toddler, sunlight on his towhead, hair so blond it was almost white. She held him and felt how he'd grown so strong, and would grow stronger. She held his future to her, that Dan'l had give back to him. And to her.

Jacob Himmelfarb pumped her hand, and all the fringes on his striped shawl danced. "Is good," he said. "Is good." He pronounced 'good' in that funny way he had, to rhyme with 'loot.' He began to say something about Cossacks in the Old Country, but couldn't manage the words for choking. Dan'l patted his shoulder. "It's all right, Jacob. You said before, we're not Cossacks." We being the Vigilantes.

The party could not be contained in the Eatery. It flowed out onto Wallace street and up Jackson to the Melodeon Hall. More people joined in, beer flowed like Alder Creek, and music carried people into the dance. Even Lydia, sober Quaker that she was, looked on smiling. The toe of her shoe peeked out from under her hem, patting the floor in time to the music.

Mr. Van Fleet came in, congratulated Timothy, took her hand in both of his. Seemingly all he could say was, "Dear lady, dear lady. Thank God for your son's deliverance."

He turned to Dan'l, plainly not knowing what to say, but Dan'l stood up and shook his hand and welcomed him to the party, a cool welcome, but better'n nothing. Mr. Van Fleet bowed to Lydia, who colored a little and made room for him to sit beside her.

Con Orem, who'd made his name as a pugilist, spoke to Timmy for a minute or so, until Timmy smiled and nodded, and the two shook hands. Mr. Orem went back to his bar, and Timmy came and stood in front of Dotty with his hand out.

"What did Mr. Orem want?" Martha asked.

He turned the beam of his smile toward Martha. "He offered to teach me to box."

Oh, no, thought Martha. No fighting. The child laid her hand in her brother's, and Martha forgot her fear of Timmy fighting. She glimpsed him someday giving his hand to a special woman, on account there was a future for him, and that future meant grandbabies for her, life on down the generations. Through swimming eyes, she watched Timmy lead Dotty to the dance floor, they two as dignified as only young'uns could be when they try to act grown up.

Lydia leaned across Dotty's empty chair to shout something about handling like glass.

Over the boots' stomping, the rising laughter, the rhythms banging out from the upright piano that jigged across the floor under the piano player's pounding fingers, Lydia shouted to Martha, who couldn't catch more than a few words, "Good ... so many people ... happy ... deliverance." A lull in the noise as two strong men dragged the piano back to its place let Martha hear Lydia's next: "There is joy in Heaven for thee and thy son. 'The hills clap their hands, and the heavens sound their trumpets.'"

A Psalm. Martha couldn't smile any wider. She might have said something; she was thinking, Praise the Lord, but Dan'l shed his coat and vest. The music started again, he held out his hand to her. "Shall we take a chance that I won't fall over?"

Martha rose up to dance.

~32~

SPRING RUNOFF had not entirely stopped. In the high country gleaming snow waited to melt and flow down cold into the channels where miners stood in two seasons, their feet in new-melted winter, their shoulders in summer. They flung their shirts on the bank and by mid-morning worked in their one-piece underwear, by noon they stripped the tops down and knotted the sleeves around their waists. Their trousers were mud-crusted and torn, but they covered as convention dictated because little girls came down after school with their old hairbrushes to clean the rockers and sluice-boxes and cradles, all the contraptions miners built to wash dirt and small stones away from the gold. A woman who came down here, Dan thought, would have to be impervious to shock. The men did not care who saw them. They had one thought – to get the gold. They drove their shovels into the creek bottom and brought up streaming loads of mud and gravel to be cradled, rocked, smashed, and washed into giving up the gold. Most of them had waited all winter and well into the spring from ice to ice melt. In early June they knew the summer would be all too short. A mile up, the nights were sharp.

Dan and Jacob stopped on their way upstream on the road to Summit City. Jacob led the pack mule loaded with surveying gear, chain and tripods for the transit and compass. Dan's mount tugged at the reins. He had not yet enough clients to stop the surveying, and he could not bear to wait in his office, idle, for clients who might come. Surveying would always be his best love; it brought chaotic nature into mathematical order. The law, which sought to bring order out of human chaos, would always be messy.

Tim, bent to his digging, did not see them. He had made a combined sluice box and rocker of his own design, a three-stage device ten feet long, with crosswise slats that trapped larger stones. The usual rocker was open-ended, so water ran in and out, carrying away the gravel and dirt but leaving gold trapped against crosswise slats. Tim's device was closed at the far end, and an additional two floors below laid with differently sized screens in front of slats nailed down in a square U-shape. The water washed the dirt over the slats, which held smaller pebbles and gravel, while the much heavier gold fell through to a removable, triangular tray at the bottom. It worked so well that other miners clamored for him to make the box for them.

"It won't work for long," the boy said.

"Why not?" asked Dan.

"I aim to go underground this summer. Me and a couple others, we'll have the top pretty well worked by the middle of July. We'll sink shafts when the water's low." He stood at the bank, and talked faster than usual, maybe from excitement, or the miner's dislike of stopping for anything. Summers were short here, perhaps ninety days in a good year. Ice would rime the water's edges soon enough. "Put a dam across there," a wave at the upstream edge of his claim, "and channel the flow around."

"Shore it up with timbering?" When Tim nodded, Dan said, "You'll need help."

"We'll do it in trades." By which he meant he and the other miners would take turns helping each other.

"Your mother will worry."

Tim rubbed his arm across his forehead. "Mam knows mining's dangerous. 'Sides, they'll watch out for me, like I do them."

Something made Dan add, "Make sure the timbering's solid." At the irritation that tightened Tim's mouth, he said to himself, So this was why fathers gave their sons unnecessary advice, because they could not say what they meant. Tim would go his own way, just as he had done and still did, and no one to tell either of them the obvious. What would Father have said if he had known about jumping into the quarry?

"I think I'll ride over to the nugget claim later," Dan said. "Want to come?"

"I got plenty here."

Dan threaded the reins through his fingers. The horse shook his head, rattled the bit chains. "I can't stay till the ice comes back. There's a limit to how long Van Fleet will wait, and it's best to get this trip behind me. Are you up to managing both claims?"

Tim shrugged the underwear top off, tied the sleeves around his waist. Sweat glistened on his chest, and he moved his shoulders to keep them loose. "I can't hardly keep up with this'n. How the hell am I going to manage two claims?"

Or three, Dan said to himself. Depending on how the cards fall. My claim. Mine. He rubbed the back of his neck, shifted in the saddle.

Jacob said, "I can help. You do not worry, Daniel. Timothy and I, we work good together."

~33~

ONE HAND RESTING between their bare breasts, the other holding the draperies that covered their loins, the carved ladies on either side of Con Orem's long bar mirror smiled down on the poker tables as if promising a reward to the winner, to open their hands and let the draperies fall.

Would they open for him tonight, Dan wondered.

His back to the wall, he sat at a table tucked into the corner between the bar and a window. Jacob leaned against the bar at his right shoulder, to block the view of anyone trying to see in the mirror when he checked his hole card. He would not check it. He knew what it was, the ten of diamonds. In front of him his three up cards, the nine, six, and seven of diamonds, lay in a sunbeam filtered through a smoke-clogged window. All he needed was the eight of diamonds. The blessed eight.

The hope of it had kept him in this game. More than once a bad hand had turned to gold for him on the last card.

Van Fleet watched the game from the window side. Occasionally, he would scratch an ear, or cough, but mostly he held his hands behind his back and studied the play down the length of his nose. He made no side bets.

Con Orem leaned his elbows on the bar behind Jacob. He flexed his hands, cracked his knuckles, made fists. His nose wandered on its own path over his face. Now he waited, as they all waited, for the last deal. They could not know this one card might fill an inside straight.

A beam from the setting sun lighted the chips in the pot, showed them battered, worn at the edges, cracked.

"All right, gentlemen, here we go." The dealer, Jim Sloan, minus the odorous buffalo coat, flicked a card to each of the players.

Dan's card slid toward him, face down. He turned it over. A three of clubs. His hope splintered. The wooden ladies clutched their draperies.

Jacob said something in his own bastard German.

Van Fleet snorted, "Bah!"

Con Orem said, "Too damn bad. I thought you had a straight flush going there."

"So did I." Dan shrugged. He'd lost fifty dollars tonight, and had yet to play for the claim. The cards had suckered him, one card wooing him, the next tantalizing him, promising him, building his hopes, until this. Lady Luck was laughing, sure. He needed to get out.

Chortling, a man stretched across and raked in his winnings. Thirty dollars of Dan's money. The fool did not know a man never gloated, because the cards could as easily turn against him.

"Bad luck, Stark," Sloan said. "Maybe next time." He retrieved the cards, and stacked them, aligned the edges.

"There's always next time." Ignoring the pressure inside, Dan commented on how long the days were even this early in June, nine o'clock, the sun just setting. Across the street, a dog barked. Canary. "Maybe I'll quit now." Ordinarily, he would. The cards were running against him, had been running against him all evening. He should have quit, would have quit, an hour ago, after the first loss, but he could not quit, and he knew it. Fitch was sitting in, grumbling that the cards were against him, cursing Dan because he'd forced him into this. "You can't quit. We have a deal."

Pretending not to hear him, Dan yawned. "Then again, cards always turn." In his own ears, his voice sounded confident, calm, with no hint of the frustration seething in his stomach.

He stood up to go outside. Someone hissed, "Mudsill." More of Fitch's friends come to cheer the Major on. Con Orem and his bartender were busy pulling the handles on the beer kegs.

Tim and Van Fleet followed Dan around to the back of the building. He had not wanted Tim there, but his authority over the boy extended just so far. Sam McDowell had taught his son about saloons. He could do nothing about Van Fleet, either, except wish him far from here.

Tim said, "You'll quit now, won't you?"

"I can't. I have to play them."

Van Fleet said, "I don't see why. You've been gambling with other people's gold. The Bank's gold. And losing."

"It's damn well not the Bank's gold, it's mine. Mine until I pay the debt. You hear? Mine, dammit, mine." Exploding at the banker did him good. Van Fleet could represent God, and still not tell Dan what to do with the gold. Some of the tension left his neck.

Tim slammed his palm against the wall. "The damn cards are eating you up."

Don't I know that? Dan wanted to yell. Given any other night, without a challenge, he would have walked away. As he'd said, the cards always turned, but how or when no man could say, and wanting made no difference.

"If I could walk away, I would have. Long before this."

For anything else, he could wait for a better time. Not for this game. He stood in the building's deep shadow, willed the carping voices to quiet, and knew that even if he could quit, he would not. To quit would be to forfeit the claim, and that he would not do without a fight. Whether the cards turned in his favor, or not, he could not quit. If he won, the claim would be wholly his. His own claim. He wanted it, and felt himself stiffen with the wanting, his back straighter, his shoulders more square.

Van Fleet began to lecture him, but Jim Sloan, coming around the corner, interrupted. "You here, Stark?"

Dan said, "Did you put that coat out of its misery, at last?"

"Nah. It's too warm for it. I'll bring it out this winter, though, just to hear the bad jokes you like to make." In twilight, his teeth gleamed. "Ain't going so good, huh?"

"No." Dan buttoned his trousers. "At least tonight, I don't have to play with a revolver on my lap. That's an improvement."

Van Fleet gasped. "A – a revolver?"

Dan ignored him as Sloan said, "Sure enough. There was more at stake that night."

"Yeah?" Dan walked toward the saloon's front door, Sloan just behind him.

"Your life, that's all. Just your life."

"Oh, that." Dan pulled open the door. His palms were sweating.

They took their places at the table, five men for this game, and a dealer from Con Orem's staff, as agreed, who would not play but make sure the game stayed fair. They removed their coats to play in their shirts, and rolled their sleeves nearly to their elbows. Fitch's short arm lay on the table as if a hand still ended it. The stump was a tidy pad of flesh folded over the bone. When Dan glanced at it, Fitch said, "The surgeon took pride in his amputations. He said it wouldn't do to offend the thin-skinned."

"No one here answers to that description," said Dan.

"Especially not us, Blue."

Dan nodded, made himself smile. That would be the last friendly word they said tonight.

Con Orem had given them a new deck, and the dealer, breaking it open, said, "The boss is being generous tonight."

Hypocrite, Dan thought. The five-dollar table fee they'd agreed on would more than make up for the expense of the new deck.

"Hell," Sloan said. "It's about time. We've been using the same decks since Discovery." Meaning for a year, going back to the original discovery of gold in Alder Gulch.

Behind Dan, Jacob laughed. Orem, setting two overflowing beers on the bar, said, "Careful, Jim, or I'll ban your coat this winter."

The dealer, who was new to the Gulch, looked shocked at the other men's laughter.

It would be a short game, one hand, winner take all. One way or another, win or lose, this would end his business dealings with Fitch. Because he would not – by God, he would not – be partners with Fitch in a dog pile. God, how he wanted that claim.

Fitch, seated at the dealer's right, cut the cards. The dealer scooped up the stack, and dealt the first hole card to Sloan, at dealer's left, then to Dan, then to Fitch.

As his hole card fell, he heard Tim's ragged breathing. He lifted a corner of the hole card, shielded it from Tim as from any onlooker, and smoothed it down. Ace of hearts. That and a pinch of dust will buy a piece of pie, he told himself. The first up cards fell, a queen of spades to Sloan, a nine of spades to himself, a queen of clubs to Fitch. One of the new men picked up a queen of hearts. The other had a ten of diamonds.

The onlookers were still, and the music came from far away.

A motion from the end of the room, among the dancers, caught his attention. He peered down beyond the dealer. Father walked toward him out of the heavy cigar smoke. The hairs rose on his forearms, and he looked down at his cards, closed his eyes. When he opened them, Father stood behind the dealer's shoulder, his face alight with the gleam of play.

The second up cards floated to the players. Sloan held a five of clubs, Fitch the four of spades. Another ace, of spades, landed in front of him. He had a pair of aces. He'd done it! He had beaten Fitch. He owned the claim. Just two more cards to go. For safety, he checked the strangers' hands. One had the eight of clubs, the other the six of diamonds.

Father disappeared. Dan took a shallow breath. The third up cards sailed out. Dan's card landed face down, about two feet away from him. When he reached for it, Father stood behind Fitch, who rubbed the back of his neck. "Somebody got some ice back there?" Fitch, holding the king of hearts, frowned at Sloan's ace of clubs.

Dan laid his card face up: four of spades. Not that it mattered, he had the pair of aces. Only one more card to go, and no one had anything to beat him. He could feel the jubilation building up inside him: He would own the claim. One more card. He took a quick glance around the table. One stranger had a queen and a pair of eights. The other held a ten, a four, and a six. Sloan muttered over a five, a three, and a ten. Fitch glared at a queen, a four, and a king lying before him. Only the stranger whose eyebrows had grown together over his nose, had a pair. Eights. The other man, even if his hole card doubled his ten, could not win this. The claim was his.

The last card came to him, planing across the cigar smoke. A five of – what did it matter? He held a pair of aces. He looked around. Sloan stared at a king of diamonds, the single brow smiled at a two of hearts. The other stranger shook his head at a jack of clubs and threw down his cards. Fitch grimaced at his five of spades.

They spread out their cards, turned up their hole cards. He turned to Fitch, to ask for a meeting to sign the claim over to him, when the one-browed man whooped. "Lady Luck, I'm in love tonight!"

Not believing it, he stared at the cards laid out on the cracked wood surface. Two pairs. A pair of queens, a pair of eights. The winning hand was not his.

He looked toward the bar mirror, where the ladies kept firm hold on their draperies. Damn.

Father appeared behind the dealer, and as if he had spoken, Dan heard, 'That's my boy,' before he faded into the smoke.

Tim swore, and someone – Van Fleet? – made a growling sound deep in his throat.

God damn it! He had lost the claim.

Taking his notecase out of his coat pocket, he drew out the agreement and handed it to Fitch. Let the one-brow deal with Fitch about it now. He and Fitch were quits. Except for McDowell's other shares, that Martha held.

Barely aware of the stranger and his pals celebrating around him, Dan shouldered his way out of the saloon. You son of a bitch, he scolded himself. You arrogant bastard. All this time he had thought himself better than Father, but he had just proved to himself, to everyone, that he was just like him. As Father – or his ghost – had said. He did not believe in ghosts, though what had it been? A figment of his imagination? That's my boy – bull. Yes, like Father, he had plunged, and the result was as bad as could be.

He had hoped to have something of his own out of this, but he'd left himself with nothing. When he finished in New York, he would have even less. When the debt was paid he would have nothing to show for all his months in Alder Gulch. A year's hard work and monumental risks, to his life, his very soul. What? He would have to start all over.

Worse, he would have to face Martha. He had nothing.

He lifted the latch and went into his house, pulled the latch string in. Martha, in her bentwood rocker, looked up from her knitting and put her finger to her lips. "The child's asleep."

Standing before her, he said, "I lost the claim."

"Oh." Martha finished the row, wrapped the excess yarn around the ball, and thrust the needles through to hold ball and knitting together.

"I lost fifty dollars, too."

Her eyes were cast down, unreadable to him, as she rose to light a candle before blowing out the lamp. "It's late," she said. "Past bedtime." Taking the candle, she walked away from him.

~34~

A SPASM CAUGHT MARTHA while she was taking a pie out of the oven, and only by the Lord's mercy did she put it safely on the table and stick her head over the slop pail before her clenched jaws lost the battle with her stomach. She vomited until she thought she'd heaved up everything she'd ever eaten in her whole life. Shaky and weak, she sat down and rested a spell before she made to get up and chew some dried mint to settle her stomach and refresh her mouth. When she had her legs again, she took the pail to dump it down the privy and rinse it with clean water she pumped at the well.

Dear Lord, no, it can't be that, she thought as she swirled the water in the pail.

But she knew it was. Knew it with a horrid certainty because she had missed May altogether, and now she was way late for June. She flung the water out as far as she could.

In the house, she set herself down on a chair near the stove to try to think, but fear clawed at her mind. She's started a baby by a man she wasn't married to, a man who was set to leave in just a few weeks, and while he'd said he loved her and promised to come back, he'd be seeing the angel again. Rocking forward, Martha buried her face in her hands. She'd be ruined. Ruined. Disgraced and ruined. There'd be no more strolling the town on Dan'l's arm, while gentlemen touched their hats to her and their wives made pleasant remarks about the weather.

The shelf clock pulled back its striker and bonged the hour. Martha flinched. She'd promised that pie to Lydia in time for supper, and she'd best be carrying it to her so's she'd have time to fix supper herself. She knotted the pie in a dish towel and left the house. Canary stretched and wagged his tail like he was hoping to come along, but not feeling up to fetching him back if'n he hared off somewhere, she left him tied up.

All the way down the slope, folks smiled and said how-do, and their friendly greetings pricked at her soul. When she showed, they'd turn their backs and shame her.

Holding the pie by the knot, Lydia inhaled the scent of apple and cinnamon. "Delicious. My, my. Still warm. Are you quite well? Thee had better set thyself a bit."

Martha followed her to the back of the Eatery, though the stove was far too warm for such a fine day. Tabby, stirring something savory in the largest cook pot, nodded to her and paused to wipe her face with a towel hanging from her belt. Would even Tabby nod after she knew? Would Lydia be her friend, or would she draw her skirts aside as from someone not fit to associate with?

Lydia unwrapped the pie and gave Martha the folded towel. She turned Martha's face up to the lamplight. "Thee are looking downright peaked."

Trying to smile, to pass it off as nothing, Martha said, "It'll pass. I drank something that didn't agree." If her trouble was so plain to see, even in this dim room, what must she look like in the sunshine?

Tabby snorted, and at the look Lydia gave her, said, "Yes'm, that's it, no doubt." But her tone of voice denied the words.

Martha tried again. "Mr. Stark isn't leaving for another three weeks, but I think I miss him already." Saying that much, Martha felt as if something gave way inside, and a tear ran down her cheek. "I'm so afeared he won't be coming back here."

"He be coming back," said Tabby. "That's a good man, and he be lovin' you something awful, and he be here before the snow flies."

Lydia said, "Of course he will, but we all know what's plaguing thee, Martha McDowell, there's no point in trying to hide thy condition from thy friends. Thee has started a baby, and he is making thee unwell." She patted Martha's hand.

Martha burst into tears.

She had no defenses against kindness, seemed like she could stand up under whatever hard words anyone wanted to use toward her, but sympathy undid her so that she could only lean on her friend's shoulder and weep into the black ruffles of her dress while Lydia patted her back, saying, "I know, I know. Thee will be just fine. The Lord is with thee." When Martha could, she sat up straight and wiped her eyes and blew her nose.

Lydia made a show of fluffing her shoulder ruffles again until Martha had put away her handkerchief. "Thee are not only bothered by the baby."

Martha shook her head. It was everything along with it. It was not being married to Dan'l, being pregnant with his baby growing inevitably bigger and displaying her disgrace for the whole town, the entire Gulch, to see and know, and him being in New York City. All this, Lydia's face showed she knew without being told.

"Thee are married," said Lydia. "Except for words, except for a piece of paper, thee are married. He is a good man, and he would marry thee if he could. If thee could divorce McDowell. If McDowell were known to be dead. If there were a preacher, he would marry thee."

"I don't know." Martha knew she was close to breaking down again. It wasn't just that, but how could she tell Lydia about the picture in the bottom of his valise, the picture of the angel, Yours, Harriet. He was going back to her, Martha felt it in her bones and along the beating of her heart. Dan'l was going back to Her.

"Especially knowing about the baby, he would marry thee. Has he not said so?"

Martha could only shake her head.

"He has not? I don't – That isn't like – Oh." Lydia lifted Martha's chin until she could look her in the eye. "Thee has not told him?"

Martha shook her head.

"Thee must. Thee must not let him go without knowing he leaves his own child behind."

"No," Martha managed to say.

"He must know. He – He must."

"No."

"But why? Why do thee not tell him?"

It was all Martha could stand, Lydia pressing her and pressing her, and trapping her in this awful corner. "Because. I don't want him obligated."

"Obligated? To his own child? Any man is obligated to the child he fathers, and Daniel Stark is a man who feels his obligations."

"Oh, yes, he does. I know that. I've seen how he feels his duty in New York. How he feels his duty to the law. But I don't want to be a duty to him. If he comes back, it has to be because he wants to.

"I been through obligation before, I obliged Sam to bring me with him, and look how that turned out. I won't have that again." She took a deep breath. Almost, she added, I want him to come back because he loves me. Not because he has a child.

"Daniel Stark is no Sam McDowell, to raise his hand to thee. He'd never—"

"I ain't afeard of Dan'l hitting me. Or the young'uns. It ain't being beat that scares me with him. It's how he'd feel, tied to a duty day after day, years without end." While Lydia thought that over, Martha added, "It's since he lost that claim. If he'd won it, I'd know he was coming back. But without it, he's got nothing to come back to. 'Cepting me."

"That will bring him back," Lydia said. "Thee will see. I think thee are wrong to suffer so. Have faith, in the dear Lord that brought him to thee. Daniel Stark will come back." When Martha said nothing, Lydia sighed as deep as coming from her toes. "We have mint tea. It should have steeped enough now. Would thee like a cup?"

It helped, the tea did, to settle her stomach enough that she could take some nourishment herself and keep it down while she walked home and got busy with their own supper, feeling considerably better. About everything. Except Dan'l coming back.

Have faith, Lydia had said. Have faith.

Lying beside Dan'l in the bed he had bought for them both, his smell resting mellow at the back of her throat, she prayed for faith.

~35~

SHIVERING, MARTHA HUGGED Dan'l's duster to her. The rising sun, low on Mt. Baldy's left shoulder, hadn't begun to warm the day, but it might as well be night creeping over her soul. Dan'l was leaving. He crouched on top of the stage, stretched for this box and that bag, lifted them and set them down without standing up, moving easy though sweat already glistened on his face, him being weighed down with all that dust she'd sewed in the seams of his clothes. When he put the duster on, he'd have more gold weight on him.

Tonight his side of the bed would be empty. She'd wake in the night without him beside her, his breathing, his feet sliding between the sheets, the squeak of springs as he turned over. How would she sleep in that stillness?

Dotty stood beside her, for once without a fidget, just now and then a sniff. A proper Mam would tell the child to use her hanky, but she didn't trust herself to speak, her control was so thin.

From the top of the stage coach he called, "Ready." Albert lifted the big wooden box up as high as he could, and together Dan'l and Timmy, on their knees, stretched down for it, hefted the box onto the top by the rope handles at either end. It was longer than wide, like a box made for rifles, Dan'l having decided to pass for a drummer of long arms. Taking care of the criminals around here and Bannack didn't mean the Vigilantes had turned the whole world into an easy place for transporting gold.

Lord, bring him safe and sound to where he's going and back again. She'd strung that prayer already on a cord long enough to reach clear to Bannack, and was like to be adding to it considerable before she saw him again. If ever.

"Has anyone seen Van Fleet?" Dan'l called.

The driver spat a long stream into the street. "He was at Miz Hudson's tying on the feedbag last I saw 'im. He'd better get here. I ain't waitin' all damn day." For Martha's sake and Dotty's, he touched his hatbrim. "Begging your pardon, Miz Stark. Missy."

"I'll roust him out if need be," said Sheriff Fox.

Another man laughed.

Timmy looked up Wallace Street. "No need. Here they come now."

Martha turned. Mr. Van Fleet strolled along like he had time and time, his small traveling trunk on one shoulder and his valise in the other hand. Beside him Lydia kept up with no trouble at all, and seemed so confidential with him that Martha stifled a cry: Oh, no. There had never been any question of him coming back to the Gulch.

Lydia joined Martha and the child while Mr. Van Fleet stopped by the coach. Dan'l reached down, and Albert took the trunk off Mr. Van Fleet's shoulder and lifted it up to him and Timmy, but he kept the valise. "I'll keep it with me," Mr. Van Fleet said.

"Suit yourself," said Dan'l.

When they had tied everything secure, Timmy jumped to the ground straight from the top, while Dan'l stepped onto the driver's seat, then the wheel hub and down. When Sheriff Fox offered him the Spencer rifle he'd been holding, Dan'l shook his head.

"Good morning." Mr. Van Fleet looked mighty pleased with himself, probably on account he had got Dan'l to leave. Dan'l mumbled something Martha did not catch, and the banker's satisfaction left him, a balloon pricked. Turning his back on him, Dan'l put him outside the circle of men while he shook Albert's hand and Timmy's and Jacob's. What sort of traveling companions would they be? Not comfortable together, surely. Not a bit.

Martha heard her boy say to Dan'l, "Don't worry about nothing while you're gone. We'll be fine."

Dan'l said, "Take good care of your mother and sister."

"You won't have to worry on that score," Timmy said.

Jacob nodded so he set the fringe on his shawl to waving. "Everything will just fine be, Daniel. You do not worry. Just come home. Posthaste." He smiled, his cheeks lifting almost to his eyelids.

Dan'l punched him lightly on the bicep. "Just don't break the transit while I'm gone."

"It is so much time I have to survey, now that I am a miner." Pretending to complain, Jacob could not hide his pleasure. He and Albert would help Timothy keep the claims going, mining on shares, taking their dollar a day wages from the dust they washed, and putting the rest aside for settling up when Dan'l came back.

It all looked so ordinary, Dan'l readying himself for the journey, the men talking of his return, that Martha might almost believe he would come back instead feeling like quicksand waited for her under a thin crust of firm-seeming ground She couldn't shake the notion that she was seeing the last of him.

Mr. Van Fleet looked over at Lydia and smiled. "I shall miss that man," whispered Lydia.

"Mr. Van Fleet?" Martha wished she could have kept the surprise from sounding so plain in her voice. Considering how Joel Van Fleet had pestered Dan'l to hurry up about making this journey, she hadn't been able to warm up to him, herself.

"Indeed. He has been very forthcoming to answer my questions about banking. I have found him a pleasant gentleman of varied business experience." Lydia dabbed her handkerchief at the corners of her eyes.

Martha thought, Glory be, she cares about him.

"I have hopes," said Lydia.

Startled, Martha slid a glance toward her friend.

"Not of that sort," Lydia said as if reading Martha's mind. "I have hopes of his soul opening to the light of the Lord."

"Of course." Martha didn't believe a word of it. She prayed Lydia's feelings had not gone very far, because her friendship with Mr. Van Fleet hadn't progressed near enough for her to think of seeing him again in Alder Gulch.

"No, truly." Lydia dropped her voice to the merest whisper. "Thee still has time to speak."

"I can't. I just can't."

Dan'l shook hands with each of the other men who had come to see him off. Sheriff Fox, Mr. Pfouts, Mr. Sanders, one or two others from Nevada City. They were all there, wishing him a good journey, and come back as soon as might be. Even Major Fitch offered his left hand, and Martha held her breath as Dan'l hesitated before shaking it. "Good journey," the Major took a deep breath. "Safe return, Blue."

"Thank you." Dan'l said.

Timmy led Dotty toward LeBeau's window – "Give them a minute" – and Dan'l's shadow came between her and the sun.

"I don't want to leave you." His blue eyes, that she had come to read his feelings, showed his pain at going, but not like her own.

"Stay, then." At that moment, a voice inside her spoke: Tell him. Tell him he has a baby on the way, but she closed her lips tight to keep the words in.

"You know why I have to go," said Dan'l.

Martha couldn't miss the irk in his voice, and she didn't want him to go like that, so she gave him his duster, and when he had put it on, she slid her hands under it and around him, and laid her cheek against his waistcoat, even though they'd agreed there'd be no public displays at leave-taking, as not being seemly. He held her, and she breathed in the smell of him, clean from his bath yesterday, and warm leather from packing all them pokes into the box this morning, and under all that himself. Just himself.

The driver, finished taking the feedbags off the horses, called out that he'd leave with or without Dan'l. She stood away from him, and they laughed together, his face as red as hers.

Dan'l shook hands with Tim again without speaking. Was it because, like hers, their words were all blocked?

Dan'l gave Dotty a quick hug around her shoulders and said to Martha, "Stay well."

Sheriff Fox handed him the rifle in its scabbard, and he climbed into the stage, and a man slammed the door. As Dan'l's head poked out of the window, the driver shook the reins over the horses' backs. The stage rolled forward. "I'll be home before the ice comes," he called.

The driver cracked his whip over the horses' heads. They pulled into the street and trotted to the foot of Wallace, where they turned the corner around the Leviathan Hall onto the road down the Gulch, and he was gone.

Dotty said, "Mam, he'll be back like he promised. He'll be back."

Would he? Or would the streams freeze over the gold and he not be here?

PART II:
THE GOLD ROOM

~THE ROAD HOME~

AT A TROT, the coach rocked Dan against the coach wall and back on the man to his left. He clutched the Spencer between his knees and wished he were not beginning this infernal journey. His last glimpse of Martha stayed in his mind: how she pulled the shawl tight around her shoulders, raised one hand. Goodbye.

Six men in the coach. Van Fleet in the opposite corner, sitting backwards, facing him. Two drummers selling elixirs for perfect lives, a rancher heading home after contracting his beef to Con Kohrs' butcher shop, and a sharp-eyed man who claimed to be a mining speculator. The rancher smiled. "Ain't everybody some sort of speculator around here?"

They changed horses at Daly's, the outlaws' former headquarters, then at Ramsey's. Bob Ramsey greeted him and shook his hand while stable boys ran to hitch up the fresh team. His half-Indian children played near the house by Alder Creek.

"It's a good summer." Dempsey watched his hands unhitch the traces, lead the team aside to unbuckle their harnesses. He yelled, "Not so rough, there. That's a good horse." Spoke to Dan, "Yessiree, better'n last summer by a long shot." Dan thought the Irish brogue gave his speech an added music.

"Do you ever hear from your old partner?" asked Dan.

"Nope. That darky knew it was too hot for him here, once you fellas hung his pal." Again the wink. "He won't be letting me know where you can find him. Thinks I've the wrong friends."

"He doesn't know, does he?"

"Hell, no. I've kept it dark."

"No one will ever learn it from us," Dan said.

Dempsey clapped Dan on the shoulder. "You fellas are good at keeping secrets." His face hardened. "My wife's uncle was a good man."

Back in the coach, Dan lowered the leather curtain against the dust blowing in on his cheek. You had to admire Dempsey, he thought. The Irishman had played bog-ignorant to perfection, protected his wife and family from his partner's outlaw friends, and silence protected them still. No one would guess how the Vigilantes had come by the evidence that hanged the murderers of his wife's uncle. Old Snag had been a valued man among his people.

The stagecoach rattled and tossed on the rocky, pitted road. A small craft on a restless ocean, thought Dan, only his ass had never taken such a pounding in a boat.

Van Fleet spoke over the creak and rattle. "You'll have to talk sometime, Stark. It's a very long way to New York."

"That where you're going?" asked another passenger. "I'm bound for Salt Lake, myself."

Polite conversation was beyond him, too much effort in this coach, but he offered a minimum and pretended to listen to the others. Like most people, they wished to talk about themselves and loved an audience.

All the time, Martha's sorrowing eyes accused him. Dempsey protected his family, but he could not protect Martha all the way from New York. What if Jacky Stevens made more mischief? Would she bring in the dog and pull in the latchstring? What could he do? Pray? Even if he could, that seemed too paltry, to delegate her safety to a God that might or might not be.

At Bannack they stayed over night. He and Van Fleet left the box in Chrisman's store, behind Henry Plummer's old desk, out of sight. Chrisman's slave, George, would roll some blankets on the floor. "He often sleeps in the store," Chrisman said. "It will be no hardship."

His aching muscles and complaining joints kept him from sleeping well. Martha stood in his dreams. It's only 80 miles, she said, not too late to come home. Against her, Grandfather shouted at him,

You're late. Do you hear? Late.

Van Fleet shook him awake. "Hurry. We'll be late. We'd better eat breakfast quickly." They ate at the same restaurant where he had eaten after the first hangings. As then, men nudged each other and pointed their chins toward him, greeted him on their way out: a nod, recognition in their eyes. Because Van Fleet, the stranger, sat with him, they kept to themselves what they might have said. It was enough. They understood each other, and Van Fleet washed down his flapjacks and bacon with coffee, oblivious to the silent conversation swirling around him.

It didn't have to be this way, memory whispered, and Dan countered: You chose it, you forced it. Not I.

After Bannack, they traveled south round the clock, stopped every seven to ten miles to change horses, sometimes to pick up a new driver and lookout. In the high cold nights Dan welcomed a drink of whiskey to warm his gullet, at every day stop he refilled his canteen with water. His thoughts concentrated on the aches in every part of his body, the constant jolting that broke his sleep, the dust and the heat. Martha's voice calling him home grew fainter.

At Salt Lake he agreed with the driver that they had been lucky. Nothing broke, the horses stayed sound, some hard-looking characters had left them in peace. "Of course –" the man turned his head to spit, "– you look like you're handy with that long arm." He nodded toward the Spencer slung on Dan's right shoulder.

"I don't know about you," said Van Fleet, "but I can't go another mile without rest. Let's stay a day before we go on."

They carried the box to a hotel and put it in their room, took turn about to go to dinner. Dan ate first, returned to wake the banker, undressed, and fell into bed. He woke mid-afternoon to find Van Fleet reading a newspaper.

"The Times," Van Fleet said, "and only two weeks old." But while he gave Dan the main section, he did not share the business news. From that, Dan surmised gold was rising. But to what level? Where was it now? He had to find out without giving himself away to Van Fleet. As long as the banker thought him ignorant of the rising value of gold, and the fall in the value of the greenback, his plan – hardly even a plan, more an idea – was safe.

The next morning they boarded a through coach to Fort Laramie, where they would change to a line bound for Independence, Missouri. Each time they stopped, he or Van Fleet watched to make sure the box stayed safe on top, took turns on guard until the coach was once more on its way. The roads were some better across the plains, and he slept some, but twice they broke an axle. He helped the driver change axles with the spare carried in the boot, and his bruises from the crash screamed as he took his place again. At the hog ranches, where the drivers change horses while the passengers hogged down beans and bread washed down with beer or coffee, it felt like rest to stand up for the few minutes it took to change horses. Then back into the stage. At one ranch, cowboys at play rode a bull that twisted in mid-air and came down on its front feet, threw its heels, and its rider, toward the sky. Dan did not think the cowpoke had a worse journey than he did. The only blessing in the rough ride was to spare him Van Fleet's conversation, save for a few shouted words here and there.

Onward, always onward. At Independence, they switched to train travel. If they had figured the connections right, they would change trains sixteen times before arriving in New York. Van Fleet sent a wire before they boarded the first train. Soot and cinders from the engine blew in through open windows, but when they were closed the train cars, crowded with refugees from the War, became unbearably warm and rank from the stench of used diapers and tobacco juice and unwashed people. Now and then catching a whiff of his own odor, Dan vowed that he would burn everything he wore when he was home. And then pan the gold Martha had sewed in the seams.

Martha. When he dozed, she called him home, but her voice drowned under Grandfather's shouting: Damn you, you should have brought the gold months ago.

The trains made for faster travel, ungodly fast, sometimes twenty-five miles an hour, or even thirty on a down slope. In St. Louis he escaped outside the rail station into the hot and humid afternoon to find a newspaper. People eyed his dust-laden, soot-black duster, the sweat pouring through his beard, and walked wide around him. An urchin in a ragged jacket hawked a newspaper: "Latest news of the war. Five cents. Get your latest war news here."

Dan overpaid with a bit piece that widened the child's eyes. The value of gold, he read, was rising.

No time to stop and enjoy the luxury of a bath. For once, Dan was as eager to arrive as Van Fleet, although he had his own reasons for wanting the business over with. Exhausted though he was, he was keyed up, a race horse coming to the start, a fighter about to enter the ring. The papers he managed to see along the way told him the value of gold was rising, the greenback falling. That meant more greenbacks for the family after he paid the Bank.

Each connection took valuable time. Once they missed a connection because the baggage handlers did not unload their box quickly enough, and he sat up with Van Fleet overnight in the men's waiting room, his feet on the box. Listening to Van Fleet snore, Dan thought of what awaited him at home. He must have dozed, because he saw Grandfather pacing the floor, studying his thick gold pocket watch to see if the minute hand jerked forward, holding it to his ear to listen for each tick that showed the watch still worked. Soon enough he would face the old man's ire. Daniel, come here. He jerked awake, relieved to find himself as himself, a grown man with his feet on a box of gold, a rifle against his shoulder.

Another time they missed a connection because a battle delayed their train. The station agent offered them a room in the hotel while his cousin looked after the box, but Dan misliked the look of the man and the room's location. Judging it better to stay in public with the box, he sent the scabbard up to the room with Van Fleet, kept the rifle, and took the first watch in the lobby. They gave him a comfortable chair by the fire, and he put his feet on the box and leaned the Spencer against his shoulder. He watched a game of seven-card stud, and the hard characters round the table reminded him of some he had helped to hang. When they offered to let him sit in, he smiled. "I'm not much for cards." Yawning, he pretended to fall asleep. Sometime later, feeling a movement at his knee, as if a cat brushed past, he opened his eyes to see a man with his hand outstretched toward the rifle. Dan cocked the Spencer and the ratcheting sound froze the room.

"Sorry," the man muttered. "Don't get your whatsit in a knot."

Dan said nothing, but the Spencer's single eye followed the man to his seat. He let the hammer down easy.

"Whatcha got in that box, anyway, mister?" asked another card player.

"Books." This time he did not have to fake the yawn. "I'm a book drummer." From behind the wall of his smile, he told them silently, Gold. Just gold. More gold than you can imagine. "My friend and I are traveling drummers. We sell books, but we also have a nice little sideline in rifles." He pretended to sigh. "These violent days, though, people would rather have the rifles, so we're still stuck with the books. Nobody reads any more." He patted the Spencer and whined about having to make his own bullets, shot for the gun being scarce, otherwise he'd be pleased to offer them a demonstration, gentlemen, if they were interested.

They squinted at him through the smoke. He imagined he perplexed them, him being a stranger who carried an odd rifle that had no flintlock or any way of loading that they could see, never having known anything but a musket in their misbegotten lives. "No, thanks," they said.

Dan dozed at the fireside and cursed the deal he had made with Van Fleet to let the banker sleep first, for Van Fleet slept all night. I'll sleep in New York, Dan promised himself.

Someplace after Chicago, as they waited in a station for their next connection, Van Fleet asked, "Why don't we rest a night or two? At this rate, we'll be exhausted. It won't do anyone much good to have one of us drop dead."

"The sooner we're in New York the sooner we can finish this infernal business of ours."

This time Van Fleet bought the newspaper and fobbed Dan off with war news, but by now Dan had deduced a connection between Union successes and the rising value of the greenbacks that funded the War. It seemed that when the Union cause prospered, greenbacks rose against gold; with every Union setback, the value of the greenback sank. He bought another newspaper and took it with him to the privy.

By the light filtering between cracks in the three-hole necessary, Dan paged through the paper until he found what he was looking for: Latest Gold Prices. He ripped the page out, folded it, and put it in his inside breast pocket. He tore the next page into narrow strips as if to use the shreds to clean himself and so provide a reason for tearing out the pages. Hearing steps, he swore, but when a stranger entered, Dan was pissing into the hole next to the wall, the paper under his arm, the shredded strips in a pile by the hole.

Back in the station waiting room, he said to Van Fleet, "Washington was nearly taken, but the Rebs retreated."

"Damn." Van Fleet held out his hand. "Do you mind if I read about it?"

Dan gave him the paper and prepared to make himself as comfortable as possible on the wooden bench, grateful that at least it backed against the wall. Tugging his hat down to his eyebrows, he stretched his legs out on the long box and folded his arms across his chest. The Spencer in its scabbard leaned against the wall by his right arm. He wanted to know what the gold prices were, but he could not look while Van Fleet sat across from him. Would the damned man never use the privy?

"I shall return in just a few minutes," said Van Fleet.

When Van Fleet's steps had faded across the gravel yard, Dan took the newspaper page out of his pocket to read the "Latest Gold Prices." It was a small table of gold values in greenbacks for the preceding two weeks, July 5 - 19. Reading the numbers, Dan felt unsteady, and a light shimmered in a jagged curve at the edge of his vision. On July 11, the day Jubal Early's forces surrounded Washington, the value of $100 in greenbacks had sunk to $35.09 in gold. Jesus Christ! Six months ago, the greenback was worth $64 against $100 in gold. It was now worth 55% of its January value.

Dan's mind stuttered among parts of calculations, and he could come to no answer. How much was his gold worth in greenbacks? Twice as much as he had thought? But he would not know until it was minted. How could he estimate it? Sweat ran down his ribs. He would tell Van Fleet he had caught a fever. The son of a bitch would stay away from him then.

From afar he felt a vibration, next heard the rumble of large wheels, and the baggage man called out from the doorway to the platform that their train was coming. Dan refolded the paper and tucked it into his breast pocket. He and the baggage man were carrying the long box to the baggage cart when Van Fleet returned. "You missed a button," Dan said. Van Fleet faced the empty room while he corrected the mistake. When he returned for his valise and the Spencer, Dan was satisfied that his knowledge of gold prices was safely hidden away. He wiped his face and neck, tucked away the handkerchief, but Van Fleet, mounting the steps into the train car, did not notice anything odd.

The conductor punched and tore their tickets, and gave back the stubs, but Dan hardly knew it. He searched among calculations, the arithmetic of gold. On the Exchange, thirty-five dollars in gold would buy $100 in greenbacks. The gold he brought from Alder Creek might be worth nearly three times as much as he had thought. More than $100,000. In greenbacks. Paper currency.

North of the Harlem River, they changed to the last train, the New York and Harlem Railroad, saw to the loading of the box and valises into the baggage car, and settled onto the plush seats. The clack of iron wheels over the rails beat the same phrase along Dan's veins: Greenbacks and gold. Greenbacks and gold. His heart caught the rhythm and beat along with the train. He stared out at the changing landscape. The city was growing; small farms yielded to encroaching buildings. The train ran down Manhattan alongside carriages and drays whose horses shied from the great iron horse that overtook them. Would the day come, he wondered, when a man could travel in such speed and comfort all the way West?

The buildings stood closer together as they rumbled farther south. The smells of New York, compounded of smoke and horse dung and thousands of meals cooking, blew in with soot on the warm damp air. Someone had opened a window ahead of him. At Twenty-First Street the train slowed for Union Place, where they would get off. Mother, out of mourning black and wearing purple, held a parasol to shade her face and sought him among the windows. He waved. The train, slowing, passed them, but she saw him and pointed. Not caring about cinders blowing back from the engine, he raised the window and leaned head and shoulders out to wave. The entire family had come to meet the train. Mother picked up her skirts and fairly ran toward him. He had never seen her so forgetful of her dignity. Grandfather, more stooped and leaning on a walking stick, Grandmother's hand tucked into the crook of his elbow. Florentine, his sister – in a delicate condition – let go of her husband's arm, and Arthur snatched his hat from his head and pelted after the train, never mind his clerical collar, his parson's black suit. He left them all behind, dodged a small dog and its owner, jumped over a porter's step-stool, and ran alongside, waved his hat in the air and shouted into the shriek of brakes something that Dan could not hear. After Arthur, Nathaniel ran, leaving behind the two small children, the offspring of his parents' later blooming, who ran as fast as they could, jostled each other like puppies.

He could not see for the blurring in his eyes – those damned smuts. God! How he loved his family! He had done it all for them, and here he was, home with the gold at last.

The train jerked to a stop, and he staggered, regained his balance, and reached up to the luggage rack for his case. The porter hardly had the vestibule door opened and the steps lowered when Arthur bounded in, shouted, "Daniel! Daniel! Welcome home!"

As the two men pounded each other on the back, Dan thought how much he liked Arthur, had liked him from the first because Arthur was human despite his profession, and he liked him even more now that Arthur had sheltered the family after the debacle of Father's disaster.

"Did you get it?" Arthur asked, because Dan, fearing that letters could be opened by robbers – as they often were – had not written about gold.

"Yes," Dan glanced around. Van Fleet had descended to the street, and the other passengers gathered their parcels and wraps. No one seemed to listen, but his habit of secrecy went too deep.

"Thank God," said Arthur. "Thank God!"

Dan pointed out Van Fleet, who stood looking toward the baggage car. "The bailiff."

"So that's the one," Arthur said. "The Judge said the Bank sent a representative." He looked at Van Fleet with no liking in his eyes.

"Apparently, they didn't trust me to return," said Dan.

"It wasn't only you, Daniel. It's all of us." He held Dan back. "They've been convinced that we had a plot to defraud them."

"Son of a bitch," muttered Dan. "Still, it stands to reason, doesn't it?" He slung the Spencer on his left shoulder, put on his hat and draped his duster onto his left arm. "After Father, we have little right to expect anyone's trust."

In the street, he introduced Arthur and Van Fleet, then turned to greet the children. He wanted to gather them all into his arms one by one, toss each one into the air as he had used to do, but they had all matured into miniature adults, and were shy of him. The older boy, Nathaniel, was now fourteen, and of them all looked the most like Father. He offered his hand for a handshake, and called him Sir. Dan resisted an urge to ruffle his hair: None of that 'Sir' stuff, young man. But he shook hands with both of his brothers and hugged his youngest sister for a moment with his unencumbered arm, and knew an instant's grief that she would never again be the little girl who had climbed into his lap for a story. He had missed a year of her life and she was taller, a ladylike seven.

Near the head of the train, baggage men unloaded trunks onto large hand carts. He did not see the box. Yet. He turned back to the family, and found Florentine, dear Flo, smiling at him. Never one for the more useless proprieties, she drew his face down and laid her cheek against his, whispered, "Dearest brother. How I have missed you, this horrid year."

He replied, "As I have missed you."

She laughed, her palm against his bearded cheek. "Oh, I doubt that. You have been far too busy with your peculiar Western adventures."

He hardly heard her, for he was looking into Mother's eyes. All his questions flooded into his mouth: How have you borne this year of Father's disgrace? How have you fared? He had hated to leave her at the mercy of Grandfather and the city's harpies, who would tear her heart to bits. Wanting to gather her to him, but mindful of his stink, he murmured, "I'm back."

Smiling, she dabbed a handkerchief at her eyes. "Thank God."

Looking over her hat, he glimpsed Grandfather's white head. The old man stepped along, more slowly, but with the imperious carriage of a lifetime near the top of men's affairs, when other men courted his good opinion. Before Father's crimes became known.

"I had better see to the goods." Dan gave his arm to Mother, and walked the four or five car lengths to the baggage cars.

And as he watched the box being wrestled out of the baggage car, heard the curses of the baggage men at the weight of the damn books, his father's elegant form appeared in the back of the car, dim among the things yet to be brought out. His father raised his gloved hand to his eyebrow in a salute to his son, but as Dan heard Grandfather's voice, Father vanished.

"You're late," Grandfather said. "You should have returned eight months ago."

Dan laughed. He could think of nothing to say, but as his laughter boomed out over the box now being hefted onto the carts, he knew that after this outlandish greeting, nothing Grandfather could ever say would touch him. The silly old fool. The silly old fool who thought his own perspective was the only one, himself the world around which other worlds rotated, if indeed there were any other worlds at all.

Van Fleet said, "I shall arrange for the goods to be brought to a suitable storage."

Dan smiled. "Your bank, perhaps?" Before Van Fleet could do more than begin to nod, Dan said, "No. We will take them to the Assay Office, and they will remain there under my signature. They are still my goods, however they will be disbursed later."

"You can't mean that! You —You —" Van Fleet sputtered.

Moving the scabbard-held Spencer from his left to his right shoulder, Dan said, "I assure you, they will be better guarded at the Assay Office than anywhere else." The family gathered in a small group a few feet away, and in the periphery of his vision he was aware that Mother's hand wore only one ring, that his younger brothers' trousers had been let down, that Florentine's parasol needed mending where the lace edging had come loose, but that Grandfather's shoes gleamed. Father's crimes had been enough for them to bear; he would not let them be the Bank's victims by allowing Van Fleet to take possession of the gold.

"The Assay Office is closed until Monday," said Arthur.

Dan had lost track of days and dates. He raised an eyebrow at his brother-in-law.

"Today," said Arthur, "is Saturday, the thirtieth of July, in the year of our Lord —"

"I do know the year," Dan said.

Arthur smiled. "And the time is seven forty-eight of the clock. In the evening."

Van Fleet glared at Dan. "Have I your word that you will —"

Dan moved close enough to the banker to catch his smell. "Do you think I've done everything with any intent but to make restitution? Do you think I would have risked everything to commit another fraud? If you think that, your time in Alder Gulch was utterly wasted. You learned nothing." And between them, as the crowds thinned and the baggage handlers moved the loaded cart toward the rank of taxi-carriages waiting for custom, there was the sound of ice breaking.

~2~

THE FAMILY LIVED in Arthur's house, the manse to St. David's Episcopal, where he was the rector. The house, three-storied and topped by a servants' attic, was narrow, and flanked on either side by taller brownstones. It stood on the north side of West Fourth Street, a few doors from Mercer Street. When they had been forced to sell their own house, Arthur offered them shelter in the manse. Dreadfully inconvenient, Mother had complained to Dan, but its location, near Washington Square, stopped her from complaining where Florentine could hear.

Arthur had saved them from squeezing into a rat-infested tenement walkup, Dan thought; he probably exaggerated, but not by much.

With Arthur hovering close just in case, and Van Fleet following them, he carried the box up the front steps and into the foyer. He set it down and escorted the banker onto the stoop. "The gold will be as safe here as in your vault." When he would have protested, Dan closed the door on him, picked up the box and carried it into the dining room, where he set it in a corner behind the door.

Grandfather thumped his stick on the floor. "That gold belongs to the Bank."

He rounded on the old man so fast that the scabbard flung

outward from his shoulder and knocked against the sideboard. "No, it does not. It belongs to me. I earned it, I brought it home. It is mine until I pay the debt."

"You were merely acting as an agent of the family."

"Do you want to prove that in court?" Without putting the thought into speech, Dan told him, I am as familiar with the law of agency as you are, and I have practiced law where losing meant death.

The old man's stare broke. "How much did you bring?"

"Almost seventy-five pounds." Not counting the gold on my person, Dan said in his silence.

Grandfather, always quick at sums, groped behind him for a chair and sat down. "That is not enough. Do you mean to tell me that in nearly a year that's all you were able to gather?"

"How do you think gold is acquired? It's not picked up off the ground in chunks. It has to be dug or blasted out and washed from the soil or broken out of the rock."

"You had a year. You could have brought it all," Grandfather said.

Sunlight through the window ricocheted from a mirror and splintered red, blue, purple shafts into his eyes. He swayed, and the rifle in its scabbard slid from his shoulder. He leaned on it. A fog thick as felt lurked at the edge of his thoughts.

"Jason." Mother's voice pierced the grey felt. "How dare you? Can you not see how weary Daniel is, how he has suffered to bring this fortune to us?" She held up her palm. "No. No more. He must rest. There will be time enough later."

Arthur took his free arm, and turned him toward the door; Nathaniel on his other side carried the rifle. Grandfather's voice, arguing, followed them upstairs, to the top floor, the servant's attic. They showed him into a gabled room where he could stand up straight only in the center. Nathaniel stood the rifle in a corner, and Dan heard his footsteps clatter down the stairs.

Arthur said, "You're exhausted. What would you like? A drink? A bath? Food? Name it. Anything in our power is yours."

"All of it." Dan eyed the narrow bed. "Later."

"I'll come back."

He stopped Arthur with his hand on the latch. "Wait. The gold."

"It will be where we left it when you awaken. Have no fear."

Dan tossed his duster on the floor, where it landed with a thud, stripped off all his outer garments and tossed them onto the pile, slid his underwear below his knees. Two pokes of gold dangled below his waist from galluses over his shoulders. Unbuckling the pokes, he laid them on a schoolboy's desk placed directly under the room's only window. He picked at the ties that held a wide, thick pad of gold like a money belt, made of oilcloth, around his waist. A memory of Martha's smooth dark head bent over her sewing in the lamplight sent a spasm of homesickness shuddering through him. She had worked these close stitches, and they had held this gold for nearly 3,000 miles. Trembling, he laid the belt on the desk, too, and leaned on both hands. How soon could he go home? Be with her again?

Naked, he stretched his arms out wide, arched his back. Without the gold, having only his own body to carry, he felt almost weightless. He yawned, his jaws crackled. He ought to have a bath, shave, and wash his hair, but the hell with it. Just as he was, he put his body, freed of the gold, between sheets that smelled of New York, somewhat smoky with a resonance all the city's own, as the flavor of some wines lingers on the soft palate. Outside, a carriage horse whinnied, shod hooves clopped on paving stones, carriage wheels rattled, a young woman called to a friend. In the house, footsteps climbed up and down the stairs, but none approached this aerie. Weary as he was, he lay listening to these unfamiliar sounds as if he sat up in that smoking pit of an inn by Erie. The habit of keeping watch stayed with him.

He smelled apples cooking. Martha took a pie out of the oven; she held it in her towel-wrapped hands and offered it to him.

~ALDER GULCH~

TIM LIFTED THE SLEDGE HAMMER high over his head, brought it crashing onto the rock, raised it again and smashed it down, and the rock split apart, the pieces tumbling into the stream bed. He wiped his arm across his sweating forehead. He could manage the durn thing now. He knelt and dipped his cupped hands into the stream, for a drink. A fella worked up a powerful thirst at this. He tossed the pieces of boulder farther up onto the bank and climbed up after them. One by one he broke them into ever smaller rocks. When he had dirt and small pebbles, he would shovel them into the sluice box and release the water flow dammed at the top of his claim.

All the time, his mind picked at a problem. He'd soon have to go underground, dig a shaft and tunnel outward, to follow the pay streak. That took two men at least, and maybe as many as four. He could do it in shares with the men on either side of his claim, but did he trust them? Some folks thought he was just a boy, wet behind the ears.

After breaking up the smaller rocks, he took up the smaller sledge and broke them as small as he could, then shoveled the dirt and pebbles into the sluice box. He bet that new stamp mill broke up rocks real fine. One of these days he'd have to look into that.

"Tim! Timmy!" A girl's shout caught his attention as he opened the wooden dam to let the stream flow through. Dotty. Smiling, he leaned on the shovel to watch her, in her oldest dress and apron, skip toward him, hairbrush in one hand, a poke in the other. She was coming to help him by cleaning the sluice box. Whatever gold she cleaned out, he let her keep.

"Hey, Miss Dotty," called a man at another claim, and his cry echoed upstream and down as other neighboring miners stopped their work to shout a greeting and wave.

"Hey, Mister Bob." Dotty waved and greeted each man by name, seeming not to notice where her feet landed as the bank grew steeper, and she leaped from rock to rock. Landing with a plump a few feet from him, she said, "Hey, Timmy."

"Hey, Dotty."

"What can I do?" She raised an arm to shield her eyes from the sun, and a seam ripped. "Oh, Lordy." She dropped her arm to hide the tear. "I'm growing too fast." Her eyes filled.

"Now, come on." Tim shoveled more dirt and new made gravel into the sluice box. "Mr. Dance and Mr. McClurg have new stuff. You can take a pattern and —"

She interrupted him. "I'll have to take a pattern from an old dress and sew it, and Mam will make me rip it up if the stitches aren't small enough because the seams have to be strong, and she won't let me play outside till it's done."

"Go on with you. Mam won't make you sit in all summer." Shoveling fast to keep up with the water flow, he heard her say, "By the time I finish it, it'll be too cold to wear cotton, and next year I'll be grown out of it before I wear it, but it won't matter, it was out of style to start with."

"You could make it a size or two larger and have it ready for next year."

She acted like she did not hear him, but knowing Dotty, he figured she ignored him. "Of course," she added, "when Dan'l comes home, he may bring me something from New York."

He heard her rattling on, speculating on what Dan'l might bring her, like New York was the Heavenly City and he would bring her the grail, but he paid her no mind. She was always going on about something, and he added another thought to his pile of worries: What if Dan'l didn't come back? He'd never let on to Dotty or Mam he was afeared of that, but he was.

At last, when the water had washed the dirt and gravel out of the box, he closed the dam to stop the water flow. Gold had fallen through and lay shining on the bottom tray. He pointed. "Ain't that a pretty sight?"

"Ooh, yes." She hunkered down to admire it. He lifted out the tray. Its triangle shape made it a workable funnel for him to pour the gold into his poke. "Are you coming home for supper?"

"No. I want to catch as much daylight as I can." The summer solstice was a month back, and the days were already considerably shorter.

"Then let's clean out this washing, and I'll fetch your dinner to you."

Together they cleaned the sluice, until Dotty complained, "Isn't it clean enough now?"

He allowed as to how it was, and went back to digging into the stream bed while she brushed at the cracks around the slats. When the dust was safe in her poke, she said, "So long. I'll bring your dinner down."

Nodding to show he'd heard her, Tim picked up the sledgehammer to smash a large rock. He had nearly broken it when he heard her shriek. Dropping the sledge, he scrambled up the bank and saw Jacky Stevens, knife pointing at Dotty, his other hand out for the poke. Men ran toward them, but none as fast as him. He got there first, ran straight into Jacky and knocked him to the ground, rolled over with him, grabbed the smaller boy's wrist until he dropped the knife.

Tim raised his fist. Jacky squirmed and struggled at the end of his other arm, lips drawn back in a snarl, looking like a mad dog fighting to get away.

A man bellowed, and Dotty's scream penetrated the roaring voices inside urging him to hit Jacky, smash him to a bloody pulp, and he remembered Dan'l lying still in the mud. He opened his hands. Snarling, Jacky backed away, until he bumped up against the wall of men summoned by the commotion.

"You bother that little girl again, and you'll answer to us," said a miner.

He would never want to be the one the miners' growl was aimed at. He put both arms around Dotty, who huddled against him, shivering and sobbing.

"You come near her again, or any of mine, Jacky Stevens, and I won't stop."

"Yeah? You watch out, y'hear? One of these days you-all won't be so high and mighty. That Dan Stark ain't never coming back, y'hear? Never. Just like your Pap."

~NEW YORK CITY~

SOMEONE KNOCKED at the door, but why did the dog not bark? What bed was this? The knocking sounded louder, and Dan came awake. He was in Arthur's house. In New York. When he lay down, the setting sun had been shining, as it did now, on the opening door. Had he not slept then? Why would someone wake him already?

"Come in," he called.

Arthur stepped into the room. "How are you?"

"Is anything wrong?" Dan stretched, relaxed. "What time is it?"

"It's time you cleaned up for dinner."

"But I just got to sleep."

Arthur laughed. "You slept all night, and all day. It's Saturday evening. We can't wait any longer to hear about your adventures. And see the gold."

He eyed the pile of clothes on the floor, and from his expression Dan decided he must look like a wild man from Borneo – unshaven, his hair long and matted. He flung back the top sheet, swung his legs over the edge of the bed. The chamber pot in its discreet wooden box occupied a corner, and he needed it urgently.

Arthur cleared his throat. "In order not to discommode the servants too much, we have a bathroom on the floor below. I've asked to

have it filled for you. If you need anything else, just use this bell pull – "
he nodded toward a thick velvet rope that hung on the wall "– and either
one of the servants will come as far as the landing below."

Dan rose, bumped his head on the sloping ceiling, sat down
again.

"Have you something to cover yourself with?" Arthur asked.

Looking down at himself, Dan shook his head. He had forgotten
he was naked.

"I'll bring you a large towel and a robe." Arthur bent to pick up
his clothes.

"Leave them," he said. Arthur dropped a garment and
straightened, his face shocked at the sharp tone. "Sorry. I'll deal with
them later."

"They're fit for nothing but the trash," said Arthur.

"I know, but they're full of gold. I'll burn them outside and pan
the ashes."

In the painted cast iron tub, which, unlike his own galvanized tin
one, did not leak, Dan soaked the travel grime, the dust and smoke
and cinders, out of his skin, and washed his hair and beard three times
before he was satisfied that they were clean. Wrapping himself in the
large towel, he found his room again. Hot water stood in a pitcher
ready for him to shave, and the clothes from his valise – along with
the suits, trousers, shirts that he had left behind in New York – were
hung in the cupboard. His underwear was put away in a small chest.

When he realized that someone had stacked the belt and the
pokes on an empty bookshelf, he sucked in a breath and could not
exhale until he had counted them all.

He looked at himself in the mirror and decided that a barber
would attack the beard and his hair. He dressed and went downstairs.

So much about home he had not thought of. How lamplight
gleamed on cut glass, how silver glowed against a polished cherry table
top. His mother smiling through candlelight. Summer air stirring
burgundy-colored drapes. Children squirming on their chairs through
endless adult conversation, glancing sideways at Grandfather, whose
presence at the head of the table repressed everyone, as always.

But in the refraction of light through crystal, he noticed that the
corners of Flo's eyes were pinched. Grandfather's head had sunk
toward his shoulders, and his back was more stooped. Mother's face
had deep lines from her nose to her mouth, and a new furrow creased
the skin between her eyebrows. Someone had lengthened little Peggy's

sleeves by turned back cuffs long out of style; she tugged at the sleeve hems. Grandmother dabbed at her eyes with a patched handkerchief.

A drape caught on the box in the corner. The lining had been mended at least twice.

There was not enough gold.

Grandmother, across from him, asked how he had slept, and Dan made the required polite reply, though he was thinking of the gold in his clothes and on the desk. He would not give it to the Bank. Grandfather, seated at the head of the table, grumbled that the wine was inferior, as if Arthur, who for charity's sake had taken them all into his house, should provide better. Anger flared in Dan's belly. The old bastard sat in Arthur's place with Arthur at his right, and Flo at the foot. Mother sat across from Dan between Jeremy and Peggy, while Nathaniel sat between Dan, next to Flo, and Arthur.

The seating was wrong. In Arthur's house, Arthur should sit at the head of the table. Perhaps Arthur's Christianity did not allow him to claim his proper place, but turning the other cheek had turned him out of his chair.

The drape struggled against the wooden box.

Grandfather grumbled about inferior cooking. Buying cheaper cuts of meat was obviously the result of inefficient housekeeping on Flo's part, and Arthur's eyelids tightened, his mouth opened. Flo shook her head. Arthur closed his mouth, but a pulse beat in his temple.

Breathing a silent apology to Martha, Dan said, "Florentine, you really must congratulate your cook. This joint is done to perfection. I have not had so well-cooked a meal since I went West." Dearest Martha, you could make an elderly buck tasty and tender.

Grandfather said, "Your tastes have been seriously lowered by your sojourn in rough country. You have been keeping low company."

Daniel regarded the old man over the rim of his glass. The wine was a truly inferior burgundy. "Not so, Grandfather." He carved a bite of meat, loaded a bit of spinach leaf onto it, and held it. "I have been eating the best of wild game, much of which I shot myself. There is nothing so succulent as a two-year-old buck, or a young antelope, or a buffalo cow's hump. Beef can be quite bland after that, but this –" he inserted the bite into his mouth and chewed, pretending to savor the tough cut while they all waited, mocking Grandfather's habit of keeping them waiting so. Mother's mouth twitched at the corners, and Florentine hid her smile in her napkin. Arthur choked on a swallow of wine, and Nathaniel pounded him on the back. The children watched

Dan with round eyes and mouths. When he judged the joke had gone far enough, he swallowed, sipped wine. "This is excellent."

"Do you really hunt like that?" It was Nathaniel, curious about the West, and perhaps, Dan thought, envious of his older brother's adventures. God help him.

"Yes, if I want to eat. We have a few stores, but they are hard pressed to keep enough goods for all the people who need them. Fortunately, game is plentiful."

"Why can't they keep enough stock?" Flo asked.

"Because the closest supply centers are Salt Lake City, 700 miles south, or Fort Benton, 300 miles north. Both routes cross high mountain passes. This winter, deep snow blocked the passes for more than a month."

"What are the amusements?" Mother asked.

"We depend on ourselves, and there is a wealth of talent. The Drama Club puts on plays, and we have a Philosophical Club, a debating society, a community band, and a choral society." He leaned aside for the maid to clear his plate and gather the silverware he would not need for dessert. "I'm a member of the Union Club, and the Confederates have their own society, I understand. The miners court is sometimes a source of amusement."

"Miners court?" Flo rested her knife and fork on her plate for the maid.

"Yes." He smiled. "I have resumed the practice of law as well as my surveying business."

Grandfather asked, "There is much contract law, then?"

"More than you might think, Grandfather, but my main practice is criminal law." He swirled the wine in his glass, and Mother pushed the decanter toward him. "This past winter I prosecuted murderers and robbers."

"Oh!" Grandmother laid her fingers over her mouth. Smiling at her, Dan thought of her long marriage to a man who believed that women's delicacy was warped by reading newspapers.

Sure enough, Grandfather's face reddened. "This is not fit conversation for the company of ladies and children. We shall not speak of it in their presence again."

"The women of Alder Gulch stood up to the subject with a most becoming courage."

"I notice you speak of women, not ladies. Such subjects and experiences unsexes them."

So had he once thought, and to his shame Dan remembered having said the same thing. A warmth crept into his face that he felt sure the beard could not hide. Memories of Martha: in their bed, kneeling astride him, her face turned up, her eyes closed. Her fierce attack on a rattlesnake. Dan said, "The ladies of my acquaintance are not unsexed because their courage equals a man's. If anything, they are more interesting."

"Bah!" Grandfather gestured at Dan with his fork. "What sort of place did you come to?"

"A place of good intentions. During the winter we instituted certain reforms, though a stable system will have to await the outcome of Chief Justice Edgerton's mission to Washington." He hoped no one recalled the saying that the road to hell was paved with good intentions.

Arthur said, "Then you don't know? I read – oh, about two months ago – President Lincoln signed an Act making a new Territory. Montana, I believe it's called. Does that affect you?"

"Yes." Dan sat back in his chair. Montana Territory. So Edgerton had succeeded.

"I don't see how it could." Grandfather dabbed at his mouth with a white linen napkin patched in one corner. "It is not as if Daniel's place were out there. His place is here. With us. This is his home." He glared at Dan as though challenging him to deny that.

The maid brought in the dessert, apples and cheddar cheese on a board, with coffee, and as she opened the door, a breeze through the window blew out a candle. Dan rose to shut it, and freed the drape from the box. Turning to sit down again, to cross six feet of highly waxed floor, he seemed to see this family he loved as if on the other side of a great canyon, and his stomach tightened. He could never again be at home here. Home was at the foot of a wind-blown knoll where five hanged men lay in a row. Home was a little brown sparrow of a woman who knew what he had done and forgave him. Home was Montana Territory. He tried the strange word on his tongue, rolled it about with the wine. Montana.

~2~

EVENING SUNBEAMS SLANTED across the table and caught the glistening stream of gold that Dan poured from the poke, shimmering flakes collecting in a glittering pile on white paper. Setting aside the poke, he looked at their faces. Wonder turned them into caricatures – parted lips, wide eyes, and a stillness to their breath. Especially the children. Even Grandfather.

Dan tore another piece of paper into pieces. He put about a teaspoonful of gold on the bigger ones, a pinch into a couple of the smaller, and twisted them closed. The small twists he gave to the children, the larger ones to Nathaniel and the women. "A souvenir," he said, "of Alder Gulch, Montana Territory." As they grasped the papers, their dazzled eyes thanked him.

"Now to business," said Grandfather. Arthur opened the dining room door. Shepherding the children ahead of them, Mother and Florentine, with tightened lips, followed Grandmother out. In the hallway, Mother looked back and caught Dan's eye. He winked, a silent promise to tell her and Flo everything. She smiled.

Arthur brought the decanter of port, with glasses, on a silver tray. As he set it on the table, the declining sun turned the room to shades of red and silver – Arthur's carroty hair, the deep red wine, the cherry table, the silver tray and candlesticks. Through the open windows, a cooler breeze carried the city's pungent smell of roses and horse droppings.

Pouring wine, Arthur could hardly look away from the gold.

Dan stood, tilted the decanter upward. "Better let me pour."

"Oh. Right." By the absent tone of his voice, Arthur might not have registered that Dan took the wine away from him. "Do you know how much it's worth?"

"No exactly. The assays in the Gulch were crude." He lied, but saw no reason to recant.

"How much did you bring?" asked Grandfather.

He reseated himself where young Jeremy had sat, his right shoulder toward Grandfather, and stretched out his legs. The old man preferred to have other men sit square to him, as the center of their attention, but Dan would not give him the satisfaction. The imperious hawk nose, brows pulled into one above his close-set eyes – Grandfather's face showed that he had hardened instead of mellowing. He had not grieved, that Dan knew.

He remembered Grandfather's three-part tread behind him as he ran to Father's closed door after the shot, how Grandfather had pushed him aside as he held breathless in the doorway, fighting nausea, at the sharp cordite smell scratching at the back of his nose through the reek of blood. He'd heard a slow drip, and Grandfather cursing. Cursing Father.

The port lay sweet and thick against Dan's soft palate. He inhaled its colors along with the flavors of the city, swallowed, and put the glass down. He did not like port any more. It was like the air of Manhattan Island, heavy and cloying. He longed for crisp, dry mountain air.

"Well?" Grandfather prompted him.

"As I said," he replied, "nearly seventy-five pounds."

Arthur brought the port to his lips, but did not taste it. His eyes met Grandfather's. "Is that enough to pay the debt?"

"No." Grandfather touched the top of the smaller heap of gold. A few flakes dislodged and slid down, as if a live thing shuddered.

"What is gold worth here?" asked Dan.

"Who knows?" said Arthur. "It fluctuates daily. Yesterday the premium fluctuated between 258 and 253. Today being Sunday, of course, the markets are closed."

As if the big standing clock stopped, its pendulum poised

between tick and tock, Dan's flow of thought broke, blanked, started again, echoed Arthur: between 258 and 253. And on July 11, just twenty days ago, according to the *Times* article, it had traded – he made a rapid calculation, divided $100 by $35.09 – at 285. And now it traded at 258? That meant the value of gold had dropped 27 points, which in turn meant the greenback had to be worth about $39 rather than $35.09. No wonder Van Fleet had pushed him for an early meeting to pay back the debt. The bank would want to pay out greenbacks. If this downward trend continued, they would increase in value and the exchange would be worth less to the bank. And to him.

Dan said, "It's dropping, then." That confirmed his suspicions during the journey.

"Yes." A few flakes of gold stuck to Grandfather's fingers. He brushed them off onto the pile. "You should have brought it sooner and saved us some of the interest." He glared at Dan. "You've failed."

Arthur set the small glass on the table so hard that a few drops splashed over and pooled on the polished surface. He brought out his handkerchief to mop the spill.

Failed, had he? A pulse beat in Dan's eyes. "In the first place, earlier I would have had even less gold. Second, had I tried to bring it home then, I and the gold would have been lost."

"Lost? What do you mean?" Grandfather demanded.

"Killed," Dan said. "Murdered. For the gold."

"You can't know that," Grandfather said, "not for a certainty."

"I do know it. It was certain. Anyone who traveled with gold took a grave chance."

"Pah! Such dangers are greatly exaggerated."

Inside, Dan yelled at Grandfather: you damned old fool, you know nothing of that danger, and because you know nothing you choose not to believe. Your atheistical attitude condemns you to ignorance.

"We must arrange a meeting with the bank before gold sinks further," said Grandfather.

God damn it, fumed Dan. You and Van fleet might as well be in cahoots to rob the family. Across his thoughts, boots swung and kicked in mid-air. In order to bring this gold home, he had done what he had done. In order to ensure the family's future, he would do as needs must.

It is my gold and I will disperse it as I see fit, he vowed, and seeing his opposition clearly, as in court or outside, he became calm. "Have you any Scotch?" he asked Arthur in as mild a voice as he could muster. We will settle this tonight, he promised himself.

"Yes, I do. I laid in some single malt because Florentine said you liked it." From a lower cabinet of the sideboard, Arthur took an unopened bottle of Scotch.

"Thank you, I do like it." He would repay Arthur, who could ill afford good Scotch. Good thing the Episcopalian church had no prejudice against liquor. Dan recalled Arthur saying, Jesus changed water into wine, after all.

"Scotch is not a drink for gentlemen after dinner," said Grandfather.

Dan ignored him. "We'll take the gold to the New York Assay Office in the morning. I assume it's still on Wall Street, next to the Sub-Treasury?"

Arthur, setting the bottle and a glass before him, nodded.

"No!" said Grandfather. "It will go to the bank for safekeeping."

As if he had not spoken, Dan opened the bottle and poured himself a drink. "Join me?" he asked Arthur. In the fading light, Arthur's face seemed thinner. How worn he is, Dan thought. The difficulties of housing so many people, of bearing up under Grandfather's carping, would try any man's soul. Savoring the Scotch, he was reminded of peat smoke and purple heather-covered hills. Scotch was a mountain drink, the color of gold.

"Join me?" he asked Arthur.

Under Grandfather's glare, Arthur shook his head.

The old man thumped his cane on the floor. "I said, it goes to the Bank."

"We can't just pay the debt with raw gold, Grandfather." He would try to appear reasonable, as long as he could.

"Why not? You have seventy-five pounds of gold. Van Fleet told me that they would accept that amount as full payment."

He sipped more Scotch and held it in his mouth. So Grandfather had talked to Van Fleet. The Bank was so eager – desperate? – to take the gold that it would forgive almost thirty percent of the debt? Where would that leave the family? What was Grandfather's object?

The questions churned in his brain. To camouflage them, he spoke as if explaining a process to a less intelligent toddler. "First the gold must be assayed, and then formed into Government bars or Double Eagles, and only then we'll know what we have. It's the normal procedure that the Bank should require of us." Another sip. "Van Fleet's idea is extremely irregular." What was it about talking to the old man that drove him into such stilted phrasing, as if he laid on words like bricks on a wall?

"You need not lecture me on how raw gold becomes money." Grandfather held out his hand, palm up. "I'll take the rest of that gold."

If he gave in on this one small thing, he yielded all. Nothing would be changed. The habit of obedience ran too strong in him, in all of the family.

"Begging your pardon, Grandfather, it will go to the Assay Office with the rest. As gold dust it's useless." He smiled at his brother-in-law. "Besides, there must be something for household expenses, now that you have another mouth to feed."

"Oh, no," Arthur said, "I can't let you do that. Truly I can't. You need it to pay the debt."

"You can. It's –"

Grandfather cut in. "He certainly may not have it. Arthur is quite correct. We must repay —"

"Do you expect him to support all of us indefinitely? On a churchman's salary? He has done more than his share. I'm back now, and I shall repay our debt to Arthur, as well as to the Bank."

"That's fine." Grandfather s eyes gleamed through the shaggy white brows. "We will repay the Bank first, in gold, and then concentrate on lifting the family from our financial straits."

"You would let Van Fleet have it all? With no regard to the family?"

"Of course not." Grandfather stroked his heavy white mustache. "Hear my plan."

Rising, he carried the scotch to the window. A gnawing in his stomach told him he would not like Grandfather's idea.

"Sit down when I'm speaking to you."

Day stayed at the window, watched the amber liquid swirl against the glass.

"Repaying the Bank – in gold, mind you – will restore our honor."

Mothers and nannies called their children in from play. A small boy rolled his hoop around a hitching post. An open shay pulled up before a house across street. A young man jumped down and handed out an older woman, then a young one. At the sight of her blonde hair, Dan thought of Harriet. Did her husband squire her to the theater, perhaps to a concert, on this warm evening?

Over his shoulder, he asked, "You, Arthur, do you favor paying back the debt in gold?"

"Yes." Arthur's voice sounded clogged. He cleared his throat. "Yes, I do."

"This gold does not belong to the Bank. It is mine. I earned it. I sweated for it, and froze for it." He spoke to be heard across the ropes creaking on the beam, boots swinging across his thoughts. "I will not turn it over to you, to let you impoverish this family all over again." He swallowed Scotch, and the drink comforted him. "I will repay the debt myself."

"Very well." Grandfather's eyes narrowed. "That might be a good thing. Yes, indeed. A good thing for you to be the one to repay the debt. You should be seen as the man who repaid it. That will give more credence to the firm."

"The firm?" Yet he did not have to ask; he could foresee what Grandfather wanted. He replaced the glass on the tray, clasped his hands behind his back to keep from striking out.

"Honor is an asset more valuable than gold." Grandfather shook his finger at Dan. "The firm cannot be re-established on a solid basis without honor." He smiled as if at something beautiful but far away. "Jonas Stark & Company," he murmured. "Attorneys at Law."

He could not speak. That was the fate the old bastard would arrange for him. To remain in the city and rebuild the law firm.

Grandfather said, as though Dan's silence signaled his surrender, "My boy, when you repay the debt in gold, the best men will again bring their most lucrative cases to us."

"You need me to rebuild the law firm, is that it? I am the cornerstone of your plan?"

Grandfather's chin lifted, and he stared down his long straight nose. He said nothing, but Dan did not need words to tell him the fate the old man planned for him. Grandfather would consign him to choke on dust and ink. Repaying the bank in gold was not a matter of honor but of re-establishing the law firm so that he could preen himself in the best clubs, hobnob with men of affairs, judges and Senators, the business elite of the City.

What of Martha? Dear God, he would not give her up. He would not sacrifice her on the altar of the old bastard's pride.

He sat down. The little boy had been made to stand when Grandfather took the stick and yanked down his pants. He gripped his thighs under the table to stop his hands shaking and flung a single syllable across the cherry wood. "No."

"What do you mean?"

"I mean 'No.' You will not sacrifice me as you sacrificed Father."

"Pah! My son was a thief and a suicide! I expected better of you, my boy. I have always thought you were more like me than my son was."

"Perhaps I am." His fingertips dug into his thigh muscles, and the pain steadied him. "I have other plans."

"You cannot!" roared Grandfather. "I won't allow it."

Dan took his upper lip in his teeth. The damned old son of a bitch was his grandfather, and he could not pummel him as he might an enemy his own age.

"I will remain long enough to repay the Bank in full, with interest, and secure an independence for Mother and the children. I will repay Arthur for his generosity. When that is done, I am going home."

"You can't." Grandfather aimed his middle finger at Dan. "You have not enough gold."

"I will repay the bank in greenbacks."

~3~

BELOW, AN UPROAR OF VOICES and hurrying feet, swift heels knocking on hardwood floors, thumping on carpets. When Grandfather first erupted, Dan had let Arthur thrust him from the dining room until they had calmed the old man. Standing at the dormer window in his room, he let the air cool him while the moonlight stripped color from the night. Outside, all was silent except for distant noises of city traffic and a battle between two tomcats on a neighbor's fence.

Inside, Grandfather's voice rose. "He is no grandson of mine. I will not have him in this house." Entirely forgetting that the house belonged to Arthur's church. Other voices sounded, but too low to separate them beyond male and female or know what they said, but the entire household, it seemed, was trying to calm Grandfather. He wished them well.

Grandfather damned him in a shout, and there were murmurs, and he damned Dan again, and Arthur's rumbling base ordered him to cease swearing in his house. Grandfather shouted again, "I will not –" and a door slammed on the rest.

Children's crying sounded closer, with footsteps on the stairs.

Dan went to the door and opened it to find Mother, who had changed into a plain housedress and no hoop. She held the little ones by the hand, and Nathaniel stood at her shoulder, his chin jutting out at Dan.

"May we come in?" Mother asked. "We need a refuge someplace."

It was cramped for five people, even when two of them were children. Mother sat on the bed and hitched herself back to lean against the wall. She gathered Jeremy onto her lap and Peggy into the circle of her arm. Nathaniel took the chair. In his silent challenge, Dan recognized a miniature version of himself as if Mother and Father had decided to duplicate him.

Mother laid her cheek against Peggy's hair.

"Are you all right?" Dan asked.

"Yes. Just very tired."

"I'm sorry, Mother."

"Not sorry enough to give in, though."

Did she want him to? "No. Don't ask me to. I will not sacrifice your future and the children's futures to help Grandfather salvage his own honor."

She took a deep breath, and tears flowed down her cheeks. He squirmed onto the bed and held both her and Peggy. Her body shook against him, and somehow he knew that her tears came from a place deep inside her, that they had been a long time coming.

After a moment, he felt a pounding on his shin. Jeremy beat at him with all his small might.

"Jeremy!" Mother searched her pockets for a handkerchief.

Dan captured the boy's small hands, and the child shouted, "You made her cry, you made Mama cry."

Mother wiped her eyes, turned Jeremy's face to hers. "No, darling, he did not make me cry. I am crying because I have waited so long for someone to stand up to your great-grandfather, and now Daniel has done it, and we'll be all right now. We will be all right."

She soothed Jeremy, who climbed back to her other side and snuggled against her. They stayed that way for some minutes while Dan's arm went numb and the little boy laid his head on his mother's lap. When Peggy yawned, Dan got off the narrow bed and shook his arm to wake it up. There were dark shadows under Mother's eyes, but she held Peggy as the little girl went to sleep. Dan slid the pillow from under the coverlet and put it behind Mother's back.

There being no place to sit, he crouched on his heels.

"I don't understand," Nathaniel said, "Why didn't you just give in?

Why don't you just do what Grandfather wants instead of upsetting everyone so?"

"Because everyone has always given in, thinking that would bring peace. Because Father gave in and it destroyed him. Because giving in is not good for the rest of you." He wished he had brought the scotch with him.

"You are a much harder man than when you went away," Mother said. "Someday you must tell us everything that happened to you in that wild country."

"Someday." Mentally, Dan crossed his fingers against the lie, for he could never tell his mother about booted feet kicking out a life, the swollen strangled faces, the whispers that threaded his nightmares.

"Oh, Daniel, not you, too?"

"What do you mean?"

"Are you one of those protecting men? Your father was. I begged him to say no to Grandfather Stark. But he said it was better to give in, and I never knew what he did or where he went. I asked him, to be sure I did, but he would stroke my cheek and kiss me and tell me not to worry." She shook her head. "Of course, I worried more. It almost drove me crazy. It would any woman. Telling me not to worry when all the time I knew things were deeply wrong someplace and all I could do was wait for the sword of Damocles to fall. And pray." She gulped, dabbed at her eyes. "Promise me you will not protect your wife, when you marry, to that extent. Promise —"

He thought of Martha, risking the typhus to care for the sick, risking her good name to live with him. She knew the worst of him, but she had come to him, joined with him anyway. He wondered what he could protect her from, except poverty. Yet he had not done so well at that so far. This journey, and his plan, might well be his last chance to strike it rich enough to protect her. He opened his mouth to tell Mother about Martha, but a tapping at the door stopped him.

Arthur poked his head in. "Perhaps you might like to come down for a nightcap? Florentine wishes to bid you good night, and she dare not make this climb in her present condition."

~4~

"YOU CAUSED QUITE SOME EXCITEMENT, dear brother."
Florentine patted the seat beside her, and he lowered himself into the
sofa; it was soft enough for a feather bed.

"I shall find another lodging tomorrow."

As if with one mind, they all spoke together. "No."

Startled, he looked around at their firm faces.

Arthur said, "You've opened my eyes. Before tonight, I thought
that your Grandfather strove for the greater good of the family in his
desire to reestablish the law firm. Now, I see that reestablishing the law
firm would entail a sacrifice we would all be forced to make." He paused,
and his eyes drifted toward his wife's extended figure. "Were that
sacrifice for the good of all, I could not in conscience oppose it. After
tonight, I am not so sure."

"It would always be Jonas Stark and Company," Dan said.

"I don't understand," Nathaniel put in.

"The firm could not change its name after Grandfather died
without causing confusion and some loss of business." After a second,
he added, "Perhaps a considerable loss."

"And if he died before it was well established," said Florentine,
"it might prove impossible to rebuild it anyway. He's seventy-six."

233

"A remarkably vigorous seventy-six," Mother said.

"Nonetheless," Flo said, "that's past the allotted three score and ten, and it will take years to rebuild it, to regain the trust of people with legal business. It might be better to start all over." Flo patted Dan's hand, touched the rope scars across the backs. "Your poor hand! What happened?"

"Nothing much. I helped with a bit of hauling and forgot my gloves." He turned the hand over and grasped his sister's fingers. They were rough from doing much of her own housework.

Arthur asked, "Have you truly considered the implications of what you plan to do, pay the debt in greenbacks?"

"Yes," said Dan. "Depending on the value of the gold, repaying the Bank in greenbacks should leave plenty to provide for all of you."

Mother said, "Are you sure that is a good —"

He overrode her. "Mother, I haven't enough to repay the Bank in gold, but in greenbacks there's plenty. Arthur has been uncommon good, but this situation can't last. There must be enough as well to secure your future. Once I am sure of that, I'm going home."

"I can't say I like the idea of repaying in paper," Arthur said. "It smacks of sharp dealing."

"Just like a man," said Mother. "And a Christian. All for honor and honesty while we women worry about making a thin cut of old meat stretch among eight people."

Arthur started. Had Mother never spoken up to him before? Perhaps not, Dan thought, as he realized that he brought the number of Arthur's dependents to nine.

"Why don't you reestablish the law firm?" asked Nathaniel. "What else do you have to do?"

What else, indeed? Martha's face emerged from his memory, and the feel of her skin was on his fingertips, her smell of sage soap and something indefinably her own was in his nostrils. "I have made a life in the West. I have responsibilities in a new country."

"Good Lord," said Arthur. "What responsibilities could you have acquired in a year?"

He pictured Martha, brushing her hair before bed while he lay watching in the mirror the lift of a breast with every stroke.

"I am married, for one."

As they stared in blank surprise, he added, "Besides, I have a law practice and a surveying business. Alder Gulch is home now."

Flo coughed. "Married?"

"Yes. Her name is Martha and she is a widow with two children." He smiled at Nathaniel. "Timothy is a couple of years older than you."

"She is so much older?" Mother sounded indignant.

"By just two years. She married at fifteen. Not uncommon among her people."

Arthur cleared his throat. "Her people?"

"She grew up in East Tennessee." Dan heard his voice harden. They were not congratulating him for having found happiness in a godforsaken hell hole that had become home. They were questioning him as if he had bought a nag thinking it a thoroughbred. Very well. He would give them the rest of it. "She is one quarter Cherokee, and she heals the sick and wounded." To himself, he added, She healed me.

"An Indian?" Mother sat bolt upright. "You cannot expect us to receive her."

"When I bring Martha to New York, you will receive her or you will not receive me." Martha had warned him about this attitude, but he had not expected it. He compressed his lips, felt all he had done to bring them the gold throbbed in the scars on his hands.

The hall clock bonged out the hour. "My goodness." Florentine sounded relieved that the time diverted them. "Midnight? We must retire or we shall be no good tomorrow. Daniel, what shall you do about the gold?"

Gold. Dan took a moment to recover himself. Yes, he must follow through on his plan, though just now he was in a mood to leave it. Let them give it to the Bank, and take himself back to the Gulch. Yet he could not do that. He would do what he had planned. Along the way, he would persuade them to accept Martha. "First, I'll have to move it to the Assay Office." Remembering the scotch in his hand, he drained the glass. The drink warmed his gullet, and his regard for them. "Perhaps it would be better if I found a room somewhere else."

"Indeed not," said Arthur. Mother and Flo echoed him, as an afterthought, it seemed.

Nathaniel added, "Stay, please."

Mother said, "You must not be a McClelland, my dear." When he raised an inquiring eyebrow, she said, "You must not rout the enemy and then retreat from the field."

"It will be awkward if I stay," Dan reminded them.

"Most awkward, indeed." Flo laid the back of his hand against her cool cheek. "But you cannot leave us to establish the new order of things without you, or I'm afraid we should soon be back in the old order."

"What do you want me to do, Arthur?"

"I think you should regard my house as your house as long as you wish." Arthur's tone left no doubt that he meant what he said. "Is that settled?" He looked around, as if compelling their agreement. They all nodded. "I have Holy Eucharist at seven o'clock, but I shall be free afterward, and can arrange for transport then. Can you be ready by ten o'clock? We can load the box and haul it to the Mint before your grandfather quite realizes where it has gone."

"Of course." Dan rose to his feet. That sofa was entirely too soft. In another minute, he would have gone to sleep.

Florentine tilted her cheek for his kiss, but as he touched his lips to her smooth face, she drew back. "Ugh. If you don't find a barber tomorrow, I shall refuse to recognize you as my brother. I quite loathe beards, although they are all the fashion among gentlemen."

~5~

SO LONG HAD DAN LIVED where neither church nor clergy were known that he was caught flat-footed, stooped over, muscles gathering to lift the box, when Arthur placed a hand on the lid, bowed his head, and closed his eyes. Mercifully, the prayer was short. Before Dan's back could complain, the drayman swooped down, took hold of the rope handles and hefted the box. He let out a whistle. "Lord love a duck, gents, what you got in this, anyhow?"

"Gold," said Dan.

The man's face collected into circles – lifted brows, wide eyes, a round mouth. "Ooh!"

The Assay Office stood on the north side of Wall Street. It would have been an imposing building, except that the Sub-Treasury, next to it on the corner of Nassau and Wall Streets, was far larger and grander, a modern Parthenon with Corinthian columns supporting the roof of the porch that lay atop a flight of steps as wide as its front. Down the long Nassau Street side, the supporting columns made a fine array. Next to it, the Assay Office appeared modest, with its second-story porch of only four columns. Beyond the Assay Office, a three-story building sported a large sign over the door: Henry Clews & Co., Gold Trading. Jumping down from the wagon, Dan made a mental note to see if Peter still worked for Mr. Clews.

He sniffed. A distinctive smell oozed out of the Assay Office doors and barred windows, adding its own sharp flavor to the air, as bitterness adds danger to an argument, Dan thought. The next moment, he spotted Van Fleet standing near the doorway.

"Christ," Dan muttered as he picked up the box. "There's Van Fleet."

Arthur said, "Language, Daniel. You've no need to take the Lord's name in vain." He peered toward the banker. "What do you suppose he wants?"

"Keep us honest."

"Us?" Arthur fingered his Roman collar and looked down at his black wool suit, shiny about the lapels and elbows. Dan laughed, first to think that Arthur, an Episcopalian priest, could be considered dishonest, and second, that Arthur believed his profession automatically insulated him from suspicion. Could he be so naïve?

As he paid him, the drayman said, "Thank you, sir. You from somewheres else?"

"Yes," said Dan. "Montana Territory."

"What's that? Never heard of it. Where in hell is it? Out west someplace?"

"Yes. Out west someplace." For fun, Dan tipped the drayman a nugget the size of a marble.

"Here, what's this, then? Gold?"

"Yes. Take good care of it. Someone worked hard digging that out of the ground."

"Hmph. First thing I'm doing is changing it for money. Gold don't do me no good."

Still smiling at the man's ignorance, he seized the rope handles and carried the box up the steps and inside, Arthur and Van Fleet following.

The acid smells of assaying lay on the air, but no testing went on in this room. A set of closed double doors in the back wall apparently led to the laboratories. Here, where clerks officially received the gold, men wearing green eye shades and black sleeve protectors worked with ledger books the size of a newspaper and ten times as thick. Each page was narrowly ruled and covered with the handwriting of spiders. Pens scratched over ledgers, paper crackled as a clerk turned a page, feet shuffled, someone slammed a desk drawer shut, men's voices murmured. The acid smell stung his nostrils. On either side of him Arthur and Van

Fleet took quick, shallow breaths. A man who sat in sunlight, facing away from Dan, mopped the back of his neck, and the handkerchief left streaks of black on his skin.

The clerk who brought over a ledger book boosted himself up to look over the counter. "Now. What have we here?"

"Gold," said Dan. "About seventy pounds of raw gold." Early this morning, he had burned his clothes and panned the gold collected among the ashes while the children watched, but he would see if Henry Clews could change the dust before he gave it to the clerk. He needed expense money, and he would pay Arthur something toward his keep.

"Aha! A significant amount." The clerk wrote the amount in the first column of a new row. He smiled. "Of course how significant will have to wait for the assay." He dipped his pen in an oblong ink bottle and poised it over the next column. "Who is the owner of this minor fortune?"

He brought the pen close to the paper.

"I am," said Dan and Van Fleet together.

The pudgy fingers raised the pen. "Both of you?"

"No." Dan, who had been leaning both elbows on the counter, straightened. "Just me. I am the rightful owner. The only rightful owner."

"That is not true." Van Fleet's voice rose. "This man owes a great deal of money to the bank I represent, and I am taking possession of this gold on their behalf."

Two armed guards standing inside the double doors came alert. Dan felt their watchfulness in the hairs at the crown of his head. "Until I pay you the amount I owe, you're committing grand larceny." He faced Van Fleet, just as he had done on Wallace Street. "You do not want to challenge me in court, do you?"

Van Fleet said to the clerk, "I tell you, this gold is mine."

The armed guards moved two steps closer. "Is there any way you can prove ownership?" asked the clerk.

"Yes." Dan controlled his voice, used what Martha called his "sweet reason" voice. "Open one of the boxes." He gestured to the guards. "Open any of them or all of them. I'll prove that I own this gold. I earned it by my own work, as a surveyor and a lawyer, in Alder Gulch, Montana Territory, and I can prove it."

Van Fleet said, "Someone may have tampered with the boxes. I have not seen them since Saturday."

"Arthur," Dan asked, "did anyone tamper with the boxes while they were in your house?"

"No." In that one syllable resounded all Arthur's authority as a cleric, backed up by his Roman collar, as rector of St. David's. Dan recognized a force in his brother-in-law he had not known existed, an intolerance of dishonesty in any man. Van Fleet's forehead shone.

The clerk spoke to a guard, who brought a crowbar and pried up the lid of the box. "Oh," said the guard. "There's just a bunch of leather bags in here. Small'uns. With tags on 'em."

"Put two or three on the counter, if you please," said Dan. "Read the tags." The clerk read out his full name, the number of ounces, the date, and Lydia Hudson's initials from each tag. Dan recalled the smells of candle wax and venison stew cooking, the occasional splat of melting snow onto the table in the Eatery as he weighed the gold in each poke and rewrote the tags, his fingers cramping and his eyes watering from the smoke of the kerosene lamp.

"If you have a Bible, give it to me," said Dan, "and I'll swear on it that I am Daniel Bradford Stark, the only legal owner of this gold."

"I promise you that this man is Daniel Bradford Stark," said Arthur.

"I believe you, Mr. Stark," said the clerk. The mischief lighted his eyes once more. "Besides, no New Yorker would go about town with that beard and hair. You have to have come from the West."

Dan laughed. "The next time you see me, I'll have a city haircut and the beard will be gone."

The clerk announced that logging each poke would take some hours.

Arthur said, "I cannot stay, Daniel. I have a diocesan meeting that may test my endurance today. Shall we see you at dinner?" He lowered his voice. "Are you all right for cash? Raw gold is not commonly accepted in barber shops, I'm afraid. They wouldn't know what to do with it."

"I'll change some of the other gold. Don't worry about me." He looked a question at the clerk, who pointed the feather end of his quill pen toward the door. "Henry Clews next door will change it for you. They'll charge a fee, mind you, everything costs these days."

When Arthur had gone, Van Fleet said, "When the gold is minted, deposit it in my bank."

"Like hell," Dan said. The guards watched. "The gold will either stay at the mint or I'll deposit it safely elsewhere. I will not trust it to an interested party."

"We'll see about that," said Van Fleet.

"Let me say this one more time. You do not want to meet me in court."

Van Fleet's laugh was strained and false to Dan's ears. "You think because you won a few cases in a rube court you can win here? In a proper New York court? Don't be daft, man. If you try to pay the debt in greenbacks, I shall bring suit, and you'll have the best attorneys in the city against you. It's you who should be afraid to face the Bank in court, not the other way around." Van Fleet nodded to himself. "I thought that might stop you. Think about it." His laughter trailed behind him like smoke as he went out the door.

He felt as if the banker had seized him by the short hairs, shaken him, and tossed him aside. The Legal Tender Acts made greenbacks legal payment of debts incurred before their passage. What if the bank's lawyers challenged him on the grounds that the debt was incurred with Father's suicide? Father had killed himself after passage of the second Act. But wait. He could argue that Father robbed the firm's clients before the first Act was passed. There was no record of the thefts. Father had written nothing down, and covered his tracks thoroughly. A judge might rule against him, but he could not afford to worry about that now.

Leaning on the counter, he watched the clerk and a helper weigh the gold. Part of his mind appreciated how they turned the pokes inside out and brushed any remaining flakes and dust with a fine wire brush. "Every grain, sir. We retrieves every single grain."

Another part flung up a new question: How had Van Fleet learned that he intended to pay the debt in greenbacks? Someone had told him. Who? Arthur? No, Arthur understood and agreed with his reasoning. Then who else? Was the spy one of the servants?

The clerks poured the gold onto a funnel-shaped container on a scale. His mind scurried about, looking for the answer to one question. Who had told Van Fleet? The dial hand on the scale rose, bit by bit. Seventy-two pounds. They poured on more gold. Seventy-seven pounds, some ounces. So much? The scale reported seventy-nine pounds, and in the midst of his surprise, he knew: Grandfather. He had showed his hand to the family, never thinking that Grandfather might favor the bank over the family. Fool that he was, he should have known. Damn it, he should have known.

Grandfather had warned Van Fleet.

~6~

THE SUPERVISING CLERK wrote a careful receipt. "Mind you, sir, this is a preliminary receipt. You can come back for the permanent receipt in two days."

"Two days? That long?"

The man laughed. "Aye, sir, it'll take that long to weigh it close and do the preliminary assay. We'll destroy the leather pouches, and add what gold is left to the total. We won't know how much gold there is, not to the last grain, until we know the percentage of other minerals amongst it, sir, though I do say it looks uncommon pure. You ain't bringing us ore, no sir, you're bringing us gold. May I guess that it's placer gold, then?"

"It is. Washed out of Alder Creek, in Montana Territory." The phrase still felt odd in his mouth, as if he learned a new language and tried it on a native speaker.

"That new territory you mentioned? I read about it in the papers. Gave me a proper distraction from war news, thank you. Congress had themselves a time to make that happen. Haggled for days over the name. Of course, Congress couldn't agree on where their pinkies was, if you takes my meaning." He winked and chuckled as if Congress were a music hall turn, rather than a law-making body.

"Getting back to your gold, sir, if you call before close of business Wednesday or at opening on Thursday, we'll give you the final receipt."

Dan put the temporary receipt in his notecase, replaced it in his inside breast pocket. "What will it tell me that this one does not?"

"It tells how much gold you've deposited with us and how pure it is."

"Will it tell me the dollar value?"

The clerk gave him a pitying look. "No, sir. Not to say exact. There's no knowing the dollar value until after it's refined and formed into bars and Double Eagles. They're .900% pure on account we have to add a base metal for hardness."

Then an ounce was worth twenty dollars, about two dollars more than in Alder Gulch. "How long will it be before I know how much money it yields?"

"Two weeks. That's a mort of time to wait, I know, sir, when you're anxious like, but a good assay takes time. Still figuring $20 per ounce, you'll have around $19,100."

Not enough. Not nearly enough. Nineteen thousand in gold. And he'd have to wait two weeks to collect it, while the greenback rose against gold. Every day he needed to make up more of a shortfall if his plan were to work, or he'd have to give it all to the bank.

~7~

DAN STOOD IN THE PORCH of the Assay Office building. On the sidewalk below, men hurried up and down Wall Street on their own mysterious errands. Was there nothing he could do to make money in the meantime? Midway down the steps, a thought stopped him. His gold was not worth twenty dollars per ounce here, no matter what the clerk said. It was worth its current market value, and what was that today?

He pushed open the door to Henry Clews & Co. Here he would change his raw gold, learn the market value of his gold, and perhaps locate Peter, all at the same time.

Three clerks behind a counter waited on customers lined up four and five deep. Dan choose a dark-haired clerk who sported a waxed mustache. Ahead of him, a tall man who wore a top hat, a cutaway coat, and striped trousers bent his head to hear the clerk better. At his feet lay a carpetbag. A boy of about ten hurried from a back room carrying a metal cash box in both hands as if he brought the Sacrament to a priest.

One of the clerks turned away from the counter and busied himself at a pair of scales, weighing gold as carefully as justice. The third clerk, balding and spectacled, whose collar points jutted out, carrying his beard, explained fluctuations in the gold premium to a stout customer in a bowler. Dan caught a word or two over the other conversations, but not enough. As he watched, a telegraph rattled and yet another clerk jumped up from a desk and chalked numbers on a blackboard: 254 ½. Gold was now trading at 254.5.

That meant his deposit of gold, with a face value of $19,100, might be worth – running the calculations in his head – $48,609.50 in greenbacks. His mouth dried. Plenty to pay off the debt and leave roughly $18,000. In greenbacks. He put his hand to the breast pocket of his coat. The note case was safe, with the Assay Office's receipt for the gold. Prudently invested, it would be a small nest egg for the family. In greenbacks. In gold, it was a shortfall of $10,000. It would leave nothing for the family. If he had to pay in gold, it would all go to the bank.

The family would have nothing.

Nothing to live on, nothing to educate the boys, provide a dowry for Peggy.

Moving to the head of the line, he realized by the clerk's dissolving smile that he frowned. Quickly he rearranged his features to be more pleasant. "I am newly arrived from the Far West, and a clerk at the Assay Office told me you can exchange gold into money." Taking the poke from his coat pocket, he placed it on the counter.

The clerk opened the poke, moistened a finger with his tongue and thrust it inside, peered at the gold flakes on the end of his finger. "I think you had better talk to Mr. Yates," he said. "If you wouldn't mind stepping aside, sir, I'll have someone fetch him." He brushed the gold into the poke and put it on Dan's outstretched palm while he put his head around a partition. "Would Mr. Yates be so good as to attend to a customer?"

Mr. Yates could only be Peter. He waited in front of a partition with a glass window until he heard a high-pitched shout: "Daniel Stark! Dan!"

A thin man, some inches shorter than himself, put one hand on the counter, hopped once, and stretched himself across it, extending his right hand. "How the hell are you?"

"Peter, you son of a gun." Dan pumped the smaller man's hand. He could not have been happier to see his school friend.

Peter smiled, his mouth stretching across his face. "Danny boy, when did you get back?" He snatched his hand out of Dan's grip. "I don't know that I should shake hands with you. You haven't even sent round a note."

"I arrived on Friday, and I've been somewhat preoccupied."

The mustached clerk cleared his throat. He must have been

trying to get their attention.

"Yes, what is it?" asked Peter.

"This gentleman wants us to trade raw gold for money."

"Well, do it. I'll vouch for him. Put it to my account."

"If you wouldn't mind, sir." The clerk slid a form along the polished counter top. Peter scrawled something on it.

"I hope that satisfies you."

"Indeed it does, Mr. Yates. Now, sir, if you would just relinquish your gold, we'll weigh it and exchange it for coin." He smiled. "Or would you prefer greenbacks?"

Peter said, "Don't be daft, man. Give him real money. Make that a full exchange." To Dan: "He'll do right by you." Glanced at the wall clock. "I must get back to the floor. Look, come down to Gilpin's when you've finished here. I'll be there until closing."

When Peter had gone, Dan asked the clerk, "What is Gilpin's?"

"Why, that's Gilpin's News Room, sir. It used to be just a coffee house where men went to hear the latest, because it has a telegraph. Being handy to the Customs House, it's a sort of sub-Post Office, for international mail. The Stock Exchange kicked the gold traders out because they thought it unpatriotic to speculate in gold, so some of our fellows did business on the curb, but that didn't serve in a snowstorm, so they found a basement room, a dank, foul place, make no mistake. They called it the Coal Hole, but it attracted more as wanted to trade, until they had to move out when their numbers grew too large. They made an arrangement with Gilpin's, and now they call it the Gold Room, too. Mr. Yates is one of our best traders. He has a nose for gold, he does. Uncanny sometimes. Even Mr. Clews says so."

"And where is this Gold Room?"

"Southeast corner of William Street and Exchange Place." The clerk winked. "You can't go wrong with Mr. Yates, sir. He'll steer you right."

Thanking the clerk, Dan thought, I hope so. By God, I hope so.

~8~

DAN WALKED TOWARD the East River. All along Wall Street, on both sides, banks and insurance companies and office buildings, some with Grecian columns supporting the roofs over porticoed entrances several steps up from the street, rose four and five stories, dwarfing horses, humans, and carriages. His stomach growled, and his tongue felt like house dust, but this near two o'clock, he wanted to see something of the Gold Exchange before it closed at three. At the corner of Wall and William Streets, with a silent curse at Van Fleet's Bank of New York opposite him, he crossed Wall and walked southward on William, tugged his hat brim a fraction lower to shade his eyes against the glare of sunlight on pale stone. Under the rumble and clash of traffic, horses' hooves and coachmen's profane shouts, he heard a low murmur, as of an underground river that boiled beneath the cobblestones. It came from near a building farther down. So large a crowd of men gathered that the sidewalk could not contain them, and they spilled well out into the street, where blaspheming coach drivers and draymen maneuvered around them. As he walked closer, the murmur became a rumble and then a roar.

A riot in the making? He paused to listen. He heard no slogans chanted, as when the city had protested Lincoln's draft. Amid the shouts and gestures, he could make out no discernable unity; they shouted at each other, seemingly without cause.

On a window above the crowd, he read, "Gilpin's News Room" in curved white lettering. A young man ran out, arms pumping, dashed out into the traffic, dodged among shying horses, yelling teamsters, and outraged pedestrians. He turned left on Wall Street and vanished into the pedestrians. Had he robbed the place? Why did no one call the police? Why was no one chasing him? A boy fled the building, this time running straight toward Dan, who thrust out an arm to fend him off, but the runner chopped down hard on it and darted on, fleeing west on Exchange. Dan rubbed his arm as running feet came up behind him, and a youth sprinted past him toward the building, yelled over his shoulder: "Damn you, get out of the way!" Ducking another runner coming out, the youth disappeared into the building.

All the boys and young men ran with purpose, human bees on mysterious errands to and from the hive, papers bulging from their jacket pockets. They sweated and ran, not caring whether they stepped on a man's feet or threw him aside; they dared their own lives among the carriages and cabs and trucks driven by men with upper arms as big as draft horses' legs.

Curved lettering in the window proclaimed, "Gilpin's News Room." So this was where Peter worked. A dial contraption with a single hand like a large weighing machine hung in the window. The hand jerked up, and some men in the crowd booed, while others began to sing "Dixie." A fight broke out, but Dan ignored it. He was not a Vigilante here.

At the right moment, he leaped into the traffic, crossed the intersection, and shouldered into the melee. A fellow running out knocked him backwards, but hands at his back saved him from falling on fresh horse manure and thrust him forward, never breaking the cadence of trade: "Buy." "Sell." "Sell two at 256." These, then, were the curbstone traders the clerk had mentioned. Edging through the crowd, he dodged boys coming at him from inside and outside at once, and made himself a space inside against the wall.

A man nearly his own size screamed in his ear: "You trading? Twenty-five dollars."

Dan shook his head.

The man pointed out the door. "Get lost."

Dan bellowed, "Peter Yates."

"You his friend?"

"Yes." Dan yelled his name.

The doorkeeper shouted something and pointed into the room. Dan, pondering the man's accent, decided he had permission to watch but not to trade.

If the noise outside was a river, here were the headwaters, a bedlam of men shouting, screaming, bellowing. All around him, they waved their fists in the air, jumped up and down, shrieked, not a single word intelligible. It seemed a mob so near to letting loose that he checked the exit and gauged how long it would take to beat his way out.

His height let him see much of the room. Across, three blackboards hung on the farther wall, and to his right a two-faced dial with a single hand on each face hung in the window. The hand ticked upward and then downward, to numbers and fractions. He picked out occasional phrases. A man near him screamed: "Selling three: Fifty at a 5/8." An answering shout came back: "Buying three: fifty at 3/5." "Sold: fifty at 3/5." Another voice sounded farther into the melee: "Buying twenty at three-fifths." "Sold." The dial hand twitched downward. From another: "Selling three, fifty at five-eighths. Selling three. Fifty at five-eighths." "Buying three. Fifty at five-eighths," came the response yell from the room. "Done!" The crowd shifted about as buyer and seller pushed toward a meeting. The dial hand twitched upward. So, he figured, it gave the current price of gold.

Everything happened in a matter of seconds. Through a parting in the crowd, he saw two men scribble on small pieces of paper, and exchange them. Tickets of sale, he assumed. They gave notes to a pair of boys. Again the crowd shifted. One boy, perhaps eleven years old, pushed past him and ran out the door. Across the room, an older boy who looked about Nathaniel's age ran up a ladder and scribbled numbers on a blackboard. A clerk at a desk between a blackboard and the dial hunched over a telegraph key. He wore an earpiece, operated the key with one hand, and transcribed the signals with the other. Without looking up, he tore off a paper and waved it. A boy ran up, glanced at it, and handed it to another boy who wrote on another blackboard, "Peters – US" and an upward arrow.

The dial hand ticked downward, from 258 to 7/8, then 3/4. Men cheered and bellowed out a chorus of "John Brown's Body," while other men cursed and shook their clenched fists. Around them, the bidding went on. Men shouted out their bids, waved their hats, and the dial clicked downward to 1/2, and boys ran in and out, up and down the ladders. On the blackboard, the scribe wrote a new, lower, number, 257. The dial hand twitched downward.

A man leaving the floor wiped sweat from his forehead. "Shit, it's another damn bear on the loose," he told Dan. "I'm ruined. Gold is dropping like rock. God, I need a drink."

Dan watched him plow his way toward the door. The dial stood at 256 3/5. The ruined man was right. With every tick of the hand, his gold bought fewer greenbacks. Even as he thought, his mind turning gray and hopeless, the dial hand ticked down to 256. Where would it stop? He wanted to join the ruined man, find a drink. For his plan to work, he needed gold to rise in value, so he could buy more greenbacks. Damn the fucking market, anyway.

The noise bombarded him, he breathed the steamed air thick with chalk dust and sweat as the dial ticked downward, ever downward. He could stand it no longer, and struggled through the crowd, heedless of other men's toes and curses, past the lookout in the doorway.

The curbside crowd mirrored the bedlam inside. Men shouted out their trades, sang "John Brown's Body," cheered. Others booed the dial's tic. He pushed through, crossed to the shady side of William Street, unbuttoned his collar and loosened his cravat. He'd wait here for Peter. Fanning himself with his hat, he felt his earlobes tingle as though from the onset of frostbite; his fingertips itched. Everything around him seemed sharp, etched on the thick, hot air. The blue granite of the U. S. Custom House diagonally across the intersection shone like lake water under a clear sky. Every detail of the portico's scrolled Corinthian columns was as sharp as if he looked at them through a telescope. He thought of finding a cool, dark bar and a cold beer, but he knew he could not sit still to drink it. Gold was dropping. He would not have enough greenbacks.

"Dan! Dan Stark!" Peter called to him, waved, and darted between a hansom cab and a carriage at full trot.

Shaking hands, Dan said, "Gold is dropping."

"Don't worry. Meet me tomorrow." Peter flapped his hand toward Gilpin's. "We're working overtime today. The market's in chaos." He rubbed his hands together and chortled. "Yes, gold is going down, dropping like a rock. Good for the Union and good for us. The Petersburgh mine success has done us a service. Join me here tomorrow morning. I'll show you something about gold trading, and we'll go on to supper before the Evening Exchange." He scribbled on a card and tucked it into Dan's handkerchief pocket. Waiting his chance with the traffic, he said, "You look like a wild man, you know. I'm not sure I ought to know you." Flashing a smile, he fled across the intersection, to disappear among the crowd of curbside gold traders.

Peter did not care that gold was down? And would show him something of gold trading? Peter, who had dared him to jump into the quarry. "Double dare you," he'd said. Peter had stripped. "Count of three." They had catapulted into deep water together, the only ones to dare the thirty-foot dive into unknown water. It did not surprise him that Peter traded in gold.

~9~

HE WALKED SOUTH on William Street and crossed Beaver Street, heading for the Hanover Square Station. Three things he needed: beer, a shave, and a haircut. Paying his fare with a three-cent silver piece, he boarded an omnibus and immediately regretted it. There was no place to sit for the mass of people jammed onto the car. He stood hemmed in near the driver's seat and listened to the running, cursing arguments between the driver and three or four passengers, over their change, the tickets, the stops. Two women tried to fight their way toward the exit. The car was so crowded that one, who wore a hoop, could not get through, until her companion screamed, "Let me off. I'm going to be sick!" The passengers squeezed aside, and she led her friend off the car like Moses through the Red Sea. Bending, Dan caught a glimpse of them out the window, giggling together. Their mirth would be short lived when they saw the tear on the hoopskirt. The horses clopped on, until Dan, debating between the hot damp streets and the hot, airless car, forced his way off.

Standing at the side of Bowery, he vowed that next time he would pay an extra three cents and ride one of the City Cars. Or else he'd walk. If necessary, he might even hire a hansom cab, although he could not do that very often if he were to shield his funds. Gold was going down.

When he came to a lager beer saloon, he gave up a half dime for a pint of inferior beer, but it helped his thirst. Sitting alone at a shadowed table with a second beer, he thought about the scene at Gilpin's. Despite Peter's confidence, his idea of making money out of the rise in gold looked impossible. Gold was worth nearly thirty points less than a month ago. Further, he knew nothing of gold trading. If he attempted to stand on that floor, he'd go broke in seconds.

Peter had not been worried. Perhaps he would have an idea.

Draining the beer, he rose. As he left the saloon, he glimpsed himself in the bar mirror. Long, tangled hair fell almost to his shoulders, and his beard had come out thick and sandy. On all that hair, his plug hat looked absurd, as if someone attempted to civilize a beast.

Before he went back to Arthur's house, he'd find a barber. He quickened his pace, hurried north on Bowery. Was Old Tom still in business? On Chrystie, before he reached North Street, stood Old Tom's Barber Shop. He entered the shop, but Old Tom was not behind the barber's chair. Another barber looked up from whisking hairs away from a customer's neck, and nodded pleasantly. "Be with you in a minute, sir."

When he was in the chair, Dan asked, "Where's Old Tom?"

"Dead and gone, sir, six months this very day. Dropped down on the floor right where I'm standing, behind this here chair. Terrible thing, it was. Just terrible. Heart, they said. His heart give out. Course it would, wouldn't it, him being eighty-two, though a fine strong-looking man he was, to the very end. They say as losing his son and grandson both to the war was what done it. Now, sir." The barber stood back to survey Dan. "Been awhile, has it, sir? What can I do for you today?"

When the barber was done, Dan smelled pomade and shaving soap on himself. He used to take that odor for granted as he took the East River for granted. Now it smelled odd to him, reminded him that he was again a City man. Another man's face looked back at him from the mirror the barber held, a face somehow unfamiliar, at once his own and not his own. Leaner, weathered below a pale forehead, the eyes harder. Not a City face. He paid the barber a dime and a half-dime, tipped him another half-dime. The man had done a good job. "Best shave I've had in months," he said, with an internal smile. He had shaved himself in cold water most of the year.

Crossing Houston Street, Dan debated going back to Arthur's house. He must reek of sweat and cigar smoke, after the Gold Room. Never could stand the smell of cigars, he thought. He thought of the dial hand dropping down. Why was Peter not worried? How could he increase his gold? A train's toot brought him to himself.

He had walked along the New York and Harlem railroad tracks and stood on a block-long triangle of grass in a tangle of intersections. Unthinking, he had let his feet bring him here. His New York. The intellectual center of the city. Of the nation. He had missed this in Alder Gulch. No place in the Americas, perhaps in the world, held more books. On the next block, on Lafayette Place, stood the Astor Library with more than 100,000 volumes. Across the north boundary of this little park, the Cooper Institute presented its arched and windowed front to the world. Its library held several thousand volumes, and its free Reading Room had been a place to escape Grandfather after he gave in to the old man and began to study law. North of the Cooper, across an angled intersection of three streets, rose the far larger Bible House, where people labored to translate the Bible into the languages of the world. The Mercantile Library, with a collection nearly half as large as the Astor's, occupied most of yet another triangle.

He knew them all: stately edifices, architectural masterpieces, they were temples to the worship of books and ideas. Scattered among them lived the learned societies for the advancement and preservation of knowledge.

In Alder Gulch men were so desperate for something to read that anyone who owned a book could dismantle it and rent it out by the chapter or even the page. Some thought him bizarre because he would not demolish his few books for the dust they would bring.

As he started across the street, a hansom cab rounded the corner at a fast trot, and Dan sprinted out of its way. "You trying to kill yourself, pal? Watch where you're going, for Chrissake." Flapping his hand at the driver, he fetched up on the sidewalk to stare at the glass-filled arches of the Cooper Union. So much glass, and a single pane twelve inches by nine inches cost a dollar in Alder Gulch. He shook his head. He wouldn't even begin to estimate what one window had cost, let alone the entire building. A year ago, to wonder about the price of windows would not have occurred to him. How Martha would marvel at the building. Some day he would show her New York.

Inside, Dan took off his hat. Sunlight through the tall glass windows shone as bright and warm as outside. Perhaps warmer because there was no breeze, despite the fans and the few open panes. People, intent on their business with the shops and offices that rented space here, bustled past him. At the entrance to the Exhibition Room, where Abraham Lincoln had delivered the speech that carried him to the Presidency, he thought of looking in, but women's laughter echoing from above distracted him. What made them laugh? Thinking to satisfy his curiosity and then look into the Reading Room, he climbed the stairs. On the fourth floor the Institute proper began, with classrooms and the Reading Room and an art gallery arranged in alcoves. In one of them, two ladies viewed a crude painting of a mountain done in thick oil. The brush work, visible where Dan stood, made the mountain look like a pyramid of sticks, a green wickiup. One woman murmured, "— so primitive."

The second woman, a statuesque blonde, tittered. "Do you imagine the artist thought to start a new school? Perhaps the primitive brush school?"

The first woman put her fingers to her lips. "The crude school?"

Perhaps hearing his heels on the wood floor, they turned, their hoops so wide that they swung against each other and rose a couple of inches, to show more ankle than decorum allowed.

Dan waited, his hands at his sides.

The blonde let out a small shriek. "Daniel! You came back."

Harriet. A vision in bold apple green plaid, her hair caught at the nape of her neck in a pink net. He hoped he did not gape, for in a year she had matured, grown beautiful. As she came closer, hand outstretched, he saw a knowing expression in her eye.

"Harriet." As he bowed over her hand, her perfume caught at his nose and clogged his throat. She introduced her friend, all the time appraising him as she might a painting to hang on her wall.

He said, "May I offer my best wishes on your marriage?"

She blushed, but at what – his good wishes or her own broken faith – he could not tell.

"Thank you," she glanced sideways at her companion, whose name Dan had not heard. "The Major is at the Front."

The other woman, short, plump, and plain, had kind eyes. "My brother holds a command under General Grant."

So he might have been at Petersburgh, among those responsible for the successful mining of the Rebel lines, the very Union success that was driving gold values down. Dan drew in a long breath. "We shall hope for his safe return."

"Thank you," said both women, speaking almost together. "We pray daily," said the sister.

"But you are safely returned," said Harriet.

"As you see."

"And your mission was successful?"

"Yes. Rather."

She laughed. "You are quite the Sphinx, these days. I should like to hear your adventures."

A whisper in his mind: It didn't have to be this way. "Oh, I assure you they are quite dull. Mostly a great deal of digging."

People walked around them, and from the alcoves disembodied voices and footsteps echoed against the hard stone floor. After a few more polite sentences, Dan bowed to the ladies, made his excuses. Harriet stopped him before he could escape, and handed him her visiting card. "Perhaps you and your mother would come to tea? I'll send a note around."

He cleared a constriction in his throat. "Thank you. It would be our pleasure." He had not forgotten her, after all.

He looked into the Reading Room, browsed among the shelves. A few workingmen in dust-whitened boots and rough jackets, women in maids' uniforms and the plain dark dresses that signified shop clerks, sat at the long tables, absorbed in their books, improving their minds in hopes of escaping their tenement homes and drab jobs. They handled the books with reverence and clean hands. He touched books of mathematics, advanced algebra and calculus, and above all, trigonometry, the mathematics of surveying, that brought him the delight in bringing order out of nature's chaos. Would that human chaos were so easily dealt with.

As he walked north, Harriet stayed in his mind. Marriage had given her an indefinable something in her air, an attraction that had not been there when she was single. She had used her fan to great advantage, rapping a young man's wrist, stroking it down his sleeve. He did not recollect that she had objected to him looking down the neckline of her gown when she sat at the piano. Of course, he had taken care to be discreet. But now? He dashed across a street. Reaching safety, he understood the impression he'd had and dismissed it out of hand. Not Harriet. She had welcomed him as an old acquaintance, nothing more. He was mistaken in reading anything more into her glance.

At any rate, he thought as he climbed the stoop to Arthur's front door, he did not believe Mrs. Browne would invite them to tea. The Starks were social pariahs, and would be until the bank was paid. He would not see her again. He raised the iron door knocker and let it fall.

~10~

"YOU LOOK SO MUCH BETTER, Daniel," said Florentine. "But where have you been, besides a barber shop?"

"I explored the city a bit." In the foyer stood a hall tree, a bench seat long enough for three people to sit and put on their boots in dirty weather, with brass hooks in a row up either side of a full length mirror.

"Do you find it different?" Flo looked as if something about him puzzled her.

Hanging his dusty hat on a hook, he saw what his sister saw, a City man but with something off kilter about him, a quality not quite New York. He'd become a Western man with a City haircut. He no longer belonged to the City.

"The omnibuses are nigh to unbearable." He smiled at her.

"They always have been. You just forgot."

"Perhaps. We regulate such things far better in the West."

"Hmph." Flo let out a snort of laughter. "Where there are few people affairs may be very easily regulated, I'm sure."

"There are some difficulties." He looked around. "Where is Grandfather?"

"Out. He went out to his club. He was invited to dine there."

"Then he has not been shunned altogether."

"It helped that the court went into summer recess after – afterwards, so that he was able to lay it all to Father's iniquity. He took to calling him 'my Absalom.'" Florentine sniffed and smoothed her apron while she regained her composure. Dan reflected that King David's son, who had tried to overthrow him, had been called Absalom. "He stands for re-election in November, and he is dreadfully worried about that. The Republicans are out for his blood because of his Copperhead views on the War and President Lincoln. And gold." She took his arm. "We're all dying to hear of your Western adventures, and I should like to know more of your wife, too. She must be a very courageous woman, and if you think she's good enough for you, I think so, too."

"The question is, am I good enough for her?" Martha. Possessed of courage, yes, and integrity – qualities not often assigned to women, or that he had not considered as belonging to the fair sex until Martha taught him otherwise. Just by being Martha.

"Mother will be wondering who came in. She is in the sitting room. Let's go up to her."

Supporting her with his arm, he escorted Florentine to the first floor. Seated on a sofa under the window, where the afternoon light fell on her work, Mother sewed what appeared to be a christening dress in white cotton. The sight stopped him on the threshold. Mother could not sew. Even to his masculine eye, the stitches looked crooked.

Seeing him, she stabbed the needle into the cloth and held out both hands. "Daniel! Come and give me a kiss."

Obedient as a schoolboy, he bent to kiss her smooth, cool cheek, that showed hardly a wrinkle though she had seen her fiftieth birthday. Her hair had grayed in the last year.

"Stand off a bit," she ordered, smiling. "How much better you look! Do you know, you're quite a handsome man?"

He could not hold her gaze with the heat rising in his face.

Florentine giggled. "Mother, you've embarrassed him." She cocked her head to one side. "I must agree with you, though. Ladies will swoon."

"Stop it, both of you," he said. "You're being silly."

Mother patted the seat beside her. "We're sorry, dear. It is an excess of happiness. Sit, and tell us about your day. We've been hiding from the heat, and we are quite dull."

He wanted to ask how Grandfather had conducted himself, but could not think how to broach the subject. "After a most tedious wait at the Assay Office, I went to Henry Clews, the gold trading firm, and found Peter Yates. He's a gold trader, you know."

"Yes," said Mother. "And while your grandfather is at home, please don't mention gold traders. They are anathema to him. Positively anathema. In his view, they manipulate the price of gold to drive up the value of greenbacks and extend the war. If Mr. Lincoln's paper money had no value, he would have to negotiate with the Rebels and bring an end to the bloodshed. So your grandfather says."

"Any peaceful solution would mean dissolving the Union," said Dan. "He can't favor such a treasonous result."

Mother cocked her head to one side. "I don't believe he has thought it through. He only thinks of the gold being, uh, devalued. Is that the right word?"

"Yes." A pause came over the conversation. Dan thought of the ladies' turned hems, the anxiety they could not conceal. "Are you sure you would not rather I took a room elsewhere?" Saying it, he realized how much he wanted to move, and not have to face Grandfather every minute he was here.

Florentine did not hesitate. "Absolutely sure. I was so proud of Arthur when he returned from the Assay Office. He told Grandfather again that this is his house and you are welcome here as long as you wish to be here." She worked herself to her feet. "Should you like tea? Coffee? Or something stronger?"

"Whiskey." Last night's bottle stood on a tray with two short glasses. "I can get it." He half rose, but Flo said, "I'm already up." She poured an inch into one and brought it to him. "I'd better see to dinner," she said and left the room. Hidden by the door, she gave him a look full of meaning that he could not decipher. "Thanks for the whiskey." He rolled the Scotch around on his tongue.

Mother frowned. She disapproved of spirits before dinner, but when she spoke, it was to talk about Grandfather. "I'm afraid your grandfather may be considering mischief. He has been an autocrat far too long to leave off easily." She flicked a speck of dust from his coat sleeve. "You have offered him the strongest challenge he has ever had."

"I don't wish to cause unpleasantness."

"If there is to be unpleasantness, you won't be the cause of it, my dear. Believe me." She sewed an inch before saying, "He ordered me to take the receipt from the Assay Office into my own keeping." The needle drove into the fabric and up, and she pulled it out, thrust it in for the next stitch. "I think he meant to get it from me afterwards. So I shall not ask you for it."

"No, Mother, do ask me for it. Now." Grandfather would use Mother against him, would he? Rather than demand the receipt himself, he would put her in the middle of this. Would he stop at nothing to acquire the gold?

"How stern you look, Daniel. Very well. May I have the receipt?"

"No." He made himself smile. "I'm keeping it safe, and no one needs to worry about it."

"Thank you." She squinted at her sewing. "I should never have made a seamstress. Ah, well. Pray tell me something of your life in the West."

"I hardly know where to start. What would you like to know about? The climate? Gold mining? The people? The terrain?" When he stopped, his mind ran on with the list: The murders, the robberies, the hangings.

"None of that, so much. I want to know how you live. If you do go back, I want to imagine you there. What sort of house you live in. Whom you associate with." She paused, and as he was about to answer, she bent her face toward her work, hiding her expression from him. "What is your wife like?"

As he hesitated, surprised, Martha's face rose up in his mind's eye as if she stood in the room. The beauties of her heritage had molded her features: the high cheekbones and luxuriant dark hair, the deep brown eyes from her Cherokee side, the narrow face and complexion like thick cream from her Scottish ancestry.

He became aware of Mother's voice, and understood that she apologized. "I spoke in haste, before." Her hands stilled, and she laid the sewing aside. "I traced your probable journey on a map one day last summer. I put my finger on a spot west of the Mississippi, along the Missouri River, and something struck me." Her voice thickened as if she spoke through tears. "The map was so vague out there, and it struck me that you could disappear into it. Indians, and bad white people. Wild animals. Floods. Blizzards."

Her eyes shining, she pulled a handkerchief from her sleeve to dab at their inner corners. "That day I thought I would die if you did not come back. I could not have borne it had you not returned. Nothing else mattered. Not the houses, the furniture, my jewels. They were all gone, but they were just things. Acquired with money. We had lost your father, and with him our good name, our standing in society, our reputation. Everything that makes life bearable in this city, I thought. Until I understood we could lose you.

"I could not have endured that. You are my first son, and a mother always feels special about her first son, though I hope I have not treated your brothers and sisters less well because I love you most." She blew her nose and tucked away the handkerchief.

The glass stopped without touching his lips. She loved him most? In his whole life, she had never spoken of loving him. All during his growing up she had been preoccupied with her charity work, her benefits, her social round. He had felt she hardly noticed him. Besides, he was a boy, and boys were reared by their fathers, not their mothers, whose job was done when he grew out of baby dresses and his curls were cut off. He had gone from a nurse to a governess, and then to school. When he was almost fifteen, Nathaniel had come, and ten years after Nathaniel, the babies.

He sipped the whiskey, wished he could escape. What did it matter now, this talk of love?

Perhaps he made a sound, or moved, because she raised one hand, palm toward him. "I shall be happy to receive your wife whenever you bring her home. Tell her –" a moment's pause "–I look forward to welcoming her as a daughter. Please tell me about her."

"What do you want to know?"

"What does she look like?"

That was easy. "Martha is small." Her shoulder came under his arm, as if they had been fitted to each other. "Her hair is almost black, and she has a slight figure. Her two children, a boy and a girl, take after their father, who was of Scottish descent. Much like her own father, I understand. She is a woman of great courage."

He swallowed some whiskey, and she asked a question, and then another until he yearned to escape lest she force him too near the truth of his non-marriage. To break the chain of question and answer, he said, "By the way, I ran into Mrs. Browne at the Cooper Institute."

"Mrs. Browne? What was she doing there?"

"Looking at pictures with her husband's sister. She mentioned that she would send round an invitation to tea."

"Indeed." An odd look crossed her face. "I suppose I shall accept."

He wondered about that look. "What is it?"

"She is acquiring something of a reputation, I'm afraid, with her husband at war."

So that was what he had felt about Harriet. "I understand," he said.

Mother nodded. "I rather thought you might."

He watched her take careful, crooked stitches. Martha could sew much better than that, and pictured her head bent over yellow cloth, candlelight flashing on the needle.

"You're very different now."

He jumped. Dreaming of Martha, he had lost himself. "What?"

"I'm your mother. I know your expressions, still, even though you are changed."

The sunshine on his neck was uncomfortably warm. He could think of nothing to say.

"You have a quality of stillness now that you did not have before. I have seen that look among veterans home from the war. As if you have nothing to prove to yourself or anyone else." She sighed. "Your father never achieved that."

The thread tangled into a knot. With an impatient sound, she bundled the whole thing up and thrust it into the sewing basket. "Come. Let's take some air. Walk with me in the garden. I am so happy you are home safely, I can hardly contain myself."

Downstairs, a parasol stood ready at the drawing room door, and when she opened it, to shield her complexion, he thought of Martha, Little Sparrow, who did not own a parasol.

They walked to the maple tree where a bench stood in its shade. When she lowered the parasol, her hands shook, and he saw tears running down her cheeks. She grabbed his lapels in her fists, and he leaned the parasol against the bench so as to hold her. Her tears came hard, and her shoulders jerked as if she fought him. He had not seen her cry when Father died, before the funeral or afterward. When they had to vacate the house, she had walked out carrying her one valise, back straight, without looking back, and left everything to the bailiffs. But now she sobbed in great wrenching gulps, the pent-up emotion of too much happening.

He wished himself far away, but he held her without speaking, and somehow it was enough.

Tomorrow he would meet with Peter and begin to learn how to keep her – all of them – safe.

Grandfather could go to hell.

~11~

FROM BEHIND THE BARRIER of his newspaper, Grandfather pounded his fist on the table. The breakfast dishes jumped. "I tell you, a sound economy is based on gold, and that madman's paper money will be the ruination of this country." Crumpling the paper to glare at Dan, he said, "Mark my words, those devils in the Gold Room will drive down the value of gold until worthless paper is all we have, and then — ruination, I tell you! Ruination!"

Holding comments behind his lips, Dan washed his toast and jam down with coffee, and left the table as soon as he could. As he prepared to go out, Mother stopped him in the foyer to tidy his cravat. "Can you endure him?"

"Yes, by seeing as little of him as possible. I'm going to the Exchange today. Peter Yates is a broker. He has invited me to observe and have dinner later. I'll be back late."

"Then you must have a key. We can't exhaust the servants by making them wait up."

Not until he left the omnibus at Trinity Church and looked eastward along Wall Street, did he admit to agreeing with Grandfather's tirade. The more gold went down, the fewer greenbacks it would buy. His idea could not work.

Despite the warm morning sun, a chill whispered across his face. Would he have to remain in New York? Work off the debt? Deep in morose pondering, he walked down Wall Street until he stood across from the Sub-Treasury, on the corner of Broad. All around him, tall buildings rose, and the air, warm and heavy, pressed down on him. He straightened his shoulders. He would not stay here, where brick and stone cramped the air. He would go home. Marry Martha. Have children of his own. Crossing Broad, he walked south. In the middle of the block, across the street, stood the New York Stock Exchange, four stories tall, with a fifth, penthouse, story on top. A palace of marble, arched windows on every floor, it dwarfed the buildings on either side.

He walked on, down Broad onto Exchange Place and turned left to Gilpin's, where a shouting throng gathered. Mingling with the outside traders, he listened and watched, occasionally going away for a beer, to buy a pretzel or a sausage, to answer a call of necessity. His uncertainty grew with every downward tick of the dial in the window, every chorus of "John Brown's Body." The Union must win, but the greenback must go down. He felt like a traitor.

At close of business, knowing he had wasted a day, he accompanied Peter to his office, a space enclosed by short walls, and crowded with a desk, two visitors' chairs, and a hat stand. Palatial compared to a store-room, he thought. He watched Peter tot up the day's trades, each buy and sell, demand note and ticket, and enter them into a ledger. That done, Peter rang a bell, summoning a clerk to collect the lot.

"He'll check my figures against the tickets." Peter leaned back in his chair and stretched. "I'm famished. What do you say we get dinner now?"

"I'm hungry, too, but I have a question."

"A fairly urgent question it is, too, by the look of you." Peter stood up. "Whatever it is, I can't think on an empty stomach. Come, I'll buy your dinner and we'll celebrate your return."

~12~

"I WOULD HAVE TAKEN YOU to Delmonico's on Fourteenth," said Peter, "but we'll save that for when you make your first million."

They faced each other in a high-backed wooden booth in a German beer restaurant two blocks from Tompkins Square Park. The tavern doors and windows stood wide open to let in hints of cooler evening air, and along with it came City sounds and smells: clopping hooves, squeaking axles, and the stench of manure piles festering in the dissolving heat. The City, he thought, should find a new contractor for street cleaning.

"Is that possible?"

"Of course it is. I've seen men do it in a week. And go broke on one trade." Holding up two fingers, Peter caught the bartender's attention: "Zwei dunkel bier." He smiled. "I speak atrocious German, but they understand me."

A waiter brought their beers in tall steins carved with domestic scenes in elaborate detail. They gave their orders and picked up their beers.

He leaned one elbow on the table. "How?"

"How." Peter clinked his stein against Dan's, and drank. His brown eyes gleamed with fun over the rim.

"I meant —"

"I know. You want me to answer your question and tell you how to make a million. You're always in a hurry. We'll get to that. I promise. First, tell me what you've been doing."

He drank half the beer at once and set down the stein. How could he ever answer that question? Could he say: Hanging criminals. Living in harm's way. Loving another man's wife. "Oh, nothing much. Seeing the country. Getting the gold. Bringing it home."

Peter struck his fist on the table. "You did it? By God, I see from your face you did it."

He patted the air, dampening Peter's enthusiasm. "Not so loud."

"Don't worry. They don't speak English here. If they did, there's too much noise."

True enough. Waiters and cooks shouted at each other, and two accordions, one inside and one outside, contested for market share among the people bellowing German songs and pounding their steins on the wooden tables. "Yes, I did it. I brought it to the Assay Office on Monday, and waited while they weighed it." He fished into his inner pocket, brought out his notecase. "Here's the receipt."

Studying the receipt, Peter's smile grew. He pounded the side of his fist on the table faster and faster, dropped his voice so that Dan almost could not hear him. "Eighty-two pounds. This is wonderful, by God." He gave the receipt back. "Guard this with your life." Lifting the stein, he saluted Dan. "Here's to you."

They drank, and set down empty steins. Peter signaled for refills.

Peter said, "You could deposit that receipt with us for safekeeping." Shook his head. "On second thought, you'd have to keep the key to your strong box. A key is easier to lose."

The waiter took away the empty steins.

Peter leaned forward. "Raw gold?"

"Raw gold."

"Flakes, nuggets, that sort of thing?"

"Exactly that sort of thing. We call it dust."

"Dust. Good God in heaven. Dust. You brought back eighty-two pounds of dust? Like in that pouch you had at the office?"

"That was dust."

The waiter brought their dinners on heaping plates and went away.

"Isn't gold embedded in rock?" Peter loaded sauerkraut onto a forkful of wurst and shoveled it into his mouth.

He cut a bite of his schnitzel, savored the combined spicy flavors with the veal.

The waiter returned with the filled steins, pale foam flowing over his hands.

"Sometimes. When gold-bearing rock is eroded by water and lies at the surface, that's called placer gold. It may be embedded in rock, or just mixed freely in the soil. The rock holding the gold is called country rock. Men dig dirt out of the streambed, or they crush some rock with sledgehammers and wash away the dirt. Gold remains because it's heavy."

Peter washed down wurst and kraut together with beer. "My God, I wonder what it'll assay at. When will you know?" Glancing at Dan's plate, "No sauerkraut?"

"In a couple of weeks." He forked cold potato salad into his mouth. "I hate sauerkraut."

"Have you any guesses?"

"About twenty thousand. I don't really know." He sipped his beer, and thought of the pandemonium at Gilpin's. "It'll depend on the market, won't it, and in any event it won't be enough for what I need." Remembering how Mother had broken under the strain at last, he laid down his cutlery and leaned against the wooden back.

"What do you mean?" Peter crammed in another loaded forkful.

They had been friends since they were both in dresses, yet he considered how much to tell. With a jolt, he realized he had lost the faculty for easy trust in Alder Gulch, when he had fitted the noose around the neck of one who had claimed to be his friend. If he could not trust Peter, who had remained his friend through everything, though, whom could he trust?

"I haven't enough gold to pay Father's debt, so I intend to pay it in greenbacks. With gold dropping, though, after paying the Bank, there won't be enough greenbacks left over to secure the family's future."

"Pay the debt in greenbacks?"

"Yes." Waiting under Peter's stare, he thought, Christ, what if Peter disapproved? He had never considered that his friend might not help him, or that, like Grandfather, he would think it immoral to pay debts with paper money. A drum beat in his left ear.

"I suppose you know that only debts incurred prior to passage of the Legal Tender Acts are payable in greenbacks."

He knew his ground, having read all three Acts. "The operative term is 'incurred.' If the Bank fights me, I'll argue that the debt was incurred prior to passage, although it came to light afterwards." He spoke in an even tone, as if he discussed another man's debt, another father's self-murder. His ear throbbed.

"Are you a good lawyer? Can you win against the Bank?"

"I've learned a few things about trial work." The winter cold settling into his bones, the threats shouted from the dark, the fists raised by torchlight.

Instead of answering, Peter waved his fork. "Let me think. Eat. This is the best schnitzel in the city."

Not rightly tasting the food any more, Dan ate, while Peter stared at a spot over his shoulder, on the brown wooden seat back. When his friend's eyes darted from side to side, he knew an idea had struck him. Around them swirled accordion music and singing, mingling with smells of food and beer, music and smells together riding cooler air coming through the door and windows.

At last, Peter set his knife and fork on the plate, pushed it aside, and took hold of the stein, his face altogether serious. "I can make money for you, because I understand gold. You needn't raise your eyebrow at me. Not mining the metal, but gold as money."

"I'm listening."

"You understand, there's a considerable risk. Every day, fortunes are made in the Gold Room. And lost."

The risk. A tingle in his tailbone flared up his spine, and his face grew warm.

"Aha!" Peter pointed at him. "You're still diving into quarries."

"You, a man from the Gold Exchange, would say that? You live by diving."

"I live well, too, old friend. I have draped Cleo and my mother and sisters in diamonds and silk, sent them and our babies to the Poconos to escape this infernal heat." He wiped his forehead with a napkin. "It may kill me yet." Tossed the napkin aside. "How much risk can you stand?"

Almost, he laughed. Risk. Twice he had traveled nearly 3,000 miles over wild trails. Played poker with a loaded revolver on his lap. Fooled thieves by lying that the box contained books. "Some. I'm not sure. Does anyone know until he must stand it?"

"All right. In brief, to answer your question, the rise in the value of the greenback does not affect your goal. Granted, the gold market is going down. It's a bear market, but men make fortunes even so by selling short. And as Union men, we want a bear market. We are bears."

He opened his mouth to ask a question, but Peter's upraised palm forestalled him. "Let me be your broker, and I'll teach you what I know. You could even to trade for yourself. "

The hairs rose on the back of his neck. No wonder Peter had asked him about his tolerance for risk. Facing a hostile mob jury armed with loaded shotguns, he had been frightened, but he had endangered only himself, his own life. Now, the family's future depended on him. He did not know enough to trade on his own. Even with Peter's help, how could he learn it in time?

Peter was saying, "By selling short, we turn your gold into a fortune. Then you convert most of it to greenbacks, even at 250 to one, pay the debt, and invest the remainder in government Treasury notes. They are redeemable at par in gold."

Out of the maelstrom of questions, two spun clear. "You're willing to trade on my behalf? How can I repay you?"

"Oh, I don't work for free. My regular broker's fee is $12.50 for every thousand I trade."

"Win or lose?"

"Precisely."

"What if I run out of gold?"

"That's rather unlikely, but the beauty of the market is you don't actually have to own any gold. You're buying and selling promises. Of course, now and then someone wants the real thing, so you have to come up with it as promised, but by then you will have sold the promise to someone else. You're rather a rare bird, you know, having gold in your possession. You and Mr. Clews, and Daniel Drew."

If he had felt before as if he dove into the quarry, now vines entangled his ankles and held him under. To save the family, he would have to place their future in Peter's care. He had no choice. He had to trust him as he would never trust anyone else. Besides, as the clerk said, he had a nose for gold. "All right, though I don't understand selling short."

Pulling out his pocket watch, Peter snapped open the lid. "Damn. We'll be late. Drink up." He slid out of the booth, and tucked a three-dollar gold piece under his plate. "Your education, Danny old boy, begins tonight. At the Evening Exchange." He slid out of the booth.

Snatching a final gulp of beer, Dan followed.

~13~

ON TENTH STREET they caught a City Car uptown and walked westward on Twenty-third to the Fifth Avenue Hotel, a magnificent pile that filled the entire block. Waiting for their chance against the traffic, Peter said, "Mr. Gallagher established his Evening Exchange in the small building behind the hotel." They dived behind a fashionable equipage into a swarm of pedestrians crossing from the other side, beat their way upstream, sprinted almost under the noses of a pair of matched grays, evaded a charging omnibus, and landed on the sidewalk.

Gallagher's Evening Exchange, where trading went on until midnight, was much like Gilpin's in the same frenzied buying and selling just shy of chaos. At the entrance to the trading room stood the biggest man Dan had ever seen, several inches taller than his own six feet and fifty pounds heavier, who planted himself wide-legged in their path. Peter spoke to him under the muffled grumbling from the other traders. The behemoth glanced at Dan and nodded.

In a muted shriek, Peter said, "You can watch as my guest, but stand where Joseph puts you, or you'll have to pay the traders' fee. $100 a year." Joseph led Dan into a long rectangular room, and gestured toward a steep flight of stairs to a raised platform fenced with a carved wooden balustrade. He joined other observers watching the pandemonium below and looked for Peter, but the men's black plug hats, like his own, concealed their heads, turned them into ravens, bobbing, twisting, jerking, impossible to distinguish.

A bar dominated the left end of the room. The mahogany nudes at either end reminded him of those in Con Orem's saloon, but these lacked draperies. Lights from the chandeliers twinkled over the bottles arrayed before the mirror. There was constant travel from the trading floor to the bar and back. A sure recipe for losing a fortune, he thought.

On the opposite side of the room, a railing fenced off two desks beneath blackboards perhaps nine feet wide by seven feet high. One blackboard bore three repeated columns: "Gold," "Premium," and "Greenbacks." A short man wearing a plaid cap ran up a rolling ladder, down again, moved the ladder a foot or so, and ran up once more. Each time, he wrote the changing values in three columns. A tall man, equally thin but sporting a hat nearly as tall as the President's, wrote on the other blackboard, labeled "War News."

To Dan's right, stood a third desk beneath a sign, "Western Union." A machine's sudden clatter startled a corpulent man smoking a cigar. He squinted at the emerging tape, scribbled on a pad, tore off the sheet, and waved it at the tall man who snatched it, scrambled up his ladder, and scribbled "Peters – Disaster," "Grant – Retreat."

"Damn!" He glanced around to see if anyone heard him. On Saturday, Union forces had blown a giant crater near Petersburg, Virginia, and on Monday the *New York Times* first reported it as an "eminent success." Now, late on Tuesday, it was a disaster? A whisper circulated among the men on the balcony: "Union forces wandered into the crater and the Rebs slaughtered 'em." "Grant's pulling back at first light."

Copperheads and Confederates linked arms, cheered, and sang, "Dixie."

Union men booed.

Rumor or truth? It didn't seem to matter. The trading took on fresh fuel and steamed ahead.

Close under him, two men screamed in each others' faces: "Buying two: 50 at 1/8." "Buying two: 50 at 1/4." "1/3." "Sold," shouted a third man, the seller, "Buyer two: 50 at 1/3." Converting the fraction to decimals, he realized that the bid was for $50,000 in gold at a premium of – a glance at the board – 257 1/3. Calculating it, he clutched the balustrade. That $50,000 in gold was worth more than

$128,666 in greenbacks at the current premium.

He asked a man standing near him, "What does it mean, 'buyer two'?"

"Deliverable in two days." The other man flicked Dan a sideways glance that told him plain as words to ask no more questions.

Shorty recorded 257 1/3. Gold was headed up, rather than down. Nearby another bidding war got underway. Someone offered "200 at 1/6", which he figured meant sell $200,000 at 257 1/6, well below 257 1/3.

The first answer came: "Buyer three: give 3/16 for any part of 200."

Through the din, he picked out an offer shrieked from somewhere in the mob. "Buyer three: 1/5 for two."

A third voice: "One-fourth for two."

Then, "Three-fourths for two."

The seller took the last offer: "Seller three: Three-fourths for two. Done."

As if he had been surveying through a transit set to the wrong focus and now had adjusted it, the blurred pattern of bid and counter bid came clear.

He understood: The man who had bid for $200,000 delivered in three days for 257 3/4 had won over his rivals, and driven the premium up at the same time. As fast as a man could speak, the seller had earned an extra $1000 between $514,500 at 1/4 and $515,500 at 3/4. The news had driven up the price of gold, and sent the greenback down.

On the basis of the new Petersburg report, the premium on gold was rising before his eyes, and the greenback was worth ever less. He ground his teeth. For their idea to work, gold had to go down and greenbacks had to rise in value. Contrarily, Union victories were sadly few these days, and the price of gold went up, while greenback values sank.

Another idea clicked into place: he and Peter could win whether values of either gold or greenbacks rose or sank. It was so beautiful, he laughed aloud. The man he had questioned moved away a few inches.

The big room was hot, despite the open windows, and the air mixed human smells, tobacco smoke, and chalk dust. From the back of his head rumbled the distant echo of a headache. He searched for Peter to take his leave, but could not single him out from all the other jostling ravens. He put his hand under his coat to massage the tight muscle across his left shoulder. The Western Union man flapped a piece of paper that Tall Hat retrieved. The room hushed so that he heard a voice: "Seventy for 5/8," but not whether it was buy or sell. Tall Hat wrote on the news board: "C retreat."

In the hush a man whooped. Peter waved his hat in the air, and kissed the paper he held.

Another tore up a paper and bulled his way out of the room. A heavy man swept off his hat to wipe his sweating forehead on the crook of his arm and forced his bulk toward the door. A third caught Dan's eye; his cheekbones stood out sharp over pallid hollows. In the moment before he clapped his hat on and was lost among the multitude of hats, Dan thought his despair rivaled that of a man on the gallows.

Heat and breathless air drove his headache pain so high that he felt ill. He climbed down the stairway and pushed through the throngs that crowded the hallway, jammed the stairs, and spilled onto the sidewalk. Hoping the cooler air would ease him, he decided to walk to Arthur's house.

This day he had learned how men made money trading gold. A Union victory drove gold values downward, because men had renewed faith that the Union would be preserved and its greenbacks would sustain the nation's economy. When gold dropped a fraction tonight, Peter had made money. A Rebel victory drove gold up, but he bet that Peter made money then also.

When at last he reached Arthur's house and climbed the stairs to his attic room, he was asleep almost before he lay down, but he dreamed of flying fractions and premiums that he tried to catch like butterflies in his bare hands, and failed.

~14~

SITTING IN ARTHUR'S GARDEN after a Sunday meal of ham, roast potatoes, three kinds of vegetables, and pie, Dan fought sleep to study his notes.

He should not have eaten so much, but after a few days of infrequent hasty meals, he'd been hungry. His head drooped forward, and he jerked awake. Over the brick walls surrounding the long garden, came the Sunday sounds of children playing, piano music. Someone yelled, "Shut up and let a man sleep."

Think, damn it, concentrate. He had to learn how to trade, and fast. Time was short. The final receipt for the raw gold rested in his notecase: 82.031 pounds, estimated at almost $20,952. In nine days, on the 16th, he'd have the minted gold, coins and bullion. He would have three days, then, to pay the Bank.

The last two days, gold had hovered between 258 1/5 and 258 1/2, but Peter refused to worry. There was money to be made either way, but it could not stay up, it must come down. The tide of war would turn in the Union's favor, because it was in the right, against the Confederates. "The bulls will have their day, but the bears will prevail. The greenbacks will rise in value." Peter might have a nose for gold, but no man was clairvoyant. What if Peter were wrong and gold rose?

What if, God forbid, the Union lost?

Peter's wide looping hand sprawled across pages, interspersed with the daily tables of values Henry Clews & Co. issued to its traders. Dan studied them. During the past six days of trading, gold had hovered between a low of 256 and a high of 259, with the high mostly at 258 and a fraction, as if the gold traders fought to a stalemate as well as the armies of Grant and Lee.

"Look at the fractions." The voice sounded so loud that for a split second he thought it was real. Glancing around, he saw nothing except the curtains moving at the windows looking out on the garden. Hairs rose on the back of his neck. Was he being watched? After a space, when nothing more stirred, he pulled his attention back to the chart.

It must have been a breeze.

The fractions told the tale, just as they did in Gilpin's. On Tuesday, August 2, gold had closed at 258 2/3, on Friday 258 1/2, and on Saturday 258 1/5. It had slipped, fractionally, but decidedly. Dan divided $21,000 by each. When he had finished, he reached for the lemonade and stared at what he had written. In those five days, his gold had lost nearly $100 in value, from $54,195 to $54,098 in greenbacks.

The *New York Times* reported mixed war news. Sheridan's pursuit of Early protected Washington, but the Petersburg mine was known for a failure. The *Times* had also reported that Farragut's campaign in Mobile Bay was a disaster, the rebels had wantonly destroyed Chambersburg, and fought Sherman to a stalemate in front of Atlanta. God, he did not want the Union to lose the war, but he needed more gold. Much more.

Could Peter really make enough money without him having to risk trading? Mother and the family, Martha and her youngsters. The children he might have with Martha. God, how he wanted them. He listened to the squeals of laughter from the children next door, where the little ones had gone to play. He wanted that music in his own home, with Martha.

His chin sank to his breastbone. I'll be the richest man in the Territory. Who said that? He started awake, his lagging memory caught up. Fitch had said that, the God damn greyback.

Forcing his attention back to Peter's notes, he read: "Dan sells Thomas $10,000 in gold at 260, deliverable in three days." That was the "Seller three" he'd heard in the trading rooms. "If the price of gold falls to 250 on the third day, Thomas nevertheless pays him 260, and Dan profits by $1000; if the price rises to 270, Thomas pays him 260, and Dan loses $1000."

All right. That was easy enough. Dan turned over a page. Under the heading, "Principles of Selling Short," Peter had written: "1: Buy for less than you sold it for. 2. Sell for more than you bought it for. 3. Each sell price must be less than the previous sell price."

As he reached out to pour himself more lemonade, something crinkled in his shirt pocket. Pulling it out, he felt the thick, creamy paper. Harriet had kept her promise and sent an invitation. Not to tea, but to a musical evening, to hear a soprano sing selections from the Magic Flute. Mother and Flo had been all a-flutter, stitching, hoping their clothes would not be too out of date. Someday, he vowed, they would not have to worry about such things.

He drank more lemonade. A tabby cat stalked a small brown bird hopping about in the grass. "Hey!" he shouted, and the bird flew. The cat glared, sat down in the sun to wash its paw.

The back door hinges squeaked. A bee flew into the lemonade pitcher and began to drown. Reaching to pluck the bee out, he glanced up. Grandfather came clumping toward him over the grass, Joel Van Fleet following. He scooped up the bee, flung it aside, and rose to meet them.

Grandfather leaned both hands on his walking stick. "We want to know when our gold will be ready for collection."

Van Fleet, dressed in his city suit, with his tall hat in his hand, had already regained most of the plump aspect he had lost in Alder Gulch. At least he had the grace to look embarrassed by Grandfather's abruptness. "Good afternoon, Mr. Stark." He nodded at Dan, summoned something of a smile, and put out his hand for Dan to shake.

"I've just rescued the lemonade from a bee. My hand is sticky." The liquid dripped from his fingers. "You appear to have recovered from your Western ordeal."

"I have, thank you. And you?"

"Quite well." He looked at Grandfather, whose chin, jutting out at an angle, appeared almost to meet the tip of his nose. "Whose gold, did you say?"

The old man glared up at him. "Mine, and then the Bank's. Mr. Van Fleet will deliver it to the Bank."

"Van Fleet deliver it? How?"

"That is not your concern," Grandfather growled. "Your part of this is finished."

"The hell it is. I earned that gold, and it is mine. When I pay back the debt, I will consider my part finished and not before."

"You can't do that," said Van Fleet. "You are not the legal representative of your family. Your grandfather is head of the family. He has made agreements that legally bind you to —"

Dan looked at the old man. "What have you done?"

Something in his bearing, perhaps, or in his expression, or the very quiet tone in which he spoke caused the old man to step backwards. "What did you think to obligate me to?" He viewed Grandfather as through a film, oil spreading on water. An inner voice warned, This is your Grandfather. Behind his back, he doubled his fists, crumpled the papers.

Van Fleet began to speak, but one glare locked him out. This did not concern him.

"I have agreed that as soon as it is minted, you will turn the gold over to Mr. Van Fleet, who will transport it to the Bank of New York."

"It is my gold, I earned it, and I have made other arrangements."

"Daniel, you can't!" Grandfather reared up to his full height, a full head shorter. "It is not your gold. You were sent West merely as an agent, to act in the family's behalf."

His mind raced to recall the law of agency. There was no contract or understanding, written or unwritten, between himself and Grandfather that bound him to turn over the gold, just that he should try to get enough to repay the debt. Which he had done. No agreement obligated him to pay the debt in gold, either. Just to pay it.

"Do not begin an argument with me over the law of agency," he said. "I am a better lawyer than you ever thought of being." And then Grandfather's words caught up with him. Our behalf, he had said. Our behalf. He had changed it to the family's behalf, but if that was what he had meant the first time, why change, unless he had meant something different by 'our.' Grandfather had said, *We* want to know. And *our* gold.

Remembering that Grandfather had told Van Fleet he intended to pay in greenbacks, he realized that far from having an adversarial relationship, as debtor and creditor, Grandfather and Van Fleet were allies.

Against him.

"We" and "our" meant Grandfather and the banker.

"I went West on behalf of the family." He spoke low, with a hard edge. "I am still acting on behalf of the family. Including you, sir, including you." He turned to Van Fleet. "I will deliver payment to the Bank. Just tell me where and when."

"Very well." Van Fleet's face settled into downward folds. Taking a paper from an inside pocket, he read, "You are ordered to appear on August 19 at three-thirty in the afternoon to tender repayment in full of $29,637."

Eleven days, counting Sundays. Nine days of trading. And he was nearly $10,000 short of full repayment. In gold. Not in greenbacks.

"I'll be there," he said. "You'll have your money on time."

~15~

AS IF HE HAD CROSSED a parched plain to reach the oasis at last, Dan sank into the music as into a pool of cool water. Unable himself to play an instrument, or to sing, except adequately, he had not realized how much he missed good music in Alder Gulch. Saloon music was dreadful, played on fiddles out of tune in the dry mountain air, or pianos whose sounding boards had cracked. If the instruments were not good, neither were the players, but here, in Harriet's drawing room, Mozart's "Magic Flute" washed over him.

He sat between Harriet and Mother, with Flo on Mother's other side, and the rest of Harriet's guests grouped around and behind them. As a guest of honor, Mother's face glowed with delight.

The soprano, a stocky, plain-faced woman, had no beauty except her voice, but that alone must have compensated her for all other beauty life had denied her. She launched into the Bell Song. Harriet dropped her fan.

Retrieving it for her, Dan smelled her perfume, sweet but afterward teasing. Taking the fan from him, her fingers stroked across the back of his hand, and her lips curved in a smile as loaded with meaning as his Spencer rifle. When she sat back, he controlled his breathing, but was helpless against the thumping in his ears and his aroused interest. Damn her. She had enjoyed this game, before, and so had he, because it added a bit of spice to life and yet was safe as long as they stayed within the social boundaries. But they were different now. He was not the same man who had set out for the west a year ago. He had scars on his hands and on his soul. She had experienced intimate life with her husband. She knew where a flirtation led, or did she think she could control the outcome?

She stirred in her chair, and her scent wafted toward him, caressed his cheek, then nipped. He crossed his legs, and tried to fix his thoughts on Martha's aroma, cedar wood and sage, as if from weeks and miles away it could calm his mind.

The soprano's voice bounded from note to note, as if the dangerous intervals were no more than spaces between stair steps, but it seemed to him she dared each leap knowing she might slip and send her career tumbling into the chasm.

He wished Martha could be here. He wanted to hold her hand while they listened, and afterwards make love to her with the glory of it still playing in his ears, to taste the joy on her lips, feel it in her hips moving against him, with him, in the ultimate dance. Someday, he would bring her to New York, but until then, could he bring New York music to her? Did the coloratura ever tour the West? Perhaps he might speak to her man of business. Martha needed to hear good music, and not just from the Alder Gulch Choral Society. Recalling their concerts, he winced. Beside this trilling, leaping, lark, their voices galumphed over the music, but never having heard better, Martha loved it.

We should have such music at home, he told himself, before a realization stopped his thought: He had never heard Martha play the dulcimer. Sam McDowell had smashed it in a rage, so Tim had said.

The coloratura's final clear tone hung suspended high above. For a few seconds the audience was held, until they leaped to their feet, cheering as if to drown her in their appreciation. They clustered around her, and in the momentary crush Dan felt Harriet's fingers slide under his suit coat, into his front trouser pocket. The room seemed to darken, as if the sun had moved. At his other side, Mother said something about the music, how the music made her think of long waterfalls from high cliffs. "Indeed, Mother," he said, adding something that pleased her, judging from her happy glow, though he had no idea what it was. He edged away from Harriet, so that her hand came out of his pocket, her fingertips trailing across his flank through the fabric.

Turning on her hostess smile, she turned away to talk to the other guests, leaving Dan to smooth the jagged edges of his breathing and assure Mother that yes, he had enjoyed the concert very much. Yes, Mrs. Browne had a lovely home. The room brightened, and he hoped to God his color did not give him away. All the while, Mother's phrase echoed: A certain reputation. Damn.

A movement caught his eye. Between a parting of her guests' shoulders, her eyes sought him out. In the quirk of her lips, a raised eyebrow, the tilt of her head, he read a challenge as real as poker, or a profit in a bear market.

~16~

DAN CLAWED HIS WAY off the railcar at Hanover Square and joined the stream of men flowing northward, toward Exchange Place, and Wall Street. At Beaver Street, the stream separated into tributaries. Men trotted up the steps of the Cotton Exchange, through the doors. Another flowed in the direction of the Produce Exchange near the Bowling Green. At the corner of William and Beaver, a crowd around the Telegraph Office spilled into the intersection, forced drays, carriages, and pedestrians around them. Dan dropped a shoulder to bull through; he was damned if he'd risk getting run over. Other men cursed him as he shoved past, but he did not care.

He crossed William, walked a short block, paused to admire the rhythm of sunlight and shadow on the blue fluted columns of the Custom House. A blow on his upper arm brought him around, a fist cocked. Peter laughed at him. "Are you ready for a fight?"

"I've sometimes had to be."

"Indeed." Peter took him to one side, out of the doorway. "Did you look at my notes?"

"I spent all afternoon yesterday with them."

"Good." Squinting at Dan's face, shaded by his hat brim, he said, "You look alert enough. Do you understand what we're doing here?"

Not waiting for an answer, he said, "Let's have a little quiz. What are options?"

"Options confer the right to buy or sell for a preset price during a specific time period. Futures are obligations to buy or sell on a specific day for a preset price." Dan paraphrased Peter's notes.

"And that means?"

"If I have an option to buy $10,000 in gold from you at 256 and a half on August 13, and the price drops that day to 256 and a quarter, I can buy or decline."

"Good. And what if you hold a futures contract in that case?"

"I can't decline. I have to buy at whatever the premium is at that moment. If it's 256 and three-fourths, I've made $2500. If it's 256 and a quarter, I've lost $2500."

"How could you recoup that in a bear market?"

"I memorized your principles, but I still don't quite understand how to make money in a down market."

"Think, man. We're in a bear market. How do you profit on $100,000? Hurry. We're losing money as we stand here."

Dan thought, while around him men jogged past, and Peter bounced on his toes. The answer came. "Buy $100,000 at 256 1/2, sell at 256 5/8, and buy it back at 256 1/4, then sell it again at 256 1/2."

"You have it." Peter punched his shoulder and laughed.

He was not so sure. "The proof of the pudding," he reminded Peter, who nodded: "Is in the eating." Thinking, Dan did not hear him. "If I have an option contract I can decline to buy or sell if the premium goes the wrong way, and if I have a futures contract I must buy or sell no matter what the premium is."

"Exactly." His friend beamed up at him. "What an apt pupil you are! Everyone always said you were the smartest boy in school."

"Hmph. If that were the case I'd have had better marks."

"You couldn't be bothered with anything but maths." Jostled by the surging crowd, Peter stumbled, and Dan caught him. Steady again, Peter asked, "When will your gold be ready?"

"They've promised it on the sixteenth, and the meeting with the Bank is on the nineteenth."

Peter whistled. For several seconds he stared into space before nodding once, as if coming to a decision. "Eight days. Seven to trade. That's infernally tight, but if you're willing to risk it, I think we might just do it, if luck is with us."

"What are you talking about?"

Peter tapped Dan's breastbone with his index finger. "It's time for you to trade."

Now? The vines clung to his ankles, and he could not speak, but only stared at Peter.

His friend laughed. "Think of your first fuck. We're all virgins the first time." With that, Peter wheeled about, leaving Dan to hurry into Gilpin's after him. Peter stopped to speak to the floor manager, a beefy man who looked as if he ate and drank too well for the safety of his waistcoat buttons. "Have you got $25?"

Dan drew out his notecase.

The beefy man sneered, "Greenbacks at Gilpin's?"

Stupid. He should have thought. Putting away the notecase, he reached into his trousers pocket for his poke, gave him two Eagles and a Half Eagle. Twenty-five dollars. The price of a year's admission to Gilpin's as a trader. A month-and-a-half's wages for a Union foot soldier.

The floor manager asked his name and wrote it in a book, along with Peter's name as his sponsor. Before releasing Dan to go onto the floor, he stared hard at him, and Dan thought, He'll know me again, anywhere.

"When you're ready, dive in." Peter worked his way to his usual spot on the floor, looked to the board, the outer door, the clock-shaped indicator, and moved three steps to the right. Dan took up a stance a little distant and watched his friend over other men's heads. Lifting his chin, Peter shouted, "Selling three: sixty 256! Sell three: sixty at 256!" He offered a futures contract to buy $60,000 in three days at a premium of 256. As he took a deep breath to shout again, a response slid in between other men's trades: "Buy three: sixty at 256!"

"Done!" Peter jumped and waved his hat for the buyer to locate him among the mob. They exchanged tickets, small preprinted cards with blank lines for the date, the amount, and their signatures. A boy squirmed through the crowd, and took a copy of the transaction, another preprinted form with both signatures, the date and the amounts written in.

Dan put straight in his mind what Peter had done: he had sold the buyer the obligation to buy gold with a face value of $60,000 at a premium of 256. Thinking in money, at 256, $60,000 in gold would be worth $153,600. If the premium dropped to 254, the gold would be worth $152,400 and the buyer would lose $1200 on the deal. But if it went to 257, the gold would be worth $154,200 and the buyer would be $600 ahead. Whether the gold premium were 257 or 254, or any other number, he was obligated to buy at 256. Unless he sold the contract on.

Dan laughed aloud. Everything seemed clear to him now. Changeable as a cloud, but plain, though it was like selling clouds, too. Traders sold gold they did not possess and made their money in the differences between up and down premiums. If the buyer wanted gold, Peter's customer would have to supply it in three days. If he did not now have it, he would have to buy it from someone who did. If he bought it for less than he was obligated to sell it for, he made a profit. Otherwise, he took a loss.

An elbow jabbed his rib. "Quit mooning and pay attention," said Peter. "I've made $3350 in fourteen minutes." Back to trading, without breaking the rhythm of buy and sell, he plucked a folded paper from his handkerchief pocket and gave it to Dan.

Dan glanced at the paper. It was a draft to him on Henry Clews for $5000, signed by Peter Yates. Peter was advancing him $5000 out of his own account to begin trading. Their eyes met, and by a nod the deal was made.

He seemed to see the prospector panning, sledgehammers rising and falling to break the rock and smash its pieces, the rockers and sluice boxes washing gold out of the smashed rock, and the long journey overland, the gold – his gold – transformed into bullion. This mayhem was the end of that trail; the value of gold rose and fell and rose again minute by minute while chalk dust and cigar smoke thickened the air. His pulse beat in his eyes, and his breathing shortened, as if the final card in a royal flush floated toward him. He could do this. He could make money trading in gold, options or futures or the metal itself made no difference. He could do it, he would do it, he knew it as sure as he stood in this chaos and felt the energy rising in him.

Everything around him seemed to slow, and out of the chaos came order, the order of the marketplace where men understood exactly what they did and why, and fought man to man as on the battlefield, the object not to kill but to make money. A man in a dusty brown suit sold an option to a bearded shrimp; a man with mutton chop whiskers bought from a clean-shaven man in funereal black; another man's shoulders slumped as he watched the clerks scribble numbers upward, then lifted as the numbers edged downward penny by penny – gold rising and falling in response to news from Grant and Sheridan in the Shenandoah Valley, from Sherman in Atlanta.

He ran numbers, prices, amounts in his mind with the beautiful clarity that mathematics had always had for him, and bellowed, "Sell two: twenty at five-eighths. Sell two: twenty at five-eighths. Sell!"

From deep in the crowd came the answer: "Buy two: twenty at five-eighths."

His first sale. $20,000 in gold futures at a premium of 255 5/8 deliverable in two days. He completed the transaction, exchanged the tickets, and watched his sale go up on the board. Yelling out the next sale, he thought beneath his trader's cry: A man could love this.

~17~

"TOMORROW YOU CAN TRADE at the Evening Exchange." Peter looked over the tickets for Dan's transactions in Gilpin's. "But this is a very good start. You can't win them all, you know, it's like – " His voice broke off, as if stranded, not wanting to speak of Father, and his inability to think of anything else.

Dan rescued him. "Yes, I know. Like poker. I can't win every hand, but I can do better than evens." Thinking of the lost claim, his smile twisted. "I have to, but don't worry. I don't plunge." Not again. Never again.

Peter cuffed him on the shoulder. "Go home. See your family. I'll call for you at 6:30 to go to the Evening Exchange."

Sweating, squirming bodies pressed into his own on the omnibus, and the ride took longer because of the crowds from the demonstration for McClellan for President. Shouting and whooping, groups of people carried signs into the streets and shouted at every stop, "Little Mac for President!" "End the war!" "Down with Lincoln!"

Damn, he said to himself. Once the commander of the Union Army, General George McClellan had to have been one of the most useless generals ever, always refusing to press forward when he had the advantage. If he were elected, it would be the end of the nation, and Negroes would forever be locked in slavery's chains.

Was Sherman marching on Atlanta, or did the Rebels still hold him a few miles outside? Could Grant prevail against Lee? For Lincoln, for them all, they desperately needed victory, or the Union was done.

At last he could stand the rub of other bodies no longer. He edged through the crowd, past a man arguing with the driver about tokens, and at last stood beside the street. Straightening his cravat and his waistcoat, he felt in his pockets even while he told himself that it would be too late to catch a pickpocket if anything were missing. His notecase, with the precious receipt from the Assay Office, rested in his inside pocket. Without that receipt, he could not claim his gold. He did not know when he had been so weary.

He walked the rest of the way home through the heat and the dampness from the harbor. As he crossed Washington Square toward Arthur's street, he heard his name: "Daniel. Daniel." Nathaniel waved and ran toward him.

"Nathaniel, what are you doing here?"

"Waiting for you." Looking up at him, the boy shielded his eyes against the sun. "I came to warn you. Joel Van Fleet visited Grandfather this afternoon, and since he left, Grandfather has been pacing about and shouting that you're a – a –" He stopped.

"Go ahead, tell me." Tears stood in his young brother's eyes. Damn, this could be serious. Was it a legal challenge? Was Grandfather accusing him of stealing the gold?

The boy's words came in a rush. "He said you're a vigilante. You're not, are you? Like those guerrilla thugs in West Tennessee who lynched that Union man?"

"No. Not at all like that."

"It's not true, is it? It's not true?"

Putting both hands on his younger brother's shoulders, he looked him in the eye. "It is true, but it was not how you think."

Nathaniel's face showed all the disappointment he must have been holding at bay.

"Then what is it? Vigilantes lynch people, don't they? You did that? You?"

The boy twisted out of his hands and ran back to the house. Damn. He took off his hat and wiped sweat from his forehead with his thumb. He had feared Grandfather knowing, but he no longer cared about being in the old man's good graces. As long as he had the gold and could use it for the family, Grandfather could think what he wished. But he did care what the rest thought. Mother. Nathaniel. Damn Van Fleet.

Raised voices came from the first floor sitting room. Dan walked up the stairs, trailing his hand on the banister. Where was Nathaniel? On the landing, he paused, listened.

"It's not true!" Mother's voice. "Daniel would never, never do —"

"Joel Van Fleet told me!" Grandfather, drowning her protest in volume, the voice that had cudgeled the opposition among legislators in Albany, achieved order from the high bench.

"We must hear his side of it." Arthur, using a tone Dan had not heard before, firm as a sword blade.

From across the landing, a door opened, and Flo peeked out. "I'm keeping the children," she whispered. "Dear Arthur thought I must not be upset." Yet her red-rimmed eyes pleaded with him to deny everything.

Martha had said not knowing was far harder than knowing. He went to her. "May I talk to you when this is over?" he whispered.

"Of course." Stepping back, she lifted her chin. "I know you would never do anything dishonorable, whatever the provocation." It was partly a question, partly a hope for reassurance.

"You must judge for yourself. We set the law in place where there was chaos, and the situation was desperate."

Her fist went to her mouth, and she bit a knuckle. He recognized her dismay because he had not fulfilled her hope for denial. From behind her, Grandmother's querulous voice called her in again. Florentine laid her palm against his cheek and closed the door.

Dan paused long enough to draw a deep breath, then pivoted on his heel and crossed the landing to the sitting room.

He opened the door on a tableau: Grandfather, sitting in a wing chair next to the screened fireplace, aimed a forefinger at Arthur, who stood opposite, shaking his head at the old man. "Mark my words," Grandfather said. Mother perched on the edge of the sofa, clutched handfuls of her skirt in white-knuckled hands. Nathaniel stood behind her. Their faces turned toward him as he closed the door.

The air smelled of acrimony, bitter as gall, and threw him back in memory to another room, where booted feet kicked the air. He moved to the center of the carpet, and stood, legs apart, and spoke before the old man could accuse him.

"I understand that Joel Van Fleet has accused me of being a Vigilante. That is true."

"No!" Mother shook her head so hard that a pin flew out of her hair.

"Lucy!" Grandfather barked. "Leave the room immediately." Mother only turned a little more toward Dan. "Lucy! Do you hear me?"

"I hear you, Jason. I shall stay." She looked at Dan as she spoke.

"I forbid it. This is not a fit discussion for a female."

Arthur said, "In my house, mother-in-law, you are welcome anywhere. Although I do agree that this subject is not suitable for feminine consumption."

Mother sat, if possible, even straighter, and raised her chin. Her nostrils were white around the edges. "This last year I have been subjected to the consequences of gambling, suicide, financial ruin, and war. I do not think justice, however achieved, will be too much for me."

Arthur made her a slight bow. "As you wish."

As though he had never caused the interruption, Grandfather chortled, "Van Fleet was telling the truth. I knew it!" His eyes were gleeful, triumphant. He sneered, "Vigilante."

Resisting the temptation to let the flames of his temper burn free, Dan said, "Van Fleet knows nothing. Just gossip, some rumors, but he does not understand the necessity." He took in a quick breath. "Alder Gulch has gold, wealth beyond dreams for the digging, and men's greed has been limited only by their own consciences. We acted for the law. We established the law where there was no law, only the rule of greed."

"Nonsense," said Grandfather, "there is always the law."

"No. Not in Alder Gulch. The Constitution did not apply because Congress did not assign it to Idaho when they created the Territory. It has only now been in force with the creation of Montana Territory."

"I don't believe it," Grandfather said.

Arthur said, "You must have had something."

"Until we agreed on the Common Law, we had no ultimate governing body of law. We had a miners court in each mining district, but their primary interest was to protect property. Gold and gold claims. The rules they administered were set by the miners in mass meetings. Other than that, we had the Ten Commandments. It was not enough."

"Well, then. You had the miners courts," said Arthur. "That was the law."

"They had no power to enforce even such rules as they put in place, and their very structure worked against them. They seldom used a twelve-man jury, but something called the jury of the whole that could change its mind after the verdict and declare it, along with the sentence, null and void." Their faces were unbelieving, as if he described life on another planet, but he charged on. "More than one murderer was freed just that way." His smile at Grandfather was a baring of teeth. "Writs came from a popularly elected court judge entirely ignorant of the law except the mining district rules." He looked at each of them, collected them as he would a jury. "We estimated that more than a hundred men disappeared or were murdered."

Mother gasped. Grandfather shook his head, no, no, no, denying what Dan said. Arthur stared at him as though he were a strange species he had never encountered before. But Nathaniel's eyes shone, and he no longer frowned.

"I explained all this to Van Fleet. He knows it."

Grandfather grumbled, "He knows you had a sheriff already, and deputies, and a court."

"That sheriff was a multiple murderer who killed a man when he broke out of prison in California. His deputies were armed robbers and murderers." He pounded his fist on his open palm. "They committed their murders in broad daylight, in front of people who were too frightened to resist them." Thinking of the Indian, Old Snag, and the honest deputy.

"You could have voted him out of office," said Arthur. "That is the civilized way to replace a crooked official."

Tired as he was, his frustration building up inside him, he forced himself to moderate his tone to reasonableness. "He had been elected sheriff of the entire area at a time when there was only one mining district. After gold was discovered in Alder Gulch, miners formed their own mining districts and elected their own sheriffs, recorders, and presidents. Mining districts have no jurisdiction in other mining districts, nor on the roads between them. Alder Gulch is fourteen miles long, yet we have five different jurisdictions. Did Van Fleet explain all that?" Seeing his Grandfather's bewilderment, Dan nodded."I thought not. Had we not acted, I might well have met the common fate of those who tried to go home with their gold."

"Which was?" asked Arthur.

"To be robbed and murdered." Dan let the ugly words drop among them.

"You can't know that," said Grandfather.

"Oh, yes, I do." Spacing the words out one by one, Dan remembered the false friendships, the affable killers who asked why he didn't leave the Gulch before winter set in, who had offered to ride with him. He had come closer to death than he wanted the family – especially Mother – to know. The bullet scar on his right thigh itched.

"I won't have a vigilante under my roof." Grandfather glared.

Dan's anger set a pulse throbbing in his eyes. He clamped his jaws shut.

Arthur cleared his throat. "Begging your pardon, sir, it is not your roof."

Grandfather turned the glare on Arthur, whose face remained calm above his clerical collar, though some color seeped from his cheeks. "Daniel is my guest. As you are." A subtle reminder that but for him the family might have had to settle into one of the horrid tenements not far away.

Grandfather said, "Then you must choose." He clamped his jaws together, his small old eyes aglow with the crafty look of one about to outflank an opponent.

"No," Arthur said, "I will not choose among the members of your family any more than I would choose among my own."

If he did not move, Grandfather might well declare himself homeless and call for a cab that very evening to take him and Grandmother to a hotel. People would think it unconscionable to throw an elderly couple out of their home.

The old man's mouth opened, and Dan thought he was about to see just that challenge, when his expression changed as a new idea gripped him. He watched the old man think, lips pushing out and in until his upper lip curled as if he had mistakenly bitten into a bug. "I spoke in haste, Arthur. You are correct. It is the height of presumption for me to dictate your hospitality." His features twisted, as from a twinge of arthritis. "I apologize for my ill temper."

Arthur mumbled that the apology was accepted, but Mother was not satisfied. "You should apologize to Daniel."

Grandfather clambered to his feet and leaned on his cane. "I do not apologize to criminals, and vigilantes are nothing more than common criminals." He thumped his way to the door. "We will take our dinner in our room."

As he seized the handle, Arthur said, "That would make too much work. Dinner will be as usual, eight o'clock in the dining room."

Grandfather glared, and his mouth opened as if to argue, but Arthur held firm, his jaw set against any argument. "Hmph." Grandfather stumped out, slammed the door behind him.

"Whew!" Arthur sank onto the wing chair, and Mother bent forward, her face in her hands. Dan perched sidesaddle on the arm of the sofa.

"Would you really have died if you hadn't become a Vigilante?" Nathaniel asked.

"Probably." Dan rubbed his forehead where another headache was starting. "Almost certainly, if I had tried to come home last winter. Fortunately, I did not have enough gold to come home." He felt them watching him. "It wasn't only that, although fear of being murdered was a large part of it." Looking at Arthur, he said, "I had a responsibility that I could not leave to other men. I could not let them risk everything while I kept safe." He was talking to Arthur now, willing him to understand. "How could I do differently?"

"You did not have to join," said Arthur.

"True. No one put a pistol to my heart, but I could not have lived with myself if I had let them take all the risks."

"What did you do, as a vigilante?"

Dan relaxed his hands, that crushed the brim of his hat, smoothed it out. "I am not at liberty to say." He had taken an oath of secrecy, and he would keep it.

"And you practice law," Arthur said.

"Yes. I am not the only lawyer among them."

"I see." Arthur eyed Dan, who wondered just what it was Arthur thought he saw.

After a moment, Mother rose to her feet. "You will excuse me. Betty needs help with dinner if we are to eat tonight." She paused at the doorway and looked back. "I think you have had a far more difficult time than you have been willing to tell us. But I trust you have done nothing dishonorable."

"No," he said, but as the door closed, the whispers of memory set up their clamor.

~ALDER GULCH~

LEGS DRAWN UP, knees touching a bundle the arms clutched to the chest, the body of a tall, big-boned man lay on its side. Hanks of dirty blond hair strayed over what had been the face. Gagging, Tim crawled backwards out of the cave. Sheriff Fox helped him to his feet.

"I warned you," said the Sheriff.

Cold as winter, even in the warm August sunshine, Tim shivered. "Yes, sir, you did." He walked away from the mouth of the cave and stopped to breathe in, down to the bottom of his lungs. On the rim of the gully, Jacob Himmelfarb held the horses. Tim saw him bending over the edge to see, heard the horses blow out their nostrils and small stones rattle like they was moving around, skittish. They didn't like the smell either. He'd long known that horses could smell a catamount a long way off, maybe hear it, too.

Jacob called down to them, "Is it maybe —?"

Tim had to swallow two or three times before he could answer. "It's him. It's Pap."

Not that he could tell from the features, the face being gone, but he recognized the long butternut coat with bits of a small insignia that looked like a cannon, and the belt buckle. A heap of things a man would need lay outside the cave, and Sheriff Fox sat on his heels to look closer at them. Tim walked back to kneel beside him, his quivery leg muscles making him glad not to stand for a bit.

"No, don't touch anything," the Sheriff said. Tim snatched his hand back like it had got burnt. "Let's just look at these things like they are. We don't want to disturb anything." He went on drawing on a piece of paper.

Tim reckoned he meant a snake, or maybe a mouse, and that made him content to just look at the pile of utensils. The burlap sack they'd been toted in had rotted mostly away, and scraps of it lay among the tumbled household items. A dented, rust-flecked coffee pot; a cast iron frying pan, rusty but not too far gone; a cooking pot, a fork, a plate, a white stoneware mug. He knew them all, just like Mam would.

Sheriff Fox took off his hat, ran his fingers through his hair, put the hat on. "We might as well sort through this stuff, see what else there is." He lifted up the coffee pot. "This is heavier than you'd expect." He lifted the lid and turned the pot over. A dried, dead mouse tumbled out, then a small deerskin poke dropped onto the ground. The Sheriff picked it up and hefted it. The poke was almost the same brownish-yellow color as his deerskin gloves. Handing it to Tim, he said, "I'd guess about three, maybe four ounces."

Weighing it on his own callused palm, Tim nodded.

"Aren't you going to look?" asked Fox.

"That's Pap's knot. See? Square knot, bowline, square knot. He always tied that way."

Pap's knot, but Mam's gold. He couldn't speak for thinking of Pap, rummaging around the house, gathering things together, with Mam lying unconscious on the floor.

Sheriff Fox picked up the frying pan and passed it to Tim, who set it aside with the coffee pot. Next came the cooking pot. The lid was still tight, but something rattled hard inside when the sheriff picked it up. He wrestled the lid off and handed the pot over to Tim. Inside was a fancy silver picture frame, tarnished black with the glass splintered, but the tight lid had preserved the picture inside. They'd had the likeness taken in Asheville before the war: Mam, Dotty, him, and Pap. He'd took it with him when he went to war, and Tim had not seen it since.

He'd had some feeling for them, then.

Tim buried his face in his arms and sobbed.

~NEW YORK CITY 18~

"AH, YES, MR. STARK. We have your gold, sir. Five thousand in Double Eagles and the rest in Government Bars, just as you requested." Rubbing his hands together, the beaming clerk in the Assay Office bowed to Dan. "I think you will find everything in order. Here is the original record of how much raw gold you brought, something over 82 pounds, was it not? And here is the assay. Your gold was remarkably pure, if I do say so. Ninety-seven, ninety-eight percent. Easily processed, yes, quite easily processed indeed, my oh my. If you would step through here, sir, and your friend, too?" He raised the counter flap and stood aside to ushered them through. Looking at the two very large men who had come along from Henry Clews, he lifted an eyebrow.

"Wait here," Peter told them. "We'll need you when we come back. We'll have the gold then."

Other men, waiting for attention, watched them, their faces lit with envy.

The vault was a long rectangular room whose walls were lined with six rows of metal doors, that looked like a gallery of blank photographs. Each door closed with a handle that joined two metal loops; a padlock secured the loops together. In the middle of the room long high tables stood end to end. Men perched on stools counting gold coins and bars, and packed them into plain canvas bags with wooden handles like a valise. Pausing in the middle of a side wall, the clerk brought out a key ring, selected a key, opened a door in the second row from the bottom, and began to pull out numbered canvas bags. As he pulled each one out, Dan or Peter lifted it onto one of the long tables. When there were no more bags, the clerk gave them a paper with a carefully printed list in several columns.

The clerk pointed to the first column. "You brought in quite a bit of raw gold, and we divided it into several lots. This is the amount of raw gold in a particular lot." His finger moved to the right. "This column represents the assay results for that lot. The purity. Yes, yes." He pointed to the third column. "This is the number of Troy ounces of refined gold in that lot." At the fourth column, he said, "This is the type of coinage or bar your gold was made into, whether Double Eagle or Government Bar. As you can see, nearly all of it went into bars and coins because of its purity."

Dan looked down to the bottom row of the table, to the totals, and made swift calculations to check the arithmetic of the clerks. When he had finished, he released the breath he had held all unknowing. At last. He knew exactly how much gold he had. $20,816.20. He was more than $10,000 short. In gold. Damn.

Only one calculation remained, ephemeral as the next trade at Gilpin's, but he asked Peter, "What's the premium?"

"Two fifty-five and three-fourths." Peter's whisper hardly stirred the air.

He could make no mistake about this. Slapping his pockets, he located a pencil and scrap of paper in his trousers pockets, fished them out and scribbled a calculation. When he was finished, the total read: $53,237.43. He tried to whisper it to Peter, but his stiff lips would not form words. He pushed the paper across to Peter, who checked it, nodding, "Okay."

After paying the debt he would have $23,600 to ensure the family's safety. Invested in Treasury notes, it would be five years before they could begin to redeem them. What would they do in the meantime? He needed more, much more. Enough money to provide a decent living until the bonds matured. Enough for Peggy's schooling and her dowry, for the boys' education. This was a fine start, but only a start. From across the table, Peter leaned forward, smiling, to shake his hand. "Congratulations."

Shaking hands, Dan said, "We're not finished yet."

"No." Peter's smile faded. "We're not finished. You'll have to be a damn good trader." The smile returned, broadened. "That won't be so hard. You've had a damn good teacher." He poked his thumb into his breastbone. "Me."

Could he do it? Could he be that damn good trader? Commodities trading ruined men as well as made them. His stomach fluttered at the thought. Think of it like poker, he told himself. The odds would be in his favor. They had to be.

~19~

HE REMEMBERED THAT a few days later when he jumped off the omnibus feeling battered and bruised, and longing for nothing so much as a bath and a cold drink. The day's trading, leaving him down $2500, had taught him the hard way about the risks inherent in selling short. As the saying went, experience was a hard teacher, but fools would learn by no other. He'd been a fool, and he could only hope and pray that he could recoup his losses tomorrow. For a moment he paused in the shade of a half-grown maple tree, but it was not much cooler than the street. He tapped the notecase safe in his breast pocket, a reflexive gesture to reassure himself that he guarded it well.

Within a few strides of Arthur's front door, he remembered that he was due to dine at Mrs. Browne's this evening. Just this afternoon, a servant had brought a note to the brokerage asking him to rescue her by making up an even number at dinner. About to refuse, he had found the invitation intrigued him. She could have asked any number of men, so why him? Purely from curiosity, he accepted.

The maid opened the door almost as he let the knocker drop. "Judge Stark asks would you see him in the drawing room, Mr. Daniel."

Pausing before the hall tree mirror to straighten his waistcoat and slap a little of the dust from his shoulders, Dan swore. Grandfather was the last man he wanted to see right now, but he put his head into the drawing room anyway.

"Come here." Grandfather crooked a beckoning finger. "Sit down. You hurt my neck standing there. You're too tall."

Dan stifled a laugh. He pulled up a straight chair and sat on its edge.

"The Bank meeting is in three days."

"I know that. But we can't pay in full. There isn't that much gold. We're about $10,000 short. " He could not delay the meeting, and Grandfather knew it, but it didn't hurt to offer a delaying tactic.

Grandfather waved that aside. "You've been spending too many evenings in the Fifth Avenue Hotel." The blue eyes above the imperious hooked nose challenged him.

Dan said nothing. How did the old man know they traded there at night? Sometimes, he had thought he heard or sensed someone following them, but each time he looked around, he lost the presence. Had he been correct? Had Grandfather hired someone to find out where he went after dinner? From now on, he would try to see the follower, although in New York's nighttime crowds it was nigh to impossible.

Beyond the partially open door the sounds of the household went on, at a remove from him. A woman's quick heels crossed the hallway. A child's voice upstairs shouted, "I don't want to!" Arthur called out, "Has anyone seen my —?" Dan lost the word, which probably meant some piece of ecclesiastical garb. And amidst it all, a man's footsteps walked quietly down the stairs, along the hallway, and he heard the sound of the front door opening and closing. Florentine asked, "Who was that, Nellie? Did Nathaniel go out? He has no business going out now. Has Daniel come in yet?"

"I'm in here." Dan raised his voice. "With Grandfather."

Flo poked her head around the door. "Good. Grandfather, dinner is in half an hour." She smiled at Dan. "Enjoy your evening."

"How —?"

"The servant called here first, silly. I sent him to Wall Street."

"How did you know I would accept?" He ducked as Flo reached out to ruffle his hair.

"Don't be silly. No one refuses Mrs. Browne." Flo tugged his hair. "When do we receive the honor of your company for an evening?"

Dan put his sister's hand to his lips. "If I stayed in every night, you'd be sick of me."

"You men," said his sister with a mock sigh.

Grandfather grumbled, "I don't want dinner so soon. I won't be hungry yet. If you ran this house properly, we would eat at a civilized hour."

"We can't put it back, Grandfather. Arthur has a council meeting tonight." To Dan, as she left the room, "Enjoy your evening, my dear."

Gathering his feet under him, Dan stood up.

Grandfather demanded, "Do you still intend to carry out your dishonorable plan of repaying the debt in greenbacks?"

"I do. For one thing, I see no reason why the Bank should take all the gold and enrich themselves with it. Repayment is all we contracted for, and that's all they get. And – " he held up his hand when Grandfather tried to interrupt – "if we repay in gold, we're short."

"Bah. If you thought of the family instead of yourself, you would even now be starting the firm. You could earn the shortage in a few years. But no, you have no regard for this family."

"Of course I do. The family is the reason I'll repay them in greenbacks." Dan consulted his pocket watch. "I have to change for dinner. This suit is disreputable." He took a couple of steps toward the door.

"How dare you? I have not dismissed you."

Over his shoulder, Dan said, "I'll be at the meeting. Tell Van Fleet they can expect repayment then in full." And the devil in him could not resist adding, "In greenbacks."

He ran up the stairs, into his room. Shutting the door, he leaned against it to catch his breath. Something was not right. The room smelled different. He inhaled slowly, against his body's demand to breathe faster, more deeply.

Cigar. Not the smoke, but an aftertaste of cigar, as if a cigar smoker had been in here. Someone who smoked had been in here. Grandfather smoked cigars, but not often. He would not have been able to climb all this way. Why had someone come in when he was not at home? Perhaps he had not known he was out and wanted to ask him for —? The hell with that. Someone had come in because he had not been at home.

Perhaps he was wrong.

On first glance, everything looked to be as he had left it. His bed was as unmade as before, but the impression of his head was no longer on the pillow. On the desk, papers lay straighter than he had left them this morning. Same with the books on the nightstand.

The intruder had not been able to resist his impulse to tidiness.

Had it been the intruder's footsteps on the hall carpet? Had he closed front door, let the latch click into place? He'd been quiet but not stealthy.

Dan opened the door and hollered down the stairs: "Nathaniel!"

Hurrying feet, and Nathaniel's anxious face appeared on the landing below. "Here I am! Is anything wrong?"

"No, just making sure I wouldn't have to go looking for you."

"I've been here all the time, reading. People keep yelling for me. What do you want?"

"You haven't taken up smoking cigars, have you?"

"No! Dreadful things. They stink. Besides, they cost too much. I'd rather burn greenbacks and have done with it."

"You're not turning into a Copperhead, are you?"

"No, I only meant —"

Dan laughed. "I know what you meant. Thank you." As he turned back to his room to dress, he thought, All right, so it wasn't Nathaniel. He flung up the window sash to let out the cigar smell. Who had searched his room and left while he was talking to Grandfather? And why?

And for what? Removing his suit coat, he emptied the pockets, laid everything on the desk. What had he been looking for? He took the wilted handkerchief from the breast pocket and tossed it onto the bed. It did not need laundering yet, but he should brush the coat before he hung it away. His fingers closed on the notecase, pulled it from his inside pocket.

He dropped the notecase on the desk, but it slid onto the floor. Bending to pick it up, he stopped with his fingers touching it and the blood rushing to his head. The receipt. The cigar smoker had been searching for the receipt. Whoever held the receipt could claim the gold from Henry Clews. His fingers closed around the notecase.

As if dizzy from the great leap his thoughts had taken, he sat on the bed, his fingers white-tipped around the notecase.

The searcher had been after a piece of paper, so he looked only where paper might be hidden – into books, under the pillow, among other papers. But he smoked cigars, and he could not restrain his impulse to tidiness. He'd had the effrontery to come and go out the front door.

Grandfather found stairs too difficult, but was he so determined to pay the Bank in gold that he would stoop to burglary?

Dan wiped his hand across his sweating face. He feared the answer was yes.

~20~

HE HAD NOT WORN his evening suit in more than a year, and it was tight across the shoulders. He must have added muscle during his time in the West, and he supposed that was to be expected, when a man dug his own hole for the necessary, shot and dressed and packed his own game through winter snows and spring mud.

Harriet, resplendent in white, long gloves above the elbows, wore a plume and diamonds in her hair and carried a decorated Chinese fan. She met him with an outstretched hand and a smile that seemed genuine. "Daniel! Mr. Stark, how good of you to come." As he bowed over her hand, she murmured, "I was so afraid you'd stay away."

Almost, he had. His first thought had been to decline, but he had not been able to resist the shiver of chance, not quite a risk, in seeing Harriet again. One hand in the crook of his elbow, she guided him among her other guests, her other hand occupied with the fan in a language of its own. Open and fluttering or languid, closed and touching another male guest on the knuckles, tapping another man's shoulder to claim his attention so she could present Dan.

The feminine arts.

He spoke to this one and that, acknowledged their greetings, admitted that his Western expedition had met with success. The men pumped his hand, their eyes full of envy; the women offered him their admiration. But he met them all, talked with them, as if in a bubble, their smiles bounced off his shield. Why, after all, had she invited him? She could have invited another male to make an even number at her table.

After dinner, during which he entertained them with accounts of the Far West, he tried twice to take his leave. Each time she opened her eyes wide and murmured, "Don't go. Wait." She had not, then, invited him in order to entertain her guests.

So it was that he sat beside a fireplace in her large drawing room, and drank his second whiskey of the evening. She had excused herself on some pretext, and he imagined how she would reappear. When she returned, she had shed her hoop and perhaps some layers of petticoat. She walked around snuffing candles. "No point in wasting wax."

"I thought you were rich enough not to concern yourself with saving wax."

"Little you know, my friend. Rich people are rich precisely because they do concern themselves with saving wax."

"True enough. You can't spend it and keep it at the same time."

Harriet said nothing, as if saving her breath to blow out the candles, but Dan noticed how she displayed her figure to its best advantage while she did so. Martha would have simply blown them out. He closed his eyes to picture her face, but it would not come. He hunted for it, as he might search among papers for the deed to a claim.

"Are you falling asleep?"

He opened his eyes to find Harriet smiling at him. "Perhaps I was. It's late enough." He pulled the watch from his pocket, snapped open the lid to see the time. A miracle it had not been broken in his travels. "Good God! Look—"

"Don't go." She walked around to stand behind his chair and spoke almost in a whisper. Her fingertips tickled his neck at the base of his skull, twined in his hair. A tingle ran down his spine. Was this how Harriet was earning her reputation?

"I must." His voice was hoarse. Her fingers stroked up and down the nape of his neck.

"You're a different man than when you left." Her voice was barely audible. One fingertip insinuated itself under his collar.

"I grew up," he said.

"It's more than that. You have a certain something about you, which intrigues all the women in our circle."

He laid back his head and laughed. "You are joking!"

"No, I assure you, I am most certainly not joking. You do intrigue us all." She came around the chair and sank onto the ottoman at his feet, leaned forward on her locked arms so that he had a clear view down the low neckline of her dress. "You've changed."

Mother had said something similar. What did all these women think, and why did they care? Silly subject, anyway, he thought. "Tell me why you married."

"Why I did not wait for you? I wanted to. When you left, I expected to wait." She sighed.

Listening, he watched the rise and fall of her bosom, sculpted by lamplight and shadow. He did not know what to expect of her, what sort of answer she might give him. The question was impertinent, he knew, but he had left his regard for some proprieties far behind.

"Because you had no prospects." Her fingers twined together, almost as if she wrung her hands. "And because Father dislikes you. Even before, he did not like you." It was as close as she had yet come to mentioning his own father's suicide, the family's ruin. "He thought you would be killed by Indians, or that you would go wild, or any of a number of things. And I thought you would find someone else out there, someone more suited to your character. Father insisted that I not wait for you, that I accept Morton, even though he is twenty years older and had a reputation as something of a roué. He has a sizeable fortune and could provide me with the things Father wanted me to have. I agreed because I wanted to be free."

"Free! I should have thought you were freer as an unmarried woman than as —"

She interrupted him. "A husband is easier to get around than a father is. As Mrs. Morton Browne, I have nearly the entire freedom of the town, particularly in his absence. As Miss Dean, I was so circumscribed by my father that at times I thought I might not exist at all."

"You married, then, for an establishment of your own?"

"Yes, partly, and I made a good bargain, don't you think?"

"It depends on what you want."

She laughed, but it was not a humorous sound. "I have only ever wanted one thing, and that has been denied me."

"What was that?" His pulse beat in his right ear. Before she said it, he guessed what she would tell him, and he asked himself if it could be true.

"You." She looked toward his right hand, that rested in his lap, the fingers casually draped over his inner thigh. "Before, I would have defied my father to marry you. After, it was so much more difficult, and all our friends – well, you know."

She wanted him to exonerate her, did she? Pity me, her eyes begged him. She had thrown him over because she had wanted a better catch, because she had not been willing to link herself to a social pariah, a man without prospects or reputation. He understood her, all right. She, in turn, understood clearly the world they lived in – that she lived in – which decreed that a woman ally herself to the best provider she could. While he had sought after her, so had others, and she had made herself a prize to be awarded to the best prospect. Pity me, her waif-like expression said, her chin tucked, the big eyes looking up from under her lashes. She'd had to find a man wealthy enough to provide well for her, and there had been no guarantee that he would ever have been able to do that, even before the family's fall. Afterward?

She should have known him better. He would have made a life for them, and she should have known it. Blame her father all she might, nevertheless she should have known him better.

Regarding her now, as she leaned forward and rested her elbows on her knees so he could see more of her breasts, loose under the layers of cloth, he felt Martha's presence in his thoughts. Little Brown Sparrow. He could not imagine Martha displaying herself so, she whose shirtwaist buttons rose on high collars almost to her chin. He stared at Harriet's bosom, and felt himself reacting, made sure she knew he stared.

He could have Harriet. Now. Perhaps on that Persian carpet, or in her marriage bed, her blonde hair down around her shoulders, her body in his hands.

He murmured, "I thought of little else but you the first six months I was in Alder Gulch."

"You did?" The words came in a hoarse whisper between parted lips.

"Yes." He slid forward in the chair, touched a ringlet at one side of her face.

She rested her cheek against his palm. "Then what?" As if answering her own question, she took the tip of his index finger in her lips, between her front teeth, sucked on it, nibbled it, released it, and lifted her chin. Dan let the finger move downward, trace her chin, throat, collarbone, the top of one breast, to the neckline of her dress. Her breathing speeded.

He smiled at her. She had removed some undergarments, and perhaps only two thin layers separated him from the dream of his youth, when he had turned her music at the pianoforte and tried to hide his stare down her neckline from her father's guardian gaze. "Then what, indeed?" He spoke below a whisper, so that she leaned into his hand to hear him better. "I met my wife."

Her parted lips closed, and her drooping eyelids raised on what he used to call her patented blue-eyed stare. "You're married?"

"Yes."

Laughing, she inched forward on the ottoman. "We're even, then." Placing a hand on either side of his face, she drew him to her. "We're both faithless."

Blood surged in his veins. He lifted his hands away, onto the chair arms, amid visions of her struggling under him, on the floor.

"What's the matter?"

Though her face was an inch or two from his, her blue eyes huge, and her breath smelled of old wine, he saw her as though from a great distance. "I can't." At the sound of his own voice, the haze lifted.

She pulled back. "You can't?" She stared at his trousers buttons. "But —"

"Not that." A deep-voiced clock somewhere chimed three. He said, "I have an appointment at nine. Besides, your servants will be up soon." His voice sounded hoarse to him, and he coughed behind his fist as he pushed the chair back and stood up.

"You need not worry about servants. Morton taught them well to turn a blind eye. He is a fine educator, you know, along certain lines, and he enjoyed teaching me." Rising, she stood too close to him, trapped him against the chair. She put his finger in her mouth, but this time when she released it, Dan let it drop to his side. She said, "When I played the piano at our musicales you were the only boy I ever allowed to turn the pages. I knew you liked to look down my dress. Morton noticed that, too."

He had thought himself unobserved, and felt a schoolboy's flush. "What?"

"Yes. He understood us both, as I learned after we were married. Then he told me he had recognized in the way I treated you what he called my playful spirit." She fiddled with the tiny buttons at the neckline of her dress. "If there had been a safe way to do it, I would have let you see more. But that would have ruined my value on the marriage market, and Father was determined to make the best bargain possible." An unmistakable bitterness rang in her voice. "So the bargain is made, and I am as free as any woman can possibly be." He willed his fingers to remain still despite the ache in his flesh.

She smiled up at him, her eyes alight with mischief. "Morton is very understanding, too. He rather enjoys the idea that other men find me attractive." When he did not react, she sighed. "Another time, perhaps. I forgot you have an appointment in the morning. Perhaps you'd better go. But I would like to hear about your life in the Far West. I've heard your wife is an Indian." Letting go of his hand, she said, "Is she really your wife? Or your squaw?"

He spoke through tight jaws. "She is my wife, and as unlike you as a woman could be."

~21~

AFTER THE DAY'S TRADING, Dan met Peter on the corner outside Gilpin's. His friend peered up at Dan's face and frowned. In his shaving mirror that morning, Dan had seen dark pouches under his red-rimmed eyes, and now his face felt greasy, with chalk dust clinging to the stubble of whiskers sprouting in the late afternoon. At least Peter couldn't feel his headache, the hammer attack on his left ear that had steadily worsened during each trade, whether he was up or down. He'd finished down, he thought, by about $3,000. The gold premium had bounced between 255 and 251, and he had not ridden the jumps correctly. He'd been stupid and unlucky, tired and distracted by thoughts of Harriet. Some of his options could have been postponed – he had been abysmally stupid to sell them, but the futures had to be traded, and it was damn bad luck they came due today. He could not afford another day like it, or he wouldn't be able to repay the debt even in greenbacks.

He was not cut out to be a trader. He should have left it up to Peter.

"Damn it," said Peter, "you can't debauch the night before you trade, that's an invitation to disaster. You needed a clear head."

They dodged traffic from four directions. When Dan's shoe

landed unsoiled on the corner pavement, he breathed a thank you to whatever sub-deity brought fools to safe shores. Now if there were only one for the trading rooms.

"I did not debauch. I sat up late with an old friend." His tongue was a piece of felt inside his woolen mouth. In truth, he had been in his bed enough hours, but had not been able to sleep. Pieces of Harriet's conversation tumbled in his mind, and he could not banish the dream of her, how his hand had molded to her and his palm had carried away a faint scent of roses. Even reminding himself that Martha smelled of sage and juniper had not served. He could not bring her scent to mind.

"From school? Who? Why was I not invited? I'd have kept you out of trouble. I didn't know anyone was having a party, except Mrs. Browne." He snorted. "She does not invite us, because Cleo does not like her." Watching for a break in the traffic, he added, "Silly woman."

Whom did he mean, Dan wondered. Harriet, or his wife?

Men hurried past, jostled them, grumbled at them: slow-coaches. Peter gripped his elbow, propelled him up Wall Street toward Henry Clews. The Street, a canyon edged in stone and brick buildings three and four stories tall, porticoes and columns in various classical Greek styles, thrummed to the steps of men hurrying on business of vital importance. The steamy air trapped the noise – men, horses, carriages, whip cracks – and pressed it on them.

Dan shook his head, and regretted it. He wanted a bath and a long nap.

Just outside Henry Clews, Peter shouted, "Mrs. Browne! By God, you had an invitation to her dinner party." He slapped Dan's back and lowered his voice as if anyone on the Street would listen for anything except the price of gold. "You'll be the envy of all Manhattan, you will. Her invitations are the most sought after in town, even if she is rather the merry –" He broke off. "Oh, damn, I'm sorry. You and she, I mean she – I was shocked when she married Browne."

"It's all right. I married a woman out West." Dan said, and as Peter's face changed from concern to bewilderment to surprise, he led the way into the office. "Let's see how much damage I did today."

In the event, counting previous losses, balanced against more wins, he was down $7,106. He tried to swallow, but his throat closed. The Bank meeting loomed like a ship out of a foggy night. Just two more days. Damn. He would have to recoup that. Fast. He had to keep his wits about him, but the anvil in his head gave him no peace.

"Wake up," said Peter. "Think, man. You have trades due in what? A day? Two days?"

"Yes." Every day for the next week, in fact. He had to have everything in hand very soon. The tickets were lodged in the metal box tagged with his name, and he watched the clerk slide it into its compartment and turn the keys. Dan pocketed his own key.

"Maybe I can make some of it up tonight?" he suggested. There had to be a way.

"Let's go to my room." Peter meant his private office. Most of the other brokers had desks in a common room. But three or four other traders, among them Peter, had their own offices. "The Evening Exchange? Not in your present condition. You need rest and a fresh start." They spoke low to prevent their voices carrying through the thin walls.

Dan wiped his face, the handkerchief rasped on his whiskers. "Then what do you suggest?" A begging note crept into his voice, and he tried to negate it by smiling, but his face muscles would not respond.

"Truly? Check into the Fifth Avenue, and I'll call for you half an hour before trading. Clean up. Sleep. Then we'll see what we can do."

The hotel had a room available, sir, and a bath room available for gentlemen guests, sir, and an attendant at his convenience, sir. The concierge snapped his fingers to bring the bell boy. Dan sent off his suit to be brushed, ordered a clean shirt, and did not think about the receipt until he was toweling himself off after the bath. The towel wrapped around his loins, he dashed down the long hallway to his room, not caring about the screams of a woman or two, nor their escorts' protests. He unlocked the door and relocked it. The notecase lay under his pillow where he had left it. The receipt and his supply of greenbacks were safe. He slid receipt and notecase under his pillow and sank onto the bed, ignored the pounding on his door.

He must not see Harriet again. He had allowed himself to be thrown off stride: trading for a loss, forgetting about the receipt. It was not her fault, but his, entirely. He must not lose sight of his purpose here, stupid fucking idiot that he was. Even so, his hand curved, and he turned over on his side, drawing his knees up. Falling asleep, he smelled sage and juniper.

~22~

AS HE TROTTED down the stairs from his room, he passed a couple in evening dress. The man, of medium height and thick around the waist, whose tailoring did not hide the lack of muscle in his arms and shoulders, ignored him, but the woman glared as he went by and said, "He's the one. He offered me a gross insult. Go on. Do something, Charles." Expecting a challenge, knowing he deserved it, Dan heard, "A new carriage, my dear?" The woman cooed, "Oh, Charleykins, you are so sweet to me. Perhaps a brougham?"

In the lobby Peter was asking for his room when Dan walked up behind him and offered his key to the clerk. "I'd like to check out now. I shan't need the room for the rest of the night."

"Indeed." The clerk wrote up the bill and slid it across the desk. He tapped a fingernail on the polished stone surface while he waited for Dan to count out the money. In greenbacks. "You do realize, sir, that this establishment is not accustomed to—" Dan laid a three-dollar gold coin on top of the pile. The money disappeared, the greenbacks into a drawer and the coin into the clerk's pocket.

Dan smiled. As they walked away, Peter asked, "What was that about?"

"Nothing important." Only a scandalous nude run down a hallway of the best hotel in New York. He almost laughed.

"You look in fine fettle," said Peter. "Let's hope your performance improves along with it."

He pictured Con Orem's large-knuckled hands gripping the stock of a shotgun. He was a fighter entering the ring, the prosecutor facing a mob jury cursing him by torchlight. Outside the air carried a forewarning of rain. Before going into Gallagher's, he breathed deep, met the waterfall noise that rumbled upward and closed over his head.

The flow of trade carried him, and he rode the current as one swimming under water through tall weeds. Farragut had won the Battle of Mobile Bay. His battle cry, "Damn the torpedoes, full speed ahead," was on everyone's lips. The Board showed gold at 251; it had fallen from 255. He opened his mouth to announce a short, when a thought struck him. This low was premature. Too sharp, too swift. What if it rises? he asked himself. In the Shenandoah Valley, the Rebels were moving north, more were rumored to be massing at the Upper Potomac. Rumors of another riot against the draft floated on the smoke-laden air, and the city was still jittery from the carnage of last summer's riots. He cocked his head, the better to hear with his good ear.

Coughing at the dust and smoke, he bellowed, "Buyer three: thirty at 251 1/8." The answer came: "Seller three: thirty at 251 1/8."

"Are you crazy?" Peter swung around in front of him. "You'll go broke buying high."

"This low is premature." He spread his hands. For the life of him, he could not explain it.

"My God, you are crazy. Farragut has won in Mobile Bay. The war can't go on much longer. Atlanta will fall soon, and it will be all but over. Besides, trades are made for this minute." Peter jabbed his breastbone. "This minute only. Remember that."

~23~

AS THEY LEFT THE HOTEL shortly after midnight, it had begun to rain. Peter walked head down without speaking to him. He had been right, the premium had risen to 253, but Peter expected it to fall more tomorrow and the day after, expected he would lose, perhaps go broke and lose all the money Peter had loaned him.

What if Peter were right? He should have been more cautious. When he walked into Gallagher's, he'd intended to play it smart, recoup his day's losses and begin tomorrow even. Now, he doubted if he would sleep tonight for fear of the premium dropping below 251. He'd staked everything on a hunch, like drawing to an inside straight.

"And you said you never plunged. If this wasn't plunging, I'm damned if I know what it is." Peter spoke as if to the walkway; the flat crown of his hat hid his face.

"I can't explain it."

"Well, try, damn it. Just try."

"I could feel it, as strong as – as hearing thunder beyond the horizon. Haven't you ever been outside on a clear day and felt a storm coming?"

"No."

That single syllable dropped between them. Believing the premium would drop below 251, Peter had lost tonight. Peter said, "If you lose tomorrow, I won't back you any more. You'll forfeit everything, and then what? How do I recoup—"

Men's booted feet clattered behind them, bumped them, and Peter stumbled. Grabbing to save his friend from falling, Dan swung into an arm coming up around his neck, glimpsed the shine of metal, drove his shoulder at the thug, felt the stale-smelling command like a foul kiss at his ear: "Give it up." The robber slid a hand into Dan's coat, pawing at his chest, and he was falling, pain searing his neck, his heel slipping off the walkway amid voices roaring and a whistle's blast. In his nostrils a stench of filth as in a roofless building where hanging corpses slowly froze.

Something lay on him, troubled his breathing, but he held tight to it amid a formless noise that separated into words: "Let go." He held fast to an arm. He opened his hands, and the weight came off him. An Irish accent said, "This one's a stiff." Another said, "So's this one."

Torchlight caught on shiny buttons on a dark coat. Someone knelt beside him. He tried to sit up, but his head weighed too much. "What happened?"

"Bring that torch lower." An Irish accent. "You're bleedin', sir." Cloth pressed against his neck. "Lie still, you've a cut neck, and you're lucky to be alive." Pressed the cloth against Dan's neck. "Can you hold this tight? Good. Here I was, hoping you'd be telling me what happened."

"He attacked us." He put up his hand. "Help me up."

"No, sir. Best you lay still, sir." Put a whistle to his mouth and blew a blast. "Keep holding your hand there." Opened his coat and waistcoat, pulled his shirt tail out of his trousers, tore it into strips, tore the undershirt, folded it and pieces of shirt into a pad, tied it around his neck.

Men's footsteps running, a steady murmur of voices, and he knew he was a spectacle for late New Yorkers. "Move away, now, this man's hurt, move away." Men took his shoulders and legs, laid him against the building. "Keep them away." The policeman knelt at his side. He shielded his eyes from the torch and shivered as raindrops chilled his bare chest.

A woman's voice, somehow familiar, sounded from the general murmur: "Oooh, Charleykins, I think it's him."

The Irish policeman buttoned his coat. Someone gave an umbrella to the mick, who held it over them both. "Easy, there, you wouldn't want to be leaving me, now, would you?"

"No." His neck hurt, and despite the rain, he did not want to move. Only to sleep.

"Good. More help is coming. My name's Grady, by the way. Sergeant Grady."

"Take me home."

"We're taking you to Bellevue Hospital, sir. A surgeon should look at that cut."

Cut? So that was what hurt. The metallic gleam: a knife, then. Shuddering, he listened to the confusion around him, smelled blood. He raised his hand. It was not bleeding, though there was blood on it, and blood on his coat, and his back was wet – with blood? – or maybe rain water. He wanted to sleep, but the Irish sergeant insisted.

"Who attacked you?"

"Don't know. Ask Peter."

"Would that be the other gentleman, sir?"

"Yes."

"Now, then, the hard boyos ran away, and we've got two dead men here, so it seems I'm having to ask you, considering that you're the only one talking."

"Bodies?" He forced words though his tight throat: "Dead men?" He tried to get up, but the Irishman's hand on his shoulder held him. "Peter? Where's Peter?"

"Aye. Bodies. Dead men. Two dead men." Grady described one of the dead.

"He jumped me, I think."

Grady said, "The second dead man is a few inches shorter than you, and thin, and wears a lodge ring, a red ruby with a gold Masonic symbol."

"God, no. That's Peter. No." He closed his eyes to hide the starting tears. "Get me up. Let me see him."

Trembling, he clenched his teeth against the sharp agony in his neck as Grady and another policeman helped him to stand, wobbly but inwardly burning: they'd killed Peter, and he'd get them, by God, he'd get them all, one son of a bitch was already dead. Supported by Grady, he stood over a uniformed policemen who knelt by a corpse. A third kept onlookers away.

Dan pointed to the body. "He's the one who jumped me."

The Irishman motioned to the second policeman, who moved to let Dan see. "Jesus Christ." Rain drops slapped down on Peter's wide open eyeballs. A constable handed Grady a handful of small papers. Grady flipped through them. "Be careful with those. They're his trading tickets."

"Tickets?" asked the Irishman.

"For his gold trades. We —" Dan swallowed and flinched at the sharp twinge in his neck. "Close his eyes, for God's sake."

The young constable did not wait for Grady's nod to brush Peter's eyelids down.

"You were saying, sir?"

Dan shook his head, unable to speak; a sour metallic anger choked him.

"You were out for a night on the town, were you then?"

"No. We – We were trading on the Evening Exchange. Up there." Dan nodded toward the Fifth Avenue Hotel. "We were on our way home." Just minutes ago. Peter had not been happy with him. His voice dried.

"You said 'gold trades.' Would your friend have been a gold trader, now?"

"Yes. That's what we were doing. We'd been trading and we were going home. Then that bastard jumped me." He booted the corpse, which shifted to show the knife handle sticking out from the left side of his breastbone. At least he'd killed the murderous son of a bitch. It had not saved Peter, but at any rate he had sent one with him.

"It was you killed him, then?"

"He had a knife. I fought back."

"I would have done the same thing, Mr. – Now, fancy that. You haven't honored me with your name."

Surprised by such extreme politeness from a bog Irish sergeant, Dan looked directly at him. "Daniel Bradford Stark."

"My condolences, then, Mr. Stark, on the death of your friend."

"Thank you."

A hansom cab drew up beside the knot of people. The sergeant spoke to a policeman with two stripes on his sleeve. "I'll be coming back when I've seen this gentleman to Bellevue." The horse, smelling blood, shifted about, the cab rocking forward and backward on its two wheels. While the driver tried to steady the horse, Dan let Grady support him into it. He supposed the mick would close the gate and send him on his way, but he climbed in and pulled the gate to. They clattered into the street, and he leaned into a corner of the cab, savoring the darkness that hid his sorrow.

The soft Irish voice came to him like cold fog. "Your friend, sir? How would he be called, if I may ask?"

He answered from the darkness that was not so deep as he wished. "Peter Adelphus Yates. He hated his middle name." Unable to stop talking, he went on, though his chattering teeth bit the words into odd pieces. "He used to say he would never give a child of his a Classical name, he'd name him something plain and Anglo-Saxon and never anything other boys could make a word from." Rain blew on his face, the gate being a little over knee high, until the cab turned and they traveled at angles to the wind. "Cleo, his wife, agreed. Her given name is — oh. Cleo. She's in the Poconos. Peter sent the family there to escape the heat."

They had jumped into the quarry together, fallen thirty feet through the air, met the shock of cold water over their bodies. When he'd escaped the long twining weeds and broke the surface, wheezing and gasping for air, Peter had been there, treading water and laughing. Now he was dead between one word and the next. How could that be? To die in the flash of a knife?

A wheel bounced, jarring his neck. The pain broke open the raw inner wound, and he wept for his friend.

~24~

AT BELLEVUE HOSPITAL, someone poured whiskey into the cut. He gasped and jerked away. Someone laughed: "Baby. Hold him down." Other hands wrapped a fresh piece of his shirt around his neck, stripped him of his blood-soaked clothes. Gripping the notecase, shivering, he let them put him to bed in a ward filled with other men, who coughed, snorted, and vomited through the rest of the night. Dead men's eyes glimmered through his dreams, and a sensation of falling toward black water jerked him awake more than once. The last time, as he grabbed the mattress to save himself, Arthur laid a hand on his arm.

He came awake, sweating. "The notecase. Where is it?" He clutched it under the blanket, and when he would let go of it to put on the presentable garments that Arthur had brought, his fingers were stiff.

"I told the hospital to burn your other clothes," said Arthur. "They were soaked in blood."

When they stepped out of the hansom cab in front of the manse, Mother opened the door while they were climbing the stoop. "My darling boy," she said, "you're all right?" At sight of the bandage, her tears overflowed, and she said no more, but could not leave off touching him – his arm, his hand, his cheek, his back – as if to reassure herself that he was not a ghost but her live son, present in the body.

"Miraculously," Arthur said, "the attacker did not complete—"

Remembering, he shuddered: the knife's gleam, the attacker's hand on his chest, the slicing agony on the side of his neck.

"Thank the Lord." Mother opened the door to the dining room. "First you need food to build up your strength, and then rest."

"You stink of whiskey." Grandfather sat at breakfast with Grandmother, who half rose with a soft cry at the sight of Dan, leaning on Arthur's arm. "Sit down, woman, he has been on a debauch, wastrel that he is."

The old son of a bitch. Accuse him of roistering, would he? Arthur pulled out a chair next to Nathaniel, and he dropped onto it. Nathaniel got up to pour his coffee.

He said, "Peter Yates is dead."

"Oh, no!" said Nathaniel. The coffee pot rattled against the cup's rim.

The others cried out. Grandfather's face blanched. Clapping a napkin to his mouth, he groped for his stick, struggled to his feet and scuttled from the room, leaving the door open behind him.

Grandmother hurried after him.

"Florentine," said Mother. "Take the children, please." When Nathaniel did not stir, Mother spoke his name in her no-nonsense voice.

Florentine ushered the small ones out of the room, assured them that they could finish their breakfasts in the garden as a special treat.

Nathaniel shook his head. "I'm old enough to know what's happening, Mother." The boy finished pouring the coffee and set it in front of Dan.

"Thank you. Let him stay, Mother." Dan looked at the pancakes piled on the warmer's metal plate. Before he had told about Peter, he thought he was hungry, but his stomach knotted and he tasted bitterness. The metallic gleam, a sweating terror that he might die.

Arthur said, "How are you?"

"Rotten, but I'll survive." He cursed the threatening crack in his voice.

"You must eat," said Mother.

"I can't." Peter's eyes, staring open, rain falling on them. If he tried the drink the coffee, he would vomit.

A heavy knock sounded at the front door, followed by men's

voices in the hallway. A tap at the door, and Florentine opened it just wide enough to look in. "Arthur, there's a – a person wanting to speak with Daniel. He's with the police."

Arthur swallowed and dabbed a napkin at his mouth. "Have the maid show him to my study, if you please, my dear. They can wait there until Daniel is ready."

Dan pushed back his chair. "I'm ready now." Best to get this over with.

As Flo pulled the door closed, Arthur called her back. "May we have a large mug?"

The maid brought it, and Arthur poured coffee into it, then spooned in enough honey to make a syrup. "This is for you, Daniel." When he would have refused, his brother-in-law said, "You need something to sustain you, and you've had more than enough whiskey." To Mother and Nathaniel, "You'll excuse us." It was a statement, not a question, as he held the door open.

~25~

GRADY, THE IRISH POLICEMAN from last night, stood on the hearth, holding his hat. Another policeman, younger, and with no stripe on his sleeve, stood at the window. The backlighting obscured his face. Under one arm he held his cap, to free his hands for his notebook and pencil. The sun cast his shadow long over Arthur's desk.

Arthur set Dan's coffee on a piecrust table beside the wing chair nearest the cold hearth. Sitting down, Dan nodded to the Irishman, whose eyes had widened at Arthur's clerical collar and the black shirt under his dark gray suit. Standing behind his desk, Arthur introduced himself. "I am the Reverend Arthur Cunningham, Rector of St. David's Episcopal Church. I believe you have already met my brother-in-law, Daniel Stark, under very unpleasant circumstances."

"Yes, sir." The Irish accent sounded more pronounced than he recalled it. "My name is Michael Grady, sergeant of the Metropolitan Police. I am charged with finding answers to crimes involving sudden or unexpected deaths by violence. Murders, sir, in a word." The word, 'murders,' sounded like 'marders.'

"I take it you would like to ask Mr. Stark questions concerning last night's attack on himself and poor Mr. Yates." Arthur seated himself and indicated a chair in front of his desk. "Please have a seat."

"Thanking you kindly, sir, but I'd prefer to stand."

Dan took a drink of the coffee. It warmed his gullet and comforted his stomach. Arthur had been right. He drank it all. When Grady finished telling him that he'd like to go over the previous night's events "once more, sir, if you'd be so kind," he was ready.

He explained what they had been doing in the Fifth Avenue Hotel, how the Evening Exchange worked, what the trading tickets meant. He took two from his coat pocket and showed them to Grady, who knelt by the arm of his chair to study them. After fewer questions than Dan expected, Grady quieted, frowning over the tickets.

"These are nothing but bits of paper, like those we found in your friend's pockets."

"What happened to them?"

"On your advice, sir, we sent to Henry Clews and Company, and I believe they were claimed this morning."

Dan did not recall having given any advice, but the previous night was an incoherent collection of glimpses and sounds.

Grady's jaws moved as if he chewed on something. "These tickets promise to sell gold or to buy gold in three days' time, or a week. No one could walk into a bank and demand gold with any of these."

The policeman's voice faded. He felt again the robber pawing at his chest. Oh, God. They'd been after the receipt. The cut throbbed, and he tipped his head back and closed his eyes. The robber had been fumbling for his breast pocket, the notecase. He swallowed hard against his stomach's threatening roll. Who knew he carried the receipt? What to tell Grady? Think.

He opened his eyes to find the Irishman still knelt beside the chair, close enough to read his mind. The man was no fool; he would have to be careful. "That's correct. I think they must have been under the misapprehension that we carried gold, but traders don't commonly have gold on our person. That's far too dangerous. Gold is kept in the banks, or the brokerages, and transported by couriers employed to carry it between institutions."

Grady rose, moved to his former place on the hearth. "Then I wonder why you two were attacked. Thaddeus King was not one to take such a chance. He was too careful."

"Thaddeus King. Was he one of the attackers?"

"Aye, sir. He's the man you killed."

"No." Arthur cried out. "You killed a man?"

"The one who attacked me. Yes." The other's odor like sour

milk in his nostrils, the knife grating against bone before it slid through flesh, King's life going on a rancid grunt.

Grady spoke to Arthur. "He was a notorious underworld character, and I'm ashamed to say a countryman of mine. We've arrested him on numerous charges, but he was a wily devil right enough, and managed to escape without taking up permanent residence in The Tombs. Or being hanged. Although I've no doubt," his eyes brightening as though he laughed, "he's a member of the Underworld for sure now, sir, having escaped The Tombs."

The policeman at the window chuckled, and Dan smiled, but Arthur said, "A man's sudden death, any man's, is not something to joke about."

"Begging your pardon, Reverend, but those of us charged with the responsibility of keeping the public safe in these perilous times do not find King's death a cause for mourning."

Dan nodded. Uppity mick, this Grady. A man he'd want on his side any time.

Arthur said, "It was a simple robbery, but what if he had gotten the receipt? Your grandfather has been worried about you carrying it on your person."

"Receipt?" asked Grady.

Damn! He thought to deflect the policeman. "Grandfather, worried? Why? When?"

"Very worried. A few days ago. He wanted assurances you were keeping it safe."

From his trousers pocket, he brought out his pocket knife, opened the blade, scraped under a fingernail. He wished he had a stick; he thought better in court when carving thin curls of wood. "Were you able to reassure him?"

"I wasn't here. I had a meeting with some ladies of the city who are thinking of founding a free school for children of the poor." His smile lifted his homely, creased face. "We believe that education will break the cycle of poverty."

"Very commendable, sir," said Grady. "Very true, to be sure, but might I ask how, if you were not at home —?" He left the rest of the question dangling.

"How did I know he was worried? Mrs. Cunningham, my dear wife, told me when I returned home. He had asked permission for Joel Van Fleet to look into your room, Daniel."

His hands trembled too much to continue. God damn it. Closing the knife on his thigh, he put it in his pocket and clasped his hands on his lap, below the level of the chair arm. Why couldn't Arthur have kept his thoughts to himself? Couldn't he see a trail beyond the first turn? Yet how would – no, he must be wrong. For King to have been after the receipt, he had to know of it from— That could not be. There must be another explanation.

"She gave her permission, though reluctantly," Arthur said. "Judge Stark is seventy-six and arthritic," he explained to Grady. "He finds stairs difficult." He straightened some papers on his desk. "My wife would have looked herself, but she is delicate, and must limit her exertions. My grandfather-in-law can also be quite persuasive."

Arthur's voice flowed on behind Dan's thoughts. Those footsteps had belonged to Van Fleet. Van Fleet searched his room while he was with Grandfather, no, while Grandfather delayed him. The footsteps, the front door latch dropping — that had been Van Fleet leaving the house. Van Fleet smoked cigars.

His thoughts hurtled over ground he did not want to travel. When the search failed, what then? Had they concluded he carried the receipt with him? Could they have then decided to have it stolen?

King. How had they known of King, or someone like him? Much less how to find him, or – or hire him? How would Grandfather, or Van Fleet, a banker — Grandfather. Attorney. Judge. Of course. He would know how to find someone like King, and keep himself well shielded, too. Grandfather, rushing from the breakfast table when he learned of Peter's murder.

"May I see this piece of paper, this receipt?" His features set in grim lines, Grady held out his hand.

Dan brought out the notecase, well filled with greenbacks, removed the receipt tucked behind a back flap, and put it in Grady's hand. "It's just as likely they were after money."

The policeman read the receipt and whistled. "It instructs the firm of Henry Clews & Co., Gold Traders, to pay bearer $20,816.20 in gold." He crossed himself. "Begorra." It was the first Irish word Dan had heard him use, and he reminded himself that the receipt was probably thirty years' salary for him. Grady asked, "Who knew you had this piece of paper?"

The policeman at the window turned a page in his notebook, licked the end of his pencil.

"We all knew," Arthur said. "The adults in the family. Not the children or the maid."

340

"Peter knew, God ret his soul. Henry Clews & Co. is holding the gold, so some there had to know of the receipt, if not where I kept it."

"Their names?" Grady gave the receipt back to Dan, who tucked it into his notecase, replaced it in his pocket, all the time keeping his hands steady.

By the stricken look on his face, Arthur now understood what he had started.

"My grandfather, Jason Stark. Reverend Cunningham." He spelled it for the note taker. "Joel Van Fleet, of the Bank of New York." Naming Van Fleet gave him satisfaction.

Grady whistled between his lower teeth. "Judge Jason Stark is your grandfather?"

"Yes," he said.

Arthur asked, "Is Judge Stark known to the police?"

"Yes, sir. The Stark name is very well known in legal circles, you understand."

No doubt for reasons other than legal, he thought, the odor of cordite from Father's pistol strong in his memory.

He wished he could read Grady's thoughts. Did the Irishman think along the same lines, that Grandfather would know how to find King from his many years of presiding over criminal trials? All Grady lacked was a motive, and he had just given it to him.

"It could have been pure chance," said Arthur. "Like Daniel says, they were after money."

Wishing he could speak aloud, Dan willed Arthur to be quiet.

"Can you think of any reason," Grady asked, "why any of them should be wanting to get their hands on more than $20,000 in gold?"

The question dropped into the middle of the room and lay on the carpet. The policeman at the window guffawed, clapped his hand over his mouth. Grady glared at him.

Dan laid his hands on the arms of the chair. Pretending to consider Grady's question, he lowered his chin toward his chest. It could not be true. He would not believe it. The old son of a bitch was determined to rule the legal world of New York like he had done before Father – died. He wanted his power back, his standing, and to do that he would pay the Bank in gold. But not even Grandfather would go so far. Grandfather bolting from the room at the news of Peter's death.

God almighty. Could Grandfather have conspired with King to rob him? It could not be.

It fit. Damnation, it fit.

Grandfather, Van Fleet – they had not meant murder. But King had come to kill. There had been no words. No "stand and deliver." Just the silent stab to Peter's heart, a slice at his own throat: Give it up. He put his finger to the bandage, where a faster pulse beat; it might have hit the vital artery, the big vein. His hands clenched, as he remembered the desperate grappling, the thick smell of blood. He was alive because he'd fought hard, turned the knife on King.

Arthur answered Grady's question. "Who would not want so much gold?"

He asked, "Was this man King ever implicated in robbery with murder?"

"Not to say implicated," Grady said. "We've thought we saw his shadow more than once in violent crimes. Certain it is, many in the underworld, shall we say, were terrified of him." He paused, thinking, head cocked a degree to one side. "No, terrified is not too strong a word. I'm not the only one considering you've done the city a service, Mr. Stark. Unofficially speaking."

"It was just luck. It could easily have gone the other way." How true that was. A split second, a lesser resolve to kill rather than be killed, and he would have lain on the paving stones with rain on his eyes. Damn them.

Certainty was a hard ember that ignited in his mind, burned away doubt. Whether he wanted to believe it or not, it was true. Damn them to hell, they had got Peter killed. Almost got him killed. Their crime was no different from marking a stagecoach to show it carried gold, or passing the word. He had hanged men for that. They were as guilty of Peter's murder as if they had wielded the knife. Conspiracy to murder, even if they had not intended it.

Grady watched him, too closely, as if reading his mind. "If you're knowing something that would help to understand why you and your friend were attacked, it would be your duty to tell me, if I might say so, you being an officer of the court and all."

He should tell Grady, and let the law find the answer. He could tell the policeman about the debt, Father's suicide, Grandfather's passion to regain his former power. Both Van Fleet and Grandfather would be ruined. Revenge lay sweet on his tongue, perfumed his mind like the scent of summer roses. They deserved everything that could happen to them, every punishment, to the limits of the law. The Tombs and then the noose.

They were guilty as sin. Both of them.

The Irishman was right. He would tell Grady what he knew, what he suspected, and by that he would place both Grandfather and Van Fleet in the law's hands. He could do that. Should do it. It was his duty. Let the law make its own dispositions. This was not Alder Gulch. He had no standing in New York, except that he was still licensed to practice law. He was not a Vigilante here. He was an officer of the court. The ember flared.

Somewhere in the house a woman sang, from a distance, perhaps from upstairs.

Let the law take revenge on Grandfather for Father's suicide and Peter's murder. The old bastard had killed them both to further his ambition. Oh, not by his own hand, he would never have blood on his hands, would never pull his own rope, but his greed had set in motion the events that led to death.

The woman's singing sounded somewhat louder, as if she descended the stairs. A maid, probably. How could she sing with Peter dead? Why did no one tell her to be quiet?

Damn Grandfather to everlasting hell. The little flame burned higher. By God, he would do it. Tell Grady and let the law deal with Grandfather.

The woman sang in a rich contralto almost outside the door. Bracing himself to get up and shout at her, he recognized the voice. Mother. Singing.

She had not sung in months, but today she sang. The coloratura from Harriet's musicale had inspired her to sing again. A song, full of joy, from Handel. He heard the word, "Rejoice." Mother, singing for joy. Because he lived?

"I believe you had something to say, sir?" Grady leaned forward, elbows on his knees.

Mother had not sung since Father's death. Grandfather deserved justice. Even at his age, he had earned the punishment of the law. He deserved to pay for Peter's death, as King had paid.

Arthur watched him, the freckles standing out from his bleached skin like a rash. He and the rest of the family were innocent, as well. Mother did not deserve to pay for Grandfather's crime. If he told Grady, they would all suffer the consequences, and none of this was their doing.

He coughed. The wound hurt, and he touched the bandage, felt a dampness. "I'm sorry. I haven't any idea. Most of that gold will be used to pay back a debt this family has owed for nearly two years."

Grady's look reproached Dan. "That a fact, now?" The policeman tapped the brim of his hat. "Pity. I had some hopes of that line of inquiry, sir. Are you sure there is nothing you can tell me? No? Then it seems I'll have to pursue other lines." The policeman by the window closed his book, stuffed it and the pencil into a pocket of his tunic. Arthur rose, and when Dan braced his hands on the chair arms, Grady put out his hand. "You don't have to get up, sir. You've had a nasty experience, and you're needing your rest. I apologize for the intrusion."

As Arthur showed the policemen out, Dan closed his eyes. A child chanted, "Two bits, four bits, six bits, a dollar," before Flo's voice shushed the noise.

Mother sang: "Rejoice. Rejoice greatly."

His teeth chattered. King's breath in his right ear, his fingertips pinching his nipple, the blank instant when the knife sliced his neck.

Peter was dead. He'd nearly been killed. Because Grandfather and Van Fleet had given an order. They had given an order, perhaps only to retrieve the receipt, which he carried in his notecase. How had they rationalized it to themselves? As recovering what was already theirs? His hands shook and he could not stop them.

He had killed King: the knife grating on bone resonated through the muscles of his forearm, King's flesh resisted as he thrust the blade home, and warm blood spurted out, soaked him, and King had exhaled a long, curdled breath. The shivering spread through his body.

Clenching his jaws against the surging vomit in his throat, he rose to his feet and ran outside, to the necessary.

~26~

POUNDING AT THE FRONT DOOR jolted him awake. Lacking the strength to climb the stairs, he had gone to sleep again in the wing chair, and someone – presumably Arthur – had put his feet on an ottoman, covered him with a blanket. His mouth tasted vile. He longed for peppermint leaves, cool sweet water. Rocky Mountain water.

"Stay there, Daniel." Arthur strode out, shutting the door behind him.

A man bellowed, "Where is he? Where in God's name is he? I have to see him." Footsteps scrambled on the parqueted floor, voices clamored together: "I must see him."

"No, no, you can't go in there."

"Is he all right? Dear God, tell me he's all right. Tell me he's not killed."

Arthur's voice: "Calm yourself. He's all right."

From the other side of the door, a man sobbed. "Oh, thank God, thank God. I must see for myself. Please."

"No, no, you must not," Mother protested. "He's resting."

The door slammed open, rebounded from the doorstop and struck Joel Van Fleet, left a red mark down one cheekbone, that he seemed not to notice as he came in. A collar button had come undone

345

and freed the starched collar point to poke into his side whiskers, and his cravat was untied. Stopping, he panted for breath.

The fat bastard had got Peter killed. He should have let Van Fleet drown.

"You are alive. Thank God, oh, thank – but your neck?"

He coughed, flinched from the pain's jab, touched the bandage. "My throat was cut."

Van Fleet dropped onto the sofa arm, slid down to the seat. "It's all my fault. All my fault. I'm to blame." His eyes seemed sunk back in their sockets, as if he looked inside himself.

What did he see? His own soul? Under the blanket, Dan gripped his thighs to keep himself from attacking. "Peter was murdered. I killed the one who tried to murder me." Saying it, he heard another man's hard, sharp voice.

Mother, at the door, stifled a scream. Arthur guided her to the sofa, the end closer to his desk, away from Van Fleet. "Are you all right?" he asked. Seating herself, she nodded, and brushed at a few strands of hair that escaped their smooth imprisonment.

Van Fleet groaned. "My fault. All of it. My fault."

Saying nothing, he waited, listened to Van Fleet's ragged breathing.

Arthur sat in his own chair, behind his desk. His mouth turned downward at the corners, his cheeks sagged. Picking up a letter opener, he tapped the point on the blotter centered on his desk. Father's blotter had always been crooked.

In the hallway, an uneven thump and shuffle drew closer. Grandfather. Dan nudged aside the ottoman, tossed the blanket on it, planted both feet on the floor, and sat straight, hands on the chair arms, knees spread.

Nathaniel hurried in. "Grandfather's coming!" He took up a stance on the hearth, next to Dan's chair.

Grandfather paused at the doorway, and his glance found Van Fleet. "Say nothing. As your counsel, I advise you to say nothing. No one is at fault for what happened last night, except the attackers." He crossed the room to take the other wing chair nearer the window, closer to Arthur's desk, laid his hands on the top of his stick, and glowered at Dan.

On the trip West, he had joined some men hunting. Topping a rise, they had seen perhaps a mile away a grounded dust storm, felt the earth tremble and heard an almighty roaring. Two bison, each weighing nearly a ton, charged each other, separated, and charged again. Their clash echoed across the plain.

From the shadows of their torches, the outlaws' friends shouted threats at the prosecutor. King's hand stroked across his chest. Peter was dead. He rubbed the rope scars on his hands. Was this so different from Alder Gulch? He would prosecute them here, with Mother, Arthur, and Nathaniel as jury. "Close the door, Nathaniel."

When the boy had done it, Dan said, "You set them on us, didn't you?" He spoke to Van Fleet. The bisons' hoofbeats throbbed in his ears.

"Be quiet!" snarled Grandfather. "Say not one more word."

"No," Mother whispered. "Father-in-law, how could you?" When Grandfather would have spoken, she said, "Do not even think to forbid me the room. My son's throat has been cut, he survived by a miracle, and he was forced to kill his attacker, and his friend was murdered? Because you wanted that receipt?"

Before he could tell the old bastard to go to hell, never mind Mother's presence, she rose, adjusted her hoop, and sat down again, pulled her skirt aside from touching Van Fleet. The set of her jaw told them she would not be moved.

The old man made a dismissive gesture and swung his glare toward Dan. "If there's any fault in this," pointing his finger, "it's yours."

That red herring. Blame someone else to deflect attention from yourself. The old bastard. It would not work. And yet, there was some truth. "I should have left the receipt at Henry Clews."

"It would not have mattered." Van Fleet buried his face in both hands propped on his knees. His voice was muffled. "We would have needed the key."

"Be quiet!" snarled Grandfather. "Do not say another word."

Arthur said, "Why? Why could it not have been a chance robbery gone terribly wrong?"

"Because while Grandfather kept me here, Van Fleet sneaked to my room and searched —"

Van Fleet winced.

"— as you told us yourself. I wouldn't give it them, so Grandfather made up a story about being concerned for it, and Florentine gave them permission."

Van Fleet's head moved up and down.

"Am I right?"

"Say nothing," Grandfather hissed.

Van Fleet's ears reddened. "Yes. I looked for it."

"I don't follow," Arthur said. "Van Fleet searched the room, not to be sure the receipt was safe, but to steal it?" When Van Fleet nodded, Arthur went on, "Nonetheless, it is a very long way from even a gross abuse of our hospitality to a street attack."

"When they didn't find the receipt," Dan said, "they determined that I must be carrying it." He spoke to Van Fleet's ear, bright red, that was all he could see of the banker's face. "Am I right? Am I?"

"Yes."

"Be quiet, I tell you." The old man thumped his stick on the floor. "Be quiet."

"Are you sure, Daniel?" A frown creased Arthur's nose.

He would have to lay out all the tidy logical structure of this nightmare for Arthur's inhospitable scrutiny. Just as in a courtroom. If Van Fleet did not confirm it, without Thaddeus King there was no evidence. Merely logic. The theory of the crime.

"I told them both that I would pay the debt in greenbacks. The Bank wants it in gold, so they can pay their debts in greenbacks and reap a tidy profit." Almost, he laid out his reasons, the desire to insure the family's future, but Arthur, Christian as he was, would dismiss any hint of altruism as no just reason to defraud the Bank. The end does not justify the means.

Grandfather shouted, "You dishonest, greedy — Your fool of a father raised you to be a wastrel and a gambler just like him."

The bison hoofbeats shook the air. He breathed in and out to calm the flame in his gut. "It could be worse, Grandfather. I could have turned out like you."

The old man's eyes widened, then narrowed. Without looking away from the old bastard, he said, "The Judge planned to give the gold to the Bank. He's up for reelection this year, and has to parade a clean character to the voters, or the newspapers will crucify him. Many people — especially the Bank — think repaying a debt in greenbacks is immoral, even though it is legal."

"It is immoral." Grandfather sputtered, "You – you – if you did as I wish, the family honor would be restored and I would regain —"

"Yes," said Arthur. "Why are you so determined to go back to that wilderness? There's nothing there but wild animals and lawless men."

"My wife is there. My life is there."

"But we thought — "Arthur stopped.

"We thought you were just a squaw man," Grandfather sneered. "Bah! As you are. Or have you a taste for hanging men at will? You kill easily."

At his shoulder, he heard Nathaniel gasp, but he could not stop the thunder of hoofbeats. "I will tell Sergeant Grady of the Metropolitan Police about this, and you will end in The Tombs."

"You would never dare."

"Do you want to test me? Your plot to rob us killed Peter and almost killed me."

Saliva leaked down Grandfather's chin. "Think of the family! You can't do this, damn —"

"Go ahead, Daniel," Mother said.

Grandfather roared abuse of him, to drown her out, but she pitched her voice so that he had no difficulty hearing her through the tirade. "If he gets his way, he will break you on the same wheel he broke your father. Do what you must."

She had sung, just a while ago, because she was happy again, because she had been out in society, and perhaps because he was alive, and now she invited him to do something that would bring disgrace on them all. Do what you must. She sat straight-backed and square-shouldered, a soldier on a domestic battlefield.

What was right? The hoofbeats kicked up a dust cloud, and he sought the answer through it: How to neutralize Grandfather without harming the family.

Van Fleet sobbed. Grandfather's lip curled.

"What would you have gained, Van Fleet?" The banker looked at him, his eyes red-rimmed and bloodshot. "You would make a tidy profit for the bank, and for yourself?" He was stalling, looking for a way to pull the old snake's fangs.

"Yes," Van Fleet said. "A bonus, promotion. All ashes. Ashes."

Arthur rubbed his hands over his face. "Even if that were true," looking from Van Fleet to Grandfather, "it's no proof that either of them would condone a heinous crime."

"Of course not," began Grandfather. "That you could even suggest such a thing —"

"I saw it in Alder Gulch. Some of the men we hanged – I hanged – " ignored Mother's small shiver, Nathaniel's stifled gasp "– were not evil. They were weak, or they had no moral compass to tell them where was true north. Yet because they went along with evil, they were just as dangerous. They were just as guilty, being part of the conspiracy, as if they had pulled the triggers." To Grandfather, "They were guilty of conspiracy to commit murder."

"Oh, God help me," said Van Fleet.

Nathaniel said, "I don't understand. Why would they —?"

"For the money. They wanted what other men earned, and they thought they were entitled to it. The killing had nothing to do with them. Someone else did that. One man marked stagecoaches to let the robbers know gold was being transported. He thought he did nothing wrong. He didn't think his way through to the other side, where the guns were." Dan put a finger to the bandage. "In this case, the knives."

Mother chewed on her knuckles, her eyes huge, as if she had never seen him before.

Weeping, Van Fleet covered his face with the handkerchief.

"You're saying that something similar has happened here." Arthur's voice sounded hoarse.

"Yes. They set in motion events that led to two deaths."

"You have no proof," shouted Grandfather. "This is all conjecture."

Van Fleet sat staring at the floor, his shoulders slumped.

"You surmise," said Arthur.

Nodding, he admitted it. "I surmise."

"Then it could as easily have been a random attack."

"Yes. Except for Grandfather's reactions this morning. When I announced that Peter had been killed. Whatever he did, or acquiesced to, he did not intend for it to lead to a death. I don't believe he intended murder."

Arthur held up his hands as if to ward off a dangerous truth. "I can't believe it. Surely men like this do not hire thugs to commit a heinous crime against his own grandson."

"Why not?" Mother pounded her fist on the sofa between her and Van Fleet. "Arthur, you have not watched Jason exert his will on this family day after day, year on year. For decades. He ground down poor John until there was almost nothing left. He has never mourned him. His own son. He has only mourned the loss of his power, the loss of the firm. I believe Daniel."

"Woman!" Grandfather half rose from his chair.

"Sit down!" shouted Dan.

"You horrid old man," said Mother. "I believe you would hire these thugs to rob Daniel, and you would not have mourned him, had he been killed, so long as you got what you wanted."

Grandfather raised his cane, brandished it at her. "Foolish and stupid woman. My idiot son should have beaten you. You would not then dare —"

"Stop it." Van Fleet stood up, towered over Grandfather, who shrank back into the chair, his stick held as if to defend himself. He turned to Arthur. "Father, I wish to confess my guilt. Will you hear my confession?"

Arthur stared at him for a second or two. "Yes, we can go over to the church when —"

"No. Here. Please" Steadying himself with a hand on Arthur's desk, Van Fleet knelt almost on Mother's feet. "Now." Holding up his right hand, he said, "May the Lord preserve me, but Dan Stark is correct in everything he has said."

"Damn you!" Grandfather raged up from his chair, the walking stick raised to strike.

Jumping up, Dan yanked the stick from his hand and pushed him back into the chair. Arthur held out his hand, and when Dan passed the stick to him, he leaned it against his desk, out of the old man's reach.

Dropping into the wing chair, Dan caught his breath and watched what he had made.

A vein pulsed across the old man's forehead. "How dare you? How dare you ape a confession, made from a tissue of lies?"

"God help me," Van Fleet said. "God forgive me that I ever conspired with you to have your own grandson robbed of that receipt. We did, you know," he said to Arthur. "When I could not find the receipt in his room, we decided to contact Thaddeus King and have it taken from him."

"Didn't you know that you would be conspiring at theft?" Dan demanded.

"It never seemed so. We spoke in terms of recovering what was rightfully the bank's property." He cleared his throat. "I'm so very sorry. I'll gladly accept whatever punishment you see fit to give me."

Dan's head ached just behind his left eyeball, and his neck throbbed. He touched the bandage and felt the dampness. He was near the end of his strength, in desperate need of sleep, but this was almost over. He'd been right, but God in heaven, it gave him no pleasure.

The unthinkable, the only logical answer, was true. Van Fleet had plotted with Grandfather to rob him. His own grandson. The two of them had conspired together, and two men had died. He leaned his head against the high back of the wing chair and closed his eyes. He saw Father's face glowing over the cards, his ruined head on the desk top, smelled the acrid odor of gunpowder. Opening his eyes, he found his brother-in-law watching him. Father, Peter, the thief. Three deaths at Grandfather's hands, the puppet string of cause and effect.

Silence grew. Failure to report all this to Grady was obstruction of justice. But he had killed Peter's murderer, and how would justice be further served by Grandfather's public disgrace, the family's permanent sadness? Having bravely told him to go ahead, would Mother sing again?

Nathaniel laid his hand on his shoulder, and he thought, my life is not here, but the children's lives are. They must be allowed to grow up here.

The answer was before him, the buck in his gunsights, how to take the old bastard down without harming the family. "Write out a confession," he told Van Fleet. "Give it to Arthur. Describe Grandfather's role in this as well as your own."

"No," said Grandfather. "You can't. You – we – have nothing to confess. We did not wield those knives. That was not our doing." He sat forward, his eyes unrepentant behind the straggling white brows. "We hired them for a simple task, to retrieve the receipt, and they —" His voice faltered as he heard his own damning words, then caught and hurried on as though they would not have noticed. Stabbing his forefinger at Dan, he shouted, "It's you! You and your Vigilante actions. You brought this on yourself. If you had just given up the receipt, your friend —"

"That's enough!" Van Fleet rose up, an angry bear of a man. "To my eternal shame, I conspired to rob the man who pulled me nearly dead from a frozen, flooding stream. I will bear that burden of guilt all my life." He bent until his face was inches away from the old man. "I will not hear you accuse your grandson of your own crime. You and I are responsible, do you hear me? You and I. Not Daniel Stark. You and I."

Turning to Dan, he said, "I will go to the police and freely confess to them as well, even if it means that I spend the rest of my days in The Tombs."

In that moment, Dan knew the answer. "No, don't do that." He looked at Grandfather. "You will resign the bench, effective immediately. You are unfit to serve."

From a desk drawer, Arthur produced a writing lap desk, and placed it across Grandfather's legs. Pen, paper, and ink bottle lay in separate compartments around the writing space. The old man shrank back as from a snake. "No." His head turned from side to side.

"Yes. Now."

Grandfather seized the ink bottle, but could not open it. Arthur opened it and set it in its place. "On what grounds?"

"Whatever you like, as long as it's permanent. Ill health. Your age."

The fierce old eyes glowered, but he took up the pen, checked that the nib was sharp, and wrote a few lines. The pen scratched loud in the stillness.

Dan said, "Make two copies of your confession. Give one to Arthur, and leave one copy and the original with me. The copy will go in my box at Henry Clews." He turned to Van Fleet. "When Grandfather is done, you do the same."

In silence, Van Fleet obeyed.

When he had read the confessions and put them in his notecase with the blood-stained receipt, he rose to his feet. For an instant he was dizzy, and steadied himself with a hand on Nathaniel's shoulder. "As far as the police are concerned, Peter died in a random robbery attempt gone horribly wrong."

To Grandfather, he said, "We know different."

~27~

THE FAMILY had wanted him to rest today, Friday, as the doctor had ordered, attend Peter's funeral tomorrow, wait till Monday to trade, but he could not. Van Fleet had persuaded the Bank to postpone the meeting, but they could reschedule it at any time and he had to be ready. Besides, he had options and futures due today, and he had already lost opportunities. Yesterday, gold had risen to nearly 258 from 251, and settled at 257. He'd been right. Forgetting, he looked around to share the joke with Peter, to crow a bit, and found Nathaniel jogging at his heels. Damn. Peter was dead. How could he have forgotten between one thought and the next?

They turned up William, hurried in the stream of men toward Wall Street, and into Henry Clews. Somber clerks recognized him, ushered him and Nathaniel into Peter's office. A white silk scarf hung on a hat tree. For a moment he expected Peter to come in, make a joke. On the desk stood a photo of Cleo and Peter. Unsmiling, holding their stiff poses for the camera's timing, they looked like strangers. "We have not had the heart to pack his effects." A clerk laid Dan's strongbox on the desk. When he asked about Peter's trades, the clerk assured him that another senior trader, perhaps Mr. Clews himself, would act for Peter, protect his family's interests. "It's the least we can do."

His eyes stung. He would like to have done that, but others were better traders.

He would have enough to do to make good on Peter's loans to him from his own account. His pulse throbbed against the bandage.

At Gilpin's, men nodded to him as he squeezed through the doorway. They touched his arm, shouted their sympathy over the bedlam of trade. Joseph bellowed in his ear, "Pity about Mr. Yates. Who's he?" Meaning Nathaniel.

"My brother. Watching my back." Leaving Nathaniel to Joseph, he walked onto the floor.

Shouting, men waved fists, papers: "Buyer two: 257!" "Selling two: 257 3/16!" "257 1/2!"

Dan hesitated. Christ, Peter should be here now. What should he do? He needed a bear market, a sinking gold price, to sell his futures and options at a profit, but the premium held firm at 257 and fractions. He stood in a fog of smoke and dust. What to do? "Fifty at an eighth," shouted a man behind him, and the fog lifted. At the Evening Exchange, he'd sold $30,000 at 253 and 5/8. The boy on the ladder chalked 257 1/2 on the board.

Dan yelled, "Buying. Three at 257 2/5."

One eye on the board, he shouted again, and heard the answer, "Sold."

He wrote out tickets, exchanged them with the buyer, thought of the profit: $1132. The throbbing in his neck quieted as the new premium went up: 257 2/5. On to the next trade. He felt damp in his armpits.

"Seller three," he shouted. "Seventy at 7/8." He had bought the $70,000 future at 257 1/16 and must sell it now. The premium had risen to 257 7/8, for a profit of $332.50.

He exchanged tickets, the same ticket he had written before, but in different hands than he'd sold it to. A brief nod, the ticket stuffed into an empty pocket, a copy to the boy who ran to the board, and his sale was chalked up. On to the next. And the next. Through the day.

"It's like poker," he explained to Nathaniel when they waited for an omnibus after the day's trading. "Some days a man has to take his losses in order to reap future profits."

Nathaniel flung up a hand and whistled for a passing omnibus to stop. "You sound like Father. I hope you know what you're doing better than he did."

He could not endure the crowd on the omnibus, the jostling. "Let's take a hansom."

Nathaniel waved on the omnibus, ignored the driver's curses, and whistled loud and shrill for a hansom. Giving Arthur's address, they climbed in and the driver cracked the whip over the horse's back.

He was not sure at all that he knew better than Father had, but at least he was not so much in the red as he had been. If he had not traded today, he would have defaulted on some of his obligations, and he'd be damned if he'd default. He'd had one day's grace, the traders in the Gold Room granting him that because his friendship with Peter was known. But that was all.

He tried to think over his strategy for the next day's trading, even as he knew he could have no planned strategy except the goal of making money, lots of money, until he knew if the bears were truly driving the market. In his mind he ran through tomorrow's tickets, which were options and which were futures and how to trade them. In front of Arthur's house, he stumbled getting out and lurched into Nathaniel.

Seeing the coin Dan tossed him, the driver smiled. "Thank you, sir." He touched his hat brim and urged the horse on.

"You're tired," said Nathaniel. "How can you endure another day like today?"

"I don't know, but I have to do it."

"You're a fool," Nathaniel said. "Do you know you're bleeding again?"

~ALDER GULCH~

MARTHA READ TO DOTTY out of the Good Book, one of the stories the Lord told, about a farmer who went out to sow his crop and what happened to the seed. She let the Bible rest on her lap for a moment while she took a sip of tea to moisten her throat, and Dotty took advantage of that to pause with her sewing. They sat in the corner Martha favored, she in her own chair and the child in Dan'l's chair with her sewing. Between them stood the table with the pot of self-heal tea. Lydia Hudson and Tabby Rose had collected the plants in the spring, and Martha blessed both of them on account the tea soothed some of the discomforts she felt with this baby.

"Why did the farmer broadcast the seed, Mam?"

Martha thought about that. "Probably because it was a crop like barley or wheat and he had a big field so he didn't have to be careful with it, like a body would on a small farm."

"I remember you made Timmy and me walk along the furrows and dribble the seed in so's we wouldn't lose any, and you'd come along with the shovel and cover it up."

"Jesus said he lost some, though." Martha leaned over to see the child's work up close. They were making a nursing dress for Martha. Dotty hated sewing so, that Martha checked her work often. The dress had to be sturdy enough to last until the little one was weaned.

"Mam?" Dotty said.

To Martha, Dotty's voice sounded a trifle scared. She met the child's eyes, and sure enough, they were round and wide, like she'd seen a poisonous spider. Looking quickly around at the table, she almost laughed from sheer relief when Dotty asked, "What's wrong with Timmy?"

"Nothing I know of." So it wasn't a spider after all.

"The last few days he's been moping around like something's terrible wrong."

"He'll tell us about it when he's ready, I expect. Men hold things in until they've either got so bad they can't but tell, or the trouble's over. Now, look here. There's about an inch in this seam you have to rip out. See where the stitches go crooked? And they're too long. "

"Oh, Mam, it's just an inch —"

Canary, dozing in a patch of sunlight on his mat, raised his head and woofed.

Dotty brushed the dress makings aside and darted to the door, flung it wide. "Timmy! What are you doing home?" She backed away, holding the latch, so that Martha heard before she saw, "Miz Hudson? Sheriff Fox?"

Three more people made the big room seem small. Miz Hudson picked up the sewing and plumped down in Dan'l's chair, set the sewing on the table and pulled Dotty onto her lap. Timmy knelt in front of Martha with a burlap bag in his hands, and Sheriff Fox stood behind him. Before the sheriff removed his hat, Martha knew they came about something awful.

Had someone heard something from Dan'l? He wasn't coming back? He'd been killed on the trail? She chewed on a knuckle as she watched Timmy take something from the bag. A cooking pot. The kind with a handle. Her pot. She'd been missing it since winter, and Dan'l had bought her a new one. Something clattered in the pot.

Timmy nodded at her, telling her it was all right without saying it out loud.

She took out the silver picture frame with the picture of them all. There was no glass. She couldn't rightly comprehend what it meant for a space, all her hopes and fears tumbled around inside themselves, tossing up one thought and then another: Had they found Sam? Would he be coming back? Where was he?

"They found Pap." Timmy stood up and moved aside for Sheriff

Fox, who sat on his heels in front of her.

"We think he died the same day or soon after he left, Mrs. Stark. He apparently crawled into a cave in a gully and froze to death."

She covered her face with her hands, so's they wouldn't see the fierce joy threatening to break out in unseemly laughter. Sam would trouble them no more. She didn't have to be afraid. Not any more. He'd never come back. Never. But how awful that she couldn't mourn him. Poor Sam. He'd never come back. His real being had died years ago, a few months after the likeness was taken. The war killed him, and the man that come back wasn't him. She didn't have to be afraid any more.

Her laughter turned into weeping. She heard the sheriff stand, bid them good-bye, but she couldn't say anything. She felt her son's arms around her. Dotty crept onto her lap, crying, and she held her, while Lydia rubbed up and down her spine.

Out of all the turmoil, like a dust devil blowing around in her soul, a thought flung out that she could cling to. Where was Dan'l? She wanted Dan'l. Lord Jesus, bring him home.

~NEW YORK CITY 28~

"FORGIVE ME." Dan leaped from the City Car at Hanover Square Station and strode along Beaver Street toward William.

"Forgive you for what? Who are you talking to?" Jog-trotting to keep up, Nathaniel's questions came in Gatling bursts.

He hadn't wanted Nathaniel to come along, knew he'd feel responsible for the boy, but in the end he could not prevent him. He answered, "Peter. For trading today." He would miss Peter's funeral, but had written to Cleo to explain why, and he hoped she would forgive him if he resolved his loans from Peter at a profit. Peter, wherever he might be, if there was a place hereafter, would approve.

"Sometime," Nathaniel panted, "would you explain trading to me?"

Stopping in his tracks, he pivoted to stare down at his younger brother. "Why?"

"It's exciting," the boy said. "It's the most exciting thing I've ever seen." A smile turned up the corners of his mouth, and his eyes sparked. "Father never taught me about poker."

He drew Nathaniel out of the flow of men grumbling at them for stopping. He remembered: Father's hand ruffling his hair across the low table, the cards lying in the patch of sunshine. "No, I suppose he didn't. By the time you came along, his outlets were secret." He had been about Nathaniel's age when Father introduced him to Betty, the madam who thought twenty was old.

"I wish you would stay," Nathaniel said.

Dan shook his head. "I can't. As soon as this is settled, I'll be going home."

"I want to come with you."

He could not remain in New York and be a father to his brother. Somehow, Nathaniel would have to find his own way here. He would help as best he could, but now was not the time. He put his hands on Nathaniel's shoulders. "No. Not yet. Stay and finish school. Then come to me out West, and I'll help you build a life." Nathaniel, his mouth drooping at the corners, scuffed his toe at a dried dog mess. Dan said, "Now I have work to do."

He had trades from the night of Peter's murder. For the last two days, the premium had hung in fractions of 257, but now, it had sunk to 256.73, and the greenback was at $38.95. The stalemate of 257 was over. He had bought at 253 the night Peter was killed.

The clock jerked forward, the bell rang, the gavel came down. He shouted, "Sell ten at two fifty-six and two-thirds!" Waited. Would he hear? Had he pitched it right, just below the current premium? Other men called their trades, and sweat trickled down his sideburn. He opened his mouth to shout a lower price, and from a few feet away, behind stouter men, a small man appeared. "Buy," he screamed. "Buy ten at 256.67." Dan shouldered his way to the little fellow, went through the business of tickets, but not until the trade went up on the board did he remember to breathe.

Taking out a handkerchief, he wiped his eyes and blew his nose. When he turned in these tickets to Henry Clews & Co., Peter's account would be paid in full. The larger debt, though, he could never repay.

Around him the waters swirled, tossed up shouts to buy and sell that lapped at the edges of his mind, but the vines embraced him, enticed him down to rest among them on the soft pale sand. How he wanted to, but he pulled a ticket from his pocket and squared his shoulders.

He was not done yet.

~29~

IN THE EVENT, he might as well have stopped after he'd met Peter's loan. The only thing he knew for certain from the rest of Saturday's trading was that he had ended down $1750.

Sunday Dan slept late. When he came down to breakfast, the family had gone to church and the *Times* lay folded at his plate. He read it over his coffee and eggs. A woman identified as Mrs. Patterson Allan had been indicted for treason against the Confederacy, and he asked himself why had her husband denied knowledge of her activities? Was he such a coward that he would let his wife go to the gallows? Or had he truly known nothing of it? Turning the page, a headline caught his eye: Fort Gaines, one of two forts around Mobile Bay, had surrendered ten days ago.

He lay the paper down, heedless of bacon grease. His prediction to Peter had been right, but damn, he wished Peter were alive for him to gloat.

At dinner he endured Arthur's frowning disapproval for skipping church, and napped awhile in his room. Later, he played ball with the small ones in the back yard. When they clamored for horsie rides, Mother looked up from her book to object because of the cut. He fended off Nathaniel's questions about trading; something told him to put it out of his mind. Occasionally, he saw Grandfather cross the lawn to the necessary, but otherwise the old man stayed in the bedroom he shared with Grandmother, who scuttled out and back on errands. She reminded him of a frightened killdeer running along the ground. Once he met her in the hallway, but she backed away. Holding his hands at his sides open to her, he murmured, "Grandmother, I'm sorry."

As he stepped aside, she whispered, "You're not to blame."

At breakfast, Monday morning's *New York Times* reported the rebels were massing on the Upper Potomac river. An old rumor? Or would they succeed this time in capturing Washington? The Union Armies – the Army of the Potomac, the Army of Tennessee – pushed against hard Southern resistance, like boys on a playground who didn't know how to fight and could only shove at their opponents. The Union could gain no ground, or at least not enough to satisfy any Union sympathizer. Perhaps he would not have gloated to Peter quite yet.

Amid the quiet talk among the family, the children having already eaten and gone to play, Grandfather and Grandmother breakfasting in their room, Dan turned to the financial news, for the summary of the gold market. Fluctuating between 251 and 258, gold had ended the week at 257.14. The numbers had such a humdrum appearance. Ordinary readers would skim past them, or likely as not skip this page entirely. Yet men lived and died for numbers in the *Times* or on a board as surely as on a battlefield. Truly, he said to himself as a knock sounded at the front door, war was fought in the Gold Room as much as in the Wilderness.

Mother went to the door, and returned with a note for Dan. The paper was cream-colored and thick, the brief sentence written in a faultless Spencerian hand, with thicker downstrokes than upstrokes, and wide loops for ascenders and descenders.

Dan read it aloud. "The bank has scheduled the meeting for three o'clock Wednesday afternoon."

Mother touched his hand. "Will you be ready?"

He had to be. Faking confidence, Dan smiled. "I'll be ready."

"We shall pray that your endeavors succeed." Arthur's tone said he fooled no one.

Riding downtown with Nathaniel, Dan gnawed at his bottom lip. He had until noon Wednesday to trade with all the gold. After that, he would be limited to trading with the remainder of his loan from Peter.

It would all depend on his skill at trading, his judgment, without Peter to guide him. Peter, dead before he was thirty. Damn it to hell.

The market opened at 256.87, four tenths higher than its close on Saturday. Dan prowled the Gold Room, watched the trades, listened to the men around him buying and selling. He lay low, bought or sold as his tickets demanded, fulfilled his obligations at a modest profit that he hardly noticed. He was waiting. The boys ran here and there, and prices crept up and down, and chalk dust settled on the traders' hats. When it was all over the premium on gold had again moved four tenths. Just as on Saturday. He sensed something, a vibration through his feet, but it was not yet.

"You didn't trade much." On the City Car, Nathaniel spoke in his ear, under the horses' hooves clopping, a man's curse, a woman's squeal: "Keep your filthy hands away!"

"No," Dan said. "It wasn't the right time."

"When is the right time?"

Not turning his head, Dan said, "I don't know."

After supper, Nathaniel came to his room. "Are you going to want me tomorrow?"

"Yes, if you want to come."

"I don't understand what you're doing."

He did not understand, either. "I have a feeling, that's all."

"You mean you are basing all this on a hunch? All our lives?"

God, the boy had guessed what was at stake. He should not have let him tag along.

"No. I think there's a turn coming, and I'm watching for it. I'll be ready either way." The more he had to trade, the better the return. The worse the loss, an inner voice said.

"You didn't do well today, did you? You are like Father, after all."

"In some ways." Father's voice in his memory: Sometimes you have to wait and let the cards go against you so you can be ready when they turn. Because they always turn. "The time wasn't right today. I can't explain it. I have to wait for it."

His brother, who reminded him so much of Timothy, just two years older, stood with his back to the door. "Have you ever lost at poker?"

"Of course. Everyone does. Before I came back here, I lost a gold claim." Dan swung his legs over the side of the bed to face his brother.

"Then you are like Father. You're gambling with our future. How dare you? Maybe Grandfather was right. You should just pack up and go back to that place." Nathaniel opened the door. "Just go away."

"Wait. Nathaniel, wait!"

But Nathaniel was gone. His steps clattered down the stairs, a door slammed on the landing below. Half rising, thinking to go after the boy, he heard the crinkle of paper under foot. He had dropped his note about today's currency prices. He picked up the paper, scanned it. Currency prices had risen during the day. Of course. He knew that. They had not affected the premium dramatically, but by a cent or two here and there, they had gone from $38.87 to $38.93. Closing his eyes, he tried to see the board, and what he remembered from the day's trading confirmed his feeling. The greenback rising, gold beginning to sink. The bear was coming.

The next day's opening trade shook him. Gold rose. Trade by trade, by the penny and the half-dime, gold rose and the greenback sank. Moving through the crowd, his hands held low lest other traders see he had doubled them into fists, he listened, felt the bulls shaking the ground, heard their triumphant choruses of "Dixie." Under that, though, he felt the vibration of heavy paws and smelled bear, but the bulls ruled. He prowled the room, listened to the trades, offered his own when he could see a profit.

He waited. It could not last, but all around him the bulls were celebrating the rise of gold, and choruses of "Dixie" resounded from the plaster ceiling. The hairs rose on the back of his neck. He understood how to profit.

Trade had been going for over an hour, when the board told him the premium was 258.26.

"Sell," he bellowed, and men looked around because he had been quiet for so long. "Fifty at seven-eighths. Seven-eighths for fifty. Seller three." And everyone on the floor understood he was selling $50,000 at 257-7/8. The answering cry came: "Sold."

He met the buyer, wrote tickets and exchanged them. The man said, "Shame about Peter." Dan dipped his head, "Yes," and raised it to see the board. A chill swept over him, and goose bumps prickled his skin. He shouted past the buyer, "Seventy at two-fifty-seven," and another sale, this time $70,000 at 257. He underbid the premium at every turn, until it began to fall of its own accord. It was time to buy. His blood beat so hard in his neck that he put his hand under his cravat to feel for the tell-tale damp on the bandage. His hand came away dry. The calculations ran; he had the money, aside from the debt. He glanced at the board, stood at the brink of the quarry. Jumped.

After dinner, he sat alone sipping scotch in the back garden. The evening sun shone golden on the rose bushes. Nathaniel, silent at dinner, came to him across the lawn. "Congratulations."

He poured another drink from a bottle he had bought, having long used up Arthur's whiskey. "Thank you. Have a seat?" At dinner he had told the family the debt would be paid in full with an amount left over. "It went well, but there's always tomorrow."

His brother sat on the bench beside him. "I'm sorry for what I said last night."

"I didn't blame you. Sometimes the difference between a risk, a calculated risk, and a damn fool stunt isn't easy to know."

"You're trading tomorrow?"

"Yes. The debt will be paid, but we're not out of the woods yet on this."

"Will we be poor?"

"No. You may have to be careful, but you are not poor."

The boy rubbed his face, and sunlight caught the glint of reddish whiskers on his cheeks. "May I come with you?" Nathaniel's voice dropped more than an octave, and he stared at Dan, eyes wide. "To the Gold Room, I mean."

Dan smiled at him. "Come ahead. I'd like to have you watching my back again."

"I don't want to go back to school," said Nathaniel. "I don't like it. I hate the thought of being a lawyer." He stretched out his legs, shoved his hands into his trousers pockets.

A beam of sunlight found the scotch. "I don't blame you," said Dan. "I didn't want to, either. I wanted to be a surveyor."

"What happened?" The boy's voice began on a squeak, ended on a bass note.

"Now I'm a surveyor and a lawyer."

"And a gold trader."

"Yes, that, too." Not for long, though. Not for long. He would go home, soon, though he would miss trading.

"I want to be a gold trader. When I apply at Henry Clews, will you help me?"

He lifted the scotch toward the sun, enjoyed the amber glow.

"Yes."

Nathaniel blew out a great breath. "Thank you." He gave Dan his right hand.

"You're welcome." Maybe, he thought, clasping his brother's hand, it was time Nathaniel met Betty. Or someone like her.

~30~

ALREADY, BEFORE TRADING STARTED, the heat in Gilpin's could stifle the mind as it stifled breath, and the odor of chalk, mingled with men's sweat and other body odors, was enough to choke him. Forget it, he told himself, there's work to do. He drummed his heel on the floor, as keyed up to start as any racer, eager to begin his last trades before the meeting, and he had work to do at the brokerage – settle his account, change gold for greenbacks, have the old receipt cancelled, and get a new receipt for the remainder of the gold. He had less than four hours.

The board told him the premium was 257 5/6. "Buying. One hundred at 5/6. A hundred at 5/6." $100,000 at a premium of 256 5/6. Another man with a sweating face and a look of panic screamed, "Selling!" They met, exchanged tickets, and Dan, watching the boards through the haze of white chalk dust, sold it a second time at 256 7/8 , bought it back at 256 1/2, sold it at 256 5/8. Sold it again, bought an options contract, sold, bought, tickets of sale flying into and out of his hands, the increments so small, the fraction creeping down and down, the premium dropping from 256 to 255. He felt the tide of war turning, the greenback rising, though Fort Morgan, also in Mobile Bay would not surrender. The *New York Times* reported rebels were crossing the Potomac, fighting was fierce around Atlanta, but in the Gold Room confidence and the greenback were rising.

His inner tallies told him he was making money, lots of money. Like the best of possible poker hands, he drew to an inside straight, three of a kind, two pair, in a rhythm of sell and buy, each sell lower than the previous selling price, but higher than he had bought it for. The cards were falling to him. The premium dipped lower on the board. The carved mahogany ladies let their draperies fall. Nothing else existed around him, the noise of other men's trades faded into dust, and sunlight filtered through the water, the tall water vines stroked his skin.

The final call came, and he kicked for the surface. The premium stood at 254.12, and he wondered what time it was. He pulled out his watch: Quarter past three. He was already late to the meeting, but he did not much care. His pockets were stuffed with tickets, and an impossible number echoed in his mind. He would confirm it at Henry Clews. With Nathaniel beside him, he all but ran toward the brokerage.

In the portico, Detective Grady lounged against a column. "I thought I might walk along with you to the meeting." He nodded at Nathaniel.

Pointing down the Street, Dan said, "It's just down there." He caught up with what Grady had said. "How did you know it's today?"

"Easy. I looked for you at your house. The Reverend told me. It came to me that you could use a little company. You never know who might be about." Grady swept a hand at the crowds of people and traffic. "Besides, I've been wanting another word with you."

"There's no time just now. I have to tally up and go to the meeting." Nathaniel held the door for him, but as he moved toward it, an elderly gentleman escorted by a young, muscular man, shuffled through with a bare nod of thanks. "I'm late already."

Watching the gentleman and his bodyguard down the steps, Grady said, "Seeing as how you've been a target before, I'm thinking a bit of extra protection wouldn't go amiss, considering that this time you'll have the real coin."

Dan shook his head. "No, only greenbacks."

The policeman shrugged. "Still, money is money, to me and most people, to buy bread."

About to contradict that, he thought better of it. It was true, after all. "Nathaniel, wait here with Sergeant Grady, if you please."

"But, but, I thought — "

"The young man would be doing me a kindness, sir, if he stayed." The policeman's expression was all benign innocence. "I've been running out of audience for my best stories. Would you like to hear how we tracked down Desperate Dolan?"

He and the clerk met in Peter's old office to reckon up the final accounting. It was all simple arithmetic, straightforward addition, multiplication, division – the disciplines of the mind he had learned before he claimed his age in double digits, and when he was finished, he stared at the total on the paper. All his trades, and the gold he had brought: $975,167.

He could not believe it. The clerk bent his head to the final tally in a low mumble, and like a horse running behind at the finish line, looked up, and a smile spread across his face. "That's correct, sir," said the clerk. "Your figures are not mistaken. Of course, that's in greenbacks, but you can buy Treasury notes at six percent, and redeem them in gold when they mature, so taking the long view, sir, your greenbacks are good as gold."

Good God. He had never expected it. Nearly a million dollars.

He had done what he had set out to do. At the thought, something that had weighed him down so long he had not known it was there loosened its grip. He had the odd sensation of growing lighter, so that he had to rebalance as if he had been leaning against a strong wind that stopped blowing. Holding the arms of Peter's chair, he swiveled around to stare at the blank wall while he controlled the urge to weep.

The family was safe.

He had no more need of the Gold Room. And not needing it, he wanted it more than ever.

~31~

$29,637 IN GREENBACKS was not much of a weight. Not nearly so much as gold would have weighed; 1,450 Double Eagles and some odd coins would have been more than 110 pounds. Together with Grady and Nathaniel, he carried the valise from Henry Clews down Wall Street toward the Bank of New York. Before crossing William, he looked down, past the great grey-blue columns of the Custom House. Thick clots of men spilled into the street from Gilpin's, and he waited until he recognized two or three men before calling out, "What did gold close at?"

Ragged voices answered, "Two-fifty-four and an eighth." One, whose hair stuck out around his hat, said, "Gold's falling. You'll have an exciting time tomorrow."

"I suppose I will." The bear had settled in. His earlobes tingled.

They timed their crossing between two open carriages trotting in opposite directions and a hansom cab turning the corner. Grady said, "I'll stay in the lobby until you've finished."

As Nathaniel, undecided, looked to him for instructions, he saw Arthur waiting with Van Fleet. "Come along," he told the boy.

When Van Fleet saw them, red spots appeared on his cheekbones.

"Hello," Dan greeted his brother-in-law. "What are you doing here?"

"Your grandfather said I should represent the family." Arthur's mouth twisted. "I decided to see if I might be of any assistance to you. Lend moral support. That sort of thing."

Dan's eardrum throbbed. "It's all right. Glad to have you." To Van Fleet, "Let's finish this."

"Follow me." Van Fleet cut a jagged path across the marble floor, around tall tables, among the people taking care of their own banking business. Stone columns rose two stories to support the third floor, and hanging five-armed chandeliers lighted the floor.

Lines of people stretched out from tellers' cages against the left-hand wall. Van Fleet led the way along the opposite wall, past offices built of wainscoted wood to a man's waist, glass from there to Dan's shoulder height. They followed him to the back of the lobby, up wide marble stairs to the mezzanine. Looking over the marble balustrade at the people hurrying about their quiet, intent business, Nathaniel said something. Dan did not hear. He wanted to have this over.

A door stood open. Van Fleet gestured to them to walk in, followed them, and closed the door. Three men sat at a large mahogany conference table, their backs to the tall windows across which drapes had been drawn against the afternoon sunlight. In front of a thin youth with ink-smudged fingers lay a pad of paper and several sharp pencils, in precise right angles to the edge of the table. Dan took a seat opposite an older man whose dark goatee contrasted with his graying hair. Arthur sat on his right, Nathaniel on his left, opposite the young man with the paper and pencils, who gave them a quick glance, then looked down.

The goatee said, "You're late."

"Do you charge interest by the minute?"

"We will have no levity," said the second man, whose thin white hair lay in wide strands, like painted stripes, across his skull. Dan imagined it standing like a sail in a stiff wind.

Van Fleet made introductions. The goatee was a senior vice president. The white-haired man was first vice president. Dan did not bother to remember their names, nor did he rise to offer his hand, as Arthur did, too quickly to stop him. They both ignored Arthur, who sat down, his face pink. Nathaniel drew in a sharp breath.

"We wanted to see the sort of man who would commit highway robbery against this bank," said the white-haired man.

"Legal highway robbery." Dan smiled. His eardrum throbbed, and the familiar heat flared along his veins, but he sat easily. He could afford to, now. These men could do nothing to him, or to the family. Even if they sued, they would not win. The Stark name might be anathema to the Bank of New York, but the City Bank would be happy to accept a considerable sum of gold from a depositor. As would others. With the war news improving for the North, people would forget that he had owed gold and repaid in paper. Besides, as the value of gold sank, paper was worth more. As the Union went, so went its currency. Victory would come.

Van Fleet placed the valise by the pad of paper. The youth opened it, peered inside, and tipped out the contents, five bundles of greenbacks, each one wrapped in paper with the amounts printed on the sides and sealed in red wax with the name, Henry Clews & Co.

"There's one more," said Dan.

The youth held the valise open wide and upside down, shook again, and out fell a very small bundle, labeled $600. A fourth bundle, much smaller, tumbled onto the desk. The entire amount lay there: $29,637 including ten per cent interest compounded annually. Exactly as agreed.

He rested against the back of the leather chair, crossed his legs and idly swung his foot while the youth counted the money, jotted numbers on a piece of paper. No one spoke. A fly buzzed.

The young man made a clean copy and put down his pencils, realigned them, and slid the paper over to the goatee, who read it, nodded and slid it to the white-haired man. "Very well," said the white-haired man. "Have it inscribed and bring it by my office for signature."

Van Fleet stood as the goatee followed the white-haired man out. The youth strode after them. Dan remained seated, as did Arthur and Nathaniel. Van Fleet moved to the youth's place, sat with his folded hands on the table. Even with the drawn drapes, the room was hot, and sweat stood on his face.

Van Fleet said to Dan, "You may as well know this. I have resigned from the Bank effective today. This is my final act. I cannot —" He closed his eyes and swallowed.

"What about your family?" asked Arthur.

What did it matter about Van Fleet's family, Dan thought, when he'd had so little care for their own? Under the bandage, his neck itched.

"My daughter married well this winter, and my sons have good positions. My – my dear wife went to her eternal reward some years ago."

"What will you do next?" asked Arthur.

"That is at present unclear. I hope you can help me to clarify that." His voice broke. "I am so heartily ashamed of myself."

Arthur said to Dan, "He would ask you for forgiveness."

His throat closed, and his tongue filled his mouth so words could not at first squeeze past it, but after a moment he managed a single syllable: "No." Damned if he'd accept Van Fleet's facile shame. Peter was dead. King's hand slid across his chest, and blood spurted. He brought out the notecase, drew out the blood-stained receipt, cancelled an hour ago, and slid it across to Van Fleet. "You can have it now." We do things better in Alder Gulch, he thought.

~32~

OUTSIDE, AS HE ADJUSTED HIS HAT, Dan looked for Grady, but the policeman was nowhere to be seen. Just as well, he thought. He had business with Arthur, and Nathaniel, as the oldest son after he went back West, should hear it. "I need about a half an hour of your time, Arthur, if you can spare it." When his brother said a reluctant good-bye, he shook his head. "You, too, Nathaniel."

"Come to church, then." Seeing him hesitate, Arthur said, "We can be more private in my office there than at home."

As they waited to hail a hansom cab, Arthur said, "We have not seen as much of you as I would have liked. I have been hoping you would be more of a part of the family."

Dan flung up an arm and whistled. When Arthur had given directions to the driver and the three of them settled into a space ample for two, he said, "I have been on a mission to ensure the family's future."

"And have you had any success? You rather have that look about you."

"I have succeeded pretty well," he said. "Your part is coming, though. Yours, too, Nathaniel, when you're older and have gained more experience at Henry Clews." For he had spoken to Mr. Clews, and Nathaniel's apprenticeship would start on September 1, in just a week.

A cross dominated the wall behind Arthur's chair. Except for that, his office might have belonged to a lawyer. Theological books in various sizes, bound in dark leather with their titles, stamped in gold on their spines, occupied one wall of shelves. Dan and his companions sat at a round table in front of a window overlooking a square of grass shaded by a single deciduous tree that blocked the sun's direct rays. Noting the single chair and the table next to it, Dan guessed it was Arthur's refuge. So that was how he had coped with Grandfather.

A young man wearing a black suit and a Roman collar brought coffee and cookies on a black lacquered tray edged in a thin line of gold. Arthur introduced them, and the young cleric's eyes widened, but he said nothing. As he bowed himself out, smiling, Arthur thanked him. "Please see that we're not disturbed, Reginald." The door closed with a soft sigh.

Arthur poured coffee for them both and invited Dan to help himself to cookies. The coffee suited Dan's taste better than any since he had come East, and the soft cooky had chunks of chocolate in it. "Delicious."

Nathaniel said, "Thank you."

Arthur smiled. "The women of the parish are happy to indulge their clergy." He patted his waistline. "I shall grow corpulent, I fear."

A half-inch pile of clean paper, ink, and pens lay on a blotter in the middle of the table. Dan pulled a paper to him, took a pencil from an inside pocket, and began to lay out in numbers the extent of the family's current wealth. As he spoke, Arthur's freckles stood out across his nose, and Nathaniel's breath came faster.

He finished, "I intend to stop trading, but not until I have taken full advantage of this bear market." As he said that, he knew a pang of regret. Did he really intend to leave the Gold Room? He was doing well, far better than he had thought he might, but how much more could he do for the family? How would Martha look in silk?

"What do we do with this?" Arthur gripped the edge of the table, his fingertips whitening.

"We will buy Treasury notes, the five-twenties. They are redeemable in five years, and mature in twenty. The federal government has promised to redeem them in gold at par. Nathaniel can arrange to buy them with greenbacks on the Stock market through a broker at Henry Clews."

Nathaniel looked startled.

Arthur dabbed at the corners of his mouth.

"Before I return" to bring Martha to New York, if nothing else, he thought, "we'll establish Trusts, so that everyone is protected." He pushed the paper over to Arthur. "In the meantime, keep all this to yourself until I have closed all my trades. That should take about a week. Then we will know exactly what we have – given that the premium on gold is dropping, of course."

"There will have to be gifts to the poor. To further God's work." Arthur put the paper into a drawer and locked it.

"That's none of my business," said Dan. "Once the money is in your hands, my part is done. It'll be up to you and Nathaniel to manage it." He swallowed his cold coffee. "You would do well to consult with Mother before you make any disbursements."

"What about your Grandfather and Grandmother?"

A tremor ran through Dan's body: The knife gleamed against his neck, King's hand slid on his chest. "Take care of Grandmother, but the old bastard can go to hell for all I care."

Nathaniel gasped. Arthur blinked and lowered his gaze to his coffee cup. Dan took his hat and gathered his feet under himself to stand up. "I'll be on my way." What did they expect him to say?

"Wait." Arthur looked up. His freckles had vanished, absorbed in larger patches of red that mottled his features. "Please."

Dan settled onto the chair, his hat in his hand. His neck itched, and the room lacked air.

Arthur cleared his throat. "Have you no mercy in your heart?"

A knife gleamed in the dark, the ice over a stream bulged and broke, raindrops fell on unseeing eyes. He breathed in and out. Setting the hat on the table, he loosened the cravat, untied the bandage, peeled it away from the healing cut and let the ends of the bandage dangle outside his shirt. Arthur paled; the red patches disappeared. "Ask me that again." His voice, deeper than normal, belonged to a stranger. "And then tell me why I should."

Arthur's adam's apple jumped, but he met Dan straight on. "Jesus forgave His murderers while they were murdering Him."

"I am not that good a man. I am not the Son of God."

"We must forgive others if we expect God to forgive us. Otherwise, our own souls are in grave peril of eternal damnation." Arthur leaned forward, his hand open on the table, palm up.

"My soul went to the devil when I could not regret hanging murderers." He must get out of here, go where he could breathe, but a man with a cut throat would arouse too much consternation on the street. Rewinding the bandage around his neck, he asked, "Would He have forgiven those who murdered his friends? Turned the other cheek while other people were murdered? Stood by and let other men be killed?" He tied the knot on the bandage, tucked in the ends, and took up the cravat.

Arthur said, "I don't know. There's no record of that exact situation in the Bible."

He had no mirror, but the cravat had to be tidy enough. He had to escape. From out of his Sunday School past a phrase came: "'Greater love hath no man'? That's about laying down his life for his friends, right? There's a lot about that sort of thing, isn't there? Then what about risking your soul for others? Should a man refuse to save another man's life for fear of jeopardizing his own soul? Tell that to the soldiers in the field, tell them they should let the Union be damned, or Negroes be enslaved, to save their souls." He stood up.

Arthur rose, too. "Does your conscience never trouble you about what you have done?"

"Oh, God, you don't give up, do you?"

"I'm fighting for your soul, Daniel. Please let me help to save it."

Scuffed, cracked boots swung in mid-air, and memory whispered, It didn't have to be this way. "You're too late. I lost that before Christmas."

"It's never too late to accept the love of the Triune God."

"I would have to promise to sin no more." As if the hanged men jumped down from their scaffolds, the ice dissolved, the darkness lifted. "I can't do that any more than a soldier on the battlefield can."

Arthur stood on the other shore of an unbridgeable chasm. There was no way across, for either of them. It would be pointless to throw a rope. Or even to try.

"I will pray for you," said Arthur.

"That's up to you, if you think it'll do any good."

A knock sounded at the door. Arthur frowned. "I told them not to disturb us."

The young cleric put in his head. "I'm sorry, Rector, but a messenger has come. Major Morton Browne has been killed in battle."

~33~

BLACK CLOTH SWATHED the drawing room – the large mirror above the fireplace, the wine velvet drapes drawn against the life outside, the portrait of Major Morton Browne in his Union Army uniform. His bearded chin lifted, he gazed at a distant battlefield with his hand gripping his sword. Another life given for the cause.

Which cause, though? Dan studied the painting while he waited for Harriet. Had Major Browne died to free the slaves or to preserve the Union? Because it was possible to care passionately about the one while not giving a damn about the other.

A hoop touched his calf. He started. Harriet inserted her hand into the crook of his elbow. He had not heard her heels across the carpet. "Do you know how he died?" she asked.

"No." He covered her hand with his own.

"A fall from his horse. A mile behind the action, his horse shied, and my husband came out of the saddle and broke his neck. I am a widow because he was a poor rider." She squeezed his arm. "And his child will be an orphan." Pulling away, she went to the bell pull hanging near the door and tugged. "We shall have some coffee, don't you think? I have an inordinate desire for buttered toast. Perhaps a slice of cake. What about you?"

"Thank you. That would be good."

When the maid had come, taken the order, and left again, Harriet folded herself onto the settee and patted the space beside her.

She touched his black arm band. "I was so sorry about Peter Yates." Her voice held more sadness than when she had told how her husband died. "Sorry for him, for his widow – such a sweet woman – and sorry for you."

"Thank you." It was the proper return to make, though it cost him to say it. "I came to express my condolences to you, as well, for your loss." He added, "May I offer also my congratulations?" The stilted formal phrases came readily to his lips, like something out of the etiquette books his elders had insisted he learn. He had not understood why until he had been grown up; they provided proper words when a man had none.

"There's no need," she said. "I am not in an interesting condition."

"Then why? I don't —"

The maid entered with the coffee, set it on the low table in front of the settee, and vanished as noiselessly as she had come.

"Wishful thinking. I want a child. Oh, Daniel, I want a child. It's the thing I've wanted more than anything in all my life, ever since my mother died when I was small. I want someone to love me. Can you understand? I want someone to love me. You don't. I know you don't. You love that Indian woman who lives with you, but you don't love me. Not truly. My father doesn't. He had only room for one love in his heart, and that was my mother. Browne didn't. He wanted me, but he didn't love me. There is no one else. Unless I have a child. I can give my heart to a child, and it will love me, but unless I have a child, there will be no one. No one at all."

Her hand trembled as she reached forward to pour the coffee in an unsteady stream. When she had filled both cups, she held one out to him, and as he took it, his fingers closing over hers, she asked, her eyes full of tears, "Will you give me a baby?"

His mind blanked. Coffee sloshed over the rim of the cup, dripped onto his waistcoat. Almost, he thought he could not have heard her correctly, but her bright red face and frightened eyes told him he had. He set the untasted coffee on the tray.

All during his adolescence, though he had not lacked experience – Father had seen to that – he had dreamed of her. He had imagined her body in his hands, and her hair loose around her shoulders, but the night of her dinner party had shown him that his dreams lay far to the West. With Martha. And yet.

He said, "I am going home in a few days."

"I know." Her eyes pleaded with him, and her voice was very small.

"My wife must never know."

She did not look away from him, though he saw the relief plain on her face, and the redness vanished from her cheeks, leaving them pale. "Nor must my husband's family."

"It might not work."

"No." She smiled with a lift of her head. "But I think the time is right." Picking up a napkin, she dabbed at the coffee on his waistcoat. "Can you come later this evening? I shall be prostrate with grief."

~34~

THE IRISH POLICEMAN, Grady, perched at the edge of the straight chair in Arthur's study at home. He did not look at either Dan or Arthur, but at his hat, which he turned round and round in his hands. "I have been searching for evidence that someone hired Thaddeus King to attack you, and I can find none. His cohorts know nothing of that." He glanced up and back down at the hat. "However, we found a note on the body, a written description of two men who might be you, sir" — a swift look at Dan — "and your poor friend." After a pause, he recited, "'Six feet, strongly built, blond hair, narrow face, wearing a dark gray suit.' Would you say that fits you, sir?"

"And hundreds of other men in this city," said Dan.

"Very true, sir." Grady watched him.

Forcing himself to an outward calm, he wanted to shout, Yes, and give this good detective the bastard Van Fleet. But he could not give him up without exposing Grandfather, and that would do more harm to the family than anything Father had done. Protecting the family, he had to protect Van Fleet, and the thought of shielding that son of a bitch made him want to vomit. Even as he thought it, bile burned into his throat. He coughed.

Grady said, "Ah, well. Without any other evidence, sir, I'm

forced to close this case as a random attack gone very wrong."

Dan walked him to the front door and out onto the stoop, where Grady paused, smoothed his hair, and put his hat on. His cheeks and chin were dark, almost bluish from his coming beard, though it was early afternoon. "I don't suppose you'd tell me how close I've come to the right of it, sir. Just for my own information, you know. Otherwise, I might think there's a loose end."

Thinking, Dan stared at the windows of the building across the street. What to say without saying too much?

"Ah, well," said Grady, walking down the steps. "I had hopes. Safe journey, sir."

"Wait," Dan said.

"Yes, sir?"

He descended the steps to talk to the sergeant. "This family has been through enough. But from what I know of the case, you need not fear to have left any loose ends."

"Thank you, sir. I'm glad to know that. Being right is a great comfort to a man in my line of work." Grady smiled and lifted his hat. "Besides, I'm thinking justice has been served, saving your poor friend. His killer being dead, you see. No doubt by accident in the melee."

"A scuffle in the night leaves many details obscure." He offered his hand.

The Irishman looked at it, looked at him, wiped his right hand down his trouser leg. "I think we understand each other, sir."

"I believe so," he said.

They shook hands on it.

~35~

DAN WALKED THE LAST BLOCK or two through the rain, his heart beating a different rhythm from the drops that pattered on his umbrella and the hoofbeats that splashed past him in the puddled street. Harriet opened the door herself in response to his light tap, and laid her finger against his lips, gestured to indicate where to leave his wet overcoat and shoes. Padding up the unlighted staircase, he held the back of her silk skirt just below the waist to guide him in the dark. Her posteriors moved under his hand, and when he laid his little finger in the cleft between, she smiled at him over her shoulder.

He followed her into her boudoir and the door closed after him. Two lamps burning low showed the shapes of white-painted furniture trimmed in gilt. His toes curled into a deep-piled rug patterned in giant roses. Removing his suit coat, he draped it over the back of a soft, armless chair, laid his waistcoat on top. He did not need the bandage around his neck, so he had not bothered with cravat or collar. Harriet removed her outer garment – whatever women called those things – and her blonde hair flowed over the shoulders of an impossible confection of silk roses and flounces more suitable for a wedding night than a recent widow's unlawful tryst. But then, he did not suppose she would wear it for long.

He gathered her to him, pressed her close as though to memorize her body with his own. Through the doorway to her bedroom, he glimpsed a tall bed with a step-up beside it, before she reached both hands to draw his face down. Her eyes glowed from their shadowed caverns. "At last," she murmured, her breath against his cheek. "I have waited for you all my life."

So often as a boy he had dreamed of this. Turning the pages of her music at the pianoforte, pretending to watch her hands move up and down the keyboard, he had longed to explore among the shadows of her body as some men longed to explore a continent, or travel unknown rivers.

His time had come. As he savored the moment, Harriet made an impatient sound in her mouth, shook her head. Her fine hair floated around her, and she swept it back. "I did not know you liked the woman to take the active part."

"I don't."

"You will." She sank to her knees, her skirts billowing around her, and unbuttoned his trousers, while he worked at his shirt buttons, cursed his thick and stupid fingers. "You're so tall." She took hold of him.

A tremor shuddered through him. Her skin was as silken as the discarded nightdress, the rug not so deep as he had thought. He held her among the roses, her face below him slack around her avid eyes, her lips soft under his hard kiss, her thighs clamped around his waist. He was Lewis at the Great Falls of the Missouri, and he rode the white water thundering in his ears.

He carried her to the bed, where her hair, spun gold in the lamplight, lashed his face, his torso, and trailed down through the saliva and sweat, until he lay on his back while she kissed the bullet scar inside his right thigh, nibbled at his torso, bit his nipple. "Hey!" He grabbed her hair, pulled her head away, and kissed her.

"That beast might have killed you." Lying beside him, she licked at the scar on his neck.

"It's nearly healed now."

"What happened to him? Your attacker. I assume you fended him off." One hand moved downward.

"I killed him."

She twined her fingers in his hair. "Was that the first man you killed?"

"No. Why —"

She held him, and he turned to her, inhaled the scent of roses and wine and female, and she guided him, moved counter to him and with him, and they rode the white water over the cascade.

Spent, he stared up at the ceiling painted to look like a rose arbor with a white trellised gate, and a thought dropped into his mind: Suppose he stayed in New York? He could be rich beyond anything he had ever dreamed. He could be far richer, with more gold than anyone could imagine, and he had this woman, the dream of his life. The Gold Room, and Harriet. All he had ever wanted, all his dreams come true. He would master the Gold Room, daily know the heart-pounding joy of trading in gold, of sailing stormy waters in terror of capsizing. The hairs lifted along his forearms, and his blood surged in his temples. He could walk into that rose arbor.

At the gate hovered a dark-haired woman's slender shadow. When he put his arm over his face to shield himself, her luminous brown eyes still gazed at him.

Harriet whispered, "How does it feel to kill someone?"

He sat up. "What the hell kind of question is that?"

"I just wondered. I'll never do it, it's something men do, especially in war, and I wondered why. What it feels like."

He swung both legs over the side of the bed. Killing Thaddeus King had not been easier to live with than hanging men in Alder Gulch. For some men it might be. He'd killed King in self-defense, with no time to think, just act. No one could blame him, so why did his gorge rise at the sudden reminder? Self-defense was a matter of instinct, not a decision entered into after due deliberation, with infinite regret at the path the criminal had chosen. Between the first moment and King's death it had been a matter of a minute. Less.

Rubbing his face, he thought how not to answer her, but damn it, she had wanted to know, did she? He spoke with his back to her. "We kill because we must. Because the other will kill us." The malevolent gleam of metal, blood gushing over him. Boots that jerked in mid-air. The stench. "How does it feel? Horrible. The worst thing. Ever."

In the back of his mind, the shadowed woman – skirts a practical two or three inches higher than fashion warranted – paced back and forth. Martha would never ask that.

He slid off the bed. A grandfather clock downstairs sang the hour, though even without it he would have known it was late. He could see Harriet without needing lamplight.

She followed him into the boudoir, and watched him. "You've turned into a beautiful man."

Laughing, he paused in the midst of doing up his trouser buttons. "Men aren't beautiful." He looked up and down her naked body. "You are beautiful, though." Letting his smile fade, he said, "I hope you got what you wanted."

She shrugged. "Time will tell. I should know in a month or two." Before he could reach for his shirt, she pressed herself against him. "I didn't get everything I wanted. I want you to stay." He felt her tears on his chest. "When I asked you to come to me, I didn't know that. I know it now. Please stay. You belong in New York. With me."

Gritting his teeth, he set her aside. She would never know how close she had come to getting what she wanted, how he would remember her body against his, the smell of roses, the surge of his blood. He could go back to the Gold Room.

He said, "I have to go home. I promised I'd be back before ice covers the gold."

~ALDER GULCH~

"THERE'S A GOOD CROWD, Mam," said Timothy. Seeing how many people came to Pap's funeral pleased him, even though he knew they didn't come for the good memories they had of him. Some came to show their support to the family. Some, like the Stevens woman and her bastard, Jacky, off to themselves at the back of the gathering, came because they had felt something for Pap. Tim could barely look at the Stevens woman for thinking that Pap was rumored to have been one of her customers. The rest would have come for the free victuals afterwards, and for curiosity. And because they liked Mam.

For the first time, he was glad Dan'l was not here. Mam wanted him to hurry back, but Tim was glad they'd been spared the embarrassment of Mam's lover attending her husband's funeral. Now Dan'l would marry Mam. If he came back.

If he came back. If he didn't stay in New York.

There being no clergy in Alder Gulch unless the priests came through from Father DeSmet's mission up north, Mr. Dance read the funeral. He was known for a good Christian man, and no weakling, neither. What was called a "muscular Christian." Tim didn't pay the readings much mind. He figured God had already decided what to do about Pap, and nothing they could say would change things now.

The first clods dropped onto Pap's coffin. Tim only half heard the words, "sure and certain hope of life eternal," before Lydia Hudson began to sing "Abide with Me." When she finished, she joined them, along with Jacob Himmelfarb, and Tim gave Mam over to Jacob's arm. Jacob had a calming effect on Mam. Maybe because his English was still weak, he kept silent, which was a lot what Mam needed. Miz Hudson seemed like she understood Mam's vapors, too. Maybe they was natural to a women in her condition, but he didn't recall nothing like them with Dotty.

Turning to see where she was, he found Sheriff Fox behind him a foot or so. He ignored the sheriff, craned his head until he spotted Dotty hurrying along the ridge, intent on getting down to the Eatery to help Tabby Rose feed people. A short, bow-legged man walked a short distance behind her, as if he'd taken a notion to drift off toward town. Tim relaxed.

"We're looking after her." The sheriff tilted his head toward the Stevens woman and Jacky. "They won't get a chance. Neither one."

Mam, on Jacob's arm, Miz Hudson and Albert along with them, was walking toward home, too. She had her head down to keep watch on the stones and ruts of the road. Partway along the ridge, they took the trail that branched off a different way, so as not to pass by the five road agents the sheriff and Dan'l had hanged.

"I don't know an easy way to say this," the sheriff said, "but there's an indication that your father did not die from freezing to death. Or not only that."

"What – what are you talking about?" Pap? Killed? On account that's what the sheriff was saying. Only who would do it? And why?

"Before we put him in the coffin, we saw a big stain, like old blood, around a tear in his coat. It was about an inch wide, just above his belt in back. Doc Bissell says it was a knife, and it went through the greatcoat and into the body. He thinks your father was bleeding bad when he crawled into that cave, and then froze to death."

"Oh, God." Tim thought to the day they'd found the body. "He didn't get far." Only about half a mile up Daylight Creek in a dry wash. When he could think, he asked, "Who could've done it?" He'd thought Pap was drunk when he crawled into that cave.

"Have you any ideas?"

Tim thought back to that January day. "I found Mam, and then went to get Miz Hudson, and Dan'l was coming back from that Vigilante business." That had laid the five in their graves.

"I see." Fox walked along in silence.

"Yes." And then it struck Tim. For all that Dan Stark was a friend of his, Sheriff Fox had been probing to see if he might have killed Pap to get Mam. "He wouldn't have done it even if he'd had time. Dan'l Stark ain't no backstabber."

"I agree." The sheriff adjusted the brim of his hat against the hot sun. "I sure do hope he comes back soon."

"So do we." They started down the hill. "If he ain't back in a month, I'll go get him."

"You don't have to worry about him. He keeps his word. He'll be back."

That's as may be, Tim said to himself, but he figured he'd go anyway. "Do you think we'll ever know who killed Pap?"

"I don't think it's likely, I'm afraid. Not after all this time."

~NEW YORK CITY 36~

THE NEW YORK AND HARLEM train chuffed behind him, the great iron horse several cars ahead sighing like a hundred real horses impatient to be under way. Like him. A paper cup rattled along the waiting area, lifted on a dust devil, and clattered away. The women lowered their parasols against the momentary breeze. This was the end, Dan thought. His life in New York was over. The night with Harriet had been a farewell to his boyhood dreams, to all he had imagined his life would be. His future was new territory, he thought, and smiled at the irony. How many men had the opportunity to build a new world? He wished the journey home would begin.

A month, at the most six weeks, and he would see Martha again, and never leave her. Never again be parted from her. The next time he visited New York, she would come with him. He had gone shopping, Mother delighted to come with him. He'd bought books, and bolts of cloth, miners' tools, and pamphlets on metallurgy.

But the most difficult present to find had been the dulcimer that now rested in its box at his feet; he had not wanted to put it on the train with his bag. He imagined Martha's face when he gave it to her. There would be music in his house. He longed to find his seat, have these goodbyes behind him, begin the journey home, but he was bound to wait with the family until the trainman gave his boarding call. Why didn't he do it?

Around him the family, having said in private everything they could say, produced snatches of conversation, while they peered up and down the street, looking for Arthur.

"What can be delaying him?" Mother chewed her upper lip and changed the slant of her new parasol to shield her face against the midday sun. She had exchanged purple for a becoming shade of lavender in defiance of mourning convention that decreed she should spend two more months in purple, and the silk roses on the parasol reminded Dan of Harriet's nightdress. He had not gone back again to take his leave of her.

Grandfather leaned on his cane. "Arthur made me come. You'd think he would at least be here himself." His voice was dry and cracked, an old man's voice in keeping with the shawl around his bent shoulders. "Him and his fool Christian notions. They always apply to others."

"Grandfather," began Nathaniel.

"That's not fair!" Florentine stamped her foot. "Arthur lives his faith, as we all should."

Almost, Dan would have felt sorry for the old bastard, so much had he aged since his plot was exposed, but Dan sensed in him no discernible remorse, no consciousness of his own responsibility for two deaths. As if he had given an order and there had been no cause and effect, as if Peter's death, and King's, were nothing to do with him. Had he not given that order, Dan thought, I would not have had to kill King. We hang men for that sort of criminal negligence.

"If he wanted to be a Christian, he should have persuaded Dan to do his Christian duty and rebuild the Firm." Grandfather thumped his cane on the ground.

Dan, watching the trainman for signs that he could board, knew a moment's blank unbelief. Florentine clapped her handkerchief over her mouth, Mother's parasol dipped away from the sunlight, Nathaniel's hands doubled into fists. "You —" Dan clamped his jaws tight to corral the rest of it: son of a bitch, but in any event he was forestalled, because Grandmother spoke before he could gather wits enough to find words. In all his life he had never heard her raise her voice or talk back to her husband.

"Judge Stark, shame on you. You gave an order, and by it a man was killed, and our grandson was almost killed, and you have not uttered a word of remorse. Not one." Her soft, flute-like tones seemed wrapped around iron. "Nor have you ever grieved for poor John."

"Woman, be silent." He hammered his stick on the ground and small puffs of dust rose.

She had only paused for breath. "I will not. We are old. We may never see Daniel again in this life. If —"

"What are —"

"— you do not apologize to him —"

"Me? Apologize?"

"—I shall consider that I no longer have a husband." As Grandfather gaped at her, she added, "Furthermore, you will deserve whatever the Lord prepares for you in the hereafter."

Grandfather could not speak. Across his silence the train whistle screamed. They all jumped, and Grandfather would have toppled over had Nathaniel not steadied him.

"Daniel will leave soon, Judge. You are running out of time."

He waited. What if Grandfather did apologize? Would they have him forgive Grandfather's lifelong destruction of Father, Peter's murder, and the attempt on himself? Mike King had been the scum of the earth, but he had died then, too. Lay his death, too, at Grandfather's feet. Three deaths and a near miss. Because Grandfather had given an order.

Road agents had begged for forgiveness, wept on the gallows, promised to amend their lives. He had not believed in their contrition. Did not believe now. Allowed to climb down from the gallows, they would have given in to the next temptation, because they had done nothing so terrible in the first place. They had marked a stage coach, passed a message, carried a letter. What was the harm in that? It hadn't been their fault that other men used their information to rob someone, murder someone else.

Or they deserved whatever they had wanted. Had a right to other men's gold.

Did God exist? If the preachers were right, Dan said to himself, he might damn himself, but he could not forgive them. Any more than he expected to be forgiven for hanging the others. Because as surely as pulling on one particular rope, he had helped condemn all of them.

Grandfather said, "I truly never meant for anyone to be hurt." He closed his eyes as if looking at Dan, backlighted against the sun, hurt his eyes. "I'm so very sorry." He squinted at Dan. "More than you will ever know, because I have been the indirect agent of another man's death. Can you —?" The train whistle screamed again.

Surprised, Grandfather dropped the guard on his expression, and a slyness gleamed in his eyes. The old bastard. The old son of a bitch. He belonged on a gallows as much as the others.

Nathaniel, Florentine, Mother, Grandmother — all waited for him to speak. They had not seen the truth in Grandfather's eyes.

Nathaniel looked past Dan. "Here comes Arthur."

"Forgive?" said Dan. "You want my forgiveness? What will that do? Will it bring back Father? Or Peter? If you want forgiveness, ask God. Not me."

"You hear that?" Grandfather's eyes narrowed. "I should have known better than to expect mercy from a God damn vigilante."

"When could we ever expect it from you?"

The train whistle blasted, a trainman shouted his boarding call, and he had only brief moments to drop kisses on Grandmother's cheek and Florentine's, to wrap Mother in a hug that left an impression of her arms around his waist. He shook Nathaniel's hand, and his brother gave his shoulder an affectionate clout. Tears in her eyes, Grandmother stood away from Grandfather. He leaped up the steps carrying the dulcimer and the Spencer, and stood in the vestibule until the trainman came to raise the steps and drop down the floor. He found his seat, laid the dulcimer across it, and lowered the window, leaned out to wave until the train's starting jerk nearly threw him off his feet.

Nathaniel ran alongside the train. "Bring your wife next time."

"You come West," Dan called. "The latchstring is always out for you."

The train lurched along the street, and buildings dropped behind them, but at a rate no faster than a horse could trot. He could have hired a hansom to take him to Harlem Bridge, but the careful habits of relative poverty stayed with him, though he might be considered a wealthy man now. Wealth could be a blessing or a curse, because rich men were targets, and money spent too fast. He touched the money belt at his waist and hoped it did not show.

"Daniel," said a voice, and Arthur dropped into the seat beside him. "I'm sorry I'm late, but my errand took longer than I anticipated."

"I'm glad you came. I would have hated to leave without saying goodbye."

"Mine was a small service." Arthur looked out the windows, and Dan wondered what he saw – progress or vanishing fields. "When you return, you must bring your family. I should like you to present me to your wife. I have the impression she is a woman of great courage."

"Yes, she is, to take up life with me."

After a moment the two men spoke at once: "Thank you for everything," and "I'll get off at the next stop."

In the small silence that settled between them, while Dan wondered what more he and Arthur could say to each other, Van Fleet settled into an empty seat facing him.

"My God," Dan said. "What the hell are you doing here? You're not coming back, are you?"

"No. But I had to come. To tell you," turning to Arthur, "oh, I don't know what to say."

The train wheels clacked over a junction.

Arthur said, "Just tell him."

"I – I am giving my life to God. Reverend Cunningham has been of great help to me these past days, and, well, whatever time I have left, I shall spend it making amends."

It was too easy, too slick. "And that makes everything all right?"

"I don't expect you to understand." Van Fleet slumped back in the seat. "You're a hard man. If this – had happened out there, you would have hanged me."

"Yes. We would have. For conspiracy to murder."

"No, Daniel, you couldn't," Arthur began, but he interrupted: "It is the penalty of the law."

"I would have deserved it." Van Fleet looked him in the eye. "Why did you not give me up to that policeman?"

"Because I would have had to give up Grandfather, and the family has suffered enough at his hands."

"I understand. But while your grandfather is, is –" He looked at Arthur for help finding the word he wanted.

"Unregenerate?" suggested Dan, thinking of Grandfather's false apology.

"Yes. Unregenerate. I am not. It is a small and greedy life I have led, and I have but ill repaid you for saving it. Twice." Moisture came to Van Fleet's eyes; he looked as if he might weep. "I shudder at my own ingratitude." He swallowed, fell silent.

What was there to say? Did the man expect sympathy? If he and Arthur had come with that expectation, they would be disappointed. It was one thing to regret a man's death, and quite another to see the rain falling into his eyes.

At a bump of the brakes, Van Fleet grabbed the arm rest. The train was slowing.

"We'll get off here," said Arthur. Rising with him, Dan shook Arthur's hand.

"Thank you for everything," Dan said.

Van Fleet spoke fast, as if to say it all before he had to leave the train. "I feel our dear Lord calling me back to Montana. You will see that I am a changed man." He thrust out a sealed letter. "Please deliver that for me."

As the train pulled out of the station, he read the address on the envelope: Mrs. Lydia Hudson, Wallace Street, Virginia City, Montana Territory. He tucked the letter in his inside breast pocket and rested his head against the seat back, closed his eyes. At last, he was on his way home. Six weeks, perhaps only a month, and he would see Martha again, hold her, smell her scent of sage and juniper, breathe the air from snowy mountains. Home.

PART III:
ALDER GULCH

~1~

SOMEWHERE BETWEEN nowheres and nowheres else, on the road to Salt Lake City, the stage jouncing Timothy's bones out of his skin stopped at a hog ranch to change horses and let the passengers stretch their legs and grab a bite before the driver whipped up the fresh horses for the next leg south. Another stage stood there, the horses' noses pointed north. Sighing, because it would be weeks, maybe months, before he rode a northbound stage, Timothy walked toward a stand of cottonwoods where the ranch owner had told him men took care of business, there being no privy. "Too much trouble to dig," he'd said.

He stepped into the shade, grateful it was some cooler here. Glancing around, a precaution against unfriendly sorts catching him unaware, he spotted a man fastening the lowest button of his trousers. By the slump in his shoulders, he'd been traveling a goodly while from far places, and dust lay thick on his long linen duster.

Something familiar about him took away the urgency Tim had felt, but in the dappled shade, amid trailing willow stems, he wasn't sure. The other finished tidying himself, and parted the willows, stepped over a thick exposed root. Timothy let out a mighty whoop. "Dan'l!"

. . . . .

The drivers grumbled at the delay while Tim switched stagecoaches, though he climbed up and retrieved his case himself. Dan'l didn't seem to mind paying four bits extra, an outrageous sum, but at last he was on his way north. With Dan'l.

"How's your mother?" A long wooden box stood upright between Dan'l's knees.

"She's fine. She won't be half pleased to see you," he hollered over the dusty wind, the rattle of wheels and low thunder of six horses' trotting hooves. He thought to tell Dan'l the rest, but the other passengers, none best pleased at having to squeeze together for him, were openly listening, him being at least something different to break up the tedium.

At the next stop, ten miles on, Dan'l bought them both a beer. They walked a ways off by themselves. "Tell me about your mother," he said. "You're not telling me something."

"Mam's fine. The big news is they found Pap."

~2~

THE SPENCER SLUNG his right shoulder, the dulcimer under his arm, holding the valise in his left hand, Dan walked up Jackson Street from Wallace. He had told Tim he wanted to surprise Martha, and the boy smiled. "You go on ahead, then." He lagged well behind, Dan supposed, to let him have a few moments first with Martha. Progress was slow because so many people welcomed him back, shaking his hand, grinning like Christmas, as if he'd risen from the dead. Hell, he'd said he'd be back, hadn't he?

She stretched upward to tie a long cane from a yellow rose bush to the post of a new porch someone – probably Tim – had built on his house. Her back was to him, and he drank in the sight of her, brown hair escaping its bun. While he watched, she finished with the climbing rose and turned sideways, lifted her hands to fuss with her hair.

He gasped. Her belly had expanded to such a size that her skirt lifted a good couple of inches in front.

A baby coming. His child. He would be a father. A family of his own.

He put down his burdens and ran toward her, shouting her name.

"Martha!"

~ ACKNOWLEDGMENTS ~

A book does not leave the author's computer and make its way into the hands of readers without the help of other people, and that's definitely true for *Gold Under Ice*. I am especially grateful to these people:

Marge Fisher of LPL Financial, in Whitefish, MT, read the entire novel, and the trading scenes twice. Any errors, though, are mine.

Robert Brown read and commented on early drafts of the novel and taught me about inside straights.

Catherine Creel, one of the finest editors I've ever known, edited the book. I hope I fixed all the things she caught.

Martin Levy took his underwater cameras to Glacier National Park while snow piled the banks, and captured the beautiful cover photo from the midst of icy McDonald Creek.

Rob McDonald designed the beautiful cover.

Craig Lancaster not only honored me by choosing *Gold Under Ice* as the inaugural book for Missouri Breaks Press, but he made the interior design a work of art, too.

Kristin Hall, Librarian, and Mark Robertson, Library Assistant, of the Legislative Reference Library in Boise, Idaho, answered questions about the legal situation governing the area that is now southwest Montana, but in 1864 was "East Idaho."

Susan Lupton, Reference Librarian, of the Montana State Law Library in Helena, Montana, answered my questions, and located Montana's earliest legislative records from the Civil War era.

Most important of all, my husband, Dick, patiently keeps our computers running, tolerates writer's block grumbling, and keeps me laughing at his jokes – still, after all these years.

Thank you, all! I couldn't have done it without you.

Made in the USA
Lexington, KY
11 May 2013